D0500266

SHADOW CHILD

SHADOW CHILD

Rahna Reiko Rizzuto

GRAND CENTRAL
PUBLISHING

NEW YORK   BOSTON

Copyright © 2018 by Rahna Reiko Rizzuto
Cover design art direction by Anne Twomey
Cover illustration by Olaf Hajek
Cover copyright © 2018 by Hachette Book Group, Inc.

Grand Central Publishing
Hachette Book Group
1290 Avenue of the Americas, New York, NY 10104
grandcentralpublishing.com
twitter.com/grandcentralpub

First Edition: May 2018

Grand Central Publishing is a division of Hachette Book Group, Inc. The Grand Central Publishing name and logo is a trademark of Hachette Book Group, Inc.

The publisher is not responsible for websites (or their content) that are not owned by the publisher.

The Hachette Speakers Bureau provides a wide range of authors for speaking events. To find out more, go to www.hachettespeakersbureau.com or call (866) 376-6591.

Library of Congress Cataloging-in-Publication Data

Names: Rizzuto, Rahna R. author.
Title: Shadow child / Rahna Reiko Rizzuto.
Description: New York: Grand Central Publishing, 2018.
Identifiers: LCCN 2017053601| ISBN 9781538711453 (hardback) | ISBN 9781549168673 (audio download) | ISBN 9781538711446 (ebook)
Subjects: LCSH: Family life—Fiction. | Twin sisters—Fiction. | Japanese Americans—Evacuation and relocation, 1942–1945—Fiction. | World War, 1939–1945—Concentration camps—West (U.S.)—Fiction. | World War, 1939–1945—Japan—Fiction. | BISAC: FICTION / Historical. | FICTION / Family Life. | FICTION / Contemporary Women. | FICTION / Literary. | GSAFD: Suspense fiction | Historical fiction
Classification: LCC PS3568.I87 S53 2018 | DDC 813/.54—dc23
LC record available at https://lccn.loc.gov/2017053601

Printed in the United States of America

LSC-C

10 9 8 7 6 5 4 3 2 1

What if you slept, and what if, in your sleep you dreamed? And what if in your dream you went to heaven and there plucked a strange and beautiful flower? And what if, when you awoke, you had the flower in your hand?

—*Attributed to Samuel Taylor Coleridge*

Double Take

HANA

He was a ripple through the stained glass. A dark and shifting shape in an only slightly brighter lobby. It wasn't far from midnight, on the edge of Harlem, and I had already opened the outer door to my apartment building and was standing in the vestibule when he appeared. Behind me, the street was empty of everything but the occasional used coffee cup and some lazy leaves of newspaper skimming the sidewalk. There was no voice in my head whispering at me to run—not yet—though the flush creeping beneath my collar was familiar.

I was a woman alone, clenching my key between my knuckles. But when the flicker of him reached the heavy iron door handle, I looked away.

If I had chosen to stare him down, I would have had some answers for the cops when they asked me: How tall was he? How heavy? What was he wearing? I pulled back against the tiled walls instead. It was my silent deal: *I won't see you and you don't see me.* That was when he looked at me.

Twice.

The double take was for Kei. I knew it, even if I could never prove it. Even if I barely noticed it at the time. In my defense, it had been so long since I had seen my sister that I had forgotten the effect we had on others.

Kei was upstairs, waiting. Come for me, six years too late.

I slipped by the man as he hesitated, rushing through the second door and into the lobby, inflating the air and life between us with each step. I can still feel him watching me, though his footsteps didn't turn to follow mine across the marble floor. Thinking back, I can't hear any sound at all—not even the front door clicking behind him as it closed. He was a memory already, fleeing. When I finally remembered the double take, he was long gone.

Where does this story begin? My mind returns to the lobby for the safety of "before," but the truth is, there was no safety then, nor was that the beginning. If someone had told me, before Kei arrived, that I would let her drag me back through our past, I would have said that person was crazier than I am. But there are answers I need, and the strength to face them. Our stepfather Arnie used to tell us to trace each step back to the beginning if we wanted to know the truth.

Here's what I know: When Kei called and asked to visit, I said I didn't want to see her. When she booked a flight anyway, I knew I had to hold my ground. I had to show her that she didn't control me any longer, that my life here was my own. She had laid claim to our mother, our town, our home in Hawaii. The least she could do was leave me my tiny, gray New York life.

But Kei never listened to anyone, so the only protest I had was not meeting her at the airport. In a city bigger than she could have dreamed of, I let her find her own cab. I left an extra set of keys for her with Hal, my super, and stayed late at Luciano's, the Italian restaurant on the Upper West Side where I work in the back as a bookkeeper. Nick, the owner, had taken me in like a misplaced kitten a couple of years ago, when I started lingering there every afternoon instead of going to the art studio. I still couldn't bear to create when all I wanted was to disappear. I was grateful for the job, for the bustle of the restaurant. It was a perfect way to get lost in plain sight—and wasn't that what New York was supposed to be good for?

That night, once I had lingered so long that I had organized the invoices for the whole month and finished the payroll, I came out from my one-desk office and tucked myself behind a table near the kitchen for my staff meal. Usually, I take it home at six p.m., like clockwork. But that night, after I finished eating, I decided to help bus tables. At first, it was just water refills, but when the calls for "Check, please!" began playing around me like background music, I started running those, too. Some of the waitresses eyed me, though no one asked me what I was still doing there. I hadn't told them about Kei, and could not even begin to imagine how to do so. Instead, I smiled to deflect the occasional spark of concern.

Nine o'clock passed, and so did ten. I can't say now if I was hanging on to the last, untainted minutes of my life without Kei, or if I was simply preparing myself to face her.

I had worked hard to leave my sister behind. I traveled five thousand miles to find a place where no one would stare at my scars. People in New York saw so little of me that they didn't even notice my eyes—that the right one is dark brown and the left tawny, almost hazel. It gave me an ersatz David Bowie look in this big city but had just screamed *hapa haole* in our little Hawaiian town. Kei and I were two of the few privileged and damned creatures of mixed race in that watery backwater place. Not the cosmopolitan girls with the pale skin, rounded eyes, the dark chocolate hair; they were more beautiful than any one race alone. No, we were clearly a mistake: Japanese on one side, Caucasian on the other. We were the daughters of Miya Swanson, the town's crazy lady who had breakdowns in public and talked to ghosts. Hana the good girl; Kei the rebel. We were opposites but equally haunted, though by what we didn't know.

But there are only so many hours in a day that can be wasted, and it was close to midnight when I finally left the restaurant. I often liked to walk home in the early evening, especially as the days got longer, but I've always been afraid of the dark—more so now than ever—so I took the bus that night, my brain so stuck on Kei that I barely noticed the time. Was she here to beg forgiveness all these years later? What could she possibly have to tell me, now that everyone we had loved was dead? And if I couldn't bear her voice on the phone, how would I stand having her invade my apartment? We had once been inseparable, and now—part of me still hoped that I might not find her when I arrived.

Oh, Kei. If only she had decided not to come.

* * *

It wasn't until I stuck my key into the door of my apartment and heard the top deadbolt snap closed instead of open that I had to admit to myself for certain that Kei was really here. I could picture her then, fumbling with the many keys Hal had handed her and then letting the door slam behind her once she was inside. She wouldn't bother to relock it; the house we grew up in didn't even have a key. Doors were like coats; we needed them some nights and on a couple of chilly days, but most of the time we left them hanging out of sight. In Hawaii, screen doors—those banging, bouncing, fraying things—were all that we needed to keep the flies out and let the breeze in. But we weren't children anymore.

"Kei?" I called, bolting the door behind me. "You left the door open!"

I winced even before the words left my mouth. I should have started with something nicer. *I'm home*, I should have said, though I could already feel what my place must look like to my sister. Maybe, *I'm here*?

My apartment could only kindly be called a hole in the wall. It's a railroad with low ceilings and narrow doorways, opening into an eat-in living room and galley kitchen, then running down a shoulder-width hall past a bathroom to a single bedroom beyond. The kitchen has a matched set of three-quarter-sized appliances lined up side by side against the wall with gaps just big enough for cockroaches between them. After a miserable freshmen year with a revolving arsenal of roommates, my college eventually gave me special permission to move off campus, and I had picked this particular apartment for the same reasons I would later take my job. Transience. Anonymity. Mediocrity. Solitude.

Kei was the first person to step inside it in five years, except for my super. I hadn't expected her to think much of it, and clearly she didn't. She had kicked her rubber slippers, *kapakahi*, into the middle of the living room floor, nowhere near the neat line of my own shoes beside the door. My blue leather beanbag chair, which I had bought after I left college, had been shoved across the floor. She must have been hungry, because she'd also raided my refrigerator, leaving an open bottle of orange juice balanced on the tines of my gas range and some cartons with my leftovers half eaten on the edge of the sink. Kei had even claimed my spare keys as her own. I recognized them on Arnie's old key ring, the one with his rusty, hand-forged can opener, which she had tossed onto my secondhand modular couch.

I hadn't even laid eyes on Kei yet and she was already displacing me. She had always assumed the world was hers for the taking, and I guess in some ways she'd been right.

"Kei!"

Did I expect an answer? I heard the clock radio playing John Denver in my bedroom, but it couldn't have been loud enough to block my voice. Was there a chance that Kei was simply asleep on my bed? I wasn't ready to walk in on her, trespassing in my most private space. The truth is, I couldn't bear to see her face. I wanted to freeze time. To roll it back.

But Kei was here, no longer looming and potential. I nudged her slippers into line with my now bare feet and then took the six steps to my stovetop. I shook the orange juice bottle, still partially full, and smelled it reflexively before putting it back into the refrigerator.

When I moved to the sink to throw out the food Kei left and wash the fork, I felt the faucet vibrating. I listened more carefully, over the light whine of the radiator that could not decide, in the wee hours of this late March morning, whether to blast me with heat or to knock, impotently, on and off.

The shower. Of course. That was why she hadn't answered.

The bathroom door was closed, but the bedroom was open. She'd left signs of herself all over my room. My bedspread was rumpled, tugged off toward one corner. Her flowered blouse and a pair of blue bell-bottoms already threaded by a thin gold elastic belt had been flung onto my bed. Kei's duffel bag was open and spilling out more clothes, as if she was looking for something.

I folded Kei's clothes as the disc jockey took over the radio, then placed them back inside her bag. As I picked up one of her blouses, a necklace fell onto the bed. It was a piece of jade half the length of my finger on a green, knotted cord. I was surprised to see it. Arnie hadn't failed to tell me that Kei made a very good living making and selling jewelry, but I'd assumed she was hawking tin plumeria earrings to tourists. This piece, plain as it was and strangely familiar, had character. Where had I seen it?

I don't know how long I stood there, contemplating the pendant. And also my mother's leather case, of course, where she kept her small collection of mementos. That was lying on my bed, half tumbled on its side. Kei had brought it, just as I had known she would. I sank down beside Kei's things, sitting hard on the edge of my mattress. I was as careful as I could be not to disturb Mama's case. I wasn't ready to touch it again.

"I have your inheritance," Kei had told me. Was it several weeks ago when she called? "I need to talk to you."

I hadn't wanted to hear her voice because it was my voice. I couldn't bear to argue with her. Kei could make up a story for anything; she fabricated a world with her fantasies, retold the truth. That was, in fact, the thing about my sister that I feared the most. But *need*? Kei had passed the cutoff for that long ago. It was my turn to get what I needed. And more than anything, what I needed was a reality I could cling to when things began to slip away.

As for my *inheritance*, Kei knew better. Although I could think of a long list of things our mother had left us—secrets, ghosts, and insanity, among them—our actual inheritance had been settled when Mama and Arnie died six months ago. It was, in its entirety, barely enough money to "plant them" as Arnie used to say, plus the house. And the one thing I wanted nothing to do with: Mama's leather case.

Mama had named me her executor. It shouldn't have been a surprise. From the moment we were given names, I was always Hana, the good daughter—the perfect daughter, really. It was my definition. Kei was the black sheep, given to impulse and destruction. My sister was charismatic but dangerously jealous, and three times in our lives together, she'd left me painted in blood. And yet no matter what Kei did, Mama kept choosing my sister, protecting her, supporting her, while I was left to find my own way. I'd come to understand too late: The bad girl is the one who sucks up all the air in the room.

By the time Kei called to say she was coming to New York, I already knew that she had gone to the bank and managed to withdraw the leather case from the safe deposit box where I had left it. I had received a confirmation copy of the withdrawal slip. She had signed it with my name. My precise slashes, which she had perfected when we were in our teens, and then mimicked so that whenever I tried to change it, her signature was always almost my own. It was easy to see her bent over the lamp on her bedside table, her fingers shimmying across the page. It shook me, that sudden vision of her, practicing. Blackening both sides of each sheet with my name.

As hard as I had fought to protect myself against her, that forged autograph had scribbled over my new life. My nightmares were the first thing to return. In them, I am lost in utter darkness. A dark so deep I cannot find myself; I cannot even see my hand when I touch my face. These were the nightmares that drove away my college roommates, the dreams I'd fled across the country to escape. They came with middle-of-the-night screams and sleeping with the light on. In the mornings, I used to stumble to a mirror, both longing for and terrified of the face I'd see. Until the mirrors started getting broken, then going missing. Until I started having blackouts, spells disturbingly like Mama's. Sometimes, I would come back to myself to find I'd been sketching eerie portraits in a kind of sleepwalking state.

I couldn't help what I didn't see in those mirrors, any more than I could stop the nightmares. Any more than I could reclaim my memories, which are as utterly empty as most of my dreams. The moment my life hinged on was the same one my sanity had blocked for me. I could see myself standing, happy, at the mouth of the cave, surrounded by people I'd thought were my friends. And then nothing. Nothing, except Kei vanishing, and her boyfriend Eddie's whispers, and me waking up in the hospital, crusted in dried blood.

After that, my only true protection was to purge my life of feeling, and empty my apartment of all reflection. Kei had vanished, and so would I. But everywhere I turned I saw her anyway, and myself.

Exhaustion almost felled me then. Somehow, I'd found the strength to pick up my mother's case and place it, righted, on the nightstand by my bed, but I was so tired, I barely felt the piece of jade I was clutching in my hand. I pulled the hand-sewn quilt I always kept at the foot of my mattress tight around my shoulders. I wanted to curl up under it and take shelter beneath the red plumeria silhouettes on their white background. Instead, I traced the almost invisible trail of stitches that coddled the petals, encroached on the pistils and sketched each spiraling, yin-and-yang leaf in all directions.

This was my only inheritance. The only thing I cared about, and even this Kei had tainted. My mother's stitches. Her final gift to me.

But then I had another thought. I had been right about the shower. Kei *hadn't* been ignoring me since I walked in. We still had the chance to start over, to begin again. That was what I thought: that there might still be a moment of welcome, a chance to simply be in each other's company. My desire for it surprised me, bittersweet in its impossibility, but still, palpably, there.

I got up and tapped gently on the bathroom door. "Kei?"

I had been home for about fifteen minutes by that time. My sister had always loved long, hot showers, a source of constant fights when my mother was lucid. It wasn't just the cesspool overflowing, or the bright orange fat from Arnie's Portuguese sausages climbing the walls of the kitchen sink while my mother waited to wash the dishes. Every morning, when Kei emerged from the bathroom, the hot water tank was empty. This went on until we were about thirteen, when, one day, my mother decided to clean up from breakfast *while* Kei was showering and discovered that by turning the cold water on, she could burn Kei—just a little, but enough to remind her that her time was up. Standing outside my New York bathroom, the sudden memory seemed funny—my sister's squawk, the smile on my mother's face that only I could see.

I smiled to myself and knocked again, a louder warning, and opened the door.

The light was off. I turned it on. The warm embrace of Kei's shower didn't rush to greet me; the room was cold.

The shower curtain was closed.

"You good, eh?" I asked Kei. I was doing my best: welcoming her in her own language—the pidgin she'd perfected in high school.

I drew the curtain, imagining her face bright and open under the stream of water.

All the signs I missed now fairly scream at me, but I saw none of them. I'd convinced myself she was simply washing shampoo from her hair.

Or maybe I did see the signs. Maybe by then, in the face of Kei's silence, in the room that had been dark, after so much time, I knew what I would see. I knew enough to draw the curtain, and when I did, there was no question.

My sister was lying, naked, on the bottom of the porcelain tub. Forgotten water sprayed onto her pelvis: beading her breasts, running down her belly and thighs. The tub was clear, clean; there was no blood. An inch or two of water had pooled around her, held there by a heel neatly plugging the drain. The rest of that foot flopped on its side, wrenched out of the plane of her body at the ankle, her wide, almost triangular feet looking all the more incongruous for pointing in the wrong direction. Her arms lay gracefully against her hips, palms cupped as though they had once held something too fragile to trust on its own.

I knew that body like it was mine. It was the body that would have been mine, without my scars. A long, purpling bruise pressed into Kei's ribs under her left breast, unnaturally crisp and thin. I thought, unaccountably, of hara-kiri, though it was not a blade cut. The rest of her skin was smooth, golden down to the nested black-and-white triangles over her pubic bone. She looked peaceful, except for the necklace of marks smudged incompletely into the base of her throat, dawning bruises in varying inks of red and blue.

And above her neck, my own face floated in a long, unraveling braid of dark seaweed just out of the water. The same egg-shaped head; my own stubby, unsophisticated nose. With her eyes closed, you could not see they were the exact opposite of my own—her left one brown, her right one tawny—but her full, bow-shaped lips were still mine, her barely sketched chin. Even her nails, which we learned to bite on the same day, let grow on the same day, and, I saw, though we were now living in different worlds, had both begun biting again.

My sister and I were more than identical; we had been cleaved down the middle, and each of us, against all odds, had sprung to life whole.

How many times had Kei wished me dead? In how many ways had she tried to make those wishes come true? For a flash of a moment, I feared that it was *my* body lying in the cold, rushing water. My spirit hovering to say its final good-byes.

But as I moved, I saw my own hand rising. My skin, white-white, and so cold. I clenched my fists and could feel my bitten nails digging into my palms.

I was alive and standing. It was Kei's shadow life that was over at last.

1 9 4 2

They would be traveling light. How many times did he have to tell her? He said they had to be able to move quickly, slip onto trains, to keep a tight hand on their luggage. When they got to Los Angeles, Lillie would need to carry her own cases, maybe even long distances. The whole world was at war now, and Donald had heard rumors. Who knew if they would be allowed onto a bus, or whether cabs were really refusing passage to people like them?

The original plan had been to travel east, making the long trip across the country to New York for their honeymoon. But when Donald got his mother's response to his telegram, they had decided to head south to be with his parents, whom Lillie had never met. She could tell he was worried. After that one message, there had been no word.

He had written that he was married.

His mother had replied: *Come home.*

There was no room for china—too breakable. The indigo blue sugar bowl Lillie's mother had given her was small enough and light, and it would be a nice gift for his own mother, he said, but there was certainly no room for the hand-embroidered quilt. It wasn't a real quilt, she'd protested, just a bedspread with light batting. Her mother had been working on it for months, creating patterns in bead, bullion, and bonnet stitches. The patterns, all in white, swirled off the ramps of paisley cocoons with flowers inside them, no two the same. The paisleys themselves nestled like flipped twins.

—Your trousseau. Her mother had smiled when Lillie exclaimed over the tiny stitches.

It could have fit into any reasonable trunk with room to spare, but they would take no trunks, not now. It was no longer the right time for the young bride to set up her new home. Besides, Donald didn't believe in possessions. He believed in *her*—that was what he told her—and he promised that as long as they were together he would take care of everything she would ever need. But he also believed in war—everyone was talking about Pearl Harbor and enemy aliens and espionage nets and some "fifth column"—and that made Lillie nervous. She'd felt so safe here in their home that was barely a town, with her parents' protection. What was she doing, letting him drag her into a city where simply having a face like hers made her a threat?

Watching her pack, Lillie's mother couldn't shake her own sadness. She had been preparing for Lillie's wedding for years. She wanted to send her daughter into the world with home around her.

She smoothed the quilt in her lap, still folded, unwilling to lay it back on Lillie's bed.

—We'll be back soon, Mother. And then we'll go on to New York, just as we planned. Donald will finish school and we'll start our own family. I promise I'll send for everything just as soon as we have a home.

She was twenty-two, her mother reminded herself. Old enough to make her own mistakes.

—Why can't he go himself, if he has to move so quickly? Lillie's mother heard the waver in her voice and waited for it to steady. Los Angeles might only be a few hours' ride away, but it felt like another world. "It's not safe there."

There was nothing to say to this. It was hard to know what was really happening there now that America was officially at war with Japan, but the rumors about the curfews and the FBI raids weren't comforting.

But Donald's mother had been ill, and he wanted to be with his parents, to bring his new happiness with Lillie into their lives. They might even pack his parents up and take them East, too, if the city was really as unfriendly to the Japanese as Donald said it was. What a gift that would be from the new bride to her in-laws, Lillie thought: a home, a hand extended, and later, a trousseau. She wasn't losing a mother, she told herself; she was gaining a new one.

She imagined herself in a family full of people who looked like she did.

—It was...Now Lillie's mother's voice did crack. Crying softly, but this time without embarrassment, she said, "The quilt was supposed to bring you luck."

—Mother.

Lillie had slept beneath this quilt for the last two weeks since the wedding, and each night, she fell into a deep sleep in Donald's arms. She would wrap herself in it if she could and wear it on the train. But she didn't want to anger her husband now. Why couldn't her mother understand? Why did she have to make their parting so difficult?

Their temporary parting, Lillie corrected herself. It was the first time since she had been left on the steps of their church as a nameless infant that Lillie would leave her mother's sight for longer than a night of sleep.

Now, she put her arm around her mother. *Foster* mother, she reminded herself. But she'd never thought much of their differences until she met Donald. Her mother's golden hair was shot with silver now, and her skin was like soft tissue.

—I'm my own good luck charm. Isn't that what you always tell me? I'm the one who brought the luck.

Lillie watched her mother flinch, each taking in the consequences of her words.

What had happened to their simple days? Lillie wondered. When Donald first showed up in their town, a handsome stranger with a face like hers; when he was courting her, teaching her how to pick up rice with the ends of sticks and then throwing up his hands, but with a smile, when she tossed them down, when she declared she didn't know what made less sense, eating with sticks when you had a drawer of perfectly good forks in the sideboard or trying to corral all those tiny little grains into a mouthful that wouldn't feed a baby bird. Those days, her mother would laugh at Lillie's nice young man, and he would give up and eat the potatoes she served them. And at night, when Donald and Lillie sat on the porch together and she pointed out the stars, he whispered:

—I'll show you the world someday. Your true home. Your people.

It sounded like the promise she had been longing to hear all her life. Now, surrounded by the home she'd chosen not to question until now, and her marriage, too, she felt she could be anything. Go anywhere. She was complete for the first time.

The time had come to see the world.

Lillie ran her hand one last time over her mother's stitches. "Let's put it back on the bed, Mother, and then come outside with me."

Lillie's mother shook her head. "We'll leave it in the trunk. That way, it'll be ready when you return."

Their four hands lifted the light offering, balancing it back and forth between them, then placed it into the trunk together, their hands brushing as they patted it into place. Her mother stood, heavily. "Just to the door."

When Lillie stepped past her mother onto the front porch, where her father and husband were waiting, she took in the rolling grass of the California prairie for the last time, and their little white church, next to their little white house, bobbing in a sea of green. The congregation had come on Sunday, and the hymns that Lillie always loved to sing were sad, but beautiful. There were no neighbors to say good-bye to.

Her mother hovered in the doorway as if she might dissolve if she stepped away from the house. Her father hugged her, stiff and oddly formal, and then handed his daughter over to the husband God gave her.

—It's all a mistake, her father assured them. "Don't worry about what the newspapers are saying. They'll realize soon enough that you aren't the Japs they should be worrying about."

Japs. Lillie knew what her father meant, but Donald flinched at the word and she realized that she had, too. She was a Jap now. Even her father had said it. She'd become an enemy alien, when she had always only been herself.

Donald picked up her bag and thanked her parents for their hospitality. He addressed the preacher and his wife formally, and for a moment, when the words "Mother" and "Father" refused to cross his lips, Lillie wondered if her mother wasn't right after all: He *could* travel much lighter to check on his mother if he was alone.

But the choice had been made, and her mother was holding her, her tears falling into her daughter's black hair. Lillie felt her own tears rise in response. She blinked them away. It was supposed to be a happy day, the first real day of her adulthood. Still, she hugged her mother tight, unwilling to be the one who let go first. They clutched each other until Donald gently touched her arm.

—Don't forget us, her mother whispered, finally releasing her grip. They stared at each other.

Lillie's father patted his wife's back awkwardly. "You'll be just fine," he said again, directing his words to Lillie. "War or no war. If you can't make it on your own in the world, we didn't do our job right when we raised you." He turned to his wife, gave her a pained smile. "Right, Mother? Children are supposed to leave. She is strong. She's beautiful..."

—Wait, Lillie's mother said. "Take this." She unclenched her fist and held out her balled, damp handkerchief. "See? Light and luck. You remember the song? *She'll bring light and luck wherever she goes.* And it won't take up any room."

Lillie looked at the tiny pointed stars her mother had crocheted herself—snowflakes, as Donald would later correct her, perfect for a winter wonderland on the East Coast. She unbuckled the clasp on her leather handcase and tucked it inside.

Lillie's mother collected herself and spoke one last time, as the preacher put his arm around her shoulders. "Wherever you are in the world, even if you never come home, promise me you won't forget we love you."

The future that her mother released her into slipped beneath Lillie like a startled horse. *Never come home?* They'd return in just a few weeks, as her mother well knew. Lillie almost spoke, to insist on it, but something in her mother's face stopped her. Instead, she promised, and waved good-bye as she walked, backward, to the waiting car.

HANA

Nothing that happened that night will stay where it belongs in my mind. It's a kaleidoscope. Forever shifting, without end. The shards of broken time: No matter how fast I spin my mind, I cannot fit them into the picture that I used to carry.

When I found Kei, what did I do? I knelt beside her. I know I called her name. I can still feel the spray, light on my face when I bent over; I can watch it grow on my lashes as I wonder what to do. I think my hair spilled over the side of the basin and grazed Kei's rib cage. And then I watched myself move—slowly—my hands floating away from my body as if the world no longer ran on time.

I reached out, expecting to help her, but instead, I touched Kei's neck. I felt her heartbeat quite clearly. Thank God—she was alive. As the tips of my fingers brushed her bruises, my hands felt disconnected, hovering over her, trying to make sense of those ugly, brutal marks. I flipped my hands thumbs up; I overlapped them; I faced them off against each other, nail to nail. Impossible.

How could someone have hurt my sister?

What I remember is this: her heartbeat in my temples, and the singsong running through my mind. *She left me, she left me not. She left me, she left me not. She left me...*

"Kei," I whispered. It bewildered me to look down at her, her adulthood washed off her, as if the years between us had never happened. But somehow that made it harder, not easier, to accept that it really was her. "It's me. Hana. Can you sit up?"

I thought then about lifting her so she didn't drown, but what if a rib was broken? What if I punctured her lung? I raised my hands, then dropped them. I stood, then knelt, then stood again. I was useless, unable to change even the angle of her torso. All I could do was turn the water off.

And then turn it back on once I realized my mistake.

Evidence. I was tampering with evidence. And then tampering again in my effort to rectify the problem because my mind could not keep up. Evidence meant police. And police? I left Kei with the water running and called 911.

Time started moving forward then. A woman's voice answered. I told her what I knew, that my sister was unconscious. I could hear her typing as she talked.

"Is she breathing?"

"Yes."

"Bleeding?"

"No. I don't think so. Please, can't you send someone?"

"They're on their way. Stay with me. How long since it happened?"

I knew she was trying to be helpful, but I couldn't bear to think of the hours Kei could have been lying there while I wasted time at the restaurant. "Please..." I said, letting whatever words that might have wanted to follow fade before they could be formed.

She continued typing in the background. "Any medications?"

It took me a moment to understand what she was asking. "She was attacked. I think. I don't know."

"Is the perpetrator there?"

"I don't—no." The *perpetrator*? I spun around, as if her words could conjure up a figure in the hallway. An attacker, here in the room with me still.

If he *was* here, was I safer looking for him, or letting him hide until the police arrived? What was I thinking? The hallway was empty. I was alone, of course. My apartment was so tiny, and I had been in every room.

Breathe, I told myself.

"Please. She's my sister." I dropped the phone back into the cradle and backed up until I could feel the comfort of the wall behind me. "She's my sister," I said again to no one.

Across the room, I saw that someone had shoved aside my heavy curtains. Through my large, unblinking windows, I had a clear view of the elevated subway tracks. Washed in the struggling, cellophane light of the overhead lamps, the platform was mostly empty at this time of night. None of the people waiting on the downtown platform were looking toward me. Yet.

Had Kei been the one to open the curtains? Had *the perpetrator* looked in and targeted her that way? Once it was night, my fourth-floor apartment was a beacon in the darkness. Any one of the shifting mass of commuters could look straight in at me. He might have watched me regularly if I was on his usual route, might have stepped off the train to see me drift from one window to the other as I washed my dishes or read a book any night of the week.

On impulse, I pulled the curtains shut, but it was too late. Now that he had been here, inside my private spaces, I'd never be able to get him out. It wasn't the kind of invasion I had imagined up to that point: a physical confrontation I could avoid with my double-locked doors.

The phone rang again. *The perpetrator*, I thought, with another flash of panic. No one ever called me; I only had a telephone number because I needed it to get electricity and gas. As I put the receiver to my ear and heard no voice but the distant, almost otherworldly, static in the earpiece, I had the strangest thought: my mother.

My mother was here. Somewhere in the phone. She'd come back to me. I waited to hear her curl the tail of her sentence up and into a question, just as always. What would she say to me? I had been waiting for her for so long.

"Hello?" I ventured into the silence. *Mama?* stayed on the tip of my tongue.

The static clicked off then and I could hear a male voice in mid-shout through the handset that also doubled as the building intercom.

The police.

I buzzed them in, then listened to their shoes clomp and the chatter of their walkie-talkies. There were two on the third floor already and more coming up the stairs. By the time the hall had emptied into my apartment, there were six officers, bumping into each other as they tried to avoid touching my things. I watched them separate—two down the hall toward the sound of the shower, while the others headed to the roof or down to the basement laundry room looking for clues, witnesses, the perpetrator. I took a breath as the activity eased, and then the sole female officer moved forward. I read her name tag: DETECTIVE LYNCH. She had short, badly permed hair, and about forty pounds on me.

"Do you speak English?"

"Yes."

I was her duty then: a woman, an English speaker. "You are...?" she prompted.

"Hana. Hanako Swanson."

"You're the one who called? Did you see what happened? Who are we looking for?"

Her questions piled on top of each other so fast I didn't know whether to nod or shake my head. I must have looked entirely useless, because once she figured out that I'd just come home and discovered Kei's body, she led me out to the hall so I wouldn't contaminate the crime scene. I was relieved to get away from the bustle, and, despite her assumption that I was an uncomprehending foreigner, I was grateful when she sat me down on the wide marble stairs just outside my apartment door and took out her notebook. I could feel myself shaking. I grabbed my elbows, hugging myself as she asked for my name, again. My address. Kei's name.

Hanako—I spelled it. Keiko—I spelled that too. But then the questions got murkier. Had I touched anything? What was out of place when I walked in? Who knew Kei was here?

There was nothing I *hadn't* touched, I realized. The leftovers I had tampered with, and Kei's strewn clothing...they could have been decisive clues. And the shower: I had obliterated any fingerprints that would have been on the faucets. But I'd been in a daze, surely understandable;

there was no reason to volunteer my stupidity. *No*, I kept saying, to myself as much as to the detective. *No. No.* The words echoed in my mind, threatening to take on a tune.

The ambulance stretcher arrived shortly after the police did. Two paramedics carried it, hanging vertically between them; two black bands strapping the sheets down so they wouldn't slide off the backboard as the paramedics jogged up the stairs. Both of the men were loaded down with black bags of different sizes. All that equipment just for Kei.

Why was Kei visiting in the first place? Detective Lynch was asking. I pulled my attention away from the medics, but I had no answer for her. Wasn't that what I'd been dreading to learn this whole time? Now, what if I never could?

The detective was still talking. Did she take drugs? Might she have slipped in the shower?

I reminded myself that she hadn't seen Kei or her bruises.

"You sure she knows no one here?" She flipped through her notes. "No one who would want to hurt her?"

Then another cop joined us.

"Detective Tapper," he said to me by way of introduction. "Which one's her purse? She must've had one—you said she'd just got off the plane, right?"

"I—" I tried to imagine my sister—much younger in my mind. She was cramming what little she needed into her pockets. "She doesn't...I don't think she carries a purse."

"She *is* your sister, isn't she?" He raised an eyebrow. "I mean, she must have a wallet. A plane ticket. Don't you girls always have some place to put your lipstick and a bit of gum?"

Gum, I thought, guilty. Did Kei chew gum? What was wrong with my brain?

"Sir, in here!" Another officer leaned out of my doorway. "The window."

I lost their attention immediately. As quick as that, we were back inside my apartment, and I was hovering near my bedroom door as one of the officers pointed to a dusting of white paint chips beneath the window ledge by the fire escape.

"That you?" he asked me.

"What?"

"Did you open it?"

"No." It was true.

He turned to confer with the detective. "Could be like the others."

"Others?" That was my voice.

"Break-ins in the neighborhood. Small stuff usually, jewelry, cash—easy to carry. Guy comes in off the fire escape. Did you leave it open?"

Did he really think I would leave my apartment open? Had he failed to make a connection between the relative safety of my neighborhood and the floor bolt braced through my front door? My building was on a quiet side street, only ten blocks long, and next door to a theological seminary, a park, and a church. It was less grimy, less bustling, than the bodega-lined Broadway it was tucked behind, and so inconsequential that some people who'd lived on the Upper West Side forever didn't even know it was there. But still, it was New York and nothing was safe.

"There's a gate on the window," I pointed out.

"Maybe he opened it himself, after, you know, whatever happened in the bathroom with her."

My chest caved right then, and I could feel myself slipping. I held on to my head with both hands as if they could keep me from losing my mind. That was why there were so many policemen. They were chasing a guy...and he did this to women. In my neighborhood.

When I didn't answer, he waved his hand at the sill, showing me that the window sash was indeed lifted, just a crack. He slid a pencil through the opening and pushed at the security gate. It swung outward at his touch. "Painted shut, looks like. See these flakes? That's all that was keeping anyone from getting in. These old buildings are like that. You probably didn't know."

"No." I was still trying to scrub my mind of all the new images they had just evoked. It could have happened to me, I realized. My security gate...how had it opened? I had checked it, obsessively, just like all the other locks, hadn't I?

Except I couldn't remember.

"Robbery," Detective Tapper said, with some consideration. "Did she bring anything else with her? Anything someone might have been looking for?"

My eyes fell on Mama's case, though there was nothing in it that a stranger would want. There was nothing in it for me, either, except old pain. But I didn't want them pawing through it, so I kept turning my head, hoping they wouldn't notice my hesitation. I kept turning, until I had spun myself around.

"You're lucky you didn't have anything valuable. Just the sister's purse, then. I don't suppose you can describe it?"

"No. I said that already. About the purse. I don't know." I could feel myself breaking, but they didn't have to know that there was no way I could know any of these answers, having been outside of Kei's life for so long.

Detective Lynch was explaining that they would be dusting my apartment for fingerprints and I would be more comfortable spending the night elsewhere when Kei was wheeled, feet first, out of the bathroom.

"Kei!" I said. "Oh, thank God!"

I expected her to answer. I assumed they had woken her up. They'd had so much time to do it. She was tied down on the stretcher, tucked under a layer of blankets mounded with meters and monitors. What was left of her braid had been dumped into a wet pile beside her head. Between her closed eyes and the oxygen mask, most of her face was covered. Her neck was braced.

When Kei didn't respond, I turned to Detective Lynch. "She's going to be okay?" I asked, as if she could know. She just looked at me, with the first real sympathy I'd gotten since they'd arrived.

We stepped aside as they maneuvered Kei into the hall in a cloud of radio static. "I'll drop you at the hospital. We can finish up in the car."

"The hospital," I repeated. Hospitals have never been my favorite places—less so since I spent my eighteenth birthday in an ICU.

To her credit, Detective Lynch noticed my expression. "I can drop you with a friend instead. If you want someone to be with you. Who will you stay with, in case we have more questions for you tomorrow? Where will you be?"

There was no one. She must have seen that in my expression, too.

"Friends? From college? A teacher?"

I shook my head, turning away to find my own purse. Since I had stopped meeting Dr. Shawe, the shrink Arnie had insisted I see in exchange for my college tuition, the only person who ever even checked on me was my boss, and I certainly wasn't getting Nick involved in this mess. After my own turned against me, I'd had enough "family" to last a lifetime.

I grabbed a sweater and my shoes, hoping she wouldn't ask anything more. I lived a solitary life, but the truth was, I kept myself separate by choice. Since Mama died, I'd allowed myself to be friendly with some of the waitresses, especially the ones who worked semester to semester, because I could count on them to leave. We could share a laugh, but we didn't get together outside of work, or exchange telephone numbers. It was a relief to me.

When you have no one, no one can hurt you.

But of course, a detective wasn't going to let that drop so easily. The fact that there was no one waiting to take me in at one a.m. took on a significance it didn't actually have. I wasn't going to explain how I'd never really had friends, not until high school, and then the worst had happened. As we walked down the stairs to the lobby, she asked, "What about you?"

"I'm all right, thanks."

"I meant, is there anyone *you* know who might have done this? Someone who might have a bone to pick with you?"

"No." It was shocking to think of.

"Any guys in your classes look at you funny? Maybe a special fellow?"

"No. I—" There had never been anyone after Russell. I couldn't even bear to be alone with my own body, much less become intimate with someone else. "No fellows. Boyfriends. No. No friends. I mean, I graduated two years ago."

"Work, then. Any strange characters—"

"No." I cut her off. "I don't work."

The lie just burst out of me—I had to stop her from speaking. Then I saw her face. I had already told her I worked at a restaurant and had been forced to wait tables that night until it closed. And now I realized that my story of being required to stay would be very easy to check. "I mean…it's a restaurant, not a real job…Not like I'm in anyone's way for a promotion. I'm in the back mostly, doing the books, ordering the supplies, and making sure the shifts are covered. Most of the day, I'm completely alone. I only wait tables sometimes, if I want to, which is almost never, really. Tonight was an exception. But no one there would ever…I'm mean, I've never even dumped a pot of coffee into someone's lap!" I was babbling, but only because it seemed less peculiar than the truth. I pulled the sleeves of my sweater down over my wrists so she couldn't see my skin. An old reflex. Panic bubbled in my throat, though whether it was because of the detective's skeptical expression or the suggestion that I could have been the target, I didn't know. How could I admit to her that I'd spent years making myself invisible? No one even whistled at me on the street.

It was then I remembered the double take. Kei and I got them all the time when we were growing up.

"Oh my God," I said, looking around at the empty lobby. "I know who it was. I walked right into him when I came home."

It was a gift, and I could feel the rush of thanks that ran through my body. I had something to offer after all.

Detective Lynch picked up her walkie-talkie, ready to broadcast his description. "What did he look like?"

"I—"

I couldn't quite see him, though he had been standing right in front of me. I took in the black marble-tiled floor and the wavering light from the fluorescents above. Color, could I see any color in his clothing? "Normal clothes, maybe? He was about my height. Maybe a little taller. Average height. Not heavy. You know, ah—a normal build."

She was waiting.

"He—" I couldn't say I didn't know. I walked toward the vestibule, as if being there could help me. "It was the look he gave me. I know it was him. The way he stared at me...it was like I had just risen from the dead."

"What did *he* look like?" she repeated.

"Ah..." I closed my eyes to dredge up his face. I didn't have the words to describe him, not for even the things I could almost remember. How do you describe a nose, if it's a normal nose? What about eyes that aren't squinty, or bulging, or ringed in black?

The more I pushed, the greater my sense that I knew him. He was hovering outside of my reach.

After a moment of silence, fingers pressed to my forehead, I finally came up with a word. "White?"

The word dropped between us: belly up, unmoving. It was my only offering, after destroying the crime scene, but it wasn't what she wanted. I searched for something more, a description that would please her, but I couldn't make up the kind of bad guy she would recognize. "Maybe...swarthy?"

"Swarthy." She mouthed the word like she didn't know what it meant, but in this case, other than *not blond*, I couldn't help her.

She left me... I felt panic rising and looked to Detective Lynch to help ground me before my worries could gain enough momentum to carry me away. Who knew how I must have appeared to her, in midargument with my inner demons?

Her expression gave me more than an inkling. She put the walkie-talkie down.

1 9 4 2

There were not many other people waiting on the train platform. Lillie smiled at two women she knew from church, but they turned away. Donald was furious for her. "How *couldn't* they know you?" He was right. She and Donald were the only two Japanese in this town, a nub in the rough center of hundreds of acres of farms. She'd been the only until he arrived, a passenger on the bus that broke down near their church. A broken axle, and he stayed. By Christmas he'd proposed. Until Donald, Lillie had never had a mirror held constantly to her face, and she was still not used to seeing herself through his eyes.

Once they were settled on the train, with their bags stacked around their feet and in their laps, a conductor came through the aisle, cheerfully checking people's tickets. When he got to their seats, he looked at the two of them in mild alarm.

—You're going in the wrong direction, he said.

Lillie wasn't sure what he meant—it was true they were facing the caboose—until he continued, "Once we pass into the restricted zone, you won't be able to leave."

Donald's eyes flashed as he retorted, "We're fine, thank you."

And there was her choice: to believe in her husband or a stranger. Donald would consider no alternative: He was riding to his parents' rescue. "It's us against them," he had been saying for weeks. Lillie understood who "us" was. She'd been having trouble with "them." She was American: born here, dropped on her parents' doorstep when she was only a few days old. She'd grown up in the home of a preacher. She'd taught the children music and led the Sunday choir. Surely that would prove she was no enemy to the people around her. But now, as she thought about the women on the platform, she wondered if the smiles she got when she passed through the congregation had always been as thin as they'd become since December.

Lillie could tell by the set of Donald's tight mouth that he didn't want to talk about the ticket taker's warning, so she turned back to the window as the train chugged on. When they finally crossed the city limits, she felt a mild nausea building after several hours of jostling and lurching backward on the swaying train. A pair of men in uniform whose smiles were far less friendly came through asking for their travel permits.

Donald pretended not to understand their question. Even if he had been aware they needed permits, Lillie felt pretty certain Donald would have rejected the notion that the government could tell them where they could go. Her husband was an idealist but also stubborn; he liked to tease her that she was afraid enough for both of them. She let her hand creep toward his lap, and one of the men may have seen it because he made a crack about how it was easier to round the Japs up all together in one place anyway before he hitched his head in the direction of the door and they left Lillie and Donald alone.

She could see the blocky city skyline growing bigger through the window when she craned her neck and clenched her jaw against her gurgling stomach.

Los Angeles. January 1942. They had arrived.

Donald's parents lived in a two-room apartment over a small store in the south corner of the city. The stairs in the hallway smelled of garlic, and some spices she would come to recognize later as shoyu and ginger. Not unpleasant, exactly, but cloying and sharp. The hall itself was so narrow that she had to scale the stairs sideways to get her bag up, trying not to bang her shins, which had become black and blue on the long walk from the station despite Donald's help, carrying both bags for long stretches. Here at last at their destination, he'd found a burst of energy and took the stairs quickly. He was excited to surprise his parents, she knew, and he wanted them to welcome her. By the time Lillie arrived at the top of the stairs, Donald was half inside the door, propping it open for her with one trailing foot as his body leaned forward, dragged down and into the embrace of his frail, sobbing mother. Lillie assumed the man in the chair in the living room, waiting for Donald to disengage himself, was Donald's father. Tateishi-sama. The man seemed to grimace, but nodded when Donald came over to bow in front of him.

Lillie's own entrance was less joyful. When his parents greeted her in Japanese, the sounds were rushed and slurred. Lillie froze, fumbling, unable to remember the formal Japanese phrase Donald had taught her, though she wasn't sure if it would be the right response anyway, since she didn't recognize the noises they had made. She also forgot to bow.

His parents, she was shocked to discover, didn't speak *any* English. *Belly so nice to greet you*, his mother said to her, as Lillie fought the urge to smile at the double entendre. The rest of the initial welcome fluttered over her head, punctuated by tears and coughing on the part of Donald's mother. His mother was, indeed, quite sick.

Unsure how to proceed from the doorway where she remained, hovering, Lillie felt the urge to run. When she finally moved into the room, she perched on the arm of the couch where Donald and his mother sat, barely floating her bottom in case this was not allowed, though there was nowhere else to sit. No one acknowledged her.

She couldn't tell how long they talked: Donald's mother gesturing and tearful, his father seemingly angry, and all of it in a language that dipped and dove like birds around her. She noticed that they were not offered food; she wondered, for the first time, if Donald's parents could afford to host them. When Donald's mother finally laid some bedding on the floor for them to sleep on, since they wouldn't both fit on the narrow cot that had been Donald's bed in a room barely bigger than Lillie's own closet, Lillie didn't ask him to fill her in on the conversation.

She was not ready to know.

* * *

The ticket taker had been right. The patriotic fervor of the country had trained itself on the people who looked like the enemy, and it seemed that the government released new restrictions every few days. Lillie and Donald had barely arrived when it was announced that Japanese Americans could no longer travel more than five miles without a permit. Also, they were not allowed on the streets after dark. Donald fumed—he was a citizen and this was clearly unconstitutional, but if that was true, no one in the government seemed to care. It was more than a touchy subject for Lillie. Not just because they were trapped here and a burden on his parents instead of being the support they had intended to be, nor because—even though each new rule was a surprise—it was also clear in retrospect that they'd been warned. When Lillie met Donald, he'd been on his way to New York for a scholarship to law school. After lingering for a week with her and her family, he called to let the registrar know he was delayed and learned his funding had been revoked because of the war. Donald blamed the broken axle, and a racial prejudice he'd thought he was leaving behind in California, but Lillie blamed herself. Donald could have taken another bus if he hadn't met her. Every time the word *unconstitutional* crossed his lips, which was often, Lillie only heard again that it was she who had destroyed his dreams.

Donald's father seemed to think so, too. Whether he appreciated his son's return or thought him stupid, Lillie couldn't tell, but it was clear Tateishi-sama didn't like his son's choice of bride. Maybe it was the fact that she didn't speak Japanese, which he often pointed out by cursing her, rather than isolating the words like Donald's mother did so Lillie could understand. Maybe he knew that she had distracted Donald. Maybe he had been counting on his son to find a lawyer in New York to rescue them. In the whirlwind that was their romance, it had never occurred to Lillie to ask if there was someone else his parents had picked out for him, and now that she was slowly learning about "her people," she wondered about that, too.

On the bright side, Donald's parents never ventured out of Little Tokyo anyway, so the travel restrictions didn't affect her daily life. Lillie spent her days trailing behind her mother-in-law, carrying whatever food they purchased, and letting the old woman lean on her when she grew tired. If she'd understood Japanese, Lillie could have taken over the shopping and let Donald's mother rest, but unlike Donald's father, her new mother-in-law seemed to enjoy pantomiming the proper way to do things and teaching Lillie simple words in her new language. *Please. Thank you. Excuse me. Don't go to any trouble. I'm sorry.* Lillie tried her best, but there was always another word to learn to get across the specific nuance of *Excuse me, I'm sorry* in whatever she was trying to say. She gave herself to the role: proud of the few words she learned and grateful that her mother-in-law enjoyed her company. "Living in a bubble," Donald called it, but not unkindly since he could see that her cheer made his mother feel better, especially on the days when the older woman's lungs were so weak that she couldn't get out of bed.

Weeks went by. Then months. Lillie never wrote to her parents. There wasn't time at first. Then there wasn't money for frivolities like stationery and postage stamps. Donald's parents were poor, but it was more than that: She was out of place in what felt like a foreign country, so far away that a letter would never bridge the gap between here and her former life. After a while, it had been so long since Lillie had had a conversation of more than a few sentences in English that she was at a loss for what to write. It might have been, too, that she simply couldn't bring herself to admit what she was bursting to say.

She had made a mistake.

She was tired of the strangeness, of being an outsider. She wanted to roll back time: travel away from the city, erase her marriage, unmeet Donald, be under her mother's protection once more. But it was done. Her luck had run out, if she ever had any. Could she bear to disappoint her foster parents by showing up on their doorstep once again, feeling ill and tarnished, and vaguely unworthy? *Children leave*, she reminded herself. When she returned next, she wanted to make them proud, to show them she was a woman in her own right. And yet for every day that passed here, she grew more childlike, less able to fend for herself, more dependent on Donald and his parents.

And she knew, too, that now that she was here in LA, there was no way for her to get back to the farm—with or without a sense of defeat. She was trapped: by her marriage, by her duty to her mother-in-law, by the government itself with its no-travel zones.

Then, once again, Donald and Lillie were leaving.

The posters went up in April on the telephone poles all over Little Tokyo. "Aliens and non-aliens" were being evacuated in six days' time. As their family head, Donald had to report to the Civil Control Station for instructions, where he started to point out that *non-alien* was another word for *citizen of the United States*, but then kept his mouth shut when it became clear that comments like that would get him arrested, leaving Lillie and his parents to be evacuated alone. No one was told where they were going or why, or how long they'd be gone; they knew only where to meet and what to bring, which was almost nothing. Bedding, clothes, plates, and utensils for each of them, but only as much as each person could carry themselves. Lillie had brought only what she could carry with her in the first place, but even she had not expected that that would be all she ever owned.

The much larger problem was what to do with the things they were leaving behind. Six days was not much time to sell everything the family owned. In fact, it was an impossible time frame. Everyone was having the same fire sales. Signs that read, EVERYTHING MUST GO! competed with signs that assured curious gawkers, I AM AN AMERICAN. All the homes and stores in Little Tokyo had been thrown open to loud, pink men who left perspiration all over their furniture and refused to drink the tea Lillie offered. Carpetbaggers, Donald called them. No one bought anything the first day, or the second. Panic mounted, and as the week went by, it was clear from the haggling that Donald and his family were going to get little if any money for their hard-earned possessions. The bids were getting *lower*. Some people offered, with their gloating and their false pity, to take things off their hands for free.

That was when Lillie learned how truly unconcerned her husband was with possessions. The day before they were leaving, Lillie and her mother-in-law were sorting through items in the front room. The older

woman kept trying to rescue her most precious objects, replacing bed-
sheets with a picture album and a cup with a candlestick. Her one bag
was hopelessly overflowing, and Lillie was trying to slip the candlestick
back out without her mother-in-law seeing when a man arrived. He offered Donald a nickel for whatever he could stack into one box. When
Donald refused, the man changed his offer.

—A tenner for everything.

—For what? What do you want?

—Everything. The whole house.

He was sneering at Lillie when he said it, as if she might be part of
the sale. Lillie looked away from his greedy blue eyes and wanted to
vomit. What was wrong with these people? These were their neighbors they were preying on. Poor old people, who had done nothing
wrong. She wanted to scream at him, but Donald was shoving her out
of the way hard as he moved to shield her, and she and her mother-
in-law scrambled to the bedroom as Donald shoved the man next.
Lillie and the old woman remained there through the raised voices,
the threats to call the police and the crash that followed, and even
through the held breath of silence that stretched painfully in Lillie's
chest. From behind the bedroom door, they listened to Donald stack-
ing dishes, and gathering all the breakable items in the house. These,
she knew, they could never carry. Was he taking them somewhere else
to sell them? Was he filling up a nickel box?

She knew she should go out to help her husband, but the fury in his
face as he pushed her lingered, adding to the queasy feeling she'd had in
her stomach all day. Her mother-in-law clung to her arm, so Lillie gave in
to her weakness and stayed in the bedroom with her, letting Donald take
care of the house for a change. There were no sounds of carpetbaggers.
She imagined the huge stacks of things they would have to carry, twisting
and swaying against the sky.

Lillie and her mother-in-law were still in the bedroom when the glass-
blown lamp shattered: first through the windowpane, then again from
a distance below them, in the street. Lillie leapt to her feet, startled,
until she heard Donald swearing at the living room window, breaking the

shards of glass out of the wooden frame. She could tell from the high, shattering pops that he was lobbing drinking glasses next, and found herself trying to guess which glass was which by the pitch of the sound. She knew she was numb, that there was something wrong with her reaction, even as she heard Donald's voice float out of the past: *Your world, Lillie. The time has come to see* your *world.* Donald's mother moaned, and Lillie held her tightly while she sorted through the sounds of her husband picking up each piece of china and tossing it, one by one, into the street two stories down.

She needn't have worried; there would be no wavering tower of valuables. Donald took care of everything, just as he had promised. Once the sound stopped below the window, he started flinging what was left around the apartment. Lillie heard liquid splash against the door. Her heart broke to hear him stumble into the furniture. To be filled with his braying, keening despair. Yet she stayed still, holding his mother in her arms. When the two women finally opened the bedroom door into silence, long after Donald departed, they found that carrying what was left would be simple enough. The more difficult task would be to gather it, when they couldn't even take a step through the glass and the splattered food without shoes.

HANA

It was a quiet ride to the hospital, and a too-short one. I imagined sirens for Kei, and fishtailing in the back of an ambulance as the EMTs rushed to save her, but she was gone, ahead of me, and I was bundled into the back seat of Detective Lynch's squad car with my options dwindling to none. My breath kept catching; it might have been the heater, or the protective guard between the front and back seats that shut me off from the detective and her partner, but I couldn't seem to fill my lungs.

When the squad car pulled up to the neon-lit emergency room entrance, I didn't move. Detective Lynch asked me again if there wasn't someone I could stay with, then she told me she'd check for me here tomorrow if she didn't hear from me. It sounded like a threat. Huddled families smoked in the sallow spotlights in front of the sliding doors to the ER, arms wrapped against the spring cold. I looked from her to them and then back, letting my eyes rest on the gray roots peeking out from beneath the detective's bristled perm. The light caught the sheen of a long day splashed across her nose and accentuated the soft puffs under her eyes. And still...I wanted her to hold me. I had barely touched another human being in years, and suddenly I had the urge to fling myself at her, through the barrier of the squad car, and be borne back to a safety that I couldn't even locate in my mind.

My desperation shocked me.

The air outside was sharp and cold when the car door opened. Inside the waiting area, I was accosted by that too-familiar smell of hospitals:

shrill on top, sour underneath, and in the middle, empty. I even recognized the sound of the vending machines clicking on and off, and the soap opera stars in their endless loop murmuring from television screens set so close to the ceiling that none of the grief-stricken people in the waiting room could shut them up.

Kei was somewhere behind the locked doors that read, DO NOT ENTER. The triage nurse gave me my sister's intake forms, but I could barely hold a pen. Surrounded by coughing, bleeding patients playing musical chairs as they waited for their injuries to become more urgent than anyone else's, I waited—forms in my lap, half-filled insurance papers on the chair, and a jangling in my legs that kept taking me back to the triage window.

Was Kei awake? Had she been asking for me? Did someone tell her that her sister was here?

The nurses would tell me nothing about my sister's condition. *We don't know yet. They're doing tests. They're doing everything they can.* They had questions for me, plenty of questions I couldn't answer, but they would only say in return, *Let the doctors do their job.*

"Is she dead, then?" I asked the poor nurse behind the thick, scratched glass of the triage window; she'd seen far too much of me by then and had probably been awake just as long as I had. The sharp warble of my worry unnerved me. I raised my voice. "Is she dead?" I wanted to shock her. I could feel a riot growing inside me and I wanted it to spread. We were all gathered here in the early-morning hours reserved for the furtive and the sleeping, and wasn't that what we were all thinking? Why couldn't we see the people we had come for?

I caused a ripple in the room, but barely. They probably chalked me up as someone off her meds, a patient myself, and right then I wished I still was. I was the quiet twin. The caretaker. Normally, I would never have made a scene. It was Kei who, for so much of our childhood, had been the rule breaker: the one who could slip in and out of trouble like it was the sea. We had worried for my reckless sister, even lost her, but she had always been stronger than any trouble she called to her. Now, her sudden vulnerability unnerved me. It reminded me too much of my own.

* * *

I lost some time. That night, even the hour leading up to the cave, is spotty, but I remember Kei, and her boyfriend, Eddie, and I remember standing at the dark, yawning mouth. I held Russell's hand. I can hear one voice, Eddie's, hissing, *Kei was right, we aren't your friends*, and then he switches off the flashlight and the dark rushes up to meet me. The next thing I remember, I woke up in the emergency room. I couldn't even tell Dr. Shawe how I got there.

Did I wander out on my own? Did I make it to the road to flag a passing car? That I have no idea how I was rescued, or if I was, is a blank that Kei could have filled in for me.

I still don't know how many days I lost afterward, either. All I have are mental snapshots of Arnie on a folding chair by my bed in the hospital. His head was in his hands. His back hunched, as if braced for a beating. As I waited for my blood to refill my body and fought off a massive infection, it was Arnie and only Arnie.

My mother never came to the hospital. The only visit I got was from two awkward policemen, standing a safe distance from my hospital bed, asking me questions I didn't have answers to. *What exactly did I claim Eddie had done to me? Was I sure I wasn't mistaken? Couldn't I just have gotten turned around and wandered off into the cave?*

It was my word against his, against my sister's, against my "friends'." The policemen didn't want to hear me. There was no one to take my side. One cop kept reminding me that Eddie and Ray were *good boys*. My friends. Why else would I have gone with them? Didn't I want to think better of it and drop the case?

Arnie said nothing, watching me.

My mother wasn't there.

How can a mother abandon her child like that? It's a question that can barely find its shape in words. How can a sister disfigure her sister? Mama chose Kei over me. By then, Kei was popular, confident, whereas I was just beginning to realize how repulsive my ruined body would seem to her. I was my mother's worst nightmare, and I couldn't bear to see her recoil from me again.

Every day, I still hoped for them—Kei and Mama—and when they didn't come, I punished Arnie. I made sure he saw every detail of my shredded knees. They were raw knobs, swollen mounds of poké—sashimi flecked with bits of black cinder and served up just for him. I made sure he saw my legs: shins tattooed in brick red. My arms were impressive, too: my elbows swollen twice their normal size, my forearms scraped flat and oozing. Arnie's questions went unanswered: *What happened, Hana? What kind of monster could do such a thing?* My anger was all I had; my silence the only edge I could push hard enough to force Kei to come to see me. It wasn't enough, of course. Nothing I did was ever enough.

And now, six years later, Kei and I were finally together in a hospital, and I was the one who would have given anything to escape. My mouth was thick with Cheetos dust, and my adrenaline had ebbed, leaving me nauseated, when the nurse finally called for me.

"Miss Swanson?"

The tests were over. Kei had been transferred to Intensive Care.

The ICU was full to capacity, but there was no life in it. There were no doors, no televisions, and the bathrooms were through locked doors and down the hall. They were so unused to the living that they never even turned off the lights; day and night, all the patients floated in the glow of technology, curtains drawn open so that the nurses on duty would be able to see them if they started to die. Each of the eight beds arranged in the semicircle around the nurses' station held a person so frail you might believe the machines were filtering the life out of them, not the other way around. I recognized Kei instantly by the thick, dark flag of her hair.

At last, I had access to the doctors. Kei's injuries were slight—a bump on her head and a severely twisted ankle; also a *costochondral separation*, which meant a separated rib—except that something was wrong with her brain. She had not regained consciousness, and I could measure their concern by the tangle of wires that mimicked Kei's still-matted braid, and the litany of words the neurospecialists recited as they assured me of the very many tests they were running. *Cerebellum, infarction, aneurysm. Edema, hemorrhage, increased intracranial pressure.* All the causes and indicators of coma. Was it the beeping, so many lines of jumping light that came from so many monitors, that made it impossible for me to keep track of what they were saying? I noticed they'd put socks on her, and a tube in her nose, but I couldn't see Kei's neck between the brace and the blankets. Her face was chalky—what color she had now lay in the thin surface of her skin.

Strangulation, they told me when I asked about the bruises on her neck, *can cause anoxic brain injury, though in this case we don't know if she was deprived of oxygen or for how long. There is a hematoma behind her right temple, but fortunately no lesions, no apparent areas of internal swelling in this patient. Your sister. There are no genital abrasions or evidence of, ah, a sexual assault. We have also ruled out a pharmacological cause—*

In other words, they had no idea why she hadn't woken up.

But in the list of all the things they didn't find, there was hope. She had not been raped. She could wake up any moment; all there was to do was wait. *Time heals all wounds.* Did someone really say that? What I heard for sure is that the first twenty-four hours would be decisive.

And after that, the first forty-eight.

I stood inside the ICU curtain, processing my sister. Kei's consciousness had sunken deep inside her, leaving all the angles in her face to break free and rise to the surface. I could see the architecture of her body. I knew, if I looked, that her ribs would stick out like stepping-stones to her heart. Kei had been divided, and the physical part of her that was also part of me had been assaulted and subdued, while her personality and essence were hiding somewhere out of reach.

I must have been standing there for some time. Enough that someone brought me a chair from the cafeteria. I was perched on the edge of it, a safe distance from Kei's bed, as the nurses came by every forty-five minutes to check the machines and pinch the tender skin on her belly. A pattern was quickly established: Whoever was on rounds would open the curtains and pick up Kei's chart. "Hanako Swanson?" they would ask me, as if I could be anyone else, and then they would flash a light into her pupils and begin their work. I watched as they enacted their routine without comment, which was all I needed to understand that the first twenty-four hours were ticking by, more than half gone. And once they left us alone, the growing bruise on her forearm where the intravenous fluid was needled in was my timekeeper. There was nothing for me to do, no way to help.

Perhaps I could relate. Perhaps Arnie's question, *What kind of monster would do this?* was still haunting the recesses of my mind. But seeing Kei from this angle in profile—the gentle curve of her cheekbone, the tender snub of her nose—she didn't look like a monster.

I suddenly found that I could breathe.

Kei was my sister. How quickly this feeling came swirling through me, after so many years of protecting myself against her. And when it did, I stood up and moved over to her bed. I brought my face close to hers. Nose to nose; brown eye—if hers had been open—to brown eye.

"Kei?" I asked, my voice disappearing before it could be heard. And then, "Koko?"

It was the nickname that we gave each other when we were children, made of the small, safe endings left over when our mother created *Kei* and *Hana*, the bad girl and the good. It came to me then like a call, a way to sound the depths of our past to find her.

I hadn't spoken it in years.

"Hanako Swanson?" a voice asked from behind me. I jerked away from Kei as the nurse slipped the chart out of its slot. "Date of birth?"

"April first, 1947," I mumbled.

She glanced at the chart and nodded. And then: "She can't see you."

I know a reprimand when I hear one. I pulled back to give the nurse room to work. On the outside—the part of her the nurses were supposed to be tending—Kei's hair had dried into a ratted halo, fraying and uncertain ropes of it falling to one side. It wasn't her brain, or her rib, or even her ankle, but wasn't this still their job?

I watched the nurse check the monitors. "Do you have a comb?"

"A comb?" she asked, recording her readings on the clip chart. "No, we don't have those."

Maybe you should go home and get one. I waited for her to say it.

"There's a deli on Amsterdam."

I nodded, but didn't move.

Instead, once the nurse had left, I pulled my chair across the floor until it was beside Kei's head. My fingers teased a small section of her hair loose and began pulling through the snarls, just as my mother used to do when we were girls. I started with the ends like Mama taught me, avoiding Kei's scalp, feeling my mother's ghostly hands tickle my own hair once again as I began to work on Kei's. An inch at a time, she used to say; anything more would pull the twists and tangles into knots. Do it in order—ends to roots, or all the way around the bottom and then one inch up.

Kei seemed to frown, if only for an instant. It brought out the tight edges of her skull.

I'm sorry, I thought at her.

As a girl, Kei never sat still for my mother's fingers. She wriggled, and, like everything else in her life, she made things worse. But then Mama would start humming and Kei would immediately relax. Mama made up some lyrics to that tune, something about how "the light on the other side shines on two girls." I hummed it now, even though I could barely remember how it went.

"Two girls," I told her. "Do you remember?"

I imagined I could feel her listening. And my mother, too.

Two girls.

KOKO

Two girls. Two white cotton dresses: Simplicity, size 4T. You must remember how we looked then? A-line, eyelet lace on the hem. Long-sleeved shirts underneath, and white cotton *momohiki* to protect our legs. *Tabis* on four feet.

White.

Lauhala hats, broad with brims to shelter thin, white necks. Gloves, too. Our mama tucked each fragile finger into its cocoon, and still we lost them. Still we flung them. We needed to stroke everything or dismantle it, and the gloves got in our way.

There is light on the other side.

Do you remember?

There's breath in our ears from sneaking away from Mama. And light between the leaves. The leaves are called oleander, and they are long. Green as the ground. She tells us not to come here. *Don't touch the sap. It will kill you.* But when we watch the neighbor children, the leaves must be stripped so we can see.

The boy is there, on the other side of the oleander, in denim shorts that end in fringe above his knee. We can see his dark nipples and his filled-in skin. His legs are folded. His buttocks hang behind his ankles. He leans forward slightly on his flat, bare feet. Dirt dots his skin and sleeps in *U*s around his toenails.

We don't know where his twin is. We only ever see one boy.

There is a girl, too. Also only one. She's smaller than the boy. About our height but rounded like he is, with his same bare feet, his same ropy, red-tinted hair. They have the same skin, the color of wood.

These children we spy on, toasted by the sun.

The girl crouches beside the boy. They're both intent on his kneecap. He scrapes at it with one finger, then lifts something small and dark and puts it in his mouth.

"Eeeww, gross! You wen eat um! You wen pick your scab and eat um!"

He looks at her.

"You wen eat da scab!"

"So? You eat *hanabata*. I seen you."

"Not."

"Do too. Do too. Cindy picks her nose and eats it," he sings. "Hanabata eater."

"Still yet." The girl stands, steps away from him undecided. She sees us.

"Eeeww!" She points. "Spy girls! Spy girls!"

We've been waiting for this. Waiting with our thighs pressed against each other's, savoring the heat between. It is thrilling to be caught. As thrilling as it is to be spied upon.

We look back at the children, then we all run.

It is just us, now, with the children gone. Us two, trying out the new word. Hanabata. We prance together on the top of one of the low rock walls embedded in our hill. The hill is steep, so the wall holds it back so it won't fall into the stream.

The wall is very low. Maybe three stones high? Two wide? Lava rocks. Full of spindle-sided *pukas* that tear our clothes. And pale, dusty lichen.

The air is still and hot. It clutches at us, collecting in our armpits.

We crouch: feet flat, splayed in a V toward the drop; big toes gripping. White toes, in Mama's tabis. Fingers free. Our leggings scratch as we tug them so our buttocks can drop like the boy's, and we bounce, at first only testing. Opening and shutting four white knees.

"Hanabata, *ne*?" That's how it was then. All our questions end in ne. Do we dare?

We look down the steep hill, measuring the jump. Then toward the house where Mama is sleeping. Hanabata, it is. We bounce, faster and higher until we're standing, then crouching, then standing again. We check with each other—are we ready?—feeling the sweat tickle our necks and faces, and we laugh. We laugh, laugh until one long white scarf unknots and then flies. The hat it was meant to tie down follows. It tumbles away in the still air. One matted head, bouncing and dropping. One head released, to make its own breeze.

It's time to follow.

"Koko!"

Together we leap for the hat. Arms swimming, legs cycling to drive us through the air, to spin it into something new: a cool breath beneath our dresses. We fall. The scrubby *kikuyu* grass at the edge of the stream tickles as we tumble. And when we've had our fill of flying and rolling in the grass, we crawl, crushing rotted yellow flowers with our knees as we seek the shade of the nearby hau tree. We scratch at the drying sweat on our scalps quickly, replacing the hat, entwining fingers. A puff of stink air blows over from the pen behind the children's house. Slop and manure in the heat. We breathe in, large and full. By now, our heartbeats are steady and the hot iron has worn out of our dresses, leaving the scent of Mama's soap to rise.

We lie with our hands laced on the grass, inside our mama's safety, and relive our temporary flight.

"Hanabata."

HANA

I didn't leave. Kei didn't wake. The nurses gave me their barely perceptible frowns of acknowledgment when they found me still slumped in the molded plastic chair every time they came to check on Kei. I called the number Detective Lynch had given me and left her a message telling her where I was. No doubt she would judge me, but whether as someone friendless or as a devoted sister, I didn't know. At least at the hospital, we were safe from Kei's attacker.

They added machines, more tubes, but Kei was unresponsive. I was so weary I could feel my heartbeat dragging. Though the room had no windows, the clock told me I had been there so long we had entered into another night. I could imagine the moon and the impossibly blood-orange clouds that would be floating through the dark sky in the city; I had nowhere to go, no one I could turn to, and no choice but to hope the staff would take pity on me and let me stay until morning. I could feel the pull of sleep, the toss of dreams, and the danger that was waiting there. My nightmares were still worse than my waking life, though not by much.

To keep myself awake, I went down to the cafeteria on the second floor, which was less appetizing than a vending machine and possibly less nutritious. I was ravenous, and I thought, how bad could a bagel be? But everything was closed and dark. I grabbed a paper cup off a serving station; water was free and I was dehydrated. Then I filled it with ice and carried it back to Kei's bedside.

All our lives, Kei had been my unexpected mirror—the one in which your image appears before you can compose yourself, where you must confront yourself unassembled in those split seconds before you remember who you are. Standing over her, still trying to work out the cramps and cricks from my night in the chair, I fished a piece of ice out of my cup and placed it on Kei's chest. I did it with the same stunned dissociation that I'd felt in my bathroom, which had led me to place my fingers into the bruises on her neck. I half-expected a jolt, to feel her feel me even through the ice cube that separated us, but there was no response. What was it like to be so free from fear and pain? I circled the ice inside the hollow between her collarbones until its edges rounded, losing hope that I could reach her. Then I lifted it off her perfect skin, and placed it on my own lips.

The ice was soft and almost immediately painful. I closed my eyes and traced the cube across my mouth, then drew it down my chin and neck until it became a more familiar thing. We used to do this for our mother when we were very young, in her "lying down days" when she complained of the cold but burned between us until morning. And now I wondered: Did the ice also feel like a fever? I could feel myself slipping with the ice, just a little, into tenderness, and my heart closed like a fist against the dangers I would surely find there.

I swirled the ice cube in the hollow of my own throat with caution, feeling for the ridges of my windpipe. Then I skated it down my arm, beneath my loose sleeves and in the gutters between my scars. My wounds had closed over time but long, pink keloids hugged my body like worms. My knees were buckling, misshapen little brains. I made it a careful practice not to look at them; I didn't have to see them to know: I could feel each scar, along my arms, my back, as if it was placed there yesterday. They were numb to the cold. The pain picked up only in the bend of my elbow, before disappearing in a small splash in my hand.

The ice was dripping, and half its original size, when I placed it on Kei's lips. I held it there, letting the cold water trickle into her mouth safely, until it was gone.

* * *

When Kei and I were very young, and it was still just the three of us, we lived in a small plantation house so far off the main street you couldn't see it. The house was square, divided exactly in half—kitchen and living room on one side, adjoining bedrooms on the other with a bathroom so small that the door couldn't open inward and swung out into the living room instead. Our lot was only twice as wide as the house itself; a skinny piece of land that fell down in two directions: gently toward the ocean and more steeply toward the stream that ran along its length. Because our house was on a hill, our front door was close to the ground, accessible by a short run of pavestones that led to a landing filled with shoes. The rest of it floated on stilts, cantilevered almost a full story above the sharp drop down to the stream.

Our favorite place was the long, shadowed lanai that wrapped around our house. That porch was unusual for a house like ours—a simple workers' home, identical in most other ways to the clusters of shacks that filled the nearby camps, with their raspy board and batten walls and their unlined, tin-hat roofs. We often crouched there, peering through the wide-spaced slats of the railing to survey the fruit trees and the three long, terraced plots of vegetables bound by the low lava rock walls that we used to jump off. And in the farthest corner of the property, beneath the huge, ancient hau tree: my mother's garden.

Even though most of my old memories have left me, I know there were nights when we woke up to find Mama planting in the moonlight. We still slept with her in those days, and Kei and I would wake up when the bed was cool and walk out onto our lanai where we could see her under the drowsy but plentiful stars. Perched on her knees at the edge of the narrow tears she had made in the dirt beside the broccoli, she looked so tiny. She seemed about to dive into the waiting earth, head first, then shoulders, slipping into the dark, wounded world beneath her. A world that would close around her, slick as water, and leave no clue she had ever existed.

People will disappear, girls. That was another way it could happen. Not hunted down by the strangers she was always on the lookout for, but by choice, too. All she had to do was tip, so slightly, and in a moment she could be gone.

Those were the days when Mama would lie down. She never collapsed abruptly; she never dropped anything or pricked her finger on an enchanted needle. She would set aside whatever she was doing, her movements dragging slower until they stopped. We kept a blanket on the *pune'e* to put on the floor beneath her, but she didn't always have time to get it before she went down.

There were whole days when she didn't get up.

And if I try now, what can I remember? It's an image so familiar I could draw it from memory. Three prone figures in white on the floor: the middle one tall, refusing to bend in either direction, the small ones curled. Three dark heads of hair, dark eyelash fringes—similar faces, though Kei's and mine were fatter with life. Mama's breath was shallow and slow, her skin moist and flushed red with a rash of pinpricks. Her most regular movement was her swallow—more insistent than her heartbeat—and I could almost feel the fluid in her body run past her eardrums and collect in tart pockets at the back of her tongue. She was always thirsty, so we brought her water in a large mayonnaise jar filled in the bathtub, which she drank from a length of flexible tubing. We brought her ice cubes, which she sucked on, and when her fever spiked too high, we skated them over her skin.

"Don't open your mouth," our mother often warned us. Her eyes were closed, and we had no idea who she was speaking to. "Don't swallow. They're dead, all of them in the river. They are still drinking, but they're dead."

She would be silent awhile, and then add, "Ah, you can't protect, ne? Not against the past. Not from the leaving."

Her words echoed behind the hum of her blood in my ear.

The "dead ones" in my mother's river were probably the damned. At least, that's how I used to picture it. The sinners who'd already sealed their fates but didn't know it. Sins in Mama's world were often slippery and difficult to identify. Good deeds did not return, nor could they shield you. The world was big, and uncaring, and even the most careful, most thought-out decision could send you down the wrong path. Now, I wonder if my mother's life was like that. Two bastard children; a family who must have thrown her out when she disgraced them. What else had she endured? She never volunteered any information about her life before us. I knew she grew up in California, but I had never dared ask how she'd gotten to Hawaii. Had she come with our father, or was he long gone? Now I can see that, with that sixth sense that children have, I must have been afraid we were responsible for whatever shame had separated her from her family. If I had questions that I dared to ask, it was only later that they occurred to me. Once it was too late.

But in those days, we were too young to be worried. We knew there was one thing that could bring our mother back from her ghosts and the sleeping. Stories.

"Mama?" It was usually Kei who asked for them, lifting her head so she could look at Mama with upturned eyes. "*Kudasai* Lillie please, *deska*?"

Sometimes just the name "Lillie" was enough to get Mama to move.

"Mama? Lillie and the mirror? Moon-Lillie deska?"

Mama's eyes were still closed. There was nothing in her face to indicate that she heard us.

Kei kept begging. "*Onegai?*"

And that plea, soaring in Kei's long, singing syllables, was the key.

"Once upon a time," our mother began, "there was a preacher and his wife who could not have any children. They were very lonely, just the two of them. Their church was empty, and they were also very poor." Her eyes remained closed. The words, dredged up from far away, rolled from her as slow as they pleased.

Kei smiled. She liked to be obeyed. This was the first in the series of stories, the one where Lillie was found. "Good girl," she said, reaching out a small, soft hand to pat Mama's chest in approval. "Nice, nice Mama."

Did Mama notice Kei's compliments? She might have, as she continued: "Then one day, the preacher's wife opened her front door and what did she find but—"

"A giant peach, with a girl inside," Kei said as if Mama was really asking a question. "And she has black long hair and night eyes—"

"A beautiful girl," Mama agreed. The peach was from another story.

We were drifting in our mother's voice, for we knew this story well. Lillie was a gift, a magic child—from the moment she appeared, other blessings arrived. Food came to the door in the same way Lillie did, families began to travel to the church from neighboring farms. Lillie was never allowed outside the house or the church, for her own protection, but it didn't matter because she had a family. When the preacher's wife made her beautiful dresses and taught her to sing in the evenings for her new parents, the thin line of music Mama hummed wrapped tightly around the three of us. By the time Lillie began to sing in church, attracting so many new members to the congregation that the preacher's wife decided to open a school, my mother's voice was just a murmur. But it didn't matter. We knew Lillie would reappear.

There was something reassuring in this story for all of us. Kei liked the power the girl had—that she was strong and gifted, and that she'd come to save the preacher and his wife; I was moved by the plight of the orphan and relieved that she'd found a home. My mother, though she never said so, always seemed taken with the idea of the church as a refuge.

Whenever her story was over, my mother would always lapse into sleep. Her breathing was still shallow—still sick—but we did not run to get help. We didn't even bother to stay quiet, since she would remain unconscious until she came back on her own.

Instead, we squabbled on top of her body.

"Ah," Kei said, "Momo-boy, ne?" She was choosing the next story for our mother when she woke. It was the tale of the peach, and the boy who was so strong it didn't matter that he was lazy. "Ah," she offered, lowering her voice to cajole me, "belly button yum, ne?" It was a different version of the same tale—a little girl without a belly button who saved the town from the ogres.

I shook my head.

Kei turned her charm on me then, for it was my turn to choose the next story. "Mighty Mountain," she whispered, holding my eyes with hers. This one was a fairy tale about three strong women. As Mama had always told it, about twins.

I thought about the twins and their mother, living high in the mountains where no one ever went. About the web of strength between them—their inheritance—which they could choose to share or not. It was not as good as a Lillie story, but Mama gave those out so sparingly. In the end, it was easier to give in.

"Koko, perfect," I said, and then I snuggled into my mother's sweat.

Looking back, I can't help but wonder at those two girls. At the single name we tossed back and forth between us, and our twin language, with its lack of verbs and made-up endings, that rises even now like an old song. In this still shimmering memory, the evening is what was "perfect"—having my mother under my hands, my sister's face breathing into mine.

Could I have meant that? Was "perfect" a limitation of my clearly inadequate language, or was it really my experience? Why weren't we terrified that our mother was too weak even to stay conscious? Why didn't we go next door to ask Old Harada-san and his wife for help? Even if we didn't know exactly what was wrong with our mother then, I can still see her curdled pink-and-white skin and feel the mist of sweat collecting in her hair. But in those days, all we knew was that the three of us were together. Mama always got up eventually, and when she did, we had her heartbeat and a story.

Could *perfect*, in fact, have been the right word?

I must have dozed, because the ice cubes that I'd gathered had melted when I was jolted awake. Kei suddenly went stiff, making herself as large as she could, as immovable.

Her eyelids sprang open.

I remember jumping up from my chair in confusion. She was in a different position, surely, but how could she have moved? She clearly didn't see me, and yet she moved again as I watched. This time her legs bent and straightened, grimly, like a marionette's.

She was wrestling with him, I thought. Her attacker.

I called out for help, running to her, and then to the curtain, and then back to the bed. The alarm sounded, summoning a staff of doctors I'd never met. There were words, suddenly, where there had been none, and voices. There were bodies between us: poking, pulling, applying resistance, calling.

"Hanako? Can you hear me?"

Blink your eyes, they said. *Bend your fingers.*

I stepped back. As the doctors fussed around her, trying to get her limbs to release, trying to cause a reaction, I realized that, until that moment, I hadn't accepted that Kei could be seriously injured. I had expected that she was going to open her eyes any minute and smile at me, say *jus' one joke*. She had gotten away with so much in her life that it didn't seem possible her luck could run out. Six years ago, Kei had broken me into pieces, erased me from my own life. It never occurred to me that she might, now, be as frightened as I was.

And then their voices registered. *Hanako*, they had called her.

I stepped back further, outside the curtain, no longer trying to see. As the volume of voices lowered, it became clear that she wasn't responding the way they wanted. There were fewer people around the bed. But still, when the last nurse turned to leave, I couldn't stop myself from asking, "She's coming out of it?"

She shook her head and that was when I learned two more terms: *spastic*, and *reflexive without reactivity or perceptivity*. "You should go home. Get some rest."

"I need to be here."

She caught my eyes. "Maybe a shower? You have time."

"Maybe." I let it sink in—both the shower and the time. But I would say whatever I needed to get her to leave me, because there was something that I understood now that I needed to see.

She placed a silent hand on my shoulder as if I were a crutch she needed to get by, and then I was alone. I stepped toward Kei's bed. They'd put soft pads over her spastic eyes to keep them shut. Now, there was even less of her to recognize, except her wristband, which I had never thought to look at.

There it was: SWANSON, HANAKO.

Somehow, in all the paperwork and repeated questions, Kei had lost her name and taken mine. Only then did I remember that I had given the triage nurses my own insurance card. *It's okay, it's okay, it's okay,* the voice in my head assured me, even before my guilt kicked in. What else was I supposed to do with the naked, half-dead body of my twin sister? Especially since she had no purse, no insurance of her own? Still, the fact of it sent chills through the center of my being: It had never been me they were addressing when they picked up the clipboard and read off the name "Hanako Swanson."

It is Kei, it is Kei, it is Kei, I could hear the singsong whisper.

And it was.

KOKO

There is a breeze. Can you feel it?

It's a light breeze, only a little cooler than the day. It's the kind that eddies on your shoulder.

Mama has risen. Opened the front door.

Arnie is here.

We are five. Wearing white dresses to reflect the sun.

White is the only safe color, according to our mother.

"Koko, deska?" one of us asks, checking in with the other. We have never seen a haole up close before. Not one so tall.

We link hands, look at Mama.

She isn't expecting him, either.

These are the days when both of us are still Koko. There is no one or the other. No Hana, no Kei. Nothing is set. We can go back there, to the time when we could still be whoever we wanted. It's a time of intuition, of knowing what the other is thinking so well that it doesn't occur to us that anything needs to be spoken. It is not the same with Mama, of course. She is weak and needs words, but still we love her. We love to be three with her. To take care of her when she falls.

When Arnie drives up, we are still three, sitting at the kitchen table, shredding stacks of newspaper into long, thin slivers. Harada-san needs them for his flowers. He is the old man who owns our house. His wife smiles at us more than other ladies, and brings us sweets that we never know if it's okay to eat. But the newspapers are okay. It's a job we love: the way the paper rips in straight, sure tears if we pull it in the right direction, from the tops of the pictured people down to their feet. Remember how our fingers blacken quickly? How we try to hold them away from our white clothes? When we are *pau*, we will all three jump into the large burlap bags we recycle, packing down the shreds with our feet and the weight of our bodies. We all three will crowd into the tiny bathtub. Two girls and Mama, we will lather the soap against our gray skin, scrubbing stubby hands and thin ones. Remember how we watch the proof of our labor run down the drain?

We are halfway through the stack when we hear the car engine. Old Harada-san broke his shoulder falling off his roof, so we know it isn't him. Harada-san hasn't come for six weeks, and in that time, we have seen no one. Mama leaves instead. Six times to town. She wraps our green avocados in newspaper then places them carefully in sacks, one for each hand and one for her back. Before she goes, she spins a magic circle around the house that keeps us safe inside and silent as secrets. She says it will keep the dead away. When she returns, there is rice for us and, on special days, tofu. Sometimes she gets a ride, she told us once. *But only from our kind.* We hear the warning. We know there are bad people out there that Mama needs to hide us from. But we don't know what *our kind* is.

On this day, though, there is something about this car engine. Mama continues ripping, but her motions are smaller with the sound. She is tense, even her eyes holding steady. We have always admired this about her, how she can disappear while she's still there.

It could be someone lost, turning around, going back to where the people live. Mama's hands don't stop until a car door slams and a man's shoes step up the stairs.

Mama stands before this strange man, blackened hands hanging from her wrists like fruit. Look at her light green blouse and loose, clumsy pants. Her gentle braid sways down her spine. It is midafternoon and she looks soft, weathered.

We like her best on these days, don't we? The days when she doesn't leave the house.

Mama's eyes move around the room and ours go with her. Now we can see the mound of shredded newspaper spilling off the kitchen table. We can see how close things are, how they've suddenly shrunk in size. The pune'e nudges the man's calves. He is three steps from everything else. Including Mama.

She is so small, he could tuck her beneath his shoulder.

"Girls, this is Mr. Swanson."

We dip our heads as we do to the Haradas, watching him in case he moves. Trying to guess which direction he will go in and what he will knock over.

"Mr. Swanson has come to..."

We are all three waiting to hear how he will finish Mama's sentence. He barks, cheerfully, and then says, "Just passing by. I missed you in town this week, so...I thought I'd say hello."

"Oh. Well. Sit down. Sit down, then." Mama doesn't explain his words: *I missed you in town this week.* "Can I get you something? If you can stay."

"You have RC?" he asks, and then misinterprets our surprise. "It's a soda pop. It doesn't matter. Whatever you got will do."

No one stayed. That you must remember. Only Harada-san and his wife ever came by. Can't you see them, sneaking up the front steps, *tontoko, tontoko*, and Mama always rushing to greet them? *You must be so tired. Please come in. The newspapers are so heavy. You are so good to come.*

And Old Harada-san always shakes his head, puts his hand up. *No trouble*, he is saying. He has only come to leave the newspapers, or to retrieve the shreds for packing and shipping his anthuriums. We are earning the house with those shreds. Each sack is a plank, a nail, a hinge that will make it ours.

Harada-san's wife never speaks or smiles at Mama, but she, too, is part of the dance. The escape: They must refuse each offer of food or drink until they are safely out the door. Mrs. Harada steps back when Mama steps forward. She keeps her eyes on the floor, as if the planks are terribly important, except when Mama calls for us and we two are brought into the room. Then, her eyes suck us in, her hands rising to cover her mouth or to finger the jade pendant that hangs from her neck. She loves us like she is starving. Look at her and remember. What does she want us to call her? Aunt Suzy? But we never do. We bow, we bow. Then they go.

Arnie is standing too close to Mama. In light green, her hands and hair hanging, she doesn't move as we three wait for him to withdraw his request for an "RC" and back out of the house. When he doesn't, Mama retreats toward the kitchen. Sidestepping, bouncing on her toes like she might change her mind. But instead, she leaves us with him. Just us, two girls, without her.

We back away as she did and tuck ourselves into the cane chair. We do this flat-footed: toe then heel, right foot then left. And there we wait for her return.

Arnie sits on the pune'e, near the front edge. He sinks until his knees nearly reach his shoulders. He scoots back toward the wall and sinks again, though not as deeply. His arms snake down to the cushions, where the long length of them lies.

"Koko, silk-silk, ne?"

He has not removed his work boots, which even the Haradas do when they step into the house on their short errands. His shoes are crooked. One is normal, but the other heel is much heavier and taller and it sits on the floor like a rock. These shoes are deeply creased and lined with sawdust. But as unexpected as they are, we are not staring at his shoes.

We are looking at his hair: silky gold and silver curls springing up so high he seems bigger than he is. We are looking at his skin. It's gold too, with flecks, like dirt, especially on his nose and cheekbones, but also on his forearms and peeking between his pants and socks. Even his most secret parts have been damaged. Burned, by the sun.

This is what Mama has always warned us about: Only the ones who wear white will survive.

Arnie shrugs at us, tries a smile. The wrinkles around his eyes and mouth bend and stretch, nudging his forehead up, exposing huge white teeth. We expect to see his skin rip, to peel off in sheets like in Mama's stories. "So?" he barks again. "What are your names?" When we don't answer, he drops down abruptly, his knees bouncing, so he's on our level. "I'm Arnie."

"Koko," we tell him, shocked.

"Kei." Mama is back. "And Hana."

Arnie grins, looks at us, and then he is up, adult again just as suddenly as he wasn't. "So which is which?" he asks Mama. Our eyes grow wide, but she does not answer. These are the other things she calls us in those rare times when we are not "two girls." When she is happy, the girl who is good is called Hana. But when she is angry, the bad one is Kei.

In Mama's hands, a round, scalloped tray with refreshments. A small folding table is tucked under her arm. We move to help, but Arnie is also moving. He flaps his arms and legs to stand and takes a bit of the tray.

"No, no—" But it's too late. The tray is rocking. When Arnie puts his hands beneath it, Mama lets go as if he's just plucked a dream from the air.

Once the table is set up, Arnie unloads the tray. There is tea, and juice in a tall glass. Two shallow bowls, one containing dull, wet peanuts and the other brown flower-shaped crackers flecked in black. There are several thin wafers in rice paper pouches. Another, even smaller dish that will hold the soggy peanut shells.

This food. There is so much of it, and we've never seen it before.

I missed you in town this week.

When he's finished unloading, Arnie lifts the tall glass in one hand and cups the other beneath it. He steps between the table and the pune'e, then turns, gauging the distance down before he sits square in the middle. We're still in the chair, so Mama perches beside him since he doesn't move to make more space. She is smiling.

"What language are they speaking?" He nods at us. "Do they speak English?"

"Hmm?" She's shifting, trying to find the proper place. Closer to the edge. "Yes, English."

"Oh. Some of it sounds Japanese. I thought maybe—"

Her head shakes. "I told you. I'm from California. American as apple pie."

Arnie thinks she's funny. "Do they talk this way in school?"

Whatever a school is, we don't have one. We watch Arnie rake the flower crackers into his hand, then drop a few back into the dish before putting the rest in his mouth. He's still shouting, occasionally making his barking laugh. He is saying we look like birds, so tiny. "Why don't you eat the crackers?" he is saying. *Fatten you up.* His hands move from the food, to the back of the pune'e, to his knees, and once even to his head. Mama nods for him to continue speaking, still smiling, her eyes steady on him.

"I could've worked for C. Brewer when I got here, but I can't stand hierarchy," Arnie is saying. "I had my fill of that in Pearl City. During the war. We're all people, right? It doesn't matter if we're soldiers or what. Doesn't matter if we're haole or Chinese...Shouldn't matter at all."

We see Mama shrink, and we realize that before Arnie's comment, she had relaxed. She looks away from him now. Her next question hides in a voice so flat it wants no answer. "Were you a soldier?"

"No." He pauses for the first time. "I tried to enlist but with my leg and all, well...Anyway, I came here to do civilian support. But I work for myself. Electrical, mostly. I'm a good electrician. People can call me up for *any kine* thing or stop by Bernice's store and I'll go right over to their house. Poke around, fix stuff they didn't even know was broken."

When he stops, finally, we breathe, awed by the sheer number of his words.

Mama breathes, too. "Bernice. Yes. Isn't it strange how we're always there at the same time?"

Arnie blushes and says, "I could set my clock by you."

It's sometime after that Mama notices Arnie's empty glass. "Hana?"

She wants just one of us. A helpful one. Whose turn is it to be Hana?

We split. Do you remember how that happens? One girl slips off the chair, and we are now Hana and Koko. Which is so much better than being Koko and Kei.

"Hana." Mama puts her hand on one shoulder. "There's some passion orange in the icebox."

"And some ice, too, please, if you have it."

We don't like this man who makes Mama forget things. We don't like this *passion orange* that used to be juice. He likes to poke around, he said. He goes *right over* to other people's houses. Is that why he came here, to see the shredded newspaper on our table? Is he here to spy on our crumbs, our unmade beds? Our beds are made, but still, he knows us now. The crocheted cover in Mama's bedroom—we saw him look at that through the doorway when he sat down.

Do the other people blush, too?

One girl stays in her seat in the living room. One girl walks to the icebox. Passion orange? And ice in juice? We put ice on headaches, the cool of it on our foreheads. We cup ice in the palms of our hands. It's for sucking on when it's hot, and for Mama when she's lying down.

Arnie is burned and loud and he has strange habits. We'll be happy when he's gone.

Of course...we *do* know how much fun it is to be a witness: to steal the things people do when they think no one else is there. Like the children we spy on through the oleanders. The fat, doomed children who pick their noses and eat the green ribbons and chewy nuggets they find. We like to watch them run in and out of their house, barefooted, past their banging screen without so much as tapping the dirt off their feet. If Arnie popped into that house, he would find trails of footprints hurrying to the bathroom. Pivoting in front of the icebox, skidding into unwashed sheets. We are spies, too—just like Arnie—he could take us with him, all of us wearing the hot skin of outlaws. Would we discover that the children sleep in the same bed, the way we do? Would we see their clothes droop from their shelves, the things they play with strewn on the floor? The wooden figures, the bottle caps, the bean sacks, the marbles...

The boy's marbles. In all sizes and colors. Marbles that click when he drops them, leaping off the ground, sometimes in our direction, landing so close to our oleander hedge. Marbles like stars, like fat fruit. Like Mama's dumplings bursting in a hot, salty bath and the crunch of water chestnuts in our mouths.

Oh, we want those marbles.

"Hana!"

We are Hana and Koko, and Hana is in the kitchen, not for so long, either, when Mama calls. Mama should know this, but she isn't paying attention. Her arm sweeps out toward Koko, still in the chair in the living room. Gathering her in.

No.

We've been lost again, in a daydream of mischief and marbles. Still, this should not be happening. Mama is never impatient. She has never forgotten where we are and made a new Hana when there is one already there. But in the other room, Koko is rising, both girls confused.

The juice is no longer important. The icebox door slams and the two girls run back together, sliding in beside each other, just as Mama picks up the empty bowl. United again, we are Koko. We are four arms, twenty fingers, two hearts.

Mama gives us a tiny smile. "More peanuts, please." She wants more food, for Arnie. It's his fault—*he* is the rush—and despite the visit we've just taken into the children's house with him, we are ready for him to leave.

Arnie laughs. "Which one *is* Hana?"

This time Mama's eyes widen at his question as she looks at us, standing together. "Does it matter?"

"Tricksters, huh?" he asks, leaning back to pull Mama's attention toward him. "You're lucky they're opposites, then. Easy to tell them apart."

Mama laughs and turns away from us. She is caught in a net we cannot see. We were three before he walked in, shredding newspaper. Now, we are two—two little girls—holding an empty bowl that we are supposed to fill with peanuts. Now, Mama is missing, and in her place she has left a question:

Who is Hana now?

HANA

The girl in the bed was Hanako Swanson. I was still trying to understand how that had happened when Detective Lynch reappeared. I barely heard her heavy heels, the jingle of cuffs and chains and keys on her belt that should have announced her. Coming in, as she did, just after Kei's spasms, she found me shakier than I wanted to be. Still, it was good to be needed, and I jumped at the chance to get away from my sister and clear my head.

The detective needed my fingerprints to compare to the partials they found in my apartment. I nodded a quick, awkward good-bye to Kei's prone form, and then I was being chauffeured to the station. Outside, the soup of New York accosted me—the smell of cooking and exhaust; the clouds of heat that lumber toward you only to be whisked away by an errant blast of cold. I was surprised by the midday sun. I'd lost track of time—how many hours did Kei have left in the sterile stuffiness of the ICU, and what would happen after her doctor-imposed deadlines had passed?—but the ride in the squad car was too short to worry for long. Detective Lynch's station turned out to be just a few blocks north and east of my apartment. When I was finished there, I would be only a quick walk from my home.

Detective Lynch led me into the receiving area. As we waited for the fingerprinting, she checked my statement and asked me if there was anything I wanted to change or add.

Where to begin? I thought. And what would happen if I told them about all the cleaning I had done—the clothes folding, the kitchen—or about Mama's case? Had they found that in my bedroom? But how important was it, really? I couldn't imagine any of my omissions mattered. What monster might blithely eat leftovers after attacking another person?

But that brought me back to nothing. Why hadn't I demanded Kei tell me what demons she had following her, and why she brought them to my house?

Detective Lynch was waiting for me to sign my statement, but how could I do that? What name would I use? I hadn't a clue, since she kept calling me Miss Swanson.

The man in the lobby lingered on the edge of my mind as I wavered. Who was he, and was he coming back for me? Why were his eyes, which I could sense more than see, making it so hard for me to breathe?

"What about the guy?" I asked. "Did you...has he...?" I was having trouble asking if they had leads because the "no" I realized I would hear was more than I could handle. "Maybe I could help that way? If you put me with a sketch artist, I'm sure we can re-create him."

"We don't have any sketch artists here at present. But if you come up with a more...ah...detailed description, we'll see what we can do."

Diplomacy aside, she was telling me my help was just a waste of time. I knew she didn't believe me because I had said he was white. And also because, if he had come through the window, why would he leave through the door? Or maybe it was too much work to look for a stranger with no connection to the victim.

They didn't want to know. Just like the cops in Hawaii who came to ask me about Eddie and his friends hadn't wanted to know. They didn't care, and no admitting to my shock-fueled instincts was going to change that. Since my statement would be useless, it could remain exactly as it was.

"What if it *was* about me?" I asked her, as I scrawled a signature on the paper that could have been either name. We did that in high school, too: a letter that could have been an *H* or a *K* with a little squiggle. "I mean, what if there really is someone in the neighborhood, someone I don't know but who's been watching me? You said your robberies were local, right? Maybe I could find a photograph of someone who's been lurking around who I just never knew to notice?"

It was a last-ditch idea, but I couldn't bring myself to leave without trying to identify the man I had encountered, and since she clearly wasn't interested in him, I needed to offer her a different possibility.

Looking back, I am amazed she agreed to let me look through the mug shots with such a thin excuse, but she escorted me upstairs to an alcove: a lopsided bulge in an already fat hallway with a door on each end. Filing cabinets were staggered like bad teeth along the wall behind me. Books and binders fell into one another across the gaps on the shelves. Even the few desks around me had been knocked toward each other or away like the unturned cards in an abandoned game of *hanafuta*. I sat down at one, a staggered stack of binders full of violent criminals at my fingertips. My breath caught.

What if the face of the man who had strangled my sister brought back my memories before I was ready? Dr. Shawe was no longer there to protect me. I longed for her then, for her laugh that had made it so easy to believe I would get better. I longed for her tricks, and her aphorisms, and how she rarely used a medical term if a metaphor would do. She'd explained that all my crazy symptoms, from the singsong voice in my head to my memory lapses, were actually defense mechanisms to help keep me sane in the wake of the trauma of the cave. My memories would come back when I was ready; too soon and they could trigger another breakdown. The important thing? *Don't push.*

But here I was, pushing. Here I was, teetering as if at the rim of a volcanic crater, Kei's attacker behind me, threatening to break me if I turned. If I recognized him... I could almost feel myself falling.

Breathe, I thought.

Enough. It was daytime, and I was surrounded by policemen. I flipped open the red cover and looked.

There were twenty tiny mug shots on each sheet. Ten eyes on each line; eighty on a double-spread page. Each pair of eyes was almost exclusively black, but beyond that, they came in every age and shape—thick necks and long ones, big hair and none at all, glasses, scars, muscled, grizzled, barely shaving, missing teeth. The stacks contained hundreds of men, thousands, each represented only by a staring, sullen picture. At first I tried so hard to study each one—even when I knew that the man I had seen in the lobby was not dark, could not have been fat, was never so young. They looked like my neighbors, the guy at the newsstand, even one of the security guards at the church near my apartment. And they could have been, of course. In the binder, they were flat, small, powerless, but I was beginning to realize something else. At any time, any one of the men I saw on the street might cast off his normal, daytime mask, raise his chin just slightly, and, in the same defiant pose of a mug shot, prove just how completely he could hurt me.

There were predators everywhere, and any of them could have done this—all of them could have done this—and the worst part was, they still could.

And here's the truth: I spent hours in that alcove looking at every face, into every set of eyes, and identified...no one. From time to time, I *had* felt frissons of recognition, but the one time I brought an officer over and said, hesitantly, "Maybe, I'm not sure but I think the mouth is similar," he flipped the photo over, stared at the back for a minute, and told me to keep looking. I did, but I also sneaked a peak at the back of that photo. Ramon Velasquez. Grand theft auto, 1969. Too dark, I had to admit then, realizing that the man, barely a boy, could have been in jail for the past two years.

My second time through the binders, I tried something new. I flipped the pages, exchanging binders as I pleased, laying them side by side on the desktop so that I could glance at them from different angles to see Kei's attacker in the same offhand way I had the first time. I allowed my gaze to blur, and each page to slip out of focus, in hopes that he would get cocky. It was a technique I used to use to capture an image of something I had never seen.

People disappear, my mother had taught us. As young girls, we learned to hide at the sound of footsteps, keep to our own kind, never ever to trust. When I was a child, hiding with Kei beneath the bed that Mama shoved us under in those times when her eyes went wild and she was sure that we were about to be stolen, I could only imagine what the ghosts in her head might have looked like, had they ever materialized to snatch us away. Even then I understood that there was no way to protect her, or us, unless I could see what we were hiding from.

And so I drew the monsters we were afraid of so I could save us from them. I couldn't see what tormented her, so I closed my eyes and let the images emerge from the crayon in my hand. I drew my mother's nightmares, sightless, again and again until their burned-to-ash faces were as blind as I was and the sheets of skin that peeled off the red zombie arms they held out in front of them withered; once I had leached them of their danger, I locked them into a carton with hearts on the lid and a flimsy tin lock and stowed it underneath my bed. As Mama's episodes faded, the sketches in the monster diaries dwindled, and by the time we got to intermediate school, I had forgotten them.

I didn't draw anymore, but I still imagined I could use that technique to get the man from the lobby to float to the top of my memory, his features breaking the surface—nose first, cheekbones, forehead, and finally eyes—and all the strangers I had burned into my mind would roll off his face so that I could see him. But after eighteen binders and a full afternoon, the only thing that surfaced was a truth: Once again, the police didn't believe me. After hours of trying, even I wavered and began to doubt myself.

There was nothing left to do there, and I had overstayed my time. I walked down the hallway, looking for a bathroom to pee and splash some water on my face. As always, I kept my gaze aimed carefully away from the mirror.

I wet my hands in the sink, then turned my back on my reflection, raking my greasy hair into a pony tail with my fingers. I had not met my own eyes more than a couple of times since I left Hawaii for college, and it had never gone well. Beneath them, I knew deep bruises of exhaustion would show through the blanched skin of a long New York winter. My face would be vaguely pummeled and puffy. I looked like Kei, of course; put an oxygen mask on me and we could be interchangeable. But we both also looked like our mother. Something about the bone structure; something about the grit and also the giving up that I could see in Kei's face in the hospital. And the ghosts that chased over our mother's pupils before they scuttled out of view.

I found an aged elevator to take me down to the receiving area. I descended in a fugue state, to find a new and smaller night crew. Detective Lynch wasn't there, and no one seemed to care who I was or where I was going. I made it all the way through the first set of glass doors and down the steps to the outer door.

Then it happened.

Night had fallen and the world beyond the glass was black, the street erased by the reflected light of the precinct behind me. Standing at the door, I realized it could open onto anything. I froze. Dry leaves of fear blew through me: pricking my inner ears, the backs of my knees, my instep; scraping all the soft, shielded places where I thought I couldn't be touched.

My fear of the dark had returned. I had arrived in New York with a terror of living in anything but a continuous blaze of electricity, and a timidity—okay, really a freezing—in precarious situations: stepping into elevators, walking at night, and most especially when I found myself alone with a man. I called it vertigo: an otherworldly slipping that kept me caught in one place while time and space seemed to move. *Panic disorder*, Dr. Shawe had called it, one of the rare times she resorted to medical terminology. *Tonic immobility, a normal part of the defense cascade.* But her reassurance that it was a common response to trauma didn't make it any less psychotic or unfair.

But that was then, and over time, I had stopped freezing at every corner until finally I couldn't precisely remember the last time I'd found myself unable to move. Until now. Standing in yet another vestibule, I could no longer raise a foot to slide it forward. I couldn't lean ahead to force myself to leave. My mind and my body were two distinct creatures, and one couldn't understand why the other would not respond. Although I could no longer step out onto the street as I had done just hours before, the truth was it was that earlier freedom that now seemed so inconceivable.

Take a step. Take a step. Take a step. I tried to coax myself into moving.

It wasn't working. Neither was the obvious fact that I was standing in the door of a police station; one of the safest places I could possibly be. There was no way I was going to be able to step into that dark night.

I heard a new voice in my head. *"Don't let go."* It was hauntingly familiar; in fact it was my own: six years earlier, giddy and young. Something twitched in my brain—loosened—and Russell, my first and only boyfriend, was pinning a flower to my dress. His fingers entwined with mine. His hands soft and slightly damp. We were all going to the dance; at least that was what they told me. My first dance, even though I was a senior, almost finished with high school. It was everything I ever wanted. Everything, but this also: *"Promise me you won't let go of my hand."*

We were such children.

Just like that, my mind had tricked me: turned me around, then delivered me back to the night of the cave. There I was, about to get into the car. I closed my eyes, refusing to remember. Blocking out my dress, yellow, a Simplicity pattern, which Mama and I had finished sewing only that afternoon. Blocking out the touch of the soft cotton on my shoulders. I blocked out Eddie, Missy, and the rest of Kei's gang, too. And Russell. My heart was pounding so loudly that it seemed a real possibility that it could explode.

No.

I gasped for breath, realizing only then that I had been holding it, and opened my eyes to bring myself home.

I was shaking. Afraid of the dark, more afraid of the monster I would see if I ever took a good look at myself. That was what happened in the cave, the night that my sanity skipped over.

I became monstrous.

I stepped backward up the stairs of the police station, as if slinking away from a predator, then when my back hit the set of inner doors, I turned, almost throwing myself against them. The officer at the main desk looked up, wary, as I burst back into the receiving area. He didn't recognize that I had just passed him on my way out.

"Can I help you—"

Several other policemen started toward me from different places in the room.

"If you could just...I was just here. Looking at the mug shots. I need..." I paused, trying to make some kind of sense. "I'm a witness. I need a ride home."

It took a while for him to sort out what I was saying. The officer's expression said he had seen people like me before. People with impossible demands. "Detective Lynch brought me," I explained to him. "She said she would be here..."

"Claremont Avenue? That's just a few blocks away. We aren't a cab service."

Could I say my ankles were weak? My shoes broken? I was weak all over, so only one was a lie. "I'm going back to the hospital. It's farther."

"The hospital?" I watched him try to decide whether I was the patient.

This was Kei's fault, I thought. She had ruined me, abandoned me, forced me to learn new ways to survive. And I had done it. Since I left home, I had relied on meticulous planning—every decision weighed exactly to ensure that it contained not a single ounce of danger. For years, I lived in the light, stayed away from strangers, skirted anything stressful or scary, and, most important, kept my past behind its obliging veil. I had begun to heal, and then Kei came back and ripped all my wounds open. And now, I was surrounded by policemen looking at me as if I was oozing, as if my damage might be dangerous, or contagious.

"Never mind. I'll just...if you could call a taxi for me, I'll just go home."

The officer looked as if he'd like to tell me he wasn't a secretary, either, but then he relented. Perhaps he could see the stinging in my eyes as I tried to hold on. There was a squad car that had to go in that direction anyway, he told me. If I could wait a few minutes, they would take me home.

Home, I thought. If only I had one. I had been run out of my home in Hawaii, my safe haven destroyed long before. There was no place for me there. I was trapped, and as the police delivered me to my apartment not too many minutes later, I could feel the danger that Kei brought with her pressing me deep into the cushions of the car.

Home. It was unbearable. But the apartment waiting four stories above me was the only place I had left in the world.

1942 – 1943

Manzanar. That was where they had been sent. It meant "apple orchard." It was an empty plain. A desert, really, once the city of Los Angeles had diverted all its water. Now it was a city of tarpaper barracks, lined up in a hurry and standing at attention. The first Japanese Americans who were sent there would build it for the ten thousand others who came after. All of them crammed into skeletal buildings without partitions, three or four families together. They were people Lillie could get lost among, but who were not, she was to find out, remotely like her.

They were given bags of straw to sleep on. They had to stand in line to use the open latrines. They stood in line, too, to eat their meals in the mess hall in their allotted thirty-minute slots of time. Dust storms blasted through the planks in the floors and the cracks under the doors and the walls and left, within minutes, a blanket of fine dirt almost as deep as Lillie's fingernail. People took to carrying goggles, when they could get them, for when they got caught outside in the sudden gray storms.

Lillie was two months pregnant when they arrived at Manzanar, throwing up on the train, but her mother-in-law was even worse off. The old woman had started coughing blood almost immediately. It was more than the dust—none of them had ever experienced such brutal extremes in temperature: blazing hot by noon and freezing shortly after the sun set. At night, they pushed their beds together to keep from shivering, but it didn't help much. Lillie had to keep opening the seal of warmth in the blankets so she could vomit in the bucket they kept outside the door.

Lillie spent most of her time going back and forth to the hospital in the compound. It had no walls. For a while it had no roof, either. The staff was mostly volunteer, and the doctors had to supply even basic medical instruments on their own. They tested Donald's mother for tuberculosis, the only diagnosis that would have qualified her for a transfer to a real hospital, but the results were negative. It was probably the dust, they said. It was probably the weather. It was seven long months of being examined and then turned away. Donald's mother kept saying she was ready to die, leaning heavily against Lillie on the long walk back to their little room in the barracks. She was only holding on to see her grandson. Donald's mother knew he was a boy, because when she whispered to Lillie's belly, brushing her hands on Lillie's tight skin in endless circles so he would know her, she could hear him answer. "Teaching him Japanese," she teased. But it was a kind joke.

The baby was a bridge between the two women, a new start for the family. In the camp, they had each other. Meanwhile, the men kept themselves busy.

There were jobs running the camp and even building it. Though they were paid almost nothing, at least the internees had something to do. There were factions forming between those who had actually lived in Japan, as Donald and his parents had, and those who had never even seen it. In the evenings, the men began to gather, and fights broke out between the Kibei—the American-born children who had gone to school in Japan like Donald had, though he had only been there for a year or two and his memories were hazy—and the "loyal" Americans who had formed some kind of league. Lillie knew little about the fights, just that the conversations got heated. Donald protected her from it, and Lillie didn't gossip, not that she had friends who would have whispered the rumors to her. What Donald did tell her was that someone was stealing the food the government was sending, and no one knew where to point fingers. Where had the meat gone? The sugar?

Donald was ever more indignant, but Lillie was just numb.

It was December when the riots began. Lillie tried to ignore them at first. It was better to keep your head down in the camps, she thought, though it was true that this was not a new impulse for her; her parents had brought her up to be humble and respectful, as befit a daughter of the church. Then one night, Lillie was in their barracks with Donald's parents when the shouting grew right outside their windows. Most of the shouting was undoubtedly in English, since speaking Japanese in the camps was prohibited, but Lillie couldn't make out what the problem was. From the tone of the yelling—something about *inu*, which meant "dog"—Lillie understood there was no fire, no emergency that they would have to contend with, and that the three of them were safer in the room. The sound eased as the crowd moved past their block toward the mess hall.

Then they heard the shots.

Lillie ducked, though she was not in front of the window. Donald, she thought, panicking. Where was he? On the weekends, he usually played cards with his Kibei friends. Donald's mother clutched anxiously at her blanket, but his father insisted there was no reason to worry. The riot must have trapped him in the hall where their game was; he would not want to cross a crowd like that to get home.

When Donald slipped through the door many hours later, di-sheveled and alarmed, he confirmed that his father had been right. Lillie didn't ask him what he'd seen. She would wait until morning to find out what happened—now he should rest. Though as the night stretched on, she could tell that no one was really sleeping. Donald's body was like ice, too stiff beside her, and the whole camp was frozen as a held breath. Only Lillie shifted, restless, as her baby kicked, regular as a metronome, against the tightening band around her womb.

She must have slept, since just before dawn, Lillie woke to a fierce contraction. She moaned, still half awake, and reached out for Donald, but he returned her hand to her and slipped out of the covers, throwing on his heavy peacoat to go to the latrine. Her mother-in-law must have been in pain, too. She was sobbing softly beside her husband, and for once, the old man didn't seem annoyed at her weakness, but propped himself up on the bed beside hers and let her cry. Lillie was too shocked by the pounding in her lower back to wonder why everyone was awake. She pulled her knit hat over her ears and curled on her side, letting the cramps rush through her. It was still dark, and the night was still below freezing, clearly not the right time to draw attention to herself. With her arms slung around her belly, she breathed, wondering how long it would be before she would be ready to go to the hospital. She longed for her own mother's arms around her, her warm hand against her skin, but she had thrown her lot in with Donald's family, and there was no one else who could help her. She was going to have to do this alone.

She waited all that morning, slow to come to the understanding that Donald was not coming back. It could have been Tateishi-sama's unusual patience with his wife, or the fact that they had no interest in doing anything, even getting food at the canteen. Neither of them looked over at Lillie, even as she stayed in bed and the fierce tightening continued, as constant as her breath, though not as quick. The neighbors next to them had been gone all day, leaving a blanket of quiet that Lillie had to work hard not to puncture, and it was in that noiselessness between her caught breaths that Lillie could almost remember Donald's dead-of-the-night whispers to his father, and the old man's measured response.

When the military police arrived, it was all Lillie could do to scramble into a sitting position. What had been a band around her belly spread through her entire torso; the pain was everywhere, pounding on the floor of her pelvis and deep inside her bones. The police informed them that a snitch had reported seeing one of the instigators of the riots sneaking into their room after dark, and it was only then that she finally understood. Tateishi-sama stood, and in a moment of quiet, reserved dignity, put his wrists out for handcuffs.

Donald didn't return.

The barracks door closed behind Donald's father, and Lillie was ashamed to feel something like relief. It was nothing to be proud of, but there it was, just an instant, when his criticism lifted, before the weight of her labor bore down again. She heard noises outside and looked up, expecting Donald, but it was only the neighbor couple, returning—of course—within minutes of the visit from the MPs.

Where was her husband? Why would he let them take his father in his place? Lillie had no time to linger on these questions—her labor was filling her body, running through the tops of her femurs and into her thighs, and now, just as she was left alone with her mother-in-law, the old woman started to convulse with coughing. It was only the tears that brought it on, her mother-in-law said, but Lillie understood she was also giving up. As Lillie tried to stand so she could comfort Donald's mother, she felt a pop deep inside her and a warm rush of fluid between her legs. She cried out for the neighbors, who gathered the two sobbing women in their arms and somehow hurried them to the hospital.

Donald never returned that night, the night his mother died, choking in her own blood on one side of the makeshift hospital room, crying out for her only son. He was not there a few hours later when, on the other side, Lillie gave birth. No one could have stayed in the latrine all day, she knew; not sitting on the holes cut into the splintered wooden benches that the internees were forced to use, side by unbearable side. Not even for an hour. But she never asked her husband where he'd hidden while his mother died and his father was taken, and his wife brought their son into the world all alone.

She didn't ask, because there couldn't be an answer.

After the riots, the camp was quiet. Whether the arrests were right or wrong—depending on whom you talked to—the atmosphere seemed to lighten somewhat, since the agitators from both sides were arrested or removed. For a few weeks, martial law kept everyone in their barracks as much as possible, whispering among themselves as if the influx of patrolling soldiers might hear them through the holes in their walls and send them off to jail, too. Which meant, as soon as Lillie left the hospital and found Donald waiting for her in their newly empty partition in the barracks, the two of them were left alone with their son.

Lillie could lose a whole day lying next to Toshi. Her son was a miracle. Lillie brushed his skin with her cheeks. She nursed him and burped him and sang to him. She whisked him away from Donald the instant he started to cry. She had no idea what to say to her husband, and she had less and less interest in hearing his excuses as time passed without even a word of regret. Donald was preoccupied—rough, and also angry—but on top of that, he didn't seem to know what to do with an infant. His son was bald, and lumpy, and easily squashed. Lillie was different, too, he complained, uninterested in getting out of bed or putting clothes on. He humored her by bringing her food from the canteen for the first week, and in return she said nothing when he snuck out of the barracks—it was becoming a habit—to "get some air."

Lillie mourned her mother-in-law, and felt her absence as a companion, but now she had Toshi. The tiny shells of his ears could easily hold all her secrets, so she confided to him the many joys and worries that she would have shared with her parents, if she could get the courage to write to them. She missed her own mother more than ever, wondering what advice she might have passed on if Toshi had been born back home. Lillie spent whole days composing a birth announcement in her head, a happy letter that could lift them out of this world of dust and sharp weather that Toshi had been born into, an announcement that would proclaim her first achievement: She was a mother, too, a successful wife with a child of her own.

She never wrote it.

As the months went by, the wall of everything left unsaid still separated her from Donald, while she was learning that it also insulated her. It was not that they did not speak; for example, Donald had traced his father to a jail being run by the Justice Department, and he made sure to tell her whenever Tateishi-sama sent a letter, though they were almost completely black with redactions when they came.

Meanwhile, while Toshi's presence gave her an excuse to avoid discussing the night Donald's father was taken, he was also a child, and Lillie had to learn how to be a mother. The volunteer nurses at the clinic gave her some useful advice but she also learned by example, watching how young mothers at the canteen treated their children, practicing certain lullabies or different positions to soothe a crying infant in the flimsy privacy of their barracks. They all seemed to understand so naturally what needed to be done; she didn't want to ask questions, because she was afraid they would think her peculiar.

Every day she longed for her mother. Lillie wondered for the first time precisely how old she had been when she was left on her parents' doorstep—it was only now that she understood how much of her life her foster mother might have missed if she'd arrived just a few weeks later. Every smile, every wild, pumping kick, even the sight of her son's closed, pouting lips when he slept was so precious. She should be with her mother, sharing it. Her mother should be with *her*, showing her how to keep a baby quiet at night. Her parents had assured her that she was capable. That she was lucky. But that luck had run out, though now she wondered if it had run into Toshi in her womb. Perhaps he was now the one who would bring the luck.

When Toshi was two months old, the internees were given a loyalty questionnaire that asked them to forswear allegiance to the Japanese Emperor and volunteer for military service. She answered yes to the questions easily, truthfully. She was, and always had been, a good American girl.

The answers were not so easy for everyone. The questionnaire divided the internees once again, raising the specter of the riots. There were those who felt it was a trap. Could you forswear allegiance to the Emperor if you had none in the first place? Were the questions designed to trick them into saying that they were foreign agents or spies? To others, it was an insult. How could a country that had stripped them of their citizenship now ask them to sign up to fight for it and quite possibly be killed? And who would take care of their parents and children left in the camps if they did so? It was complicated, and further complicated for Lillie when she learned that Donald had answered no. Twice.

That was not the worst part. Some of the "no-no boys" were being segregated and prepared to be moved to another camp. Donald had been staying up late, writing letters challenging the legality of the questionnaire, though Lillie had no idea who he was sending them to. One day, he came back to their room with great news: There was a Swedish exchange ship, the *Gripsholm*, taking diplomats and businessmen and a few hundred other fortunates back to Japan, and Tateishi-sama had been able to get them on the passenger list. Even while he was being held somewhere in custody for the riots that he'd had nothing to do with, her father-in-law still had enough sway with the Japanese Embassy to have his entire family labeled disloyal so they could be "repatriated" back to Japan.

Donald was ecstatic—with the help of his letters, his father had traded who-knew-what favors for what remained of his family and finagled their freedom—and Lillie was stunned. How could she be sent to Japan with his family, even if it was her family, if it was against her will? How could she go *back* to a place where she'd never been?

It was wrong. Whatever world Donald had thought she belonged to when she married him, he was wrong. She was American. The preacher's daughter. California was her home. Toshi was nine months old—born in the camp, true, but still a U.S. citizen. He wasn't even on the ship manifest. He should be able to stay.

Then she realized what he had just told her. "You sent those letters to your *father*?"

Her husband had schemed with his father to deport her to a foreign country. She had to stop it somehow, so she went to the director of the camp to petition to stay in America and have her citizenship reinstated.

The director didn't know her; why would he? But she got a few minutes with him by reminding one of the administrators that her son was the first child born after he took over at Manzanar. She didn't mention that her mother-in-law's was similarly the first death, if you didn't count the two men who were shot in the back by the MPs with machine guns and gas masks, which she was sure he wouldn't. It was a strange thing to be notable for, but she was here to speak for Toshi, and she couldn't be shy about using whatever she had to stay in America.

She was on the passenger list, the director pointed out, even if her child wasn't. And wasn't Toshi a Japanese if her husband was? And if not, didn't he belong to her husband anyway? Wouldn't he be better off being raised in Japan with his own kind? Regardless, the director couldn't do anything unless she had a sponsor to vouch for her and make sure she and Toshi weren't going to be burdens on America.

A burden? she'd asked. She was *American*. But she understood, in retrospect, that her voice had been too strident. He liked only the good Japs, without a blemish on their records, and the family she had married into was full of them.

She assured him that she could get a sponsor. Her parents would help. They were her only hope; neither she nor Toshi had a birth certificate. She didn't even have a marriage certificate, though that would only have placed her more firmly under Donald's family's control. She had dictated a telegram, a hasty message about their grandson so different from the announcement she'd imagined. So far, there had been no reply.

When Donald learned about her petition, he slammed the door to the barracks so hard it split.

—What is wrong with you, woman? he screamed. "*This* is America!"

He didn't care that his son was crying, nor how his voice carried through the pieces of fabric that separated them from the others. Had Lillie failed to notice that they were surrounded by barbed wire and machine guns? Their homes were taken from them. His father was in jail. Did she not remember the night he'd staggered home after the riot, eyes puffed and streaming, snot all over his face, barely ahead of the military police? All the protesters had wanted was an answer about where their food was. They were unarmed, and only asking. And now *America* wanted to throw him in front of the German army to be shot.

Lillie sat frozen beneath him, watching his spittle fly over her head. She prayed he wouldn't strike her with Toshi hugged to her chest. Donald slammed back out of the barracks and didn't come home that night, so Lillie was left alone to repair the door as best she could. But she couldn't erase his questions.

How could she want to stay here? How dare she try to steal his son?

As the days stretched on without an answer from her parents, Donald seemed to understand he'd won. Lillie begged the camp director to send a second telegram, this one marked URGENT. She could not believe her parents would abandon her. *Japs*, she thought. What kind of Jap did they now think she was? That couldn't be the answer, but surrounded by barbed wire and machine guns, how could she be sure? She thought of her mother, and the quilt that was waiting for her on the farm. She should have taken it, even if it hadn't left her enough room for her coat or a second pair of shoes. She should have done what she had secretly longed to: worn it wrapped around her on the train. *Promise me you won't forget*, her mother had said, and she must have thought her daughter had broken that promise.

Even if you never come home.

There was no response to the second telegram, either. That was what the director told her. Instead, he handed her a tin box. She had first thought this was a bit of guilt that he hadn't been able to change Lillie's status, though now she wondered if he had sent either of her messages at all. She looked at his face and imagined she found sadness in it, but whether he was sad for her, or regretting his own lies, she couldn't tell. Or maybe it had nothing to do with her; maybe when he looked at her, he saw enemy aliens to get rid of, not a desperate mother and her innocent child. Whatever the truth, blaming him wouldn't change anything. Nor would blaming her husband, who was full of his victory but smart enough to know not to point it out.

It was too late. There were no days left to receive mail.

She had been careful to keep their belongings separate just in case—hers and Toshi's in one bag, Donald's in the other—but now, it no longer mattered. In the morning, Lillie, Donald, and Toshi would leave the camp with a handful of the "special others" and board the train to cross the country. In a week or two, they would be reunited with his father in New York. There, they would board the Swedish mercy ship together: the *Gripsholm*, bound for Japan. Donald had packed nothing for his absent father—he said whatever his father had with him now would just have to hold him until they arrived. He imagined Japan as a land of plenty, where their family had property and connections.

The only thing Lillie would bring for Tateishi-sama was the tin box, which now held his wife's ashes. She has seen the pages of black redactions in enough letters to guess that he still had no idea that the old woman had died. Would he even know he had a grandson?

The tin box was light and the lid fit tightly. Lillie would have brought it for her own mother, and she owed her mother-in-law that much, though she would have to remove more of her own clothes. She'd already set aside her summer things to make room for Toshi's clothing, though he would outgrow them quickly. One season, this season, was all she could manage for either of them.

All she had left of her childhood was the indigo bowl she had refused to give to Donald's mother, and the handkerchief her mother had embroidered of the snow she would never see. And in that lost life, too, was the husband she had given up her home for. She once looked into his eyes and thought he knew her.

It seemed so long ago.

HANA

We were five. Two little girls spread out on the pune'e in the living room cutting patterns for paper dolls that Arnie had brought especially for us the previous evening. It was still afternoon, and the sky was low, unsettled—it wasn't raining, and it would not, but a skin of moisture still formed on us, even in the house. My legs were tucked under my skirt; Kei's extended. Kei was trying to make snowflakes.

Snow was a vision from Arnie, a substance we'd never seen. Mama didn't like snow and couldn't understand what all the fuss was about, but Kei was captivated by his description: as fragile as thread, balanced as a ripple, brief as a blink.

"Girls?" Mama stood in the doorway of her bedroom in her gardening clothes—a long-sleeved blouse and baggy pants made from bleached cotton rice bags turned inside out, and denim tabis. "It's time to stake the peas."

We had planted the peas together and had been checking them daily to watch the progress of the light green curls. This was an invitation, then, not a demand, but as I watched Kei tuck the scissors into the bottom of a shoebox, I couldn't help thinking we would rather she stay with us inside. There was a time when the three of us were always together. Now, though, Arnie came at night, and Mama had a different orbit. Even on those rare occasions when it was just us, now her attention wandered and she would drift away.

While Kei swept the paper scraps from the floor, I went into our bedroom and took out our own gardening outfits. Kei looked through the window at the thick cotton batting that was the sky.

"Do we have to wear hats?" Our hats were woven from lauhala. The fronds had been stripped and softened, but they were still stiff and they itched.

My mother had moved back into her bedroom. She pulled a small hand mirror out of her drawer and looked into it, touching her hair. It was loose, looped on itself in a simple knot. She had begun wearing it this way since Arnie appeared; she had given herself permission to be young. She dipped into her closet and brought out a dark blue hat, a round cloth bubble that hugged her head tightly with a thin, turned-up brim. Then she ushered us out.

"First, let's turn the manure."

Once a week, Mama lifted the round wooden lid beside the house and stirred the manure with her shovel. It was not merely dung—although we did get an annual flatbed full of that—it was her secret recipe: a striated, subterranean cauldron of compost, lime, and seaweed. As the year progressed, the mix became something richer and better than its parts, and when spring came, it crumbled like a moist cake between my fingers.

Mama had filled a metal bucket with the mixture and tucked a tied bundle of stripped twigs under her arm. Her garden was planted in three curving terraces, and now she walked along the top of one of the squat lava rock walls that held the plots in place and acted like paths in between them. Kei and I were happy to be strung out behind her, stepping off into the plots of vegetables from time to time to check for aphids and white moths. When we reached the peas, near the edge of the property, she bent to look at them, barely the length of a finger.

"Which one of you wants to help me stake?"

I would have rather sifted the black compost into a blanket for the new plants once the staking was finished. When my sister didn't move, though, I raised my hand.

"Ah, Hana," Mama said. "Good girl." She began to show me where to sink the twigs: placing two fingers between the stem and the twig to space them, then tucking the tendrils around the twigs so they would hug each other as they grew. I knew I should be grasping this crucial information as it floated by me, but instead, I was basking in my name.

Before Arnie arrived, we were merely the "girls." He used to tease Mama that she couldn't recognize us, but since all three of us were always together, why would she need to single one out? Now Mama had begun to do just that—calling us "Kei" and "Hana"—not often, and somewhat indiscriminately, though usually it was when she had a strong word of scolding or praise.

My sister heard the name, too. I could feel it in the stillness and the square of her shoulders. I knew I should reach out to her, to remind her that we were Koko, but I didn't.

Instead, I felt Mama's hands plunge into the mixture in the pail as if they were my own, felt the cool, crushed velvet of the compost against her bare palms. We never wore gloves when we were planting. Mama said it was too easy to break things, and that a little cornmeal could get our fingers cleaner than gloves ever could.

The plot was long and sat beneath the pool of still air that collected along the base of the wall. It was narrow enough so Mama could stretch to reach the innermost peas. Her hands were firm as she speared the twigs into the ground, gentle when she guided the young peas to embrace them.

I mimicked her, though my rows were not as neat and I could reach only half as far as my mother. Kei put the bucket between us, mashing the ground flat so it wouldn't tip. She waited, shaking about an inch of compost in a snug skirt around each plant when I was done. The ground was dense and resisted the twigs, so I worked more slowly than Mama, but I was happy.

I was Hana.

"How are we doing, girls?" Mama had worked in the other direction, and a crisp half of the peas had been staked. "Trade?"

I nodded. I would do anything Mama wanted me to. I handed the twigs to my sister. There was one bucket—Mama and I could share it—but first, she sat back and watched while Kei selected a twig and I sprinkled the compost around the stalk when she was done.

"Make it lighter. Not so heavy on the ground."

I rubbed my thumb against my fingers, so aware of my mother's eyes that I probed for even the tiniest clumps before I let the crumbs fall. It was right this time; I could tell by her smile. I did it again, marveling at the height and size of the halo I could create with even the smallest fistful.

"Koko!" A warning, from Kei.

I looked down at the stem I'd just surrounded and saw there was no stick there. There were four plants waiting for me, but this was not one of them. Kei sighed—extravagantly, to highlight my mistake.

Kei and I had been short with each other all week. Not angry, just missing our cues, especially when our mother wasn't there. Mama was the one we counted on to untwist our knots and fit our pieces together. We missed her.

Kei had staked the peas I fertilized and was only two plants ahead of me now. Mama and I were working together. Instead of sprinkling the manure palm down, the way I did, she held her hand palm up and sifted it with her thumb, then let it fall through the cracks between her fingers. I flipped my hand over, too, and she gave me the "good girl" smile.

For a moment, we had fallen into an old rhythm—the rhythm of a stream, of water that rushes forever over a sentinel rock, running to and away at the same moment. Then the sound changed; the bottom note dropped out, and I knew Kei had finished staking, and that she was watching me now. Watching us, me and our mother, and the twin falls of life pouring from our hands.

Mama signaled for Kei to help. I shifted the bucket to make room.

We missed our cues.

Maybe I didn't move the bucket far enough behind me. Maybe there was a rock lurking, submerged just beneath the surface of the grass, or maybe I'd forgotten to account for the hill. Whatever the reason, when Kei extended her hand, the bucket tipped.

I reached for it. So did our mother.

"Ow. *Itai.*" Kei began shaking her head: She'd drawn her hand over one eye, leaving a black bandit streak from her nose to her cheekbone. "*Auwe!* Itai! My eye! My eye!"

Mama grabbed Kei's hands, trying to keep her from rubbing more dirt and manure into her eye. "Let me see. Hold still. Let me see."

Kei held herself away, her eyes squeezed shut. Her lips trembled, bewildered, as if someone else had done this to her—one of us—and now she could not trust even Mama.

"Let me see. Open your eye. How can I see if you don't open your eyes?"

Mama's logic wasn't getting through. Finally, she released Kei's hands and put her thumbs on the top and bottom of Kei's lids to pry them open.

"Ow, ow! It's worse!"

Kei's urgency was contagious. Mama rubbed her hands on her pants in hard sharp strokes. They were far from clean, but the spigot was near the house, on the other side of the yard. She scrubbed them once more, this time on her blouse, then reached again for Kei.

"Ow. Mama." Kei was crying, shaking her head. She was shaking her hands, bouncing, anything to keep from leaping to her feet.

"Shush, shush. Hana." Mama raised her voice over Kei's. "Shush, Hanako, it's all right."

Just like that, Mama gave Kei my name. Until that moment, I was with them—in Kei's jangling movements, lending my own quiet panic to save my sister. Now, as Mama brushed Kei's eye with her cheek, trying to clear the dirt off her lids and lashes, I found I was not willing to share it. Kei was still twisting, working herself up—she appeared not to have heard Mama, but the name entered me, running from my ears into my toes, and I could only assume it was in Kei's tears, too, and in the smirk I would see at any moment that would prove this was a ruse—this dirt she put into her own eye—it was a plot to take the name Mama had given me and the love that came with it.

"Shush, shush," Mama said, and when Kei still did not quiet, she placed one hand on the back of Kei's head and the other on her shoulder.

Then, holding Kei in a vise so she couldn't move, Mama parted her lips and dropped them open over Kei's eye to lick the dirt out with her tongue.

Kei jerked, surprised; her other eye opened into Mama's hair. Mama's hands were holding Kei tight and Kei suddenly relaxed—closing her eye, closing me out. Mama's eyes were shut, too, in concentration. Her lips skimmed Kei's nose, flowed around her cheekbone, like wax, creating a seal that didn't break even as her tongue chased the timid eyeball. I could see it moving through her cheek. She was feeding on Kei the way the bees and butterflies feed on the long tongues and open throats of the honeysuckles.

And I remembered a kiss then, late at night, at our front door. Arnie was leaving. Kei was asleep, but I had gotten out of bed so I was there to watch them, Arnie and my mother, both tucked close but not touching in the doorway.

Arnie stooped and his head lunged at Mama's. I expected her to duck, but she rose up, onto her toes—she tilted her face to catch his. She held the kiss there. It went on much longer than when she kissed us good night, and was curiously singular; the rest of her body was still—no stroking hair, no whispered wishes—as if the kiss itself was enough. Their lips clung to each other's so utterly I imagined for a second their bodies had been left behind—that my mother and Arnie had disappeared, leaving their skin and bones hanging together like coats waiting for the rain on the hook by the door. I felt myself longing for her, missing her even though she was still there. And then, they pulled apart. Mama dropped back onto her feet slowly, inch by inch, exposing more of Arnie's face as she did—his blurred expression, his hopeful smile.

The next morning, no matter how carefully I studied her, I could see no difference in my mother.

But now, my mother's mouth was on Kei, and the confluence of their faces was like cool air around me, like the chill that rushes in when two people, tucked together, suddenly separate. Kei had my name; Mama gave it to her, gave her the exact space that was mine—the precise width of my wrists, the curve and pose of my slippered feet. Mama's lips were meant for me. I could smell her breath skimming my own forehead, and my blood rushed to meet it. Her tongue was rough, insistent, and it stirred up my already swirling thoughts as it probed the uncharted crevices of my eye.

Then she pulled away from Kei, and I could see the clean circle where my mother's mouth was, the lashes moist with saliva. Kei fell against her chest and Mama wrapped her in her arms. The circle hovered, pure in Kei's otherwise dirt-streaked face, and then began to dry, shrinking back into the world that, until that moment, I'd never questioned.

I was crying. I wanted my mother to take me into her mouth and heal me, too, but when she turned, astonished, I couldn't find the words.

"I have dirt in my eye," I said.

Mama considered me. The mouth I craved opened. Her teeth danced, and for a moment, I believed she'd do it.

Then Kei wailed again and Mama turned her back on me, holding my freshly sobbing sister. She whispered into Kei's hair. "Hanako," I heard. And also, "Peace."

I had disappeared.

How long did it take Kei's tears to subside? Long enough that I didn't even remember what Mama was referring to when she turned back to me. "Copycat," she called me, but kindly. "Come on girls, let's finish up here."

The bucket had been righted. My mother scooped the spilled manure and began sprinkling again. We were still coming out of her spell. I was clinging to the hope that she'd change her mind, that she would reach out and take me, too, into her arms. *It's my name*, I wanted to remind her, *you said* I *was Hanako*, but her attention was on the peas. We finished the patch in no order. Mama and Kei were in sync, fertilizing by feel, and I was the misfiring piston.

I, who tried so hard.

I remember now that, every year, Mama gave me and Kei two handfuls of flower seeds to plant wherever we wanted in the garden. I used mine to create a color-coded collar around the house. Kei scattered hers just the way Lillie did in our mother's stories, in the spontaneous, spinning romp the preacher's wife allowed her, an annual release of a child's high spirits to help her act with virtue for the rest of the year. Kei had been known to drop her entire handful of seeds in a single footstep, once flinging a drift of nasturtiums into the tomatoes. She trusted the seeds would take root, and often, to my amazement, they did.

Now, I realize that Kei was not the only one who created a garden land-scape with her eyes closed. Mama, too, believed eyes could deceive: She let her feet map paths for cinder-lined drainage ditches that would never overrun even in the rainiest weather; she let her skin find the holes in the breeze for her orchids. Where did this trust come from, that they didn't need to test, or to practice, or even to imagine the final product?

How was it that they were so much the same, and when did I become so different?

And they *were* the same, I could see even then. There I was, reaching in from the right. Kei and Mama together on the left. The connection be-tween them remained in the blotch of clean skin around Kei's eye and the fine lines of dirt smudged into Mama's lips. This was what they gave each other: soft, swollen skin and crushed lips; dazed eyes, bleary mouths; slight, immodest smiles and peace. So much peace I could not bear to be their witness.

It was the last peace we would have as a trio, though we didn't know it yet. But in the final hours of *Before*, the peas were staked and almost fertilized, and I was staring at the black dirt on my hands wishing I had the courage to smear it into my eye. Instead, I sat back and watched my mama and my sister finish the pea patch.

Neither one of them turned to look at me.

KOKO

And here is where we split. Do you remember? You don't want to—why would you?—but you need to, all the same.

Look at us. It is after dinner, after the mishap in the garden, and Mama has let us finish our dolls in her bedroom. There we are: two girls, the snowflakes, and two dolls. The dolls are creamy white, outlines cut from heavy paper. Arnie gave them to us, and Mama gave us her shoebox full of sewing scraps. We have ribbons and buttons, fabric and paste, and a single pair of scissors. One girl has been trying to cut snowflakes from the fabric, but it keeps slipping. The other girl shifts through the buttons and ribbons and the paste, and waits.

"Scissors, ne?"

Fold, *slip*, snip. The scissors snap shut. Another snowflake ruined. The fragile points Arnie showed us: One of them is sliced off.

Spindles, he called them. *Cloud seeds*. Every point a mirror of every other. We select another scrap of fabric and start over. We have to make one right.

We are two: both and neither. Is it hard to remember what it felt like to be "we"? Just like Mama always told us: four hands, four eyes, two hearts. But one of those eyes was too loved by Mama in the garden, and that is where the trouble starts.

We are the girl with the scissors. And we are the girl who waits. But the girl who waits, the one who Mama did not hold in the garden—let's call her Koko, even though we both are—she's annoyed. Her doll is lying naked beneath a blanket of uncut ribbons, a chain of unpasted buttons around her waist. Koko's hand rattles in the box, telling you to hurry. Trying to find something to trade for the precious scissors that she knows you will want.

Look at us there, lost without Mama. She should be here to help us. To smile away Koko's anger, to hold the scissors in our hands and snip the points. Instead, she is laughing with Arnie in the living room where we should have been. Balancing each other on the edges of the pune'e in their new, after-dinner positions. Creeping closer to the middle every night. Are we just now realizing that he's taken over, or were we aware of it as he slipped in? Did we notice, for example, when Arnie began to bring meat for dinner? Tonight, it was a small gray snapper. Mama's favorite. That's what she said.

"George da Silva wen catch 'um," he said when he gave it to her, forgetting Mama doesn't like pidgin. "De'ah stove wen *make* on dem."

Ma-ke: one of those crude Hawaiian words. Arnie was telling her he was paid in fish for fixing the da Silvas's stove.

Now, it is after, and the door is almost closed against us, but Arnie's voice is loud. His stories are long and high and hanging, and Mama is the only one who can catch them. We can hear her, leaping for his words, cradling them in the deep pocket of her laughter.

Every time we hear it, the scissors slip and we have to start again.

"Scissors!" Koko demands over Mama's floating laughter. Koko wants her turn.

Watch now as Koko snatches a scrap from the stack of cloth we have carefully layered. See her find the pins and scatter them across the floor. The almost-snowflake twists between the blades of our scissors. Only one cut more.

But Koko has lost her patience. She yanks her doll out from under its buttons and ribbons and tears the head from its body, then flings the head at you. She flings the arms from the body. One, then two. The paper legs fall on our scissors, and another snowflake is ruined. This one is her fault.

The head of Koko's doll is lying in your lap. Why would she destroy her own doll? Arnie starts another story in the living room and Koko grabs for your doll now. You cover it with your knee so she can't destroy it, too.

Koko's hand dips into the shoebox again. Her face is wild. Her fingers open like a flower, and there it is. A pale, pearl button in her palm.

We look at it together.

"Fish eye," she hisses.

Is it only then that you understand what is wrong?

We have seen Mama pick up the snapper's head at dinner. Seen her dig out the soft meat of the cheek and then raise it to her mouth. Her cheeks draw in. Her lips, greedy. The opaque marble fish eye disappears.

"Fish eye. Fish eye. Fish eye. Fish—" Koko's singsong now is the only sound.

Koko is the watcher, the one who can describe what happened, and she has just done so. We are back in the garden, Mama's hands clenched around your head. You are joined with her. You flow into each other. But Koko is watching, and her eyes are greedy like you've never seen.

"Not," you protest, but Koko is smirking. In her eyes, you are being stripped and sucked on. You are cast aside and left bone clean. But you are still two together, aren't you? Why then is she so mean?

"Fish eye." It's so dirty when Koko says it.

"Not!" You have to change her face.

That's when the scissors fly out of your hand. They miss Koko and hit the table next to Mama's bed.

Koko turns to grab the scissors, and then pauses. Her eyes fall on the picture frame Mama keeps there. It's a black-and-white photograph of a child standing, though she seems barely strong enough to stay upright on the skinny legs sticking out of her shorts. Her arms are raised up toward someone who is not in the picture, as if she is asking to be lifted. Her face is sharp, but shining, and her short hair whirls like a helicopter on her head.

Koko looks at the picture. Neither one of you has ever given much thought to it. You are rarely in Mama's room. But now both of you can feel the child's laughter bubbling up with so much force that it might lift her. She is tilting, as if she can't find the space between movement and stillness. But you feel sure that in the next, uncaptured instant, she will be safe and happy in her mother's arms.

You watch Koko understand that she is not this child. Then she looks at you and remembers how Mama hugged you in the garden and fixed your eye.

She throws the frame at your head.

It lifts, arcs through the air. Then it cracks against your collarbone and the glass shatters on the floor. The sound is high and compound. Mama's voice cuts off in the living room. We have her attention. She is coming. There are only seconds. And you realize: It's Koko's turn to take the blame.

You look at Koko. So jealous she is pinking from the inside.

It's Koko's turn to be Kei.

Your hand picks up a shard of glass and strikes at the photograph. The glass severs the child's head from its body—Where is Mama? Why isn't she here to stop us?—the glass slashes the child's body into rags. The battered head from the photograph floats, but not far, and settles near the body of Koko's paper doll. Your flesh is ripped, too. This is all Koko's fault. This is how deeply she has hurt us. *Fish eye*, she called you, and now she will pay for it. Your fist closes to hide the blood.

The door swings open.

Mama is finally here.

Mama is broken, barely standing. Looking at the empty frame and the ruined photograph. Arnie is with her, asking who did this.

Neither one of us comes forward.

We have seen our mother faint. We've seen her falter. But she always smiled for us when she fell, as if to promise her return. She always went down whole, not bone by bone like she is falling now, as if her insides are untied. Arnie is holding Mama around the waist, but she is hanging oddly. Her head at the wrong angle.

Move, Koko, you urge her without speaking. Koko knows it's her turn, so why isn't she moving? Move forward. Arnie and Mama are looking at us.

She'll step forward any second now.

As you wait for her to take the blame, a red stain creeps around your fingers, growing darker in the folds of your skin. You watch it gather in the spiral of your clenched pinkie until it falls—a large dark tear.

Then, everything changes.

Mama sees the blood in your hand and makes a choice. "Kei—" she begins, and then, it happens. In one sure, strong movement, she slaps you so hard she is standing.

Do you remember? Mama doesn't even look at Koko. She slaps *you*.

Look at yourself as Mama hits you. See the spring of her legs and the length of her twisting back that knocks you down. You are too stunned to cry. How is this possible?

You cannot see the bloody smear your own hand leaves when you touch your stinging cheek. You only have eyes for Mama. She has dropped straight down in the scattered glass. She is kneeling in the shards, crying, scrambling for the shreds of her cherished picture. Although she has always been so careful not to cut herself, her knees are bleeding, and Arnie is trying to tell her not to bother with the scraps, that we can clean up later. But she doesn't hear.

"Mama?" It's your voice. She is broken. Everything is very wrong. And still Koko is sitting. Like she did nothing. Like she is not here.

"Kei." You hear the name. It's Arnie speaking, looking at you. "Are you okay?"

Kei is not supposed to be a someone. She's a passing storm, a fire in the woodstove. She's a cry in the night even as the nightmare has begun to ebb. Kei is rage, and fizz. She is the pressure that spits from the bottle. But she is not the soda. Not the bottle.

She is not supposed to be *you*.

Koko threw the frame at you. She is the one who started it, and cutting at the picture should only have made her punishment worse. Mama is kneeling in the glass, scraps of her picture in her lap. The familiar curdles rise in her newly sunken cheeks. Her eyes are like whirlpools pulling her face into them until all that's left are dark, black sockets. She is already gone: to the land of the ghosts.

The blood from your hand is running off your wrist. "You!" You launch yourself at Koko. "It's you!" Your hands reach her face, her shoulders. You scramble at her, wanting to hit her the same way Mama hit you so you can be together again, but she pushes back. There is blood on her now, too. It's on her face, droplets spraying an arc across the front of her dress. You wipe your blood down her arm so Arnie will see that there is no difference between you, and so it can also be her fault. Koko ripped the doll. Koko threw the picture. And then, as you turn to try to explain it to Arnie, you hear Koko's voice on top of yours.

"Stop it, Kei," she says, even though you are no longer touching her. "You're hurting me."

Two girls are no longer. Koko is gone. Even Arnie notices.

"Oh, Christ, Miya," Arnie says, but he isn't looking at Mama. She's so still, he doesn't see how fast the pool of red is forming beneath her, or realize that she's fainting. He doesn't know there will be days—many of them—when he wonders if she'll ever wake up. She'll spend weeks in bed, unmoving, her face gray and rough with sweat. He will be told it's in her blood, but will he learn that Mama's haunted? That she sees things that no one else can, goes to places no one else can follow?

But Arnie doesn't understand that yet. Right now, *you* are the focus of his attention. You and the blood you have splattered all over you and your sister; the blood still pooling in your palm. "Let me see your hand, Princess," he says, creeping toward you with his arms extended, like you are a wild animal. "Keiko. Keiko? Look at me."

You do not offer your hand, but you don't resist him, either. He is the one who will lift you out of the glass and call a doctor. Who will let you dig your fingers into his thigh while a long sleeping snake is sewn over the red tongue of flesh in your palm.

Arnie picks you up because you are barefoot, then notices that he's the only one who's wearing shoes. "Stay where you are," he warns Hana and Mama as he turns his back on them. "You two are okay. I'll come back for you."

Over Arnie's shoulder, your sister stays. How long will she wait there—a ruined dress, a frozen statue—as she's told to? Just moments ago, the two of you were made in each other's image, but she is Hana now, forever. She has let you take the blame, and more than that, she named you.

This is how Kei is born. This is how Arnie marries Mama, how he takes your place at her bedside because of you. From this moment on, two girls are two separate people who might do anything. All that remains is to collect the severed pieces and throw them away.

HANA

The light switch inside my apartment door had been dusted with a fine black powder. It stuck to my finger, clinging to the whorls of my skin when I rubbed it with my thumb. I stepped through the door and into the living room, the yellow tape that had sealed it looped in my left hand. I snapped the deadbolt into place behind me.

I was home. But with the bald bulb on the ceiling lit, the room rose into focus, and what I saw made me want to turn and run.

Every one of my walls was covered in the same black powder. Long strokes of it on the barely taupe paint; cross hatches, circles, overeager in some places, just misted in others. Each window and sill, each door up to the height of a man's head had been systematically defaced. The police had even lifted the orange juice bottle out of the refrigerator, smeared it with powder, and left it on the table. I could smell the sour mass inside it from where I stood. Someone had dusted the cover of my unused turntable. And the two ceramic bowls on my shelf. My few pieces of left-over college furniture had been dragged around and left in the wrong position. The blue beanbag was in the center of the floor.

Hana's home. Hana's home. Hana's home. I heard it in my head but I couldn't tell whether it was a greeting or a taunt.

"I am home," I said out loud. There wasn't even a place to sit. And then, "I *am* Hana."

Silence was the only response.

I stepped farther into the living room, turning on every floor lamp and even the undercounter kitchen lights. I flipped the switches in the hall, lighting my path. The police had been just as thorough with their powder in my bedroom. Walls again; closet doors; the items on my bedside table. The handle of the latch on my window safety gate—this time, securely closed.

When I gathered the nerve to peek into my tiny bathroom, I saw that every inch was gray, even the edges of the toilet seat. My eyes went to the floor, to the octagonal coin tiles, and I was suddenly terrified that I might find the tracing of his shoes.

He must have been wearing tennis shoes. That's what came to me. I hadn't heard his step in the lobby that night. I could see them—white, old, with a slight tear in one where the canvas pulled away from the rubber toe like Arnie's used to. Shoes he had been meaning to throw away. I imagined I could tell where his feet had stopped. Was it here where he had been standing when he strangled Kei?

It was shock, these slippery imaginings. Easy to recognize. I had lived in shock for six years. How else would my poor brain deal with the fact that I was standing inches from the bathtub where I found her? A veil of black dust had fallen into it from the drawn plastic shower curtain, but I could clearly see the outline of my sister lying there. The dust was darkest where Kei's shoulders had rested, tapering off vaguely as it neared the drain like the magnet shavings in a child's science project. I ran my finger over the edge of the tub to wipe away the bit of the powder that had been left there.

But instead of the clear, satisfying arc I expected, I managed only to smudge a black, dragging trail on the porcelain.

I was suddenly too aware of my heart. I tried again, this time wadding up some toilet paper. I turned the water on, more of the blackness from the handles coming off onto my hands; I instinctively rubbed them on my pants before realizing my mistake. Everything I touched was turning black.

It was only fingerprint dust. Something the police used every day. There had to be a way to clean it. I would blast it off, dissolve it. As the bottom of the tub filled, the powder rose, filming on the surface for one hopeful moment until, when the water drained, it coalesced into black rivulets and settled down again.

The dust was defying me.

I turned to the sink, breathing, washing the bar of soap first, and then wiping down the medicine cabinet, which I had long ago covered over with strips of black duct tape so I would never surprise myself in the mirror. I used my bare hands. I tackled the porcelain basin and the knobs and faucets, before turning to my fingers. When I finished, my skin was still vaguely gray, but it didn't mark my clothes.

I tried to remember my mother's simplest recipe for cleaning. Baking soda in warm water. I pushed my long sleeves up my forearms, then put on the rubber gloves I always wore to protect my fragile skin. In the bathroom, I'd been fiddling, really, only testing the powder, but now I was determined to wipe it from my life. I took my pile of washed and folded rags and went to my front door.

The rag turned black instantly. I rinsed it in the cloudy water, and that, too, went dark. I emptied the bucket and began again; I wouldn't rinse the rags, then, I would start fresh with each one. Each stroke only dragged the dust into the scrapes and dings on my walls, the spider web cracks in the paint I'd never noticed. The paint itself looked haggard, and as I tried to move on, to declare one section pau, the rags lost their power to erase even some of the obvious smudges. It was me against them—me against *him*, whoever he was—thinking, *Are these his fingers here?*

I leaned my weight into the wall for more power. Dirty water ran down the glove and off my elbow as I clenched the rag in my hand. I was scrubbing as hard as I could, but still, I was losing.

Out the window, I could see the downtown passengers gathering on the platform. I swung the curtains shut—with more force than I should have—but I couldn't bear the thought of one of them peering in, of *him* peering in. The thousands of eyes I had immersed myself in at the precinct returned to me. My would-be attacker was everywhere and nowhere.

What about you? Detective Lynch had asked me.

I tried to picture it: Kei standing in the shower, washing the shampoo out of her hair. She would not have heard an intruder if her head was under the water.

Stay there, Kei.

The man was not coming back, I told myself again and again. If he was the one I had passed in the doorway, he would know I was onto him. *If.* The police were skeptical, but I couldn't afford to be. I had to be right, because if I was wrong, then I had no protection. Kei's true attacker would recognize me; he could be the man standing next to me in the elevator anywhere I was. Thinking of what he had done to her. And I would not know.

With all their dust, the police hadn't found a single unspoiled fingerprint. All they had needed was one perfect whorl of black. Instead, my apartment was teeming with fingerprints: thousands, millions, fragments layered so thickly that there was no way to separate them.

I had let them stay too long.

Then he slid into me, like a shadow. Time slipped, and there he was. I dropped my rag and stepped back to the spot where I had first seen Kei's slippers. Had he been the one who kicked them into the center of the room?

Double take, double take, double take.

Oh God, I thought. I was surely mad as a hatter. How else could I see Kei through his eyes? We used to play at being each other when we were little, but this was different. I'd barely slept now in more than two days. I was all of us and none of us, in the same way that our mother had sometimes seemed between two worlds: here and gone. I was watching Kei step out of the shower to greet me. Or, maybe that was her, caught between the tub and the sink, looking confused. She would have helped someone who claimed to be my neighbor; she might even have amused herself by pretending she was me. But not someone who looked so shocked to see her, and not naked. She didn't know what to do.

She must have struggled. Her ankle was twisted. Somehow, he had bruised her rib. But how had she gotten back into the shower? Was he trying to drown her or revive her? Why couldn't I see it? Too much had come between us—I could no longer see into her world.

A temporary lack of oxygen to the brain would not ordinarily cause this kind of unconsciousness, the doctors had assured me. So it wasn't his fingers around her neck that almost killed her. *There are no genital abrasions or evidence of, ah, a sexual assault.*

I picked up the bucket and hurled the water; it splashed against the wall with a white froth and ran off, weak and gray, toward the floor. I could still feel his presence, just out of reach. I threw the empty bucket hard into the space where I imagined him. It bounced and came to rest at my feet.

I grabbed a can of Ajax, a cloud of it spraying from the can as it flew. The powder bloomed into tiny blue bursts when it hit the wet wall.

I threw the can.

Then I went to the kitchen sink and swept everything out from under it. Glass cleaner. Dish soap. Drano. I let them fly. I threw them closed; sometimes hurling them straight from my shoulder, sometimes scooping them in two hands off the floor and flinging them upward.

I opened the refrigerator. My meager food glowed.

I reached in and grabbed the milk. I launched the sour liquid, then the waxed cardboard carton—my arm aiming for Kei and the man. If only I could hit the right pocket of air, I could remake the past. I flung the fermented orange juice out of the bottle, hitting him full in the face as Kei surprised him in the bathroom. Spaghetti, fettuccini, knocking his hand away as he reached for her neck. A hunk of lasagna as I wished *if only he'd made a move at me in the lobby* so I might have jammed my key into his eyes. I delighted in his head splitting open as the tomatoes ruptured against the wall—flecks of meat embedding themselves, noodles wiggling down—but then it was Kei's skull that was open, and my own, and I could see my sister in the tub, tucked into herself and cold. She loomed there, impossible and growing larger. I unsealed a gallon of shoyu, and swung it. The liquid arched, splashing again and again.

I swung it with everything I had, long after it was empty.

When it was over, I sat on the floor in the midst of it. My clothes were wet. My skin, clammy. And I was cold to the bone, as my mother used to claim to be. I could hear her, muffled, lying beside me on our linoleum floor muttering *cold to the bone* even as her body gave off a ferocious heat.

The room was in worse shape than I was, at least on the surface: the kind of mess that you would crawl away from because no one could ever get it clean again. The kind of mess you would *move* away from. Pack your bags. Leave behind.

Maybe I would, I thought. Just leave. It wouldn't be the first time. I shook off the food, left the containers and the puddle on the floor, and went to the bedroom. I was shivering like my mother used to; even with the light on, I couldn't stop. The ends of my hair smelled of shoyu and oregano. My blouse looked like it had been tie-dyed, so many distinct flavors, dark as blood, burrowing themselves into the weave of the cloth.

Take it off, and I would see my scars. Leave it on, and the craziness would crust itself around me. What could I do now that Kei was here and I could no longer turn off a light? I was too close to the edge of everything to make a decision. I was trembling; my stomach was turning over; I was not even strong enough to cry.

Mama, I thought. *Help me.* I waited, but there was no answer.

I collapsed onto the bed.

1943

Every morning at sunrise, they congregated on the deck to do calisthenics. It was a ritual for the men, but Donald insisted Lillie join them.

—The air is good for you, he would tell her as he hurried her up the narrow stairs to the deck.

The repatriates sang military marching songs as they exercised, punctuated by lusty shouts and grunts. Donald always staked out a spot near the front. Lillie knew he was eager to impress the others with his health and strength, preparing to die for the Empire or bring it glory.

The wind broke itself against the ship, hurling stinging salt spray—sometimes strong enough to rock the horizon—to greet each day. Rather than argue uselessly with her husband, Lillie stood shivering in the long shadows the new sun was not yet strong enough to erase, sheltering the sleeping, bundled Toshi with her body. What a strange pair she and Tateishi-sama were, she thought, standing here on the sidelines. She with a one-year-old strapped to her chest and her crippled, still-imperious father-in-law with the tin of his wife's ashes strapped to *his* chest, in yards of creased, yellowing muslin. All of them headed for Japan.

Lillie spent her days floating in languages she couldn't understand. Japanese mostly, along with Spanish and Portuguese once they picked up additional repatriates in Rio de Janeiro and Montevideo. Some of the foreign Japanese had been held with Tateishi-sama in the military detention camp in Utah. They were a motley group, regardless of language. There were more than thirteen hundred passengers now, including a handful of dignitaries. But Tateishi-sama was just one of so very many thin and sickly single men.

—They look so much like us, she had whispered to Donald when she first saw the foreigners.

He smiled at her, but without warmth, and cocked his head as if wondering at her ignorance. "Who did you think they would look like?" At least he didn't add, *Stupid girl*.

Still, conditions were good on the boat, crowded as it became. Women, children, and the old people had the upper, larger quarters, and the food was plentiful, though Donald pronounced it bland. White decks gleamed in a flood of never-ending light, ensuring that the word DIPLOMAT painted on the side and stern of the ship could be clearly read even at night. Lillie kept herself apart from the other women, knowing that she was the only one who didn't want to be there. Much as she had in the camps, she spent her days with Toshi, but now that he was older, and could chatter back to her and laugh, she tried to show him how to find wonder in the world. They would stand on the deck, counting the white crests of the waves, or finding patterns in the clouds. Occasionally, they saw another ship in the distance, and she wondered what country it served, enemy or friend—and how one might know the difference. At night, she held him up to the bottle-glass of the porthole in their compartment and pointed out the stars.

Otherwise it was a vast, thin horizon that surrounded them. She could not guess what future lay beyond it for her and her son.

Weeks passed this way. After running down the coast of South America, they crossed the vast expanse of the Atlantic and finally rounded the tip of Africa, heading for India. She had no chores to do here, no lines to stand in, no dust storms to duck as they swept over the empty plains. Her health was returning.

This was what she'd tried to escape, Donald could not resist reminding her. *This*, a luxury motorship with deck after deck of polished wood and bottomless supplies—look at the piles of boxes on the prom deck, so many parcels of food and medicine that they couldn't even stow them all. Their luck was changing, now that they had escaped from her two-faced land of opportunity. Life in Japan would be as plentiful as he'd promised.

Lillie hoped he was right but knew better than to voice her doubts. She looked longingly at the shores of the countries where they stopped, imagining them as places where she and Toshi could get lost, begin again, meld anonymously into the local towns; where the shapes of their faces and color of their skin might not define them. Donald might have sensed this longing of hers, or perhaps he was just wary from her attempt to escape back at the camp, because he would keep a hand on Toshi—gentle, but its meaning unmistakable—every time they docked.

Eventually they arrived in Goa, where they would be disembarking and transferring to a Japanese ship, the *Teia Maru*, to travel the final leg of their journey. Triumphant singing erupted on the *Gripsholm* when the two boats were finally docked beside each other, and the promise of Japan surged and strained on its mooring lines beside them. But Lillie wasn't the only one keeping a nervous eye on the *Teia Maru*. The *Gripsholm* remained docked for two days as the diplomats counted up the passengers to be exchanged on each ship, doing and redoing the math as if they would be able to magically balance the numbers to account for the one man who went overboard shortly after they left South Africa. The interminable heat didn't help.

When the exchange finally started and she stepped off the ship for the first time in a month, Lillie stumbled, her feet failing to adjust to the solid ground. As her body tumbled away from Donald's, she felt again the pull to disappear into the crowd. For just a moment, she savored an image of herself pantomiming her needs among a strange but free people. But she couldn't leave; Donald was holding Toshi. Even if it were possible to switch directions, or fade out of the stream of passengers and run over the packed earth and the railroad tracks and disappear into India, she wasn't willing to go without her son. Still, the yearning sharpened once they got a close look at their new home: The *Teia Maru* was even worse than the internment camps. It was filthy. Food was limited. Even drinking water was rationed and given out only twice a day.

She had had her chances, and she had left them strewn on the shores of other countries.

By the time they arrived in Yokohama, two months after they'd left New York, Lillie could feel nothing at all. The repatriates were separated, men and women, and held for processing. They took her boy—he belonged to Donald—and she clung to his absence like she would her last breath. Days went by in which she could understand nothing that anyone said to her. The language sounded different here, and ran together like an unfamiliar line of exclamations. *Ah. Oh. Eh.* She didn't bother to try to understand; she no longer cared about fitting in. She just wanted Toshi back—he was the only place she belonged. She knew the questioners would want to know where she was going—who would sponsor her and would she be a burden to their country? These questions floated up from the past, from the tight, pressed mouth of the internment camp director. Once she had known the answers. She had different answers then.

After three days of intake—spent sitting, squatting, and lying on a mat just inches from all the other unwashed women—Lillie was released, and, to her surprise, Donald was waiting for her right outside the door. He had stayed. Thank God he'd stayed. He hugged her roughly, as if it was her fault for taking so long to get to him. There was a thin, high smell of fear in his clothes. When she saw him, hard and tired, but *himself*, alive and there to rescue her, it occurred to her that perhaps things had worked out for the best after all. She and Donald had walked into this nightmare together, from the moment they left the farm, and here he was, still beside her. Was it love she felt sweeping through her, or relief, or was there a difference? Lillie grabbed her husband's hand.

She looked around her, at this new world she had never quite been able to imagine. The Japanese citizens didn't look prosperous to her. The new arrivals, fat from the Swedish ship even after a month on the *Teia Maru*, seemed the healthiest among the people she could see. The women released with Lillie were being met, tearfully, by these skinny, real Japanese in their pajama-like clothing.

Her kind, the camp director had said.

—Where is—she made a choice then—"our family?" Like it or not, she was one of them now. She knew the Tateishis were from a city called Hiroshima, a place of arcades and many rivers that meandered through the city, low, sluggish, and green. A place of swans, Donald had told her.

—Here, he said, with tenderness, and Lillie knew he had heard her capitulation. He pointed toward her father-in-law, drooping on the pile of their things. Toshi was standing in the dirt beside the old man, his feet in socks, hanging on to the edge of one of the hard-sided bags. This was everything, then. It was both impossible to conceive of living with so little, and to imagine carrying so much.

Hiroshima was a day away. There was another train in her future. Beyond that, she didn't know.

Toshi let go of the luggage and reached up, laughing, holding his hands out to her. A dried smudge of food puckered his cheek, and his palms were a map of filth. This was her family, she told herself, grateful for the light in his eyes, and the truth that at least one of them still needed her. Wherever Toshi was could be home enough for her. She put her hands out and picked up her son.

The Wave

HANA

I was dead asleep the next morning when the telephone rang again. The sound sliced into my head; I must have grabbed at the receiver as if it was an earplug: anything to cut off the noise.

"Hanako? Is that you? What's going on?"

I heard the worry in Nick's voice as I tried to understand where I was. Home, apparently, draped on top of my covers, and sideways across my bed. My filthy clothes were piled on the floor, but I could smell a mixture of Ajax and milk souring on my skin.

"Hanako! The police were here, checking your alibi. You have an *alibi*!?"

"Nick. It's okay." But of course it wasn't. "I'm okay. It...wasn't me."

Nick, my boss, was the son of the original Luciano. He was the patriarch of one of the largest extended families I had ever known. He wouldn't have understood the distance that lay between me and Kei, and I wouldn't have known how to explain, so I never mentioned her. Now, though, not only did I have to tell him Kei existed, but also that she was here and in the hospital. I kept my story vague. Something about a robbery. I didn't want him worrying that my job had been somehow responsible, or worse, have him show up at the hospital to see how he could help. That was the problem with working for a grandfather; Nick was much more attuned to family than to his business, which was how I ended up working for him in the first place.

When I was in college, I used to eat at Luciano's every Sunday. It's one of those cavernous Old World restaurants on the Upper West Side I could trust would never be trendy. I didn't socialize, but Nick of course noticed his regulars. One Sunday, close to college graduation, he came over to my table.

"You all right there, Missy?" he asked me. That was all he had to do.

I had just come from Dr. Shawe's; that was the day I had brought my therapy to an end. Our four years were up, and I'd been dropping small fibs about making a few friends at some gallery openings so she would think I was better. Still, my sudden desolation when she agreed to end it took me by surprise. I burst into tears, and Nick's response was to offer me a job organizing his paperwork and "keeping him honest." I had majored in math, and if bookkeeping was not exactly differential equations, the prospect of straightening out someone else's life was attractive. Besides, I felt comfortable with him: He never asked me if I was waiting for someone or showed any curiosity about my scars. Working for Nick meant no job interviews, no explanations for my too-thoroughly covered skin. I had no ambition left—I was fine with tucking myself away in the back office, alone.

But now, as I listened to Nick's good wishes for Kei's swift recovery and got off the phone, I recognized something else: He reminded me of Arnie. They were both wired to save people. I wondered what it was like to be so confident in the world that you could just expect to be able to.

Last night, the adrenaline that had fueled my assault on my apartment had left me shivering and puking into the toilet; the bile burning my throat a reminder of how little I had eaten in the last two days. Now that I was awake, I needed some food, as well as a shower, but first, I needed to hear how Kei was. I lay where I was and called the ICU off the number on Kei's admissions paperwork. After a brief hold, they let me talk to a doctor.

They still didn't know why Kei was unconscious, he told me, but the good news was she could breathe and swallow on her own. The bad news was there were other patients who couldn't, and they could use her ICU bed. We were at fifty-six hours and counting, and every hour she remained unconscious, her chances of a complete recovery lessened. Kei would do better on a medical floor that specialized in head trauma. If she remained stable for another day, and with my permission, they would transfer her to the Eckert Trauma Center.

A transfer would mean new forms, and new forms meant admitting— and correcting—the mistake with our names. I had no idea what all this was costing, but I knew I couldn't afford it. Hanako Swanson's insurance could. My sister had been entered into the health care system on the gold-plated insurance Arnie set up for my ruined body when I left for New York. *You can never live too well and too long*, he used to say. If there was more than a little irony in that, still, Mama had created a small fund in my name—the "flower child funds," her lawyer called it—which had continued to pay for my insurance after she and Arnie died. I had every reason to expect that she'd done the same for Kei; we might even share a family policy, and then why would it matter which one of us used which card? But I was not so far gone that I couldn't hear my own excuses. If I tried to find out through official channels and failed, I would no longer be able to keep her on my insurance by claiming shock and a mix-up in the emergency room.

I told the doctor I'd be in later to sign the release forms. Then, I did the one thing I have refused to do in the six years since I left for New York.

I called home.

My home. Ours, and our mother's, and now Kei's.

I had given Kei the house after our parents died. I knew she was living there, but it was only when I saw she'd kept Arnie's key ring that I guessed she kept the phone number, too. It was still in my fingers; the numbers never even made their way to my head. My heart pounded as my fingers ran around the dial. It was barely dawn in Hawaii. If Kei had a boyfriend, or someone who lived with her, he would surely answer. But how would I break the news to a stranger, or worse—someone I knew? I didn't want to think about who might be missing her. I didn't know what I would do if he wanted to come to New York to see her, too. Now, I don't know what I dreaded most: being sucked back into Kei's life against my will or forming the words that would make Kei's coma real. Or perhaps it was something else, something about being faced with a life of companionship and intimacy I would never have. No one would ever love me, or want to touch me, when I couldn't bear to stand naked in front of myself.

Once I realized no one was going to answer, I kept the receiver to my ear. I listened to the trill of beeps, which were not unlike the sound of a mother bird singing her babies to sleep. I could feel my heartbeat slowing almost back to normal as I imagined them tumbling out of our old desk phone that sat on the small table right near the door, then wandering across our gray linoleum floor tiles to check for life in each room. I was sliding back home with the sound, jumping on the bed-like pune'e with it. I could even see our faded cushions covered in a rusty hibiscus pattern unevenly worn by the sun. The call of home dragged me under, like the surf on the beach, and for a moment I couldn't tell which way was up or what forward looked like.

I started to dial again—my mother's lawyer, or even old Harada-san, could easily get Kei's insurance information for me and solve this whole mess. But my hand hovered over the phone.

What if Kei never woke up?

Could I bury my life with her body, killing off the self I'd tried to keep stunted in New York? It would be a relief. A reparation. Besides, I'd never seen my own birth certificate. It's not as if I had proof of which girl I really was.

A life in Hawaii could be mine again, I thought. I had Kei's keys; I knew where she lived. I had studied her scar. I knew exactly how it ran and how long I'd have to wait for a new cut to heal before returning home. I would never do it, of course, and yet these fantasies prevented me from making the calls. I didn't want to hear in their voices that it was common knowledge I had never finished college, that I had walked out on it after my last appointment with Dr. Shawe and had never taken the rest of my exams. I wanted to pretend, for just a little while, that I could start again. But the truth was, the life I wanted was so far in the past I could never return to it. The community had closed ranks against me. There was no way for me to go home.

* * *

My mother and Arnie died a year and some months after what should have been my college graduation, as the first summer of my true adulthood had turned to fall. Kei was the center of attention at their funeral. When I walked into the chapel, she had set herself up between the coffins, turning to whoever happened to be paying tribute beside her to throw herself into their arms.

She wore dark blue, which made my black seem disapproving. Her casual grace in her body, in her dress—and sleeveless, yet—felt like an insult. I had covered my scars in a neck-to-ankle New York suit, and I sat near the back of the chapel, where it should be so easy for my parents' friends to pay their respects, and I marveled. Kei's old cronies had practically surrounded her in that place reserved for viewing the bodies: her best friend, Missy; and Eddie; and a pregnant Charlene. These were the chosen four, and if I'd had any thought that I might be wrong about what happened to me in the cave, that was clearly wishful thinking. They were still together, still the town's sweethearts. If Eddie seemed a little extra jittery, at least he was smart enough to stay far away from me.

I know the ceremony couldn't have been as lonely as it appears in my memory. I'm sure some of the mourners must have come to talk to me. There would have been no family, of course, but Arnie would have easily made up for that in friends. The whole island would have been there for Arnie.

Kei had told me when she called that it was a single car accident, that they found the car on the summit of Mauna Kea in the middle of the night. My sister was such a good liar that she often fooled herself, but this was clearly not her best effort. I didn't know what to think; there were few places Mama would leave the house to go, and the top of a volcano wasn't one of them. Especially when it was blanketed in a freak early snow. But it wasn't until I was there that I first heard the rumor that it was suicide, that their bodies were recovered some distance from the car.

No one would have said such a thing to me directly, but it was always the whispers I trusted more. It reminded me of the old days, when it was hard to walk down the street without hearing the murmur of gossip about my mother.

If they had only stayed in the car, yeah?

But you gotta figa'—who goes to sleep in the snow?

Arnie's coffin was closed, but Mama's was open. She was fifty years old, but she looked younger than Kei that day. In death, her skin was translucent, and completely unlined by the sun. When I was a child, I told my mother that her eyes were like pahoehoe lava. I didn't have the vocabulary to explain then, but now I do. Her life was in her eyes, so black they were almost silver; they swirled, pocked with brittle rifts and edges. With her lids closed, she was a ghost. Dare I say it?

A shadow child.

Maybe it was that image that made me walk out of the chapel. The shadow child, the translation of my sister's name. Or maybe there was another reason I left early. Because I remember one touch in particular. At the funeral, someone did come up to me.

I was saying good-bye to my mother when he approached. He said, "Hana," in a tone that made it clear he thought I would welcome him. I can hear his voice. The way it settled, not rising in question, but falling as if to say, *At last.*

I raised my eyes slowly, preparing myself in case something about him registered. The copper-tinged curls that used to fall from a soft cowlick over his forehead had been cut short, exposing a face fuller than it should have been. Everything about him now was unfocused—his soft lips, drooping eyes—and I remember thinking he seemed strangely defeated for someone so young. But, of course, he was at a funeral. Then he said something else and held out his hands.

I felt myself swaying toward him. The stress of the day, most likely, and the heat, and the fact that I hadn't eaten much since I left New York. My legs were giving out, and I remember feeling grateful that Russell's hands were out to catch me when it struck me: He didn't want me. Russell left me, too.

What he said was, *I'm sorry.* I remember it now. Maybe it was his words—their audacity—that made me so weak. My anger at him surged and twisted, and then it overflowed to sweep in Mama, too. She had known she would die; she hadn't given me a chance to say good-bye, or wanted to say good-bye to me. I pushed Russell away and looked down at her: a woman who had killed herself before I came home, no explanation, no warning.

And that was when I saw the quilt. She was lying on it, wrapped inside it. The underside was white, and only the red and white corners of the patterned top had been brought around and placed inside her folded hands. I noticed the stitching first, so many rows and so tiny that it must have taken her forever. I reached out to finger her work and found a straight, thick line that didn't match the pattern. It was the vertical rise of a letter, stitched in red thread over white. I lifted one of her fingers and found an *H* carefully created beneath it. I picked up another finger and revealed an *A*.

My quilt, I realized in horror. I'd never actually seen it. Mama had started making it in secret, to celebrate my appointment as valedictorian. After the cave, I'd assumed she abandoned it, too. I reached into the coffin and uncrossed my mother's hands to be sure.

In death, her hands were heavier than I expected, and cool. They flopped, indifferent, as I pushed them further down onto her belly so the quilt encircling her shoulders was free. I tugged on the quilt. It wasn't particularly large, or thick with batting, but the weight of her body pinned it down. When I pulled, Mama's dress dragged up with it and into her lipstick, and I found myself yanking even harder, rolling her body as if she was asleep and turning on her side. Her hip caught; the bottom two-thirds of the coffin was closed. The agony of it engulfed me—all of it, my mother dead, her body forsaken just as I had been—as I wrenched my quilt free with both hands. I balled it up like a baby in front of me as I stared at her disarray: hands hidden now, hair floating helplessly around her, red lipstick smudging her cheek.

The first noise I registered was a wail as Kei came rushing toward me.

She looked ravaged. Disgusted. "What, are you—" she started, and I knew the next word she didn't say. At first I thought she would lunge at me, but she pushed past so she could get to Mama, rearranging her head, smoothing her hair. She was crying; we were both staring at our dead mother, so close I could feel Kei's heat.

"Crazy?" I finished her question for her. I didn't care. It was *my* quilt, and only then did I realize that it had to have been Kei's decision to cremate it. "Crazy is as crazy does." It was one of those nonsense platitudes that I must have heard in the school yard long ago that my mind had grabbed on to for the way it swung. *What does crazy do?* Crazy is not a diagnosis, Dr. Shawe used to tell me. Nor is it contagious. But of course, that was a lie.

"Crazy is as crazy does, crazy is as crazy..." I can hear my voice echo now in the chapel; I might have started screaming. I can feel myself hugging the quilt to my belly, as if I could open myself and swallow it that way. I was refusing to let go, although no one was reckless enough to try to take it from me. There might have been other things that were screamed, too. Like, *How dare you steal it? You're always stealing. You stole everything from me.* Then there were people leading me out onto the steps: Harada-san, our former neighbor, the poor old, bewildered man who had only just picked me up at the airport hours before; my mother's lawyer. I told them I was leaving. It didn't matter what the lawyer was saying. It didn't matter that Harada-san looked so broken, that he seemed to be trying to speak. I couldn't bear another explanation, and was so tired of the excuses everyone always made for Kei. It was *my* quilt, not Mama's to take, not even to the spirit world. *I* was not dead. I was the executor and I would take what I wanted—the quilt and half the tiny sum of money—I gave Kei the house because I wanted her to know how little I cared for our past. In the lawyer's office, I dumped everything I had brought with me out of my duffel bag, then shoved the quilt into it. There was room left in the duffel, but nothing I had dumped out struck me as worth keeping. I left everything I'd brought with me on the lawyer's floor.

In less than six hours I'd made it to the Honolulu airport, but it wasn't until the DC-8 finally taxied down the runway and the pressurized air flooded the cabin, lifting my blouse from where it had grafted itself onto my overheated back, that I drew my first full breath. My rage drained away, leaving me empty and nauseated. Browsing the airport newsstands in Los Angeles, I noticed the newspapers getting thicker, more full of the world, but it wasn't until I reached New York, where the Pacific Rim was barely mentioned in the "A" section of the *Times* and where no one stared at me, that I could stop looking over my shoulder.

No one tried to stop me from leaving.

No one would ever want to see me return.

KEI

Mama calls you *gasa gasa* because you are always moving. Do you remember?

You are Kei.

You are the *bad one*, the *selfish one*, the *troublemaker*, and the *one who can't sit still*. Is this what you think, or what they say? Sometimes, you feel like two people: half of you watching the other half perform. You are the storyteller and the listener; the audience and the show.

And now, you are the *dumb one*. Before they moved you to the B class, you and Hana used to swap clothes. You used to sit together in the school yard at recess, ignoring their stupid jokes. "Buy one, get one free!" and "Look at her, always talking to herself, ha-ha!" If the two of you were no longer Koko when you started primary school, still, you had a connection. Whenever yet another kid with bare feet and white fever spots on his teeth tried to do the math with his hands—*Brown eye on the left side equals Kei. Her left is my right. My right hand is the one I write with, so this must be...*—you both knew exactly when to close your eyes.

But that was primary school, and now you are in the B class. Left alone, you have to run. And you are fast, which makes it less fun for the boys to chase you. The game is to catch you. The reward is to tackle you in the grass. You thought it was about the press. The skin smell. The tumble that kept going and the weight that didn't lift even when the tumble stopped. But then they started throwing rocks at a new girl, to bring her down when she escaped them, and recess got so much darker then.

You, they like to ambush. Their favorite game is spit. They surround you like dogs since, in this game, they take turns. You fight back but eventually they throw you on the ground and pin your arms with their knees to make it hard to use your legs to buck them off. It is also hard to breathe. They work up a spitball and then hover their faces over yours and drool. They expect you to squirm away in fear, close your eyes and turn your head. Your only revenge is in locking eyes with them as they do it. The spitball spools down slow, like a cloudy spider. The longer they can make it last, the more all the dog-boys will hoot. The winner is the boy who can lower his thread of spit until it almost hits your face and still suck it back into his mouth.

There are a lot of losers in this game.

Lillie's father said, *Don't run*. You remember that story. He said the coyotes were only there for the chickens. They wouldn't chase a human, even a small one, if she stood still and looked it in the eye. But Lillie was afraid. The house seemed so far away and she had seen the spray of blood and guts in the coop last time. So she disobeyed to protect herself. She dashed for the house.

She didn't see the coyote take off to chase her. All she saw was her father's face in the window, then the barrel of his gun. His scolding that night was not about the fact that she didn't do what he told her to, or about her mother's worry that she could have been hurt. It was about the creature that had been killed because of her.

There are consequences, Lillie's father told her. Even if she's not the one to suffer them. Trying to escape to save yourself sometimes puts others at unexpected risk. But what Mama didn't seem to see was that by drawing the coyote's attention, Lillie had saved the chickens. What if you had to make a choice? you asked her. If you had to choose between lives—coyotes, chickens, yours, Hana's—how would you know which lives to save?

Mama didn't answer.

But now, you are running in the school yard. You don't want to be the boy who was sent to the hospital after they made him crawl over broken bottles, or the girl they tied to a tree. But you are not running to escape. Just as Lillie saved the chickens by getting the coyote to chase her, you are attracting the attention of the dog-boys. You can take the spit, and if you don't, they will turn on Hana. Together you two were more than they could handle, but she is as helpless as a chicken now and she is all alone.

They called Arnie on his CB. He's always the one who comes to school when recess gets out of hand. When there's dirt in your hair and snot as well as drool, and you can't get it off before the bell rings. Or when one of the other kids in the yard gets nervous and drags a teacher out of the coffee room to show him what's going on. Sometimes the dog-boys get away with it, with the magical excuse, *Jus' joke.* Sometimes, you are red with tears and anger, and you spit back hard, knowing what will happen if you don't hit your mark. On the days when Arnie has to take you, you usually ride with him while he works. *Better if we stay out of your mother's hair*, he says. *No need to tell her.* And you know better than he does what can happen if you upset her. Mama worries about you more than Hana, so Arnie helps you make sure she never knows. But today's fight in the school yard was not about the usual boredom and boy energy. Arnie was a long time in the principal's office, and he came out with a sadness that still hasn't left his eyes. He didn't say anything, but you know he's building up to it. That's why you're here. At the new lava field.

Beach chairs lounge in the backs of flatbeds. That's how Arnie first described it. Fifty cars parked along the road. Men milled between the cars, clutching cans of Primo and Oly. Little kids in pajamas hung off their shoulders, as if anyone could be too short to see this show.

And in the night in front of them, huge plumes of lava danced in the sugarcane field. Orange spittle sailed through the air. It flashed, it flickered, it tumbled down, and it could boil in your ears, too, that's what Arnie told Mama. *Come with me, Miya. It's beautiful. It's the best show there is.*

You remember when the eruption started. Arnie brought home a picture in the newspaper, where the ground cracked open four feet wide and two miles long.

"Can you imagine?" he teased Mama, grabbing her around her waist. "I would have rescued you before you fell in."

Hana looked down at her mending and you could feel it, too. The way Arnie looked at Mama, like the achy tooth you can't stop chewing on. She waved him off; she was not one for explosions, but he kept clowning around, stretching his legs apart to prove that he could save her, and when his long arm snaked out to hug her to him, the smile she gave him was cautious but bright. You know she loved him for the fact that nothing bad had ever happened to him. And the impossible possibility that nothing ever would.

But now, the papayas around you are popping, one by one, like blisters.

They ooze, too, like blisters. Their scent is thick, clogging your nose. You can see their roasted bodies lying in the cinders.

There are only two fountains now, hiding behind the ridge of cinder cones. They are short, and sloppy. The lava spits up, then blackens in midair. Like butterflies in reverse. Bright, breathing creatures returning to their chrysalises. The fishponds are gone. The old theater, too, and the Chevron station and almost all the houses.

The night show is one thing, but mostly the eruption is slow, and unpredictable. It's a fact of life. A twist of fate. You can't stop it, but it's easy to outrun.

"Here," Arnie says. He hands you a stick of pepperoni. You are sitting together on the sidewall of his flatbed Ford, looking out over the new lava field. Listening to the lazy laughter of the firemen down the road and waiting for one of the few remaining houses to begin to burn.

Their voices drift over, overlapping. They are talking about a baby luau.

"Oh, man, Alfred, he some stingy, yeah? He never like buy nutting. So I wen ask 'im, 'Where you wen get um? Da pig. You wen shoot um or buy um?'"

"Nah. Shoot a pig? Alfred neva—"

"Nah. So anyway, I go, 'Alfred, you wen shoot da pig or what?' And Alfred, he goes, 'Nah, dis pig more betta den dat. Dis one *get los' pig*. You know—da kine pig get los' and come inside your yard?'"

"So," Arnie says, keeping his eyes in the distance as if that will help him catch the firemen's story. "Want to talk about it?'"

He knows there were fists, but you don't know what else he knows. You shake your head. You can't tell him the fight was about Mama, that they were calling her a dumb cow who had had her babies on a cattle boat in the dung. It was the mooing, and the heaving, and the way they swayed their bellies and swung their *okoles* that got to you, then the way they held you down and started licking you, like they were cleaning off a baby calf. *Runt*, they called you, their legs splaying open, and you felt something bumping against you from inside their pants. *Two scrawny runts, all bloody and bony and covered in dung.*

"Your mother is a survivor, Kei."

Part of you must know he is trying to be comforting, but what you feel is the surge of shame. You feel the rage that powered your fist, how it felt good to hit that kid, even if you got pummeled for it. Now that rage flares again, but it dives around Arnie to hit its true target.

Why couldn't Mama be normal like everyone else?

"You can't let 'um get to you, Kei-girl," Arnie is telling you. "It's all in how you look at it." He gestures to the orange fountains. "Like, that's the blood of the goddess, right? And that sound...that's Pele's heart. This is a birth. It's the rock becoming. Transformation, that's what you have to remember. Everything transforms."

You feel yourself cringe when he says the word *birth*, but there is something alive in the air around you. There is a presence, shape-shifting: a dark, earthy power that has always been there.

You aren't the only ones to think so: In the lee of the cinder cones, there are offerings of flowers and canned food. People have been coming steadily to give thanks to the volcano goddess for the new earth being formed.

"You've always been the secretive one," Arnie is saying. "Like the volcano. I wonder what will come out of you when you do decide to speak?"

Like the volcano. His words. You want to ask him what he means. Mama used to be like a volcano. She used to be pink and flushed, something in her burning. She was fragile, and there was a time when you thought you had pushed her too hard and ruined her forever. That you had to carry the guilt of that forever in the palm of your hand. And though Arnie arrived and seems to have saved her, that guilt is still burning inside you. Maybe, more than the bullying or the loneliness, that guilt is what it is to be Kei.

But of course, you don't speak. After more than seven years married to Mama, Arnie is still an interloper. You bite into the pepperoni, then pass it back and wipe your hands on your pants. "Thanks."

Arnie knows that's as good as you'll give him. He smiles and sticks his hand in his pocket. It comes out with a few coins. He raises his eyebrows. "Hey, it's this year's quarter," he says to no one in particular as he pushes himself off the flatbed. "Come on, Kei-girl. I know what let's do."

Reluctantly, you trail behind him as he heads toward the firemen. There are three of them: a heavy-set man with a small white goatee leaning on the bumper and the two younger guys gesturing midstory. They are tanned. Easy. As if hanging out in the middle of a field of black rock is the most normal thing in the world.

Mama doesn't socialize with the locals. No potlucks at the girls' club. No plate lunch at the beach. The sound of pidgin, the lilting local way of talking, sometimes makes her flinch. She keeps to herself, to *our kind*, as she says it, but you notice she stays away from Japanese Americans, too. Maybe it's groups she doesn't like, or strangers. Hana is the same way. This isolation hasn't helped you get along in school. By yourself, you would never approach these men. But Arnie is different. He assumes everyone is his friend.

"So what?" Arnie asks. He is using his pretend pidgin. "Busy?"

His inflection sounds wrong. Or maybe it's his expression, the way that, when he wants to point to something, he jerks his chin at the same time. Now that you're in school, you can hear it: as if he can't quite speak their language, but if he talks loudly enough everything will be clear.

But the older man doesn't notice that Arnie doesn't belong. He puts out his hand for a hearty shake and they thump shoulders. His hard hat is almost falling off the back of his head. "Eh, brah," he says. "Wat'chu doing? No work, hah?" Arnie is introduced to one of the other guys, and then greets the last one, whom he seems to know. Arnie's skin stands out red against the other men's, and white behind his ears. They are nice to him anyway, and when Arnie jogs back to his truck, they even smile at you as they joke around with each other and poke for things in their compartments. There is something in the air, something jolly Arnie has put into motion.

When he returns, he holds an iron pipe in his hand, about six feet long. "The flow of 1960, Kei-girl," he says, explaining nothing. And then, over your head, he calls, "Eh! Got'um, brah."

Arnie takes your hand and pulls you toward the edge of the lava. You are feeling his rough hand in yours, thinking you're too old for this but thinking, too, it feels nice to be led. You do not think he will let you get hurt. The flow lies close to the road like a vast sleeping animal. It breathes on your feet and ankles. So close, you can see a few cracks in the crust a ways off, and the deep orange-red inside them. The lava is a trickster. It's still alive.

Arnie taps the crust with the pipe. *Hit it harder*, the firemen egg him on. *Break it.* He hefts the pipe above his head like a spear and thrusts it into the rock. The crust gives way. The end of the pipe sinks into the glowing lava, pulling a dark orange blob back out with it, like soft dough.

There's much excitement, and crows of encouragement. One of the firemen hugs you to celebrate this wonderful thing Arnie has done. It's a touch that's over almost as soon as you become aware of it and yet the heat of it lingers. You find yourself smiling, with the ripples of heat, and the smell of exploding papayas and sulfur and the musky smell of man all swirling into one. Arnie is shaking the pipe and the lava falls into the dirt in several blobs, some bigger than others. He drops a quarter onto the one closest to him, and the firemen crowd in, dropping their own coins until all of the bits of lava are covered. They press their coins into the lava with sticks and rocks so that it curls around their edges. There is a hose beside you. The man with the runaway hard hat sprays the coins with water and the color flickers and fades.

"Whoo whee! Nineteen sixty. It says right there." Arnie moves to pick one up, but it's much too hot to touch. "Crap." He jumps, laughing, burning himself on the steam coming off the quarter, and the fireman turns the hose on Arnie's fingers, then back on the coins. "Stupid," Arnie says, about himself, but at the same time he's dancing around, shaking his hand and dodging the bits of lava. The firefighters laugh. You are laughing, too.

When the guy with the hose goes off to get a bucket, you find yourself crouching beside the soft curl of lava around Arnie's quarter. If you touch it, you imagine, the metal will melt like chocolate around the tip of your index finger. Liquid rock. Rock that could take any shape. Your palm itself is cupped, the deep cut from the glass more than half your life ago still pulling it into puckers. You imagine how the lava would melt over it, releasing your hand to open completely and covering the scars.

It is 1960, you think. This is the turning point. The year when something sleeping will erupt to the surface, and a new life will begin.

The guy who hugged you has a shovel. He's waiting for you to stand so he can lift the quarter into the bucket to cool. As you do, his face comes into focus. His smile is crooked, and you tilt your own smile in response. His eyes have faint lines around them, and his hair sticks off his head like mown grass. You are suddenly aware of everything about him: scuffed boots, stubby, callused fingers, square nails. The way his heart beats in the indentation of his throat.

"I like try," he says, pulling a handful of coins from his pocket.

Arnie nods, but then he hands the pipe to you. "You first, Kei-girl. It's your turn."

HANA

The Eckert Trauma Center was an old redbrick building. It resembled a Catholic school from the outside; inside, the walls were bright and plain, not the sagging, paint-loaded surfaces I'd come to expect in the hundred-year-old structures of New York. After all my worries, the hospital had needed only a Xerox of an ID and insurance card for Kei's transfer. For now, we were both Hanako Swanson. Fortunately, since I was registering my sister, no one thought to ask for *my* ID.

I took the elevator to the third floor. Though the building itself aged as I rose through it—the carpet in the waiting room gave way to tile in the halls where medicine or bedpans were more likely to spill—it felt like a good place for Kei to be.

She was lying in bed, alone, no visible restraints, no eye tape, nothing except a catheter and a feeding tube in her nose. The guardrails on both sides of Kei's mattress were raised. Kei's room was small—almost filled by the bed and the single reclining chair—but like the rest of the center, it was light and calm. A large three-panel window dominated one wall.

A small hand crank lay on the sill. I'd give her some air, I thought, fitting it over one of the starburst knobs on the window casing. The pane swung easily and wide; a cool burst of spring ducked around it and into the room. In the cloister behind the Center's main building, the first signs of spring were beginning to show in the tufted grass.

Grass in New York—it has always reminded me of my home. I chose this city because it was a place to get lost in. I didn't expect the buildings to actually scrape the sky, to magnify the heat of the rotting summer, or to whip the inevitable February wind through their ruthless canyons. The town I still longed for was a place of banyans and palms, of lazy rivers; it was the trembling lip on the wide smile of the bay. While Manhattan was arrogant, claiming every inch of land in concrete and even spilling into the surrounding waters, my childhood home depended on the island's indulgence. When the tidal wave came and licked out the heart of down-town, we rebuilt further up the mountain, leaving a long green tongue along the ocean—a park for baseball and soccer and the bandstand, and for memories no one wanted anymore.

The grass below Kei's window had been wrenched out in disks around the few still-skeletal trees, and disconnected by the wide, wandering asphalt paths for wheelchairs. But it was there. And it was all I might ever have to remind me of home.

I pulled the fledgling smell of it into my lungs.

Dr. Bree Sheridan was a short, slim bit of a woman—clean faced, with blunt, fine hair and eyes that matched her beige outfit. When she first passed Kei's door, she was on her way somewhere else. I saw her profile rushing by—actually, I tried to duck it from where I stood at the window—but her face popped back a moment later.

"Oh, there you are," she said, acknowledging my resemblance to Kei, perhaps. She walked to the bed.

"Hello, Hanako, it's Bree again. I see your sister's here." Her vowels were lazy, muffled by misplaced *ew*s and *ah*s, but I couldn't place her ac-cent. She reached out a gentle hand and put it on Kei's shoulder.

"Call me Bree," she said, sticking her other hand out to shake mine. The patch on her jacket read, NEUROREHABILITATION. "I'm from Sydney. I've been here ten years but people still ask about the accent."

"Call me...Miss Swanson." It wasn't until her face shut down that I understood how offensive I sounded, but I was floundering. "It's a joke. That's all I've been called in the hospital. You can call me...Koko."

"Koko, then." Bree gave me a brief smile, then indicated that I should stand beside her at Kei's hip before she settled her right hand on my sister's rib cage. "We're going to roll her away from us and hold her on her side." I'd seen the ICU staff reposition Kei to avoid bedsores but I'd never been asked to help. Not that Bree had asked.

"Upsy-daisy," Bree said. "Here we go."

We got her positioned, awkwardly, and Bree did something I had never yet seen in Kei's treatment: She guided her body in movement. As Bree talked, Kei's arm rose, stretched, and pivoted like the swimmer she had always been. How could Bree tell?

I'd been pressing Kei securely into the bed until that point to counterbalance Bree's therapy. Then, suddenly, I felt a fraction of new heat rise in Kei's body, more unnerving than any reflexive spasm I'd witnessed so far. She lit up, and for a moment, I felt her presence there. Then, she stiffened at my touch; she bucked, arching herself even further backward. The shock of her flexed muscles fired up my own.

Had I hurt her? Could she tell from my touch it was me?

I was shaking.

Bree began easing the slight twists out of Kei's limbs. "Easy, Hanako, there's no need to be frightened," she said. Did Kei quiet at her voice? Her eyes were so blank, so much darker and more similar with the pupils shuttered open. My heightened heartbeat seemed to fill the room.

Hanako. She kept saying it. My mother didn't even like the name, she had used it so rarely. "It's Hana," I said, trying to keep the tremors out of my voice. "She likes that better."

Bree picked up Kei's hand again and began bending her wrist as if nothing had happened.

I thought of Kei twisting away from me. *What if she doesn't want me here?*

I remembered the phantom pain I felt in her body. *What if she does?*

There was so much in our past neither one of us could bear to face. If Kei did wake up, what could forgiveness look like?

At last, there were tears coming. True tears this time, the kind I had no idea how to stop. I never cry. I hadn't even cried when my mother and Arnie died.

Bree wavered, her hair dripping into her shoulders, face rippling from the tip of her nose. Her body stretched, then thickened, radiating from its own dark shadow. I felt my heart clench. I forced my eyes closed, knowing that if I let my tears continue not even Bree could put me back together.

"It might have been a reflex, or momentum," Bree said quietly. "But she might have been trying to keep her balance, too. We'll know soon enough. Right, Hana? You'll show us soon enough."

All that afternoon, Bree Sheridan taught me about my sister's body. We began with the softest parts. The bottoms of her feet, inner thighs, and armpits. Her hands. Her mouth.

"Think of it this way," she said. "You're standing next to Hana, but the only way she can tell you are here is through one of her five senses. So, one of two things could be happening: Either she's in there but somehow her senses aren't getting her the information, or she's getting it but she isn't answering back. You'll need to bring in things that she'll recognize: smells from your childhood, maybe a food she likes or a favorite perfume. Anything to give her a direction, show her the way out. If there is a consciousness of any kind, we don't want to leave it trapped alone in the dark."

Alone in the dark. I didn't have to close my eyes to imagine that. "And if there isn't?"

"With your sister, as you know, it's a curious case. We know there was probably oxygen loss, though not for long, but her symptoms are more consistent with stupor, or catatonia. The cause could be anything, even psychogenic."

Bree's explanation sounded marginally more like English than the ICU doctors'. It also sounded more like Kei. "Psychogenic? As in, she's faking it?"

"Well." Bree paused. "The brain protects itself, especially in the case of trauma. More likely there is more than one factor: underlying imbalances, even old injuries, can exacerbate an acute event. How was she feeling, the last time you spoke to her? Was she upset? Any complaints about her health? How did she look?"

I didn't answer. I couldn't even begin to explain why I couldn't. "So she'll come out of it?"

Bree looked tired, though it was midafternoon. "We don't know. Let's hope she's in there, healing. We can give her a week of intensive therapy and reevaluate, depending on how much time you can devote. But people do come back to consciousness, and some swear they knew their family members were there."

I stayed with Kei all day, learning Bree's routines for pinpricks, bells, lights. Between the therapies, as I watched my sister, I began sketching her image on an invisible page in my mind. I took inventory. We had both cut a few wisps of hair to frame our faces, but Kei's were highlighted red by the sun. Her fingers were rougher than mine, and the bottoms of her feet were callused from going barefoot. But it was her face I focused on. Did the tip of my upper lip quiver like hers when I slept? I realized that I had no idea what I looked like any longer, and even less idea what everyone else saw.

Bree told me to talk to Kei. I didn't know how to explain that I no longer knew what to say. It wasn't me who could bring her back. Our bond had broken, and broken again, so many times there were only pieces of us left. But then I remembered—Mama's case. Kei had brought it with her. I wasn't convinced that I had the courage to face the memories that would come surging back out of it, but I knew that if there was help to be had, answers, that was where I would find them.

When I returned home that night, my apartment still smelled faintly of shoyu and Ajax. I'd spent the day of Kei's transfer cleaning it. My sparse furnishings and bare walls made the job easier, but the paint was still a little dingy. I'd hung a clothesline over the windows for my rags, my clothes, and my bedspread, and though they were dry, I left them there to do the double duty of weighing down my curtains so that not even my moving shadow could be seen from the subway station.

During the day, at the Eckert Center, I'd felt like cracked glass waiting to shatter, but at least there I had something to distract me. Now, my evening stretched out before me, every minute of it bending toward the case. What did I usually do with my time? Most nights, I brought my staff meal home and lost myself in the different world of a library book as I crocheted intricate patterns into handkerchiefs, and then unraveled them and began again. Crochet was as close as I could allow myself get to artistic expression. My first and only painting in high school had attracted the wrong kind of attention, and in six years since, despite what I had told my shrink, I had not so much as doodled with a pen.

The case had been a familiar sight during our childhood. It was a beaten thing—a strapped leather box with two loose buckles filled with all Mama's secrets and treasures. She kept it on one of the makeshift pine shelves that served as her closet, out of reach but jutting far enough off the edge that we could always see it. But now it was here, in its new place on my bedside table, waiting for me.

My mother had secrets, and I was afraid of them. I wasn't scared that they would explain things—her illness, her abandonment, maybe even her death—but that they would not. Why had Mama made me, her discarded daughter, the executor of her will? And what could be so important for Kei to tell me, or give me, that she would travel halfway across the world with a case she knew I cared so little about that I had left it behind? And yet, perhaps Kei was right. I could feel the sudden urge to know who *I* was to my mother. What had she kept of me? What parts of Hana had she cherished?

I unfastened the buckles and readied myself to receive my mother.

There were fewer items than I expected. No ribbon-tied packet of letters, no outpouring of her last words. There was an old, stained crochet handkerchief I didn't recognize. A small notebook, which I flipped through and then set down for later when I saw Arnie's lanky handwriting. Tucked inside the notebook were a few pictures. Two—empty and seemingly old shots of a concrete bridge and a water tower—I'd never seen before. On the back of one, someone had penciled the word "Hiroshima," but with no date, no explanation for why my American-as-apple-pie mother might have wanted it. Also stuck between the pages was a folded clipping from the *Herald* during the aftermath of the tidal wave.

I remember the morning it came out—and the way Arnie tucked it away, tenderly and quietly, when he saw me.

Most of the rest of the contents struck me as items Arnie had believed were important, rather than talismans our mother would have cherished. The quarter Kei had dipped into a lava flow when he had taken her to see the eruption after she'd gotten into trouble at school. A wooden, hand-carved yo-yo that I didn't remember, wrapped in a curving piece of calligraphy on parchment paper. One of Kei's swimming medals. It was all old stuff, too—as if time had stopped when we were in high school. I couldn't tell if the contents were prepared deliberately or had simply accrued over the years.

There was nothing about my mother in it. No birth certificate. No marriage license. No family papers. No deed. Mama could have been dropped from the moon or washed up on shore in a woven reed basket for as much as she'd told us, and there were plenty of times when that kind of explanation would have made perfect sense. As for our biological father, there were no clues there, either, but that at least was a blessing. Whoever he had been, we didn't miss him when we were young, and once Arnie showed up there was almost too much man in the house.

There were no pictures of Mama, even as a child, and none of her family or my father. Just one of Kei and me.

The twins.

Two small girls, dressed alike, reflecting identically back at each other, even the cowlicks in our hair swirling in opposite directions. Our blue bridesmaid dresses jumped off the gray sky behind us; blue half-veils hung off our hats. It was the day of Mama's wedding to Arnie, a rainy day, so we'd gathered under the house for the vows. The ceremony was short, originally planned for the garden, and on a day that was more somber than it should have been, I remember Mama leaning on a cane and watching the clouds approaching, draped in the simple, cream wedding dress Mrs. Harada had made for her. She was thin but radiant. She had only just gotten well enough to get out of bed for the first time in weeks.

Rain, Mama said, *is lucky*.

She seemed perplexed at the possibility of good fortune.

I had never seen this photo. Kei and I, side by uncomfortable side. We hung like lost puppets, our limp fingers extending toward each other as if we were being shown how to pose—*Hold hands darlings, no, the other hand Kei, switch sides girls so you can put that bandage behind your back, that's it.* Something Arnie would say, most likely. He was always so determined that everyone in his new family should get along.

In those days, of course, we barely knew him. Mama had collapsed when Kei destroyed her picture, and later she rose out of bed a bride. In between, Arnie and Mrs. Harada kept us from her. *No place for little girls. Don't worry your heads about it,* he always told us, never wondering who had taken care of her before he arrived. Through the doorway, we could only see her sleeping, the blankets tight over her pale birds of paradise hands.

If I was going to subject myself to these traumas of my childhood, the least I could have hoped for was that the objects that Mama believed were so precious would also surround me with home. But when I saw what little there was in it, I felt more alone than ever. Of everything, it was only the final item in the case that could prove that my mother had ever really loved me. I had left it for last because I knew what it was.

She had slipped it into a plain envelope. It was her most cherished possession: the photo of me as a toddler that Kei had destroyed in her jealous rage. Though it was slashed into pieces, still Mama had kept it. Proof that she loved me once. I slipped it out of the envelope, flipping and turning the pieces to puzzle the image back together so that I could look at it for the first time since it was whole. But it was different than I remembered. Even with the shredded white lines, I didn't recognize my face. I fit the pieces together on a book cover and held it directly under the light, but the disconnect only got worse. The child's eyes were both black. And the white outfit was not a dress.

Something was wrong.

I looked for the love, the joy that had imprinted on me in the instant I saw the picture. Tried to identify the fingers the child was stretching toward, but nothing could transform that face back into my own as I had remembered it. My picture, the one Kei and I were both convinced was of our mother and Hana, wasn't.

It was a photograph of a little boy.

1944 – 1945

The night was cooler when she woke. Lillie reached out, panicked, but Toshi was still there, asleep beside her, his arms flung in both directions to claim as much of the futon as he could. Sometimes, he ended up sideways, his head against her body, his two-year-old feet kicking Donald in the ribs. On those nights, which came more and more frequently, she wondered if this restlessness was a sign of the wide chasm between her and her husband, or if it was her son's slumbering desire to keep his mother to himself.

Was he old enough to sense that his parents were separating? Would he understand and would it matter that *he* was the one who was going to leave *her?*

The plan was for Donald to slip away into the night with Toshi. The draft had finally caught up with her husband, and if he didn't report for duty in the morning, the military police who would come for him were not the kind from whom his father could save him. If Donald wanted to survive, this was his last chance to run.

She pulled her son close. Just under a year old when they arrived in Japan, he was still barely bigger than he had been when they landed in Yokohama. The war had not been good to any of them, but especially to a growing boy. Lillie had breast-fed Toshi as long as she could, but he was old enough now to leave her. All the schoolchildren up to twelve were being evacuated to the countryside, where it might be safe. Entire schools were relocating with their teachers. Toshi was too young to go with them, of course, but also, with the dwindling food and Lillie's own conscription, too young to stay.

She could see a small candle dancing in the dark of the main room; that was why the bed felt cooler. Donald was awake. Her heart fell. She could hear him sifting through their few possessions for whatever small things of value he could tuck into his clothes. She knew she should get up and help him, but instead, she pressed her lips to Toshi's ear and sang him the song he liked about the red birds. Did she see him smile, even in his sleep? Thin as he was, her son was a happy, obliging child who had an uncanny link to his mother's voice. What was he going to do without her? It was a question within a bigger question: How were any of them going to survive to the next day?

Japan was not the refuge her husband expected. The trip west from Yokohama gave Lillie her first taste of it: barren fields and long stretches of nothing. Of course, it was winter. When they got to the family house in a village in the Hiroshima prefecture, an hour north of the city, they were a sad group: a crippled old man and a baby, and a woman who couldn't speak her "own" language and had to ask her husband what everything meant. Lillie found herself living with a bunch of strangers under a thatched roof, in a building with sliding walls. It was bitterly cold, heated only by a central sunken hearth that the extended family gathered around to eat, and then pulled their sleeping mats up to in the night to stay warm. It differed from the barracks in the camps only in the constant smell of smoke in everything and the lack of electricity. And the lack of food.

From the end of 1943, the blockades had severely restricted Japan's imports. People weren't yet starving, or eating grasshoppers and rice husks, but rice had given way to barley, and with the men going off to war, the farms were being tilled by women who could not always get the seed they needed in time for the right planting season. To avoid starvation, people in the rural areas had flooded into the cities, where there was more food and factory work. After a few stunned months of trying to figure out how to use the land around the family home, Donald and Lillie had done the same, swapping places with Donald's cousins for the place in the city, where Tateishi-sama would be closer to the doctors. They had lived in their small city apartment, undisturbed, for just under a year: a young mother, her infant son, her ailing elder father-in-law, and her shadowy, rarely seen husband, who started off with a badly sprained ankle from falling into a hole during field work and never gave up using his father's cane in public.

But then Lillie was drafted, along with a group of other English-speaking women, to translate the Allied communications for the military in the basement of a mansion on the castle grounds, a place so top secret that she couldn't tell her own husband where it was. In a strange way, Donald seemed to resent her for it. It wasn't that he had lost his enthusiasm for Japan or the Emperor's victory. It was that she had a role that would not kill her.

By early in 1945, the Japanese military was running out of weapons and ammunition, as well as food. And soldiers. The military had been mobilizing children for a while, so it wasn't surprising to Lillie that once they began scraping the bottom to conscript teenagers and the elderly, they found Donald and his fake limp, too. But he thought it too much of a coincidence that he'd been overlooked by the military for a year, only to be found so soon after she herself was drafted. She must have accidentally let slip to her supervisors that he wasn't really crippled, he insisted, though she assured him she had not.

Lillie was shocked that he would think she would expose him to that. She knew, better than she could admit to him, that her husband's future as a soldier would last only as long as it took to strap a grenade to his body and throw himself onto a tank. It didn't matter that she, too, had been forcibly drafted, and that she'd fought back in her own small way, protesting that she barely knew how to speak Japanese, let alone write it, and giving in only when they threatened to arrest her for unpatriotic acts. She and the other English-speaking translators were practically held captive in their castle dungeon. The girls who lived too far away stayed in a nearby dormitory and were not allowed to leave.

He blamed her, and there was no arguing with him. His silence was as bludgeoning as he intended it, but it was a relief compared to what came out of his mouth.

Lillie held that silence as she scooped up her sleeping son and rose from bed. She took the candle from Donald to set it on the table. Then, with her sleeping father-in-law only a body's length away and her son propped in her lap, she wordlessly sat and helped Donald sew a few coins into the hems and linings of his clothes. He would need them more than she and Tateishi-sama did. She had one meal a day now, with the military no less; she couldn't remember the last time he forgot to point that out. That she was getting the best food in Japan.

They had agreed on his escape: He would take Toshi and leave the city. The mere thought of being separated from her boy—for a day or a week, let alone the possibility of months—made her head swim, but Lillie didn't have a choice. There were no other options. The Allies had begun bombing the big cities—Tokyo, Kobe—igniting the matchstick houses and turning people into charcoal, and everyone knew it was only a matter of time until Hiroshima was hit. Adolescents had been mobilized to rip down houses and create fire lanes, but no one seemed to think it was going to help, so the younger children were flooding into the countryside.

Lillie couldn't be the one to take Toshi to safety; her absence would be noticed immediately. But the military wouldn't come looking for Donald until the day after tomorrow. If he was stopped, he could say that his wife had died suddenly and he was going to leave the baby with family and return. Surely they wouldn't want him with a child in hand; it would only mean more work for them as they would have to farm Toshi out. If they came to question Lillie, it wouldn't be until days later, and she would simply play dumb and express her pride that her husband had left to die in glory for the Emperor.

Meanwhile, she would stay in the city and take care of Tateishi-sama. The old man cursed them both; the more helpless he became, the worse his temper grew. Hers grew, too. She knew Donald was right, that she couldn't care for Toshi and also for her father-in-law and still report to work. It was logical. The best thing for her son. But she also knew what she would do in Donald's place, if she were set free with Toshi—what she had tried to do already—and she couldn't bite back the sour fear rising in the back of her throat.

* * *

Besides her son, the only bright spot in Lillie's life since she left the farm was Hanako Harada. Originally from Hawaii, Hanako was Lillie's partner on the translation team. They had been paired so they could help each other, since Lillie's Japanese was so *katakoto* and Hanako's English, at least when she put her pidgin accent on, was impossible to understand. Lillie had kept her distance at first, not wanting to get involved in the trouble she knew this brash girl would attract. But that was the thing she was to learn about Hanako: She got away with everything. Soldiers, schoolgirls, even the lieutenant colonel all loved her stories. Unlike Lillie, Hanako kept nothing secret, nothing safe. In the few months they had known each other, Lillie had come to yearn for the sound of Hanako's voice every morning: the bravado and the lilt of Hawaiian pidgin; the wide grin and the barking laugh for which she had been sure Hanako would be hustled away, or maybe even jailed, when she first heard it. Hanako, more than anyone else, made Lillie feel safe.

The unit they were working for was hidden in a mansion just north of the main castle. They were intercepting shortwave radio broadcasts from the Allies. Only girls had been drafted, all Nisei: American girls who had been visiting family in Japan when the war broke out and were stranded here. Some of them were as young as thirteen. "Mo' betta than pulling down buildings to make fire breaks," Hanako observed, as if they'd been offered a choice.

Their job was to listen and to translate. They weren't supposed to talk. They couldn't talk about America because it was the enemy. They couldn't talk about what their lives were like here and now: with young boys throwing rocks at them in the streets for being American; how there had been so little for so long and now there was almost nothing. But what they really could not talk about was the truth that Japan was losing the war. They had lost Saipan, the Philippines, Iwo Jima, and reports were coming in that the Battle of Steel in Okinawa might also end in defeat. On the night shift, the Allied radio operators told stories about how the "Japs" were slaughtering their own civilians rather than letting them be taken. Women and children were walking off cliffs. It was propaganda for sure, but it was equally true that there was something in the air now of death: a sense that they had all been walking toward a cliff and it had finally come into sight. The soldiers in the south were giving townspeople grenades to kill themselves, so said the propaganda, and the soldiers in the castle complex around Lillie were muttering at the waste because there was no more lead to make bullets and few grenades left.

But they *could* talk about Hawaii. Even though Japan had bombed it, it wasn't truly America. It stood between two worlds, not a part of either. Little girls in Hawaii, Hanako said, ran around barefoot and chased tadpoles in the creeks beside their houses. There were cherry blossoms there, just like in Japan, and kids packed one *musubi* for lunch at school. On Sundays, there was shave ice with adzuki beans in the middle of a hot afternoon. There was no war in Hawaii, no internment camps. Everyone belonged.

Because Hanako was who she was, she was allowed to talk about Hawaii. And because everyone longed for a safe home. She told them she had grown up on a sugarcane plantation; she had eight brothers and sisters, but her entire family returned to Japan just after she was born. She stayed behind, *hānai*ed to her childless aunt Suzy, who owned her own home. Hanako only traveled to Japan because her grandmother was sick and her aunt had asked her to pay their last respects. She was to deliver a jade pendant that Suzy had been given when she was married, and then return to Hawaii.

With so much family in Japan, it wasn't clear why Hanako had been living alone in Hiroshima and teaching English at the school for girls when the war began. None of the monitor girls questioned her story, even though it was clear that the pendant she referred to was the one she wore around her neck and often fingered when the air raid sirens blew. It was enough for all of them to know Aunt Suzy and Uncle Joe were out there, that there was a place without prisoners and ritual suicide, a place where they could be embraced as family. It was enough to hear Hanako's lilting voice in the early-morning hours when not even the radio operators could stay awake. She was their sanctuary in the growing darkness.

Aunt Suzy and Uncle Joe love little children, Hanako told Lillie, making a space in paradise for Toshi also.

All they had to do was stay safe until the war ended. In the dark of the night, sewing coins into the hem of her husband's old coat, Lillie had one goal: that she and Toshi live through this.

If she could make sure of that, Hanako would bring them both home.

HANA

After I opened the case, just as I expected, my nightmares became constant. Me with Kei's scar in my palm. Me with my face slashed in two. I knew the photograph was causing it. Grief emanated from it, a throbbing ache that seeped through my body and into everything I touched. I wasn't the loved one. How had I ever thought I was? But that loss was only part of what was haunting me. Now I understood that there had been another child who Mama cherished, and I had no idea who he was. I took the fragments out of the envelope and mounted them on an old scrap of poster board with stick glue, matching them as carefully as I could to minimize the frayed white lines so I could see him. The answer to a question that I had never thought to ask.

What if I had gotten it wrong? I thought then. What if my mother was hounded not by spirits, but by real people? This boy, for example. What if it was *he* who disappeared? The boy in the black-and-white photo was old enough to stand, but looked fragile; at his wrists and ankles, you could clearly see his bones. His hair was thick and dark, spraying off his head like a funnel of spiked grass. His outfit was white, a long, billowing sailor suit with dark trim. It was a quick, candid photo, taken somewhere warm or at least in a warm season; I knew because his knees and lower arms were bare. He wasn't moving, and yet his hair spun around his head.

Who was this child?

Look at your hair, Mama had said one time when she was lying down, but not to us. *It's like a helicopter flying in the sky.*

It was an odd thing to say—how could hair be like a helicopter? My little-girl mind had tried to picture it. Did it hover, or pinwheel in the wind? It sounded light, the way she said it; the word floated like a dandelion in the wind, not thrumming like the propellers on the military carriers that sometimes dove in from the camp up near the volcano. And what would the spirit in her fever dream look like with this soaring hair?

Now, I knew. But knowing raised more questions than it answered. A suspicion was forming, rising along with my memories. Whoever he was, the boy was a secret, and that secret threatened to upend everything I had ever suspected about who Kei and I were meant to be.

I had learned the meaning of Kei's name one afternoon after she dropped out of the weekend sewing class Mama had enrolled us in. It was a tough year: the first year of intermediate school, and our new principal had decided that twins had to be separated and had put Kei into a less gifted class. There was no reason for it; Kei was nothing if not clever. She was *not* happy to be in the B class, so she went on strike. Anything she could quit, she quit.

On Kei's last day in the sewing class, we were learning how to cut patterns. A simple shift with darts, more fitted than anything Mama would let us wear. Once we had pinned and measured everything and were making our patterns, Miss Shima pointed out that Kei's was lopsided. She held it up—all of Kei's mistakes for the benefit of the whole class—then refit her, only to find out that Kei's measurements were meticulous. Her body was defective, not her cutting skills.

Our patterns were two sizes bigger than for most of the girls. With Arnie in the family, there was an abundance of food in the house, or maybe it was the beefy Caucasian half of our missing father that suddenly started growing, but by age twelve we were already as big as our mother, with budding but still larger breasts. We felt huge in those days—though today we stand about five foot six and our breasts and hips and thighs are all proportionate and, frankly, small—I still remember obsessing over whether my thighs would touch, or worse stick together, when I sat down. I knew, if I offered myself up, that one of my shoulders would be higher, too, my hips just as tipped, "like a little teapot," as Miss Shima had pantomimed. I could hear the happy screams of *TALL and STOUT!* that were already gathering for recess, and I couldn't bring myself to keep Kei company.

At that point in our lives, Kei and I were still sisters, if not exactly friends, and if she had announced her decision to withdraw from the class outright, I would have quit, too, in solidarity. Instead, she orchestrated a series of last-minute punishments—for a line of laundry dropped into the dirt and broken dishes in the sink—designed to get herself grounded so she wouldn't have to go. I could see the cloud wash over Mama's face every time Kei misbehaved, and I did everything I could to smooth things over between them. I folded two stacks of shirts when Kei wouldn't do hers, and convinced Mama we should switch off on chores instead of doing them together so I could pretend to be Kei. When I tried to reason with Kei, she called me a prig and told me to get off my high horse—language she'd surely picked up in the B class. She was reveling in her black sheep status, suddenly needing everything to be the opposite.

On the first day Kei left me to go to Miss Shima's alone, we were learning needlepoint, which would have bored Kei to death anyway, since her only interest in sewing was to learn how to make store-bought clothes look homemade. Miss Shima assigned us family crests: the family crest being a Japanese thing, and most of us in the class being some kind of Japanese. She was a young Japanese American woman recently arrived from the mainland—a *katonk*, some of the kids called her, slang for the empty sound that her mainlander's head would supposedly have made if you hit it. Mama would have nothing to do with Miss Shima—she avoided the "Japanese-y types" as she called them, which was strangely prejudiced, given that she was Japanese American herself. But then, Hawaii was at odds with itself about race: On one hand, everyone got along; on the other hand, there were distinctions, even within a single ethnic group. There were those who were born in the islands, those who came from the mainland (as we called the rest of the United States, having just joined the nation), and those enigmatic strangers who arrived from their originating country and had little in common with us. The mainlanders were considered to be the best—they were cultured—which meant that all the mothers except ours loved Miss Shima and overlooked her unseemly interest in a country that was the enemy just a little too recently for comfort. But the girls were different. They teased her behind her back for her perfectly haole voice.

No one wanted to make a family crest. Most of us didn't even know if our families had one. Miss Shima explained that crests should be circular—something maybe having to do with the shape of the hand guards on samurai swords. At that point in my life, I still imagined myself an artist, though by then I had abandoned my childish monsters in favor of capturing things that were actually there. Now that I was supposed to draw what I saw, I had gotten a little controlling: always sketching in one direction, from the bottom left-hand corner up. Something to do with not wanting to smudge the page. If I got stuck on something, if I couldn't replicate what I saw in a way that satisfied me, I couldn't finish. Other people could skip over it and come back later, but I didn't want to waste my time getting 90 percent of the picture right and then be unable to complete the nose. If it wasn't perfect, it was over.

But that precision was impossible in needlepoint. I was forced to create something a little more abstract than my usual pictures. It was a triad of three barely interlocking circles. I shaded them as best I could with hints of black and gray.

One of the girls swore her family crest was a gingko leaf and resisted Miss Shima's suggestion that she locate it inside a circle—maybe the frustration started there. Or maybe it was the impossibility of trying to stitch curves in a rectangular grid. When we were finished and Miss Shima was trying in vain to match our attempts to our original ideas, she came over to me.

"What is it?" she asked, after praising the subtlety of my stitches. She was overly enthusiastic whenever anyone in the class did anything right, and she tended to single me out.

"Us." I used my quietest voice. "And Mama."

Mama was the top circle; Kei and I the smaller two on the bottom. I can still see the black strokes of our hair falling through the stitches, and the suggestions of shoulders, the floor. Although those pre-Arnie days of Mama fainting and telling us fevered stories were long gone, they were still a part of me. Or maybe I was lonely.

"It looks like *chi chis*," the gingko girl muttered to her friend.

"What?"

She repeated herself in a clear voice. From the blushes and the laughter, even a mainlander should have known what the girl was talking about, but Miss Shima asked anyway.

"What's a chi chi?"

Encouraged by the snickers around her, the gingko girl cupped a hand under each of her nonexistent breasts and pretended to lift them to cradle her chin. "You know, chi chis. Big ones. Moo moo!"

"Women are not cows, Katie," Miss Shima scolded, but then I saw her make a different connection. Her eyes flicked to me, helpless.

Don't run.

It was an old Lillie story, just a snippet that Kei and I had grabbed on to. Was it a coyote Lillie encountered in the prairie, or just a threatening dog? The story was Mama's way of warning us to be obedient because there was a world out there waiting, literally, to eat us.

My face was burning, even as I pretended not to hear them. My arms inched up across my chest. I was almost thirteen then. It would have been a lot easier to perish on the spot.

Who knows what happened next? Time gets stuck there. At some point the other girls had gone home and I was left alone with Miss Shima waiting for Arnie to pick me up. Usually I enjoyed that time, with its chatter about sewing tips and tricks; I even encouraged it. But that day I could feel the bull's-eye on my chest and I understood all the name-calling that was normally directed at Miss Shima was about to be aimed at me.

I was standing just inside the doorway, looking away from Miss Shima to indicate to the other girls, all long gone, that I didn't want this woman's sympathy nor did I want to be her friend.

"It must be hard," Miss Shima said to my back. "Your mother, I mean. War is a hard thing to live through. Sometimes people...well, there are scars."

I shrugged. I had no idea what she was talking about. And yet, I did understand that she was referring to the teasing. There was something in it, something more specific than Mama's reputation as the Calrose lady, which she'd gotten for the inside-out logo stamped on the clothes she made from rice bags that she used to wear when she walked downtown. If I turned around, Miss Shima would tell me—what scars? which war? what did this have to do with the mooing?—so I held myself away stiffly, looking toward the world outside. I held even my breath until I was dizzy.

Still, she persisted.

"Your triptych is lovely, Hana. You have a gift. Not just for handwork, but an artistic eye. You said it represents you and your sister and your mother?" When I nodded, still facing away, she suggested I might want to add our names to the image, perhaps in kanji, so that the image was less confusing.

It didn't matter that crests were not supposed to be labeled. Miss Shima didn't even know kanji, but it gave her a reason to pick up the white paperback book of Japanese names and their meanings that she'd brought for this purpose, and once again to try to act like a "real Japanese." With her flip and her black-cat glasses, I realize, she was younger than I am now. That makes it easier to forgive her. She sat down and patted a seat next to her, leaving me no choice but to obey, and opened the book.

Hana, she said quickly, meant "flower."

And *Kei*—she had marked the page but she still looked at it as if trying to make up her mind before she pronounced it. Shadow. *Keiko* meant "shadow child."

I have lived with this information so long that it is hard now to remember exactly how it felt. *Recognition* is the word that comes to me, and *relief*. If it had never occurred to me that a name would have a meaning, it was comforting that mine was simple; pretty. But it was Kei's, after that tantalizing pause, that came like an answer.

Miss Shima explained that Kei was probably second born. She said she'd read of cases in which the doctors were quite surprised when a second child appeared after the first. She told me twins were often considered blessed or cursed in many cultures, and sometimes one was even killed. Twins were thought to control the rain and the weather. There was even a myth about how, if one twin died, the family would make a little statue for her spirit to dwell in, so she wouldn't try to enter the living twin.

What stuck was that Kei was my shadow. Kei was the copy. I was the original.

When I told Kei what her name meant, everything changed. All the labels that we had used to distinguish us fell away. She could be bad. *Was* bad, by name and nature, so why not embrace it?

Miss Shima gave Kei her name, and I was a fool to deliver it. But the truth is, Kei was the one who chose it. No matter what else her name could have meant, she was the shadow. It was a curse on all of us, and the worst was yet to come.

KEI

Wake up, Kei. Must we relive *all* of this? Okay, then. There is light. Do you see it? So much light through your eyelids.

And heat.

It's lunch recess. The sky is its usual soft white pillow, vaguely drizzling, and you're in the hall. Hana is home with a nervous stomach. Playing hooky on your birthday, something Mama would never let you do. But Hana is fragile. She clings to rules, and she breaks with them when they are broken. She believes being good will protect her.

You are worried about her absence, but she hasn't confided that something else is wrong. Not even late at night, in the dark, when either one of you can say anything. For as long as you can remember, Hana has been terrified of the dark, so once the two of you were too old to sleep in the same bed together, you created the ritual of your "night conversations" to keep her in the safe company of your voice until she fell asleep. Recently, you have been amusing her—counting by sevens, speaking in both pig latin and haiku. Last night, you gave her a gift: You recited all the vice presidents in reverse order. Hana's gift to you was better. Your name.

You are the Shadow Child.

In the name, you can feel that presence lurking. *The earth becoming*, Arnie said. The shape-shifter in you. A shadow can be anything: long as a road or just an edge. It is always different. Full of possibility.

A shadow can't be pinned down. It is never in one place, never stuck. It is never alone, either. Never without the thing that casts it—

It's the copy, not the real thing, Hana points out. It only follows.

You can hear in her voice that she didn't expect your excitement. But you know everything depends on where the light is. Sometimes the shadow leads.

You are still thinking about this in the school hallway when you realize you've been moving too slow. The pack of boys is outside the bathroom, between you and the yard.

The shadow is transformation, you remind yourself. And then they are on you.

This time, they will pull you into the bathroom and dunk your head in the toilet. When they leave, you will spend the rest of the recess blotting your hair dry. Then, you will clog every toilet in the boys' bathrooms with wads and wads of paper towels, pull out the stoppers in the tanks, and listen to the water run. You can almost see the dances the outraged teachers will force the dog-boys to do that afternoon when they cannot pee because the toilets are overflowing out of the bathrooms and into the halls. You could not even have hoped for the scene tomorrow when the principal takes every eighth-grade boy out of shop class to plunge out the toilets, mop the floors, and scrub the walls. But you do know that from this day forward, the dog-boys will decide you are too much trouble to deal with. The shadow tells you they will not bother you or Hana again.

After school, on your way home, you pass Missy and her friends under the tree where they always sit, even in the misty rain. Missy is cross-legged at the head of their circle, chewing on a blade of grass. She is their queen. Her hair is caramel and so smooth it's always slipping out from behind her ears. Her eyes are jet-black against her lighter features. Missy is soft. Ripening. She is a rose on the morning it begins to bloom. Even the dog-boy crew and some of the teachers fall silent when she walks by. She isn't one of those girls with a wisecrack, or a "look at me" smile. When she's in a crowd, her mind is far away from what's going on around her.

You know all this because you have watched her from a distance. But today, you can get a little closer because there is something going on. One of the girls in Missy's group is upset, Charlene Chow, and Missy is leaning forward with her hand on Charlene's shoulder. You slow down, and move close enough to hear Charlene talking about her grandmother who was swept away in the tidal wave. It was fourteen years ago today, before any of you were born.

You've seen tidal waves. One came in three years ago and it barely ran up three feet. *The* tidal wave, the one she is talking about, was a big deal—a bunch of kids and their teachers got swept out to sea and part of downtown was ruined—but that was a whole lifetime ago. You try to imagine it, how the water could be so strong. There are warnings now, but no one bothers to leave the buildings when they test the sirens.

Missy's eyes flicker toward you as you sidestep in their direction, but Charlene continues with her story. Her grandmother's car was lifted by the wave, she says, and she describes how it tumbled over and over, smashing into a building before it got sucked back out toward the sea. Her *lao lao* couldn't get out to save herself, couldn't open the door, so she was stuck in that car, tossed around like she was in a washing machine. When they found the car, it was wrapped around the trunk of a palm tree, empty. At least that was what they told her: Her grandmother had been sucked to the bottom of the sea.

It's a lie. You of all people can tell. No one would know what happened to the grandmother inside the car if she also disappeared. But it's a good one. You can see that from Missy's tears.

You stand at the edge of their circle, lingering where you don't belong. These are not your friends—you don't have friends. "April Fool!" You wait for them to scream it and shoo you away.

Instead, they don't even seem to see you. The story holds. The story is magic. As the other girls wait for her lead, Missy reaches out to embrace Charlene.

Let me tell you a story. This one is about five Chinese brothers. Surely you remember Mama's version of the story? One brother could swallow an ocean and when he did, all the children were dazzled by the flopping fish and ran out onto the sea floor to collect them. The Chinese brother waved for them to come back but they ran farther and farther out. He kept waving, until he could hold the ocean no more. The 1946 April Fool's tidal wave was like that: The first two waves pulled the water out so far that the beaches were drained, just like in the story. Twenty-three students ran out to collect the fish, and then the deadly third wave swept in and dragged them out to sea.

What did they do to deserve it? There are always tales of lucky people. The ones who are not in the bus when it crashes because they are sick that day, or they woke up late. But what of the people who are unlucky? Don't they exist, too? The ones accidentally in the *wrong* place, whom fate is not supposed to take? And what if one of those unlucky children wants to come back? What if her spirit tries, but there is already a little girl in the mother she enters, so they have to split in two?

At that moment in the school yard, you understand what Pele has been trying to tell you: You are the daughter of the dead. A spirit from the big tidal wave. Why else were you born exactly one year after they all died: April Fool's Day 1947? How else to explain your appearance? You and Hana. Half and half. Two people who wouldn't mix. Two souls who fought even then because it was your turn to be reincarnated and Hana was already there.

You are exactly thirteen, don't forget that. Doesn't every girl that age fantasize that she's adopted, that her true parents are kings and queens from another land? How much more far-fetched to imagine that you are one of the tidal wave children, so desperate to get your life back that your spirit entered the only mother to give birth on the first anniversary of your death? To imagine that you could find a way to stop being "bad-stupid-crooked-selfish-clumsy-trouble"? That there is another family out there for you, and you can try again?

You are Kei, after all. The teller of fantastical stories. In this new story, to find your real family, you will have to return to the depths of the ocean. And to do that, you will have to learn to swim.

* * *

Mama is getting better at cakes by your thirteenth birthday. This one is a three-layer devil's food cake with a rough sea of deep chocolate icing. It is ablaze: fifteen candles flashing, one for each year and two to grow on. Hana's so excited.

The singing is over. Arnie says, "Make a wish."

Birthdays are the days when wishes are granted. It is the one day when you can have anything. The trick is to ask for something that can be given.

On the fourteenth anniversary of *the* tidal wave, the cake on fire in front of you, you have chosen carefully:

"Swimming lessons."

There is, in Mama's face, a flash of our old mother. The fearful *Don't wander off too far, girls!* expression that always led to a story in the evenings in which everything turned out all right. You can almost feel her fingers stroking your hair the way they used to, smelling of soap after dinner has been put away. Time slips. If you could put your head in her lap like you did as a child, you would gladly give up your birthday wish.

"That's a great idea. Miya? Isn't it?"

Everyone looks at Arnie.

"It's easy. Anyone can swim. I can teach her."

You want to keep watching Mama's face, get back to that old life you glimpsed in it. The life before Arnie and his inventions and his laugh. But then Mama sways slightly, and you think of how much she hates the water, of her old nightmares about rivers full of the dead. You are afraid that she will fall, that she will disappear into herself for days as she did when you were little. Will it be your fault again? And still, you are ready to catch her, to lie on the floor beside her, except that Arnie keeps on speaking.

"Babies swim," he says. "It's easy as pie and safer, too."

His hand touches hers as it always does when he's about to jump in between you. He will tell her not to fret, that things will be okay, and she will believe him. *Really?* She will ask, *Do you think so?* And then he will go on about how he does, and she will listen.

And you will lose her.

"Isn't it good that she wants to get out and do something?"

"Not me," Hana says. "No way I'm getting in the water."

Mama is different, looking into you. On her face, a new expression: *Who are you and why are you haunting me?*

"It's safer," you echo. By now the flickering candles are leaving puddles in the frosting.

"Make a wish," Mama says, her eyes on the cake.

HANA

Within three days, I'd become an intimate at the Eckert Trauma Center. The ward nurses knew what kind of bagels I liked, and that cream cheese made me gag, and I knew, but couldn't quite get over the fact, that one of them ate plastic-wrapped black-and-white cookies for breakfast. My relationship with Bree Sheridan was verging on friendship—she now told me, freely and often, that I looked like hell. She had given me a nickname. From the very first day we met, "Get some sleep, Coco Chanel," was her four o'clock farewell.

Koko. I was Koko. Kei was Hana, and so was I except when I was actually at Eckert visiting Kei. If it is curious to imagine being two people at once, especially when both of them are in the same place, it was more possible than it seemed. The hardest part was how oddly exhausting it was to have to remember who I was.

I responded by throwing myself into Kei's stimulation therapy. I was giving it every minute of every day. Taking care of "Hana" allowed me to use a skill I knew I was good at, and in this case, the more I had to give the better: the more hours; the more things.

Kei's clock had reset, but it was still ticking. Bree asked for more bedtime stories, Kei's favorite songs, a different perfume. It wasn't easy to find papayas, or ukulele music, not even in the city that never sleeps, but I took the challenge.

I combed through Arnie's notebook looking for inspiration. The pages were mostly blank, and the ones that weren't were filled with lists of things to do and buy, but what did Kei, or I, know of "motor start relays" and "water inlet valves"? More interesting were the entries I recognized. *Call Torres re: swimming,* for example. There were some notes about the volcanic eruption Arnie took Kei to when we were about twelve. That was what had given me the idea for yesterday's "something familiar." The smell of sulfur, of rotten eggs, would bring the volcano back. Kei had not responded, but she seemed to have stopped thrashing—sometimes I imagined I could feel her waiting for something—and I hoped that it was some response to the comforts of home. My next task was to find some pumice, scraping like the lava rocks at the beach we used to walk on barefoot.

If Kei woke—when—I needed it to be because of me. Because of a smell or sound or sensation that I had thought to bring in, not the standard stimulation therapy of flashing lights, ice, and pricking that we still alternated through the day.

Memories popped into my head whenever I looked at my sister, and more when I was touching her, as if they were stored deep within Kei and only she could help me relive them. Or maybe they were prompted by our favorite smells and sounds, because most of the moments I remembered were more benign than I would have expected. If we were a feral, gibberish-talking duo before Arnie appeared, there was no malice then. With the exception of the photograph episode, it wasn't until intermediate school that we began to truly fall apart.

It was a Sunday afternoon in May, a day of baseball in the park and plate lunch at the beach for the rest of the town, but for us, it was another weekend afternoon of birthday swimming lessons for Kei. Most normal people would have taken their lessons in a pool, but Kei didn't want any of the kids at school to see her floundering, so she convinced Mr. Torres to take us to the beach. I understood the shame of it, since pretty much every child in Hawaii who had not been raised by our mother had learned to swim as a toddler. Mama hated the water, and I did, too: too cold, too salty in my nose, and every time I came up to breathe, the waves slapped my face and in went a lungful of ocean. I sat out with the implied excuse of female discomfort, which older girls used during gym with surprising success, and no one bothered to let me know that it couldn't be used every week. Mama did fret that I never wanted to do what Kei did, but Arnie, who was always butting in to be her mouthpiece, took my side. "They're teenagers now, Miya, why not let them decide?"

Kei swam. I got a book and read in the shade.

If we'd had a radio, maybe Mama and Arnie would have heard talk of the tidal wave, but it wasn't until after Arnie dropped us off at the beach with a toot, on his way to help a friend put a new roof on his house on the other side of the island, that Kei and I first heard the whispers. Someone's uncle had heard something, so it was declared to be fact. But we knew that if there was a real threat, we'd hear three sirens, as we learned in school. The first was an alert, the second meant get ready to evacuate along the routes we were all supposed to have memorized, and the third, that the tidal wave was about to strike land. Our house was so far above the water that we didn't need a route ourselves; perhaps that was why the whispers—*tidal wave, tidal wave*—were so strangely exciting. Even I couldn't resist watching the horizon, imagining what a hero I would be if I was the first to see the huge wall of water.

Usually, Kei practiced her strokes for an hour, after which she sat in the sun until the pruned pads of her fingers smoothed out and her hair regained flight, and Arnie came to pick us up. That day, since Arnie was away, we were supposed to catch the sampan. I expected we'd take the usual drying-off interlude, so I kept reading when Kei came out. She strolled over to me, the water dripping down her newly rounding curves—a hint of hip and breast—making them shine. She stopped just beyond the reach of the darting shadow tips of the palm trees to indicate with her head that I should join her.

"Hey. You should come in sometime. The water is fine."

On any other Sunday, she might have called out, "Hey, Rags!" or "Hey, Haole!" loud enough to get a smile from others on the beach. She would have kept her distance, too—for some reason, twelve feet seemed most comfortable to her. When we were at intermediate school, this distance wasn't really noticeable, but when we went anywhere with Arnie and Mama, she was like a stray dog, unwilling to get too far from a source of food but otherwise uncommitted. It bothered Mama; she was always sweeping her fingers at Kei to get her to come closer, but Arnie just laughed, and it was that laughter that made Kei inch over when she realized how ridiculous she looked.

I didn't respond. Kei lay down a towel and stretched her legs out, then patted the ground beside her.

I felt it, too: This day was different. I shook off my own towel and sat where she indicated, lengthening my legs beside hers, feeling the sun lift the soft hairs off my skin. We were closer to the same color than you would have expected. *The splitting image of the other*, as Arnie used to tease us. If you squinted, you probably couldn't tell who was who.

"We can't miss this."

She was referring to the wave. "Maybe Mama will let us go to the Chows," I said, thinking of the clear view of the shoreline from our neighbors' porch. Mrs. Chow was one of the few women in the neighborhood Mama visited, exchanging avocados and guava cake.

Kei's sigh was propelled by the great extravagance that came so naturally to her. "I need to be *here*, where it's happening. It's coming for me."

"Coming? What do you mean, *coming*?"

There was a pause then, for Kei to figure out how to make sense of what she was about to say, or maybe to think better of saying anything at all. "Don't you ever wonder why we look like this? Like two people?"

"We *are* two people."

"No, I mean each *one* of us looks like two people. Like half and half. There's nobody else in the whole town with two different-colored eyes. It has to mean something."

"What?"

Kei grabbed my arm, as if she could shake her ideas into me. "You're the one who told me what my name means—you of all people should understand. I came back! Ghosts, you know they can come back every year on the day they died. Maybe there was only supposed to be one girl, but there were two souls battling for the same body, and the battle was so terrible we split apart. Or maybe...maybe we *both* came back. So, I—that's who *we* are, two of those kids who died in the big wave, but we weren't supposed to, see? It was an accident, we weren't supposed to die, so when we got the chance, we came back to find our real families. I've thought this all out, you know, but the problem was always—how do we find them? How do we get back to our families? If there's a tidal wave today, then that's our answer."

I studied her for wild eyes, uncontrollable twitches. The kids in school called Kei *lolo*, especially when she came in from recess with grass in her hair, and I wondered then if they were right. Though our mother acted quite normally since she married Arnie, it was still common knowledge she was crazy. And if madness wasn't as easy to catch as cooties, despite what the other kids said in the school yard, I knew that it could crop up suddenly. Kei was looking off at the horizon, her eyes red from the saltwater but otherwise usual. There was no "gotcha" in her face, no appraising me to see if I took the bait. There was something else at work, too, a warmth that still surprises me: As ridiculous as her fantasy was, I was in it.

Even though Kei's mind was on escape, mine was focused on something equally enticing: the word *we*. Of course I'd heard how she tossed it in at the last minute to win me over, but hope isn't logical. I wanted to believe. Not in the ghosts from the tidal wave—that was preposterous—but in the fact that my sister was sitting beside me.

I missed her.

"Do you think we belonged to the same family?" I asked her.

"What?"

"Were we sisters? You know, in the other family?"

"Maybe. Or maybe we were sister and brother. Maybe I was a boy."

"A boy?" How she could think *that* was appealing, I didn't know.

I could feel the *us* slipping away. That must be why I asked, "So what are we supposed to do, then?"

Kei's eyes shone. "We're supposed to let the wave take us. And when it's over, we'll return again as April Fool's babies and be who we're supposed to be."

* * *

No—it must be said—I didn't believe her. Nor was I, who could barely dog-paddle for five minutes, interested in being sucked out to sea and drowned so that I could be reborn in a year's time. But in my defense, I didn't believe in the tidal wave, either. Sure, there had been a big one in 1946, but everyone knew there were also some pretty small ones and a lot of false alarms. We were safe. Though Mama was always worried about the end of the world, the truth was we lived in a town so slow you couldn't get hit by a car if you tried, and the juxtaposition of Mama's fear and our safety made it even harder to conceive of danger. There were none of the drugs or thieves or dark alleys I would come to dread in New York City. In our early-morning-rising town, almost all the houses were dark by ten p.m.

I could allow Kei her silly fantasy. We could spend an hour hanging around the soda fountain and maybe get some ice cream. And when no big waves came in, she would remember I stood by her. That we were together, I thought then, was the most important thing.

After a few hours on the beach, we stopped at Kress to call Mama so she wouldn't worry. Kei told her Mr. Torres had brought some adobo to the beach and that he'd bring us home later in his car. Although I couldn't hear Mama's side of the conversation, I didn't expect her to agree. She would know nothing about the tidal wave, but she'd never let us stay out unsupervised before, and with Arnie and his truck on the other side of the island, there was little chance of it that day.

Kei hung up, then dug around for some change. "We can get... some sour lemon," she said, seeing how few coins she had. "Want some?"

"What did she say?"

Kei gave me a thumbs-up. "You like? Hah?"

I ignored the touch of pidgin in her voice, and we walked along Front Street until we reached the store where the big mayonnaise jars of sour and salted lemons stood on the stairs in the sun. Kei handed over a couple of pennies and we plucked the brown, crusted rinds of fruit from the liquid, licking our fingers as we headed back toward the bandstand on the edge of the bay. It was already late in the afternoon. While I tore the skin off with my teeth—I could never eat the inside, where the seeds were, but the skin was soft and vaguely sweet—I wondered why Mama had let us stay out. It had to have been the telephone itself, I decided—Mama had just wanted to hang up as quickly as she could. Arnie had gotten it so we weren't still living in the dark ages. I remembered the first time Mama picked up the receiver and heard talking—we had a party line at first, so nothing was private, really, and you had to ask the other people to get off if you needed to make a call. I could see the words she must have been hearing chase themselves across her face, making her cheeks flare and her eyes race to follow them: For a split second, the spirit world had finally found her. Even though we had gotten a private line soon enough, she hated to answer it, and she could never get off fast enough.

A steady stream of small boats began docking at the fish market to unload their catches. The ocean was a shivering sapphire, as placid as always.

"What about names?" I asked. "What should our new names be?"

I couldn't decide whether to come back as Sandra or Donna, trying them both on with different poses and imagining the corresponding hairdos. Kei chose Marilyn. From there, we moved on to whether we should have any other sisters and brothers. Brothers were gross and sweaty, but oddly thrilling; sisters we weren't much interested in. As we waited for the wave, the baseball game in the park came to its natural close: little boys wilting in the sun in the last inning. I tried to determine if there were actually more people than usual in the streets, their cars packed, escaping to higher ground, but Kei didn't notice anything.

The lapping waves remained as safe and inviting as every other Sunday. Kei's disappointment grew. I was bored with the game of turning regular people heading home into some whispered evacuation. Plus, I was hungry.

"How long did Mama say we could stay?" I knew Kei would insist on using every last possible second, so I would have to be persuasive to bring this adventure to an early close.

"I thought..." Kei sighed, looking out at the horizon, as if the wave might still appear. "I was just hoping."

It took a minute to sink in. Then, of course, I understood. "What did Mama say, exactly?"

Kei wouldn't look at me.

"You lied!"

"I didn't—"

"What did she say?"

"She didn't answer. She must have been in the garden."

I was beside myself. Our mother was alone, worried. Had she left the house to search for us? Would it be empty when we got home? What if she had wandered away, then fallen and lost consciousness? Mama hadn't fainted for years, thanks to Arnie's cure of less work, more sleep, and red meat, but I knew that her sickness had just gone into hiding, and that the next time she might never get up. That was Kei's fault. Everything was Kei's fault. She was jealous, and spiteful. How could I have thought for a moment that she wanted to be with me? "I *knew* she wouldn't give us permission. I knew it! Why do you have to drag me into your idiotic stories?"

"I thought—"

"It's bad enough you're always in trouble. Someday Mama's going to have a heart attack and it'll be all your fault."

Was I more angry or afraid? It had suddenly hit me: What if there really had been a tidal wave? Kei could have killed us. I imagined Mama getting that news. *Your daughters are dead, Mrs. Swanson. Sucked out to sea, not even a body to bury*. I wanted to shake Kei until her teeth rattled. With all her trouble at school, the almost suspensions, and the hushed conversations in the night, was it too much to ask Kei to consider anyone else for a single second? "Leave me out of your stupid stories. If you want to kill yourself, go ahead. But I'm going home."

"Hana!"

But at that moment, Kei was not my concern. Mama hadn't answered the phone. She didn't know where we were. With Arnie gone, she could be in danger and it would be *our* fault, not Kei's alone. "I don't care,"

I said, ignoring the tears that sprang up, so fast and so unfairly, in Kei's eyes. We were missing, and I could see Mama falling. I could see her bleeding in a spray of broken glass. It was my mother I was frantic over as I lashed out. "Throw yourself in the ocean if you want to. Be a boy; leave us. It's better for Mama anyway if she doesn't have to deal with you."

Mama was in the kitchen when we got back. I ran into the house, grumbling about how the sampans were so full we couldn't get on one and had to walk, and there she was. Alive. Seemingly, she hadn't even noticed the time. I surprised her with a hug, while Kei muttered something about Mr. Torres. Kei would surely have contradicted whatever I said, so I put my hand on Mama's back and drew her over to the pune'e, offering to chop all the vegetables for dinner and clean up, too. She'd been doing laundry since early morning and she had burned her arms twice on the iron, so she was happy to let me pamper her. Kei could have helped, given that the whole senseless afternoon was her fault, but she just glared at me and claimed she had a history project to finish and there was no way for me to contradict her without getting us both in trouble.

After dinner, though, I was glad for Kei's homework excuses. Mama had a stack of mending in the front room. Helping people get an extra year out of their clothing was good business—we got a dollar an hour for it—so I sat down to help her rip out waistbands, let seams, and even add gussets.

"Good girl," she said, patting my hand after I held up my work for her inspection. I allowed myself a burst of pride. With Kei, Mama would often have to pull the stitches out. But Kei wasn't joining us. Arnie wasn't home. It was just Mama and me, alone together for the first time since I could remember.

The absence of sound closed in around us, as if silence was a vacuum that shrank the space and pulled everything closer: There were no ticking clocks, no radios playing, no kids shouting in the already darkened street, almost no cars. There must have been cicadas or birds competing with the soft rustling of fabric, but I couldn't hear them. Without Arnie's loud stories about the latest guy who let go of the hammer when he was swinging it and sent it sailing through the window behind him, the night was calm and the near tragedy of the afternoon felt erased as I mirrored Mama's quiet presence. I knew if I spoke, her startled look would only remind me she had forgotten I was there. It was enough to help her, that was what I told myself; enough to leave her with my perfect stitches. That night, the sweet, clean smell of my mother's skin assured me she was not at all afraid of anything to come.

The first siren, when it sounded, was a soft wind-up whine from far enough away we might not have heard it on a regular night. I must have been half-listening, because once it registered, it became a mosquito that wouldn't leave me alone. My first reaction was to talk over it: If I could keep Mama from hearing it, then it wouldn't exist.

"So," I blurted, "how was your day?"

Before Mama could decide what to say to this casual and entirely misplaced small talk, Kei bounded out of our bedroom.

"Did you hear that? See, it's true!"

Mama reassigned her confusion from me to Kei and then to the siren. I watched it enter her.

"Air raid." Mama whispered the words, completely white.

"No, it's not—it's not an air raid, Mama." We did have air raid tests in those days, and tsunami tests, though it was usually the curfew sirens we heard at night. But this one, of them all, hung in the air.

"It's just a test," Kei said hurriedly. "Don't worry. I mean, it's nothing to worry about."

Kei's assurances surprised me, but I was also hedging. I hadn't forgotten how the two of us had made up stupid names for ourselves while we waited for death all afternoon. A look flashed between us—*I told you so*—but who initiated it? For all my anger at Kei, I was more concerned about the red blotches that were beginning to appear on Mama's blanched face.

"It's just a test," I repeated. I wasn't lying, exactly. Just trying to keep her from falling. If it was a tidal wave, there would be more sirens, and we could decide what to tell her then.

"*Pikadon*," she whispered.

"No it's..." I didn't know what she had said. "It's not an air raid. Don't worry." I grabbed her hand.

Where was Arnie? It was a wish more than a question. We were too high above sea level and far from the waterfront for any need to evacuate, but that had never been the biggest danger we faced. And what if Kei and I *did* have to take Mama somewhere in the dark of the night during an emergency? Where would we go? Arnie would know, but he was on the other side of the island.

Kei would know.

I understood that suddenly as I looked at Mama, who needed to be rescued, and faced the truth that I needed the same thing. Kei would have to be the one to save us, and I realized, with a shock, that I trusted her to do it. I don't know if I hated or was comforted by that thought.

The siren had stopped, and once again the night was so quiet it was hard for any of us to believe what we had actually heard.

"I'm going to bed," Kei declared.

Maybe the siren was just a warning, I assured myself. Maybe it was a test for something that I had never bothered to notice. That far from shore, a tidal wave seemed like a fantasy. But whatever was true, there would be no more mending that night. With Arnie gone, and Mama agitated and asking for him, I took her into her bedroom like I used to do when we were younger and tucked her into bed. It was a game we used to play, pretending to switch places, *I'll be the mommy and you be the girl*, and if it bothered me that it seemed much less like a game now, it still worked.

I had no time to wonder or worry over Kei's withdrawal. Later, lying in bed in the room I shared with Kei, alert in case Mama got up and started fretting around the house, I was also attuned to Kei's quick breathing. I was waiting for our dark conversations.

"What are we going to do?"

It was the only thought chasing itself through my head. Though the fight we had earlier still hung between us, night was always different. In the dark, we decided not to "see" our daytime problems. That was when we talked, though sometimes we didn't talk *to* each other as much as out loud, letting our voices float between us, but still in each other's presence. Night was a time when either one of us could confess anything, without judgment, and be released. We were each other's record keepers, and it was important to have a record. However strange it may seem to someone else, the events of our lives had no weight, and might never have happened, until they were offered to the other as a silent witness.

But that night, Kei didn't answer. I was no longer thinking about how she had tried to trick me, or about her strange obsession with the wave. My worry was for Mama. I assumed Kei's was, too, and that it was guilt that kept her from answering me. First, she thrashed and muttered as if she was having nightmares. Then she quieted—she was trying to make sure I was asleep. For a long time, it was just me and Kei's smothering silence. Then I heard her sit up. I must have thought she was going to the bathroom. My back was to her bed. I wasn't to blame; that was what I tried to tell myself later. I didn't hear her get dressed. Nor did my carefully closed eyes see her creeping to the door.

1 9 4 5

Lillie slid the outer door shut and called out from the *genkan*.

—Otou-sama, *tadaima*!

She imagined Donald's father twisting in bed at the sound of her footsteps, readying the curses he had been building all day to spew on her.

—Worthless girl. You could bring me a bit of rice.

—How can a son show such disrespect for his father? How could he leave me here with you?

Her father-in-law's bitterness had grown worse since Donald fled with Toshi. A real man, he complained, would not hide behind his child. His son should be striking a blow against America, his enemy, a country that stole all he owned, arrested and tortured him, then killed his wife after he was dragged away, unable to defend her. Lillie had heard these stories every day, tossed in Tateishi-sama's mouth like small stones in a fast-moving river. She knew his version, and her own, and in the end there was not as much difference between them as she wished.

Would the old man spit at Hanako, too, when she walked in, or would he be stunned into silence by a stranger in his house? *Don't tell him*, Hanako had said. *I want to see his old coot's face when it's me who comes to give him his baby food.*

It was Hanako's suggestion that Lillie go to the country to see Toshi. Lillie had had no word from Donald since they left, and she couldn't bear to be away from her boy any longer. Besides, the doctors were saying that her father-in-law was dying. He might only have a few days more.

Tateishi-sama had hated her as long as he'd known her, but Lillie knew Donald would surely want to pay his last respects.

Hanako insisted Lillie go. She would cover Lillie's shift at the castle, spinning some story about how Lillie was deathly, if temporarily, ill. "We'll switch places," Hanako told her. "It's just for a day." Lillie felt the fierce pull of her son. She hadn't seen him in so long. But it was Hanako's help that assured her it was possible: Lillie would, indeed, be gone only one day.

—Otou-sama?

She called again, knowing he could still hear and that when she stepped out of the genkan he would be there smack in the middle of the main room, coiled in the sheet on his futon, where he had been for months. Donald had moved him there, insisting the old man wouldn't feel so lonely as long as he could watch her prepare the food and clean up afterward. Before Donald left with Toshi, the three of them slept in the small room, which she had to herself now. So much space compared to the places she'd lived in since she left the farm. She'd thought about inviting Hanako to live here with her, to get her out of the tiny room she shared with two other girls and give the friends an opportunity to talk in more than spurts and whispers. If Donald was in a good mood when she saw him today, she might ask his permission, but it would depend on what Hanako wanted.

She would raise the subject with Hanako when she returned.

Lillie had pitched her voice low the second time she called out so she wouldn't wake her father-in-law if he was sleeping. Hearing nothing, she slipped on a pair of soft house slippers and moved quietly into the main room. The old man's eyes were closed and his breathing shallow, though still steady. He had taken to dropping off in midsentence recently, dozing against his will even when he was trying to ask for something. He'd also acquired a thin, sour smell, which Lillie had worked hard to scrub away, even loosening the long length of fabric—now yellow and brown with age—that he still used to keep the tin box of his wife's ashes strapped to his chest. He had wept when she lifted the box, cursed her as much out of rage as sorrow. If he'd remembered how she had cared for his wife, how she had cleaned her and soothed her and combed her hair when she was ill, he might not be so irate that Lillie would dare to touch her now. But perhaps it was the separation that undid him, the breath of air that came between him and his wife's ashes, even for a moment, when Lillie untied the tin box.

For all her efforts, though, the smell remained. It seemed to be coming, not from the old man's private joints and crevices, but from inside.

Was it better to postpone her trip in case he was dying quickly now, or try to bring Donald home to say good-bye?

Hanako would say, "Go." It was her last word to Lillie when they parted this morning. She had pressed a small bean cake into Lillie's hand. "For Toshi," Hanako said, and hugged her hard. Lillie stared at the round confection as if she had never seen one, and indeed the first and last time was when she was still in Los Angeles, in Little Tokyo. Only Hanako could get her hands on something so precious. In fact, the most precious gift she'd received was also from Hanako: a photograph of her son.

Lillie carried it everywhere with her, took it out to look at it hundreds of times a day. It was taken just a few days after she started working at the castle. A group of journalists were coming in to take propaganda photos, and Lillie and all the other translators who were mothers were asked to bring their children in that day for the shoot. The pictures were to prove that Japan was winning the war, that it was a place of family and safety, and that the Emperor loved children so much that he would let them play on the grass in the castle garden while their mothers were working. But as soon as the journalists left, the children were hustled off into a corner to wait for their mothers to be done with their shifts. Lillie never expected to see the images. But somehow, Hanako had charmed one of the photographers into bringing her a copy of a picture of Toshi, wearing the sailor outfit they had dressed him in for the occasion, in the moment when he had reached up to ask Lillie to swing him into her arms.

Now Lillie traced the edge of the image, remembering. He was the only little boy with hair, a helicopter of it; the rest of them had just shadows on their shaved heads. It was proof that she was too American, and the only fight with Donald that she'd ever won. She wondered now if that was how Hanako had gotten the photo, if it was because her son was unusable. Embarrassing to the Emperor, who only liked good Japanese.

Hanako would just have shrugged if Lillie asked her. Just like she would shrug now about the old man Lillie was leaving in her care. *It's not like I can't roll some dead guy up in a sheet if I need to*, she would say. *Hell, he won't smell any worse by the time you get home.*

Hanako's voice was still in Lillie's head, whispering to her, as she tucked Toshi's picture back into the fold of her kimono and then stooped to pick up the indigo blue bowl her mother had given her so long ago. She washed her father-in-law's soup out of it and left it on the dish rack. The house was in order. Hanako would show up this evening to feed Tateishi-sama, and Lillie didn't want to make a bad impression. Then she closed the door again and began walking, through the hot August morning, to the train.

Lillie knew that Donald had taken Toshi to his family's house, north of the city, where they'd gone first when they arrived. She hadn't been back since, but the journey there remained fresh in her mind, imprinted as it was in the first months before the rest of Japan had overlapped it, and she followed her memory easily from the train station, past the first five turns and to the right until at last she came to a place she recognized. Or thought she did. The cherry tree near the front door had been stripped of its leaves, but she was sure she recognized the arrangement of rocks along the walk.

The windows were shuttered. The heavy wooden *amado* doors stood closed in the heat of the summer when most buildings had peeled back even their thin shoji screens to let the air circulate as much as possible. When she knocked, there was no sound, not even an echo. No one came to the door. She knew then, but still, she pounded on the doors and called Toshi's name. It came to her that perhaps this was a joke. Perhaps they were hiding from her, preparing to surprise her to make their reunion better, even though of course they had no idea she was coming. Lillie let herself imagine Toshi's face, lit with laughter, when she finally discovered him in hiding, even as she found herself sagging against the door. A truth was tiptoeing toward her, one she was not prepared to receive.

That was when the woman appeared. She came not from that house but the one next door, an older woman who looked much like Donald's mother had. Was she one of the family around them when Lillie and Donald arrived? Everyone looked so much older now.

—Aunt...

—Shame on you!

Lillie tried to explain who she was, stumbling over her honorifics, knowing she would need to sound the right note to get help. The woman's face twisted.

—Go away. There is no one.

—But, then, where? Do you know where they are?

—Gone. Never here. Go away, stupid girl.

The woman was lying. They were here, or had been. If Lillie had any doubt about being in the right place, it was gone as soon as she heard the epithet.

—He's my son. My husband. Please, I have news.

The woman was emboldened by her pleading.

—You are nothing.

—Tateishi is dying. There's not much time.

Did the so-called neighbor flinch at Lillie's words? The woman barely paused long enough to hear them. "No one," she said, the momentum of her outrage carrying her over the news. "Go away."

—No.

If he had been there. If either of them had. If the house hadn't been so strangely unused in a time of shortages everywhere, Lillie might have obeyed. But she had to find Toshi. She forced open the doors and went through every room, checking for a sign of her son, pushing the neighbor off when she tried to stop her. "It's *my* house. *My* family," Lillie said, as defiant as Hanako would have been if she had been there. By then, she was certain that Donald was on the run again, whether from the military or because he had decided to steal Toshi from her, she didn't know. But this was where he had been heading, and with the woman's insistence that she leave, she was sure he had at least been here, so there had to be a trail.

—Where is he? Where's my son?

The woman followed, berating her, indignant. Maybe it was the speed of the woman's speech, or the fact that she did not want to hear what the woman was saying, but Lillie could not make out a word. With every closet opened, every sliding partition, the search was over quickly. There were not even beds for them to hide under.

The house was empty.

By the time Lillie gave up searching, the whole neighborhood was watching her. Standing in their small yards or peering out their windows, so many heads nodding that she didn't belong there, even as they seemed to know exactly who she was. She stepped outside, her eyes drawn past the gawkers to the closed doors of the houses around her. Had Donald truly left, or was he hiding inside one of them, refusing to emerge even for his own wife?

—Toshi! she screamed. "Toshi, it's Mama!" The words ripped her throat. "Donald, it's me! Your father is dying. Do you hear me? There's no time left. You must come back."

She was airing all their ugly, dirty laundry, but she didn't care. She was American. She could be so crass, especially if there was any chance at all that her son would answer. She wasn't them, and she never would be.

The houses around her echoed back only silence.

That was when Lillie imagined planting herself in the middle of the small patch of yard, waiting motionless like a statue until her husband and son returned. It could take months, she thought. Years. She could become some kind of saint: the mother who never left. The mother who didn't make the wrong decisions, or lose too much. Who didn't fight too hard or not enough. Lillie wanted to turn into a tree, into stone, dissolve into the ether. How much easier it would be to stop, to stay there forever, frozen in time.

Toshi... She felt herself crack.

But when she got back to the train station, she couldn't bring herself to leave, either. Despite how Donald had treated her, she couldn't bear to think of her husband as a human bomb, trying to hug a tank. The smart thing would have been to flee with Toshi, and the only question was to where, and had he made it? If he hadn't... She shuddered to think about her son, orphaned and unfindable in the hands of the military, instead of with Donald's family, no matter how awful that woman had just been to her.

Donald and Toshi *had* to be together. And if they were, perhaps someone here at the train station might know which way they went. A man of military age traveling alone with a young boy wouldn't be a common sight.

No.

She held out Toshi's photo to the station workers and the few, battered travelers who came in to wait for the trains. "Have you seen this little boy?" she asked. They tried to move off in another direction when they saw her coming toward them. There were so many beggars in those days, and even those who weren't begging were out in public in patched clothing, down to their last shoes. Lillie could sometimes get them to glance at the photo if they thought it would help them get away, or if they were stuck at their posts, unable to disappear. It wasn't that she expected anyone to recognize Toshi, or even speak to her, but she couldn't sit on the wooden bench without trying.

A wave of fatigue overwhelmed her each time she heard the whistle of a train. Lillie watched them pull into the station and then go on. There weren't so many, maybe only one or two in each direction. She could no more get up to board one than she could fly.

There was an old peddler selling a few used trinkets on the ground near the station. She had shown the woman Toshi's photo twice already, but when the last train of the day passed and the peddler started putting away her things, she went back one last time. Watching the careful way the woman went about fitting each item into her single wooden box, she suddenly missed her own mother.

Foster mother, Donald would have reminded her, *who never answered your pleas for help*. But Lillie held the fading gold hair in her memory.

The hands that made her quilt. Lillie thought back to their parting: a scene that had almost never left her mind. She hadn't promised to come home, she realized now; she had promised to remember them. And more than that, to remember they loved her.

Now, the possibility of love almost knocked Lillie to her knees.

At the top of the peddler's box, already packed, was a wooden yo-yo. The crude curves splintered on Lillie's fingertips, but she could polish them with sand and stones. Toshi would be three on his next birthday. Whether it was a delusion or her own promise that she would find him, the toy made her feel lighter. She gave the peddler the bean cake Hanako had given her in exchange, thinking the old woman might share it, that she might stay and talk. But the peddler tucked it carefully into the space where the yoyo had been and said good night.

—Please, Lillie said then. "Just look. One more time."

The peddler held Toshi's photo. Lillie stood beside her, drinking in her son's wild black hair and his joyous face as he looked up at her. She remembered that white sailor suit with red trim, but even before that, she remembered the soft fat of his knees and elbows, which Japan had melted away. By now, she did not expect that the woman would magically remember him. She just needed a witness. Someone who knew he was loved.

It was a hot night. Once the station had emptied, and the remaining passengers waiting for the morning train had settled onto benches and along walls, Lillie lay down where she could see the stars. She had no concern for herself, what she must look like. It didn't matter. She was entirely alone. The stars were so close, and she looked for a new one, twinkling brightly just as her father had once showed her: that would be a new soul saying good-bye. She knew the stars well, even in that sky, and when none of them called to her, she took comfort in the knowledge that Toshi was surely alive and on earth somewhere, perhaps in Tokyo where the Embassy people had first urged them to go.

She would find him.

Aunt Suzy and Uncle Joe love little children, Hanako had said. *Forget those* inu. *I'll do your shift for you—I'll hold them off. Go get your baby. And when this war is over, we'll all go home.* Lillie held on to her friend's words as an anchor.

It was impossible to sleep.

It was early morning when she heard the first train. It was heading south, back to Hiroshima. The sun had pinked the already hot sky, and more travelers filled the waiting area. She thought about staying, continuing to search—you never knew who might have seen Donald— but what could she do now, even if she got a lead? She was already dangerously late—her morning shift was starting; the soldiers would know she wasn't there. Even if she was willing to defy the military, she couldn't leave Hanako and Tateishi-sama waiting. She had too many responsibilities.

She would return. Meanwhile, she reminded herself that Toshi was with his father. He wasn't alone; he wasn't an infant. And he wasn't in Hiroshima, either. She had done what she needed to do to keep him safe. When Donald stopped running, she would find them. So she boarded the train, comforting herself with stealing glances out the windows long after it left the station, until the jolting and the swaying threatened to pull her into sleep. Her eyes were closed and the train was still a few miles away from their destination when she heard an explosion. She thought it was a factory nearby. An accident.

The train slowed. Then it stopped in its tracks.

KEI

It takes two hours for Hana to fall asleep after the tidal wave siren. In your quiet bedroom, as you wait, you imagine diving beneath the waves. Running toward them when they are still all blue and shiny, leaving the pounding white water behind. White water that will dump you on your head and hold you down so long you can't breathe. You practice holding your breath. Swimming until your lungs might explode, until you reach the other side. Where your real family is waiting.

This time, without Hana.

It makes sense, perhaps, to leave her. Hana has always been happy being who she is, being the good one. Hana doesn't have to be Kei.

It's better for Mama anyway if she doesn't have to deal with you.

How could she have said that? That afternoon, for a few hours, you were sisters together, waiting to be saved. Didn't it feel good to know you could be anyone and anything might happen? Wasn't it nice to have nothing to do but watch some barely dressed kids chasing each other over the rocks and pretend their mothers, passing out musubi and teriyaki, were your own? So what if the bay was the same lapping, lazy water as always? It could rise up. Not everything came with advance notice.

Liar, she said.

I didn't—

Lie? Talking all along like she was there on the phone?

You thought she wanted to be there. You thought she felt the same connection and companionship you did. Didn't she miss you, too?

Hadn't you bought her a treat with your own money? Why was her only pleasure in watching you screw up?

It's your fault if she gets sick from this. She's probably going crazy with worry and Arnie isn't even here.

Hana's breathing is even now. She hasn't shifted for more than one hundred waves breaking in your mind. You sit up, test her. You'd wanted to go together, but there's no point in wishing for the moon, as Arnie says. You'll give her what she wants: She'll be happier as the only child. She said as much this afternoon:

Kill yourself.

No one cares about you.

You didn't think there'd be cars on the road this late, but their lights swing around the bends and over the rises. One by one. Easy enough to dodge as long as there's something to hide behind. A couple of the lights catch you and slow down, but you wave them away. One car stops—a woman yelling, "Girl! Little sistah!"—but she's going uphill, in the wrong direction. You duck into a driveway, as if you're home, thanks very much, and wait behind a bush until her engine starts up.

And then there's the truck, pulling in from the side just when you reach the first big intersection. You try to look casual. It's full of boys.

"Like one ride?"

In the cab, some faces you've seen at the beach and at the high school across the street. None of the dog-boys from your school. You know the driver, or know of him. Eddie. Missy's brother. Here he is at last: He has arrived in your story. He is the beginning of the end, but you won't recognize that until it's too late.

You could have made a different choice, but instead you nod. Jump in the back.

Eddie drives you all down to the singing bridge along the waterfront to see the big wave. It's not the lonely, end-of-the-world scene you'd imagined. There are lots of spectators, and a few cops and some other guys acting like everyone has to evacuate, but Eddie is friends with some of them, or cousins, and they leave you alone. Once you've been informed, Eddie says, it's not the cops' fault if you get sucked out to sea.

—What're they going to do, drag us back to bed? Then they'll miss the Big Wave.

You're only a girl, but Eddie keeps an eye on you. A girl with *guts*, he calls you, a word that echoes in your belly. It's thrilling to be out here, but you don't know what to say to these boys, or half of what they are saying to each other, and they know it, too, because they keep laughing. *No worry*, Eddie says when you blush. These boys are trouble, but they're at home on the bridge. They are known. From the looks you are getting, people here know you, too, or maybe they're judging you for the company you're keeping. You're wearing Hana's clothes. You grabbed them by accident in the dark.

You ask Eddie if Missy and his parents are coming, but his response is to snort. "I have no parents."

His gang looks approving.

Do I have parents? you wonder.

On one end of the bridge, a couple of volcano scientists have set up some instruments so they'll be the first to know when the wave is about to arrive. It turns out, it isn't due until midnight.

Time moves slow. Eddie and his gang are starting to roughhouse, shoving each other until they laugh and drift off, looking for something happening or maybe trying to stir it up. There's talk of people gathering on the bridge near the boat harbor on the other side of town where the last big wave ran up and maybe even killed Charlene's grandma, but that's farther than they want to walk.

The natural world has its own clock, Arnie always tells you, and it's much slower than man's. *Think erosion, evolution, continental drift. Be patient.* But Mama's natural world moves in quick time: the life span of new flowers open for the morning and fruit ripening by afternoon. That's the clock you've always been in sync with. It's not easy being out here without her, on tidal wave time.

The two boys with Eddie are gone now. He's alone, scuffling his feet, casting his extra-long arms in an at-loose-ends dance. From here, far enough away that you're not looking up the extra six inches he has on you, you can see he's lighter than a man. Lanky, with elbows and knees that stick out and not a lot of meat on his browned body. You want him to look for you, to notice you're gone. It must be your intensity, the way you're watching him from the corner of your eye, that gets his attention.

Mama has told you it happens that way sometimes. Do you remember? That two people can connect just through their thoughts.

Eddie looks over. Waves, then cups his hands near his mouth. "Hey, Keiko—little Kei-ko!"

You thought he'd come to you. You didn't expect him to yell your name across the bridge for everyone to hear. You scurry toward him, keeping your face turned to the water. He gets it when he sees you: You are in hiding. He says your name again but more softly when you reach him. More just for you. He stands beside you and leans his knees against the guardrail, looking at the ocean. You can tell he likes it that he has something on you, but his smile says of course he'll never use it. It's a secret to share. His smile says you should trust him, but you're not used to trusting. This is the kind of boy Mama has warned you about all your life. The kind who skips class, drives up and down beach run and not just on the weekends. His friends break down classroom doors...

The trade winds off the water chill you, but the length of his body near yours is warm.

"Want a beer, little gutsy Keiko? We got some Luckies in the car."

"I don't—"

"The guys went already. I was looking for you. Waiting. You know. For you."

And now he's trying to guilt you, to pressure you, as Mama would say. You know this. You hated the sip you took once of Arnie's beer and besides, you are waiting for the tidal wave that is going to change everything.

So why is it you want him to stay? To say it again, to sing it the way he does: *Gut-sy lit-tle Kei-ko.*

"Maybe... Later."

He cocks his head. Sees your longing. There's something in his lips that's soft, the way they curl. But then he thinks better about saying anything. He walks backward a couple of steps, still facing you, still with the smile. A space opens between you. It pulls on you, and it's everything you can do to stand there until Eddie turns and walks away.

As you turn your attention back to the wave, to the crush that is coming, you remember something you once heard Arnie say to Mama. *Fearless is good, especially in a girl. At least she'll never be at someone else's mercy.* He said it about you, but was it before this night, or after? Are you fearless now, saying no to Eddie, remembering who you are? Are you fearless facing the wave?

That night on the bridge, with Eddie gone, you feel alone for the first time. But of course, you're not. There are others here waiting for the wave, all of them restless. No one expected this waiting. No one knew what to expect. You, for example, didn't expect the people. People who might know you. People you might want to keep on knowing.

Left on your own, you realize you're not prepared. You snuck out of the house, worried more about the floor creaking than grabbing a coat or a flashlight. The most reliable light, and the radio, are back with the scientists.

Arnie would know what to look for. Like what he said about the volcano: It has to build up, to get from the center of the earth to here. You never know where and when it will explode.

Arnie would know when the story was over and it was time to go home.

"Hey," a man's voice says from behind you. "Girl! Aren't you...aren't you one of Arnie Swanson's little girls? Hey, is he around?"

It's over. He knows who you are. Except it's dark, so he might think you are Hana. You turn around. He's a regular guy in a *palaka* shirt and Bermuda shorts. You don't recognize him.

"I thought he wen—"

"Ah, yeah. No. Yeah, he's—" You look around, pretending to be surprised that Arnie's not exactly where you saw him last. "—here. He was just here."

"Yeah?" He looks around, too, then back at you, waiting for you to produce your stepfather.

"Yeah, I—I better go find him." You stay where you are, in case the man decides to tag along. If he's really looking for Arnie, it would take only minutes for him to figure it out. The bridge is narrow, and not all that long.

"Yeah," he says at last when you don't move. "So. Tell him Ralph's here. I'll be around. Tell him come find me."

It's a trick you learned from Mama, and it works. Silence and stillness. Not rejecting, or trying to get away. Just not offering. It makes the other person feel uncomfortable. They can't wait to leave, even without what they came for.

You should go home, before Mama and Hana find out you are missing. But you still have it in your head that the wave will come. All these people around you are waiting, too. Even if reincarnation was just a childish fantasy, the wave part is real. You're suddenly sure: The wave is the part that will save you.

You keep glancing toward Eddie's car. It's too dark to see whether the boys are still here. Of course, a tidal wave doesn't come on demand. It's traveling from far away, getting bigger. The bigger the better for your purposes. *Let nature take her time.*

The scientists are talking about how there's some water on Banyan Drive. Not a crest, a breaking tube as you imagine, more like a bathtub overflowing with a puddle as the result. You sit on the edge of their conversation, hoping for more, but the radio is saying the arrival time has been pushed back. If the wave is coming at all.

"They got three feet in Tahiti. That's about what we got here. And what was 'fifty-seven? 'Bout three feet then, too?"

If this is all there is, if this is all the wave adds up to, then you're in big trouble, you realize. In the cold reality that you actually live in, you snuck out of the house, people have seen you, and now you are caught.

"There she is! Arnie's little girl. Is he back, doll? Which one are you, anyway?"

It's Ralph again, with yet another guy. How can there be so many people who know Arnie, and why are they all looking for you?

His question rouses the scientists' attention.

"I thought that's who she was," one of them says. "What's he doing bringing his kid down here? And where is he?'"

Which one are you?

If you're not in trouble, Hana will be. You should have known this would happen. The town's too small. Why didn't it occur to you? It didn't occur to you to bring a flashlight, always Arnie's first line of defense. But what really didn't occur to you is that the tidal wave might be so small there would be an *after* to live through, with all its consequences.

What a fool you have been with your silly stories! You could see only up to the wave's arrival.

You are fading out of the light, away from Ralph and the scientists. If you go home now, if you can sneak in without waking Mama, maybe you can talk your way out of this one. Nothing's sure. Maybe none of these guys will ever mention that they saw you, and if they do, you can just pretend.

You need to get home and back into bed before anyone else sees you. It'll take you an hour walking uphill if you have to keep ducking to avoid the cars. You start up the smaller road that runs along the river. You're an idiot, just like Hana said. She was right, as always. It was the stupid, nonsensical fantasy of a stupid, nonsensical girl who doesn't know how to live in the real world. Now it's midnight on the day that will be known as the day the tidal wave never came and you are in so much trouble. You have so far to walk and the road is so steep.

Behind you, the bridge you left: less than a man's height off the river. The next one up the hill is the rainbow bridge. Concrete, arching between the trees and off the water maybe fifty or even a hundred feet. That's what it feels like, anyway. There are people on this bridge, too, milling around, as bored and gullible as the ones you were waiting with.

You are pretty sure no one notices you as you cross the street. It's so late. Home seems impossible, and already you just want to curl up under a tree and sleep. Or just wake up in bed and have this all be a nightmare. But it's long after midnight, and that is even more of a fantasy than your dreams of reincarnation. Of being the one who could finally slow down enough to ask or wait or trust.

Your dream of waking up not-Kei.

You keep walking. So tired. To the center of your bones. Should you sit down? Go back to one of the main streets to hitch a ride? That's when the shouting starts. The screams. It's coming from town, and also from the rainbow bridge right beside you. You run toward the bridge, tripping on the concrete curb just as you reach it and start falling. Your leg and one hand and arm scrape, always scraping, as you go down.

No one helps you up. Everyone is jammed on one side, looking down, beyond town, at the bay. You push your way to the edge. From where you are, the hooting from the bridge you just left below carries.

"What's going on?" Your eyes are adjusting in the patches of light from the handheld lanterns, the flashlights, and the streetlights.

There are policemen here, or at least there's one, trying to get everyone to leave. "We gotta evacuate, come on, everybody, let's go!" The people around you are shifting, not leaving. You are so high above the water, no one is really in danger here. You press yourself against the rail, bending your knees so you can't be knocked over by the people around you. The lower bridge looks the same.

"What's happening?"

The two men on either side of you jump all over each other now to answer. "Front Street's flooded!"

"It wen ova' da seawall!"

You can't see much from here, especially not the seawall, which is a long curve of twenty-ton boulders far out in the bay. You're trying to see the bandstand you and Hana sat in this afternoon. It's close to the shore; it would be the first to get hit. You can't make out the gray outline of the octagonal roof, but maybe the ground around it is glinting with water? Maybe the ground is higher, or the water is, you can't be sure. The ocean is its usual dark self, sleeping on the other side of the streetlights. There are no huge white breakers signaling a big tidal wave.

"Hooo—" someone next to you breathes out. "Look da water."

He's not pointing at the ocean, but at the river far below you. From where you are, the bridge looks like it's rising. The lower bridge, too, lifting up, away from the river. And then you realize: The water is dropping.

The first Chinese brother held the sea in his mouth—isn't that the way Mama told it?—and all the little children ran out to gather fish.

You are running, heading back down the hill to the bay.

HANA

Sometimes, at night, I see myself. The scenery changes, the people; sometimes it's Bree I'm talking to, sometimes Detective Lynch, or an ever-changing doctor in a white coat. It's my sense of purpose that stays the same, my need to pick a direction as if forward motion can restore certainty in a world I otherwise could not bear. I have been diligent. I have sacrificed. I have chipped away at my own silences and faced down memories I hoped never to revisit. I have done everything for Kei that I am certain I would have wanted for myself.

I am surrounded by history. I relive every episode that comes to me, knowing that even if they never happened, they are becoming real. As wrong as they seem, there is truth in them. But with every memory I resurrect, there is another possibility: that I have been wrong about how things happened, and who is to blame for them.

The morning after the tidal wave warning, I awoke to Arnie dragging the covers off me in a panic. He yanked the blanket off Kei's bed next, and then the sheets. I felt a chill through my pajamas as he grabbed me by the shoulders and pulled me standing, as if I might be lying on whatever he was looking for.

Then he was gone, checking the bathroom, the kitchen. Mama stood in the doorway, struggling to get her arms into her robe. That was when I looked for the pile of clothes I'd laid out for the morning, only to see Kei's pile alone on our single chest of drawers.

Kei was gone.

"Where is she? Where's your sister?"

This wasn't my fault. That was my first reaction. The siren never sounded again; I didn't hear Kei leave. Yesterday, wasn't it all just silliness? Sandy, Donna, Marilyn. Kei's dreams of *return*.

I wanted to ask what happened, but I was too afraid of the answer. Or rather, Arnie was the answer, one I didn't want: He was here when he was supposed to be gone for three days. He said he knew we were in trouble when he heard it on the radio. He *felt it in his bones*.

Mama was already getting into the truck in her bathrobe. I grabbed Kei's clothes and put them on. She'd be wearing my dark blue skirt and my lavender blouse. The thought came to me: *That's how we'll recognize her body.* I pushed it out of my mind. Was I more scared of finding her or of not finding her? I imagined her facedown and broken, lying on the shore.

Days later, Arnie would tell us what it looked like when he returned over the saddle road that sits between the two volcanoes high above our town. Like a giant hand had dragged itself through town, sticking its dirty fingers first down one road then the other, then swinging south and raking everything up with a flat palm. But that ride down the hill was not a time for stories. None of us could think of anything but Kei.

I could see the wave's contour as we drove. We were still far away, and the road wound behind stands of trees, so it was hard to get much more than glimpses of the swathes of brown mud. The bandstand Kei and I sat in just yesterday afternoon was still standing, but it seemed as if the wave had rushed through its open sides and then turned and surged inland through the lowest lying areas. It wasn't until we got closer that I began to understand what I was seeing. Buildings had been picked up and wrapped around trees. Cars lay smashed and twisted like a child balled them up, then threw them.

I pictured Kei right in front of me, just as she looked at the beach the previous afternoon, staring thoughtfully at the horizon, mulling the details of her death. It never occurred to me that my sister would actually try to kill herself. Had she gone down for a lark, expecting to outrun it?

I tried to imagine what she had done, what she was feeling. If something had happened to her, wouldn't I know it? I was her twin.

I warned her, I told myself, but being right didn't change anything. The idea of it smashed me: what she might have done to herself; what she had nearly done to us both.

Mama, too, was beyond speech. As we got to the barricades on Front Street, Arnie pulled over and Mama opened her door before the truck stopped rolling. I jumped out to catch her. She was so frail I could feel her ribs beneath her skin. Arnie passed us, practically bounding toward the sawhorses blocking the road. Maybe we had the same impulse: to protect Mama by knowing what happened first.

The guardsmen and police were torn between keeping the area from being overrun with spectators and potential looters, and fielding the calls on their walkie-talkies for help with discoveries in the wreckage. That was Arnie's opening: He could help. Of course Mama kept right on walking. Arnie whispered that her daughter was missing, but no one would have stopped the local madwoman in her bathrobe, even if she had been alone. It was the way she moved—I will never forget it—both unseeing and purposeful; she walked as you might imagine a sleepwalker would while being drawn through a landscape that isn't there. But that was how I felt, too: As much as we might have squabbled sometimes, I couldn't navigate without my sister. It never occurred to me until that moment what it might truly feel like to be just one.

There were already tractors and bulldozers on the other side of the sawhorses; the farmers had started bringing them in from the plantations as soon as the water receded. This part of town was spared compared to what we'd see later, but it was still a mess. The wave had taken apart the seawall and dropped the boulders into the road. It smashed windows and pulled all the stuff out of the stores. Dresses, skeins of fabric, food, shoes, books, paper, dolls, and furniture—they'd all been tossed out to sea and tossed back, and now they lay tumbled, half buried, in a thick blanket of mud. The shop owners who'd returned were already dragging their ruined merchandise into piles beneath their hanging signs and broken windows, while families were salvaging in the opposite direction:

bringing their belongings *out*. Through the open doorways, I could see the wreckage of all the possessions that had been volleyed into pieces between the walls. There was money on the ground—tens and twenties—but no one was picking it up.

There was a muted quality to the salvage in those first few blocks where the rescue was limited to possessions. Further down—where the bandstand still stood muddy and bowed in its stand of trees—it was hard to believe what we were seeing, or rather what was no longer there. The buildings were flattened, or listing, or had been spun around and smashed into other buildings. Sheets of tin were scattered, along with lumber, like pick-up sticks, and the pavement had peeled off the ground.

But the smell was the worst. The mud was slick and silky and it smelled like the sea. It smelled of dead fish, and also dead cows and chickens, dogs and cats, whole and in pieces. It smelled of broken sewage lines and gas pipes. It crawled up our calves as our feet slipped and sank into it. In my sandals, my ankles scraped on the glinting shards of glass and broken coral and tramp iron, as someone called it—nails and metal shards from the broken buildings—all of it embedded in the iridescent muck. I aimed for the sheets of tin and other pieces of debris that lay suspended in the mud to keep myself from being sucked under.

As the day progressed, I realized the smell was also of dead people. Sixty of them, when the tally was finally done. It took so long to find some of them that they were eventually located by their smell.

But perhaps all that came later. It's hard to remember just the first moments of that first day.

Arnie darted around, listening to the stories and asking about Kei. No one had seen her, but the only people in this area were the searching residents, the relief workers, and the dead. The refugees had gathered at the churches and the schools. The icehouse and the theater were being used as morgues.

It would make sense to split up, to start checking the churches. But there was the question of the morgue, the way the word echoed and the fact that there was a demand for it, such a demand they needed more than one. Morgues. We wouldn't begin there, but starting anywhere was still to begin the slow process of elimination. And once we had exhausted all our possibilities, what then?

Instead, we looked for Kei where we were. It was the same impossible impulse that led Arnie to lift Kei's flat sheets off the bed. She wasn't here, she couldn't be, and yet *here* was where we wanted her, where we demanded that she appear. Here, where we were, not just among the living, but among the saviors.

While Arnie inquired, he lifted things, grabbed what had to be grabbed. Someone threw him some work gloves for the splintered beams. As for me and Mama, we kept moving, bent over, looking for clues in the mud. Kei could not have been buried there, so what were we looking for? I remember picking up an unbroken cola bottle full of mud and sand with its cap still tightly fastened. I remember headless dolls, lonely shoes, open purses. I studied these as if they meant something, as if, if I looked hard enough, I might see back through time, to the arrival of the wave, and know where Kei had gone. Mama kept glancing around, expecting to catch her daughter strolling down what used to be the road. In my mind, I was trying to take back all the words, said and unsaid, that hung between me and Kei, though I knew that would not save either one of us. I was listening for her, and hearing nothing. I was in shock, but also hollow. I let my eyes glaze over the pyramid of three cars tossed on top of each other in the open field as the possibility that I might live even one breath without my sister entered me. Had she really chosen to leave us? Leave me?

Arnie and the emergency crews were clearing a doorway—more like an open wall into the kitchen of a crushed building—when a shout went up. Mama had drifted slightly in the direction of the ocean and I followed, so by the time we figured out they found a body, there was a crowd of people around the building.

It was strange, what we did then. Neither Mama nor I moved. I kept telling myself: It was not my sister, could not be Kei. I wasn't keen to see my first dead body, but it was more than that. For the first time, I understood something about my mother, how she could watch and wait for tragedy because there was no reason to hurry it along. How much better to observe the

rescue workers weave in and out from a distance. The crowd parted first for
the medics; then, when it was clear the person was dead, the salvage team
moved in again, but more gingerly, lifting the wreckage off the body so as
not to bruise it further, then laying the debris carefully to the side. All that
was left then was for the brave ones to volunteer to take the remains to the
icehouse so the salvagers could get back to work.

Mama and I waited out of the way, barely breathing until we heard that
the body was a man's. I don't know how long we had searched for Kei
amid the tractors and cane grabs and push rakes from the sugar plantations, but we stayed on our feet until the body passed. I looked at it,
because my mother seemed incapable of telling me not to. Exposed, it
was soft and purple. It was naked and bruised all over; the wave must
have tossed it like a ball. I could see the legs and arms under the cover
they threw over it. That was oddly shocking: damp black curls springing
off bloated skin.

Mama dropped to her knees. She stayed in that pose, like she could no
longer stand but she couldn't sit, either.

It's been a hard morning, I told myself. *She's fine. She just needs rest.* It
was up to me now. I cleared a space for me and Mama, picking splinters
of glass, wood, and metal out of the crusting mud, tugging at the broken
edge of a deep blue bowl. It was a curved crescent of indigo, nothing
special, but Mama took it from me. She placed it carefully in her lap and
was scrubbing the glaze clean with the edge of her shirt, when she looked
up and gave me a grateful smile.

It was only after she'd finished cleaning the shard of the bowl and had
slipped it in a pocket that she picked up her foot and cradled it in her lap.
I was beside her, too exhausted to pay attention, so at first I didn't notice
the blood running from her ankle to her instep.

Her foot was bare; her sandal strap broken. Although her legs were
brown with mud, the blood was turning black and beginning to color the
ground beneath it.

It was my worst nightmare. Mama was bleeding, badly, and I knew
how hard it was to stop. But she didn't act as if she was injured. She
watched the wound as if it was out of her hands.

"Arnie!" I screamed, and when he didn't answer, either, I ran for him. I could feel my body scrambling. My legs were weak so I cycled them fast, knowing beyond thought and logic that each would only hold me so long; in fact each was failing at that moment. I could see the purple hand on the dead man's body again, swollen like a balloon. The hair on it. The crusted fingernails.

I could see my mother, dying in a river of her too-thin blood.

"Arnie," I whispered, feeling my whole body tremble as I reached him. I knew if I opened my mouth any further I might start screaming and never stop.

This is what it looked like: Arnie bending over Mama, his face so close to hers; he was sitting on the ground, pulling her against him, their heads touching as they both studied her foot. The medics ran over with him. They were cupping her foot gently, friendly, consulting each other as if this injury might have some small chance of ranking as important on a day when their other patients had been dead for hours. All they could do was tell Arnie to take her to the hospital to get it looked at.

A tetanus shot. Antibiotics. Because the blood was flowing fast and freely, the cut might be deeper than it looked.

Arnie tried to help Mama stand. She fought him, trying to sink so he would let her fall, and when he lifted her entirely off the ground with one strong arm, she squirmed, kicking her feet so he couldn't force her to leave. She refused to go without Kei, refused to be the one being cared for. She was instinct. No hesitation. She was back: my former mother who loved us to the point of fainting before Arnie arrived in our lives. Blood flew off her foot and splattered Arnie's leg. His face was still close to hers as he whispered fiercely against her cheek.

"Kei!" she called, twisting her head away from his. "Kei! Kei!" She kept calling my sister's name. Everyone else knew that if Kei had been in this spot when the wave hit she would not be alive, and she certainly wouldn't be lurking in the rubble waiting to be called out. But the hush around Mama was oddly respectful. Arnie put both arms around her and pressed her whole body to him, his mouth in her ear, and then suddenly, even though she continued calling, he stopped shushing her and let her go. She stood unsteadily; then, as we watched, she started hobbling toward the ocean. If we let her continue, she would walk right into the bay, which was dark with sludge but otherwise calm. She was looking for Kei, or maybe making an offering to the God who took her daughter: to take her instead and return her child. She didn't say it out loud; she voiced nothing more than Kei's name, but I could tell from the way she spread her arms and appealed to the sky, the way she kept stumbling, stumbling toward the water.

My mother could not swim. What made her stop then and drop her arms before she reached the now-gentled lapping, and then let Arnie guide her into a waiting pickup? Perhaps it was me, hanging on her, anchoring her with my arms cinched around her legs so she couldn't move, refusing to let go, to let her go on without me. Begging her through my sobs to come to the hospital. I was the one now. The only. And I would let her pull me into the sea if that was what she wanted, but I would not let her leave me.

Please.

KEI

Sound comes before sight. A roar from the darkness. People will say it sounds like a train. It's a rumbling, from a distance and from beneath your feet, too. The ground itself is beginning to shake. There is no wall of water visible. No proud prow of a wave cresting in the belly of the bay. There's nothing to see, yet you are running toward the tidal wave. It's coming, getting louder, but the sound is being overtaken by other sounds.

Cars are racing past you, careening, as they flee from the waterfront, no proper lanes of traffic. One of them veers onto the sidewalk, narrowly missing a post that holds up the second-story awning of a building. And people, too. Where did they come from? You look for Eddie, for his friends, for anyone you recognize from the bridge. But these are not the spectators who have been waiting for the wave. There are children here, and old ladies.

The police were working so hard to empty the streets and the bridges, but the buildings are full of people.

Why are you running toward the bandstand? Before you can get close enough to the bay to see more than a pale shape forming in the darkness, something explodes, like a bomb, somewhere to your right. It lights up the sky, sets off a series of bursts as the buildings spark, greenish and crackling, before going totally black. It runs like a fuse through the town, darkness chasing light, pouncing on it. To your right, in the sudden glare, you see figures crowding in the windows. Then the streetlights are out.

Your eyes are full of the shadows of the explosion. It takes a minute to adjust to the moonlight, a minute full of screaming. The people are running past you now, and in the commotion, you hear advice—"Run, run for your life! Big wave!"—as a base note to another kind of calling. Names.

"Roy! Uncle Roy!"

"Elvin, where are you? Elvin!"

"Etsuko? Etsuko! Call back! We'll come get you."

"Elvin! Elvin!"

"Daddy, help!"

All of them pleas, and no answers.

Can you really hear this, clearly? Or is it only a story you tell? It's a clamor of screams, and sobbing, of the rushing of water and the crack of windows shattering. Water is surging up the road toward you, people on the edge of it. The wave is coming, only marginally slowing as it spreads out into doorways. It twirls like a curious puppy before the doors fall open with the weight of the water.

You expected a wall of water, like a gigantic surfing wave. This is more like the boiling pots of white water in the river, except they're getting bigger.

The water is rising. It has reached through the front row of buildings, threading through them, pulling furniture out the broken windows. Clothes. The buildings are groaning. You can hear snapping, splintering, big things crashing into bigger things, but all you can see are stores' signs rafting along the water's surface, and doors. Stores and houses are spilling into the streets, but the water isn't as much of a hammer as you expected. The walls themselves are standing. The edge of the wave has found itself, hesitating. You are standing on a small rise on the shoulder between the road and the river. The water is approaching your feet.

"Don't let go! No, Georgie-boy, hold her hand. Hold on!"

In front of you, a mother and her three children, all in their pajamas. She is standing on a stepped-up porch, trying to see out to the bay. Her youngest child clings to her hip with his legs. His head is buried in the black hair whipping around her face, his arms tight around her neck, pulling her down on one side. The railing is broken and the water is swirling up her calves but she doesn't seem to understand what's happening. She's urging her other two children out of the building.

No.

In the doorway, a boy, who must be Georgie. He's as tall as his mother's rib cage, and it's his job to hold on to the little girl who is sobbing beside him, her pajama pants wet and clinging to her legs, refusing to leave. She's half his size, but stubborn. She's holding onto the doorway first, and then the windowsill as Georgie tries to pry her off. Hand on, hand off. Hand on. They're in front of you. The water still rising, the woman still looking toward the shore.

You are far from alone. Around you, men who have come down to help—one with a rope ladder, could you use it?—others who have struggled out of the wave. Still, no one else sees Georgie succeed in getting his sister's fingers loose. You watch her float up just a little before she tips and is carried off the porch.

What of the innocents? you once wondered. *What of the children stolen by the wave?* But that was before. Now, you aren't thinking anything at all.

You are in the water, wading toward the girl. It's cold and slimy with something you don't even want to guess at. Your skirt lifts. The swirl around your legs pulls much more strongly than you expected. The little girl is a ball, tumbling. The water is carrying her toward you. You can intercept her if you don't go too deep. But between the rush of the water in, and your haste to get to the girl, whose pajamas have ballooned on her back forcing her face into the water, that is not a clear calculation. Then something big pushes past and the girl's direction shifts. She's off to your left. You need to reach her. You jump.

You've got her. Wet flannel in your hand, but your feet went out from under you and now you, too, are being carried by the wave. You have to fight to keep yourself on the surface, to get the girl turned over, get her face in the air. You are spinning like a top, but she's okay. She is coughing. She is also trying to climb on top of you. Under you go.

Your eyes sting, and the little girl's foot clubs you in the ear. You can't tell which direction is up, except maybe the girl is. Everything you can grab moves with you. You can't hold on. Your lungs spasm and there is water in your mouth and it occurs to you that you may not get to the surface. The little girl needs you, and you don't want to die.

You don't want to die.

The water grabs you like a hand and spins you up again. You surface next to a floating piece of plywood. You've got a breath now. The little girl is screaming for her mother, which is a good sign, but you can no longer focus on any noise, not even one that's shrieking directly into your ear. You are hanging off the wood, throwing up putrid water and trying to breathe. Is it your imagination, or does it seem like the pull of the wave is slowing?

Then something happens, you don't know what, and the wood is ripped away from you as you are swirled into a hedge. You still have the girl in one hand, and the hedge is in the other. The branches won't hold you unless you can get your whole body pushed inside it. The girl's little hands are wrapped in your hair. Her fists hold tight, yanking on you because there's nothing else to do, as you shove yourself into the hedge.

You will find your feet, as the water waits, then sucks back out. You will hear yourself praying, *Oh Lord, hold on,* though you have never prayed before. And when you finally stumble to safety, the solid earth beneath you, you will sit on the grass with Georgie's little sister, and both of you will sob.

Do you remember how Mama used to tell us about Lillie's nightmares when she was a young girl? Lillie dreamed she was drifting alone on a wooden raft in the middle of the ocean, with no light in sight and very far from home. Every night she would wake up screaming for her mother. Finally, one night, Lillie's mother gave her a song to protect her. With it, just when the night was the darkest and Lillie was sure she would never find her way home, an island rose on the horizon, and peeking around it was the sun. On the shore, Lillie could see two girls, hand in hand—the same girls who would someday be her daughters. Look at them. Surely you can see them, standing in a beautiful paradise, a place that could be

Lillie's home? All Lillie had to do was to find a way to get there, so she sang her song, and the two girls reached out their hands, and pulled Lillie all the way across from the other side of the ocean. And then Mama would sing that song, which sounded a lot like church music, just like she did every single night of our childhood before she turned off the light. Sing it, now. Let it pull you back out of the past. Remember why you had to come to get Hana. If you don't wake up soon, you are not the only one who will be lost.

There'll be light, there'll be light,
There'll be light on the other side.
With two girls I love, there is no more night,
There'll be light on the other side.

1945

When the train stopped, they stayed in their seats, and when there was no announcement about the explosion, no movement, the few passengers in the compartment began to look at each other. Then look away. Out the window, Lillie noticed, people were beginning to leave the other cars. A man and his wife, arms around each other, walked directly under her window, heading along the tracks in the direction the train would have taken them. Then there were others, and she wanted to call out—what had they heard? What happened and could they see it? She'd thought it was a bomb first, maybe still burning in a nearby factory, but the others didn't seem afraid. Lillie imagined an accident on the tracks, even a suicide, and wondered if she could wait it out, if she could stay safely in her seat and never have to see the wreckage, the life destroyed.

As more people walked by, the passengers around her got up to leave, and Lillie found herself rising. Better to be with the group heading for the city than to end up alone. Outside, the stream of people was thin but steady. They walked for a long time beside the tracks, passing other train stations. They acknowledged each other only by moving to make room when the clearing narrowed, but no one, not even the children, whispered about what might have happened.

By then, the glow over Hiroshima was unmistakable. August was a hot month, but this was different. The air was scorched, sizzling, rippling everything out of sight.

The black rain had already fallen. The firestorms were sweeping through anything that could still be burned, including people alive and trapped in the rubble. Lillie didn't know this yet. She wouldn't hear these stories until later. Then, she was still walking through her final steps of innocence.

They did not yet know, and they could never have imagined. Still couldn't believe, even when the black ghosts began to approach them. From a distance, the ghosts looked like people, but as they got closer, it became apparent something was wrong. Their hair, for one, puffed and frizzy even in the distance. Their color. From her vantage point, with the sun in her eyes and a strange glow behind them, they seemed to be completely in shadow.

As they got closer, Lillie could see it was their skin that was black. Some of it was burned, exposing white bone; some of it hung off their bodies. What had seemed to be a crowd when she first saw them had whittled, people falling off in the wake of the rest to sit or lie down on the ground. Those who continued walking held their arms floating in front of them like sleepwalkers, maybe to avoid the pain of rubbing raw nerve on raw nerve; maybe—with the instincts of a woman holding her hem off the ground—to keep their skin from dragging since most of them were too deeply in shock, too far beyond feeling.

They didn't even look at the passengers. No one asked a question. No one offered a warning.

It would have been horrifying, if it wasn't so clearly a nightmare.

Sometime, in the future, she would remember screams. She would remember silence. The first sight of the bodies clogging the Yokogawa river, lying like a dam that should have raised the level of the water. You could walk over them, she thought. It was how she understood they were all dead. She would remember questions, whose answers, she already understood, had no power to help her.

What had happened here?

Lillie didn't look for Hanako when she was able to get close enough to the city to skirt the edges. She couldn't get near the castle. Instead, she searched everywhere for Tateishi-sama, even though she knew he could only have been in two places: the house they lived in, which had been engulfed in a huge lake of flames, or the hospital. He was the bedridden one. Her responsibility. Yet she was wandering through streets that she knew he never would have traveled.

She couldn't think.

There was a woman with her head submerged in a drum, her long hair still swaying like seaweed in the murky water. A child huddled blind under his dead mother's arm. *Toshi*, she thought. Thank God he was not in the city. But there were so many tiny bodies. So many people of all sizes. Up close, she could see that those who had worn white clothing with darker patterns had been seared, their skin oozing in wounds that matched the charred, once-dark designs. Their faces blurred, rubbed out. People without eyes. Without ears. Without a nose.

There was no way to recognize anyone, but Lillie was afraid to stop moving—into the city, out of the city, direction didn't matter. Others were doing what she was: searching automatically just to have someplace to go. She couldn't help. She couldn't stop, either. She had seen an older man stop; she had watched the horror hit him. He'd raised his hands high to the sky, calling out for the gods to take him and return his wife instead. She had watched him crumple to the ground and stay there.

Lillie kept going.

She walked the ruined city all day, burning her hands and the soles of her feet through her sandals, before she'd ended up in the hospital. There were bodies lying in the hallways, in the courtyard. And camped outside the front door, more injured, more dying, and others just in shock, with no food and nowhere to go. *Nowhere* was where they all were, she realized. There was no outrunning it. An entire city incinerated by a single bomb.

Her son was a tiny light, in a sea of lights that she'd once believed would be protected. She had believed people had rights, that the good would be rewarded, that life was precious. And fair. But no one was safe. And in the caustic embers of the city, surrounded by the impossible, this truth that she had spent the day eluding finally caught up with her. Her hope guttered out. She sank down against the wall of the building and closed her eyes.

Lillie didn't move again until a young woman woke her. The stranger needed help carrying her father off a wooden cart and onto the ground. Lillie found she could stand. She was alive, and that was more than could be said for most of them. She could help. And so, for days, she did: dressing wounds as she could though it meant shoving her feet between the injured since there were so many of them that there was no room to walk. Her bare, slippered toes searching for the floor, sometimes forced to use their bodies as a wedge to keep her feet from skidding on the dark wet ooze. And each time she touched them, even so gently just to clean them, they screamed if they could, if it was still possible. She was awash in a new knowing, just another shard of what used to be unthinkable: Sometimes, it was better to die.

She had been helping at the hospital two days when she found Hanako in the mass of victims lying on the ground. Lillie was turning an injured young boy, when she nudged the woman's body next to him accidentally and saw the pendant on the ground behind her neck.

Hanako's face had been flattened into a white feathery ash. Her nose and one ear were burned away. Lillie wasn't even sure if Hanako was alive—her eyes were blank sunken sockets and her lips were gone. It seemed cruel that she still had hair, that her blouse was white, though twisted around her and covered with brown stains. She wasn't bandaged, which was a sign that no one had claimed her.

—Hanako.

Her best friend didn't respond to her name, whispered or shouted. Lillie tried to get help, to get salve and bandages, but one of the nurses stopped her. Lillie understood. There were those who could be saved, and then there were the rest. Hanako was beyond help. Lillie only had to look at her to know.

—Rest peacefully, the nurse said softly, before turning away to take some bandages to one of the doctors. It wasn't clear which one of them she was speaking to.

It should have been Lillie who had been there when the bomb dropped. That was why she'd never been able to bring herself to search for Hanako. Whatever injury Hanako suffered should have been hers.

Hanako's face was gone, burned away and then hardened into charcoal—

that was how Lillie knew she must have been looking out the window and directly at the flash. But her body was still pulsing, red and raw, slippery where there was no skin to cover her bones and muscles, and everything slick with pus. Lillie knew better than to try to embrace her. All those nerve endings exposed, unbearable even to feel the floor that was holding them, the rush of air when someone else was moved. No one could imagine what it was like, the moaning and the screaming—people begged to be killed rather than to be turned over. Was Hanako at peace? Lillie chose to think of her that way, rather than trapped so deeply in a body that had lost all its markings.

Peace. How much damage did people do, and how much was done to them, because of what they looked like on the outside? In this war, as Lillie had learned too well, one's face was one's destiny—looking like the enemy, looking like a friend—it made all the difference. How much better not to have one. To be no one. To slide away.

If it wasn't for the pendant, she never would have recognized Hanako. It was a testament to how little anyone could imagine a future that no one had stolen this one thing of value. The chain was fused shut; many of its links melted into each other and embedded in her best friend's neck.

It should have been her.

Rest in peace, Lillie thought. She was crying. That was strange, in all this time, with everything that had happened, she couldn't remember the last time she'd cried. But there was no peace. She hadn't had the chance to say good-bye.

Hanako's chest stopped rising almost immediately, as if she recognized Lillie's cries.

Hanako was gone. Could she still say thank you? Could she say she was sorry? If Hanako could have heard her, she had no idea what she would have said.

—Rest in peace, Lillie whispered. That was as good a wish as anything. Then she grabbed the pendant and broke the chain, tearing her own hands to get it. Hanako's body remained limp as the chain dug more deeply into her seared flesh. Her soul had been released before her pendant was. Lillie stared at the piece of jade in her palm, and then at the chain, still biting into the neck that was once her best friend's, its loose ends brushing the floor.

HANA

If Kei had stayed in bed instead of sneaking out to see the wave, we would've been like so many other little girls whose greatest loss in the Big Wave of 1960 was that their fathers disappeared for a week, coming home only to sleep, smelling of the rotting sea. It was the grown men who were supposed to bear this burden, smoking cigars to blunt the smell when gas masks ran out, operating the cranes that sometimes dredged up a body instead of rubbish. We girls were supposed to be with our mothers, gathering in home-front spirit to make food for the refugees. If my mother was willing to throw herself into the sea in exchange for my sister's life, it was because Kei had gotten it into her head that the tidal wave was some kind of fairy tale. She lived inside her wishful thinking and never once thought of how it might destroy the rest of us. She was too focused on creating her own world.

Since we'd come so far from our own truck and there was no way Mama could walk back, Arnie put Mama and me in a pickup with a guy he knew. My bleeding mother insisted that Arnie stay behind to keep looking. Although the hospital was as good a place as any to search, she believed Arnie would find Kei in the wreckage. I was given my charge: *Hana can do it. Just take her inside and tell them whatever they need to know.* It was a simple order; for the first time since Arnie appeared, it fell to me to protect my mother. I was the one they trusted.

It seemed like everyone in town was at the hospital. Everyone was

either bruised or broken or had family members who were. Either that
or they simply had no home to return to. So they stayed, on the floor, in
the halls, on the lawn around the building. And every one of them had a
story. One man had tried to hang on to a tree trunk as the wave whipped
cars and even a cow at him. The cars bounced off the trunk but the cow
wrapped around, pulling him off the tree as the wave surged inland and
deposited him on a roof. Compared to their injuries, Mama's cut was minor to the triage nurses, who kept pushing her down on the list, and no
one would listen to me when I tried to explain how serious this was for
her. Everyone besides me knew someone in authority, and as I watched
them try to negotiate themselves *up* the list, I realized Arnie wasn't the
odd one for having so many friends: Mama and I were, for being strangers
in our own town. There were plenty of kids there whom I recognized
from school, but the town's shared tragedy didn't bring us together. So I
searched for Kei on my own.

Mama was here, at least. The nurses didn't seem worried. Maybe that
was what put Kei uppermost in my mind. I asked if she had been admitted, of course, but got no useful answer. All I could do was loiter,
periodically, near the hall that led to the examining rooms where someone looking for Kei's family might recognize me. I couldn't bear to think
about the harsh things I had said. Now that she was gone, I would have
done anything to save her. I assured myself that, as her twin, I would
know if she was dead, and I couldn't feel that. But I couldn't feel that she
was still alive, either.

I had found a spot against the wall so Mama had something to lean
on, but time dragged on and her foot kept bleeding, sometimes in a spurt
of bright red, and other times in dark, thicker hiccups. I tried to keep
up with the mess by mopping around the cut with paper towels, but she
wouldn't let me put any pressure on it, and whenever I got too close,
it stimulated more bleeding. I was getting desperate for them to admit
her—but in her muddy bathrobe, she looked just like all the others who
fled on the lip of the wave when it came in, and there was no way for
a thirteen-year-old to make the overworked nurses understand that hers
was a special case. I sat beside her and felt her bones pushing into my

body, like the spines and corners of books settling inside the soft purse of her skin. She was tired. Fading. I needed to do more than hold her hand.

I had been dabbing at her foot with wet paper towels, which soon ran a deep, luxurious red; at one point the sight of my own arms—thick scarlet streams down my wrists—caught me by surprise. As I moved to clean it off, though, I had a better idea. I walked over to the triage desk where, again, I asked about Kei.

The nurse looked at the fresh blood dripping down my arms and off my elbows, onto the Formica.

"Oh my God, girl! What happened to you?"

That was all it took. I led her back to Mama, who was immediately rushed to a cot, but by that time she was too weak to give them her own version of what happened. She waved them at me. *Tell them what they need to know*, Arnie had said, but I never thought about what that meant. There were two doctors, a man and a woman, and so many questions:

When did this happen?

Was she caught in the water?

What did she step on?

Is it still in her foot?

My ploy to get the doctors' attention had worked, and now it was my duty to save her. But I couldn't keep up with the questions about vaccines and tetanus, blood type, and why her blood was so thin. *Anemia*, I said, a word I picked up from Arnie, but I'd had no idea that they would need so much information. Weren't they the doctors? Couldn't they see what was wrong with her by looking? Then they asked about family history:

Was there anything else?

It was then that everything came out: her fear of cuts and how she used to faint all the time when we were younger; her fevers and the red pinpricks on her skin. I told them how she craved water then and drank gallons of it—it was all she wanted from us. I even told them what she said when she was hallucinating. *So much blood everywhere. It won't stop.*

I told them, *She's not supposed to bleed.*

What I didn't say—because I didn't understand it at the time—is this:

My mother had a secret. It's obvious, now, that Mama was not only physically sick. Something had happened to her and she was suffering from it. That's what I can feel in all these memories: the suffering. It was as if she was too close to the veil between our world and the world of spirits; that they could reach her through the gauzy barrier, and sometimes they pulled her to them, to the other side. If that sounds insane, it's the explanation I have come to. Mama was haunted, just as Kei is now. Just as I am, by voices that shouldn't be there and memories that should and a slow accumulation of regret. I have reason to believe that it killed her. It is not random. It is inheritance.

But back then, I was thirteen and I did not believe in spirits. I just told them about the tramp iron because I liked the sound of the words.

I hovered beside Mama, white and still and no longer conscious, hooked up to tubes, and wondered if she could hear me.

Sometime after, Arnie returned. Kei was with him. She was alive. With so many victims and their loved ones crammed in around me, I barely had time to see them approaching before they were on me. I was shaking with adrenaline as Arnie scooped me into a bear hug and asked me how things were going. Just like that, like *Howzit?*, our familiar local greeting; like the morning never happened, and everything was fine. He stank of sweat and the sea, but I held on to him like I couldn't stand. I told him how I'd helped—I'd done my best and I was proud of it; if he had come back even an hour earlier he would have found Mama still on the floor. And he kept that smile on his face and an arm around me as he pulled Kei in with his other arm and faced us both toward Mama.

Were we waiting? What were we waiting for? Arnie was looking at the machines. He seemed heartened by the steady squiggles and the beeps. I thought he'd tell me I'd done well, but maybe I was supposed to assume it.

"I'll just go find a doctor," he said, and then he left Kei and me alone.

Of course, I had seen her first the moment they arrived. We didn't hug because we didn't have to; I could feel her as clear as my heartbeat, singing. But now, we had a chance to step back and welcome each other.

Kei looked tired. My clothes on her body had been wet and dried and she smelled just the way Arnie did, like the bottom of the ocean. She had a cut on her forehead, with a small Band-Aid crisscrossing it to keep it closed, and her face was hollowed by old, dried blood. She looked at me, so grave and different that I almost asked if her name was Marilyn, and when I looked down at myself, I saw that I was covered in blood, too, still red. My arms were streaked with it; it had settled into spiderwebs in the folds of my skin. Kei reached out and touched my cheek and I realized I had blood there, too. She wiped it lightly with her thumb.

I waited for her to tell me what happened. To say where she had been, and that she was sorry. I wanted to hear that she hadn't wanted to hurt me, or Mama, or herself. That she had never really been serious about her crazy idea. Most of all, I would have given anything to hear her tell me that she had wanted me with her, and that she, too, had felt the desolation of leaving me alone.

But by then, she had moved, and she was standing over Mama, who hadn't said a word since the doctors reached her. I had assumed she was still unconscious, but Kei perched lightly on the side of Mama's cot, took her hand, and reached into her slumber. Mama woke. She was dazed, of course, and at first she didn't seem to know who Kei was. Each one of us had been redrawn by the mud and the ruin, and it would take us a while to recognize the new lines and shadings. I watched that happen for Mama when Kei started to cry.

I was the one who had been there for Mama. Kei was the one whose recklessness drove her to the edge, but it was Kei, suddenly, who was in Mama's arms. All the tubes I got for my mother must have given her some strength, because I heard her voice for the first time since we got there, saying Kei's name. Mama clung to Kei's arms, raking her fingers through Kei's ratted hair. Here was her daughter, snatched from certain death and returned.

This time, it would be even longer before Mama got out of bed, but still, it was Kei who was given a seat at Mama's bedside. And that's when it truly hit me: that sharp, partial oneness that I had spent the day suffocating in was not anything Kei would ever feel. She and Mama had each other, just as they did as far back as the day in the garden when Kei got dirt in her eyes and was rewarded with my name. They fit together, these two who survived unknowable dangers. They were the same, and where was I?

Kei tried to speak through her tears, but Mama waved her words away. Then my sister's head was on our mother's shoulder. I was only steps away, but it was as if I had never been there.

Kei was the daughter Mama chose.

It's been eight days. First the twenty-four hours, then the forty-eight. Then Kei's clock was reset by Bree and she got five days of intensive therapy at Eckert. Bree told me that we could have a week, maybe two weeks if I had time to devote to my sister, but Kei has come down with a low-grade fever and Bree is concerned. I can feel the truth. We are running out of time. I have given Kei everything: more stories, more smells and sensations. We have almost caught up; my memories have crept forward to the time when we lost each other. Or maybe the truth is, I have done nothing. Nothing but follow orders, talk to myself, and pretend that I can create the world as I want it. Just like Kei, maybe all of this is wishful thinking.

Again.

It doesn't matter anymore, of course. None of it matters. Nothing, except the fact that I lost my mother, far too young. I left her. Regardless of what she did or didn't do, I punished her for choosing Kei and allowed myself to be punished. After I left for New York, I never called. I never wrote nor came home. I am the one who abandoned my mother. I stayed here in a cave of my own making for so long that there is no one left to find me. And now I will never know her, or know who I am through her.

After a while, habits form. I put up a wall, and no one tried to climb over it. It made life quiet. No friends to betray me. College was simple: The school year was timed so I could dress seasonally in an unobtrusive fashion without revealing an inch of ruined skin. *No wackos here, move on, move on, no rubbernecking.* Over time, I no longer had to hate anyone to get my privacy.

But my wall, for all my bluster, is not so tall. There were plenty of days when a smile would have done it. A sincere question. A handwritten note from my mother. That was why I never responded to any of Arnie's letters. I was waiting. Extending the grace period for my mother.

I still have them. Arnie's little notes. More than twenty over the years: updating me on the new refrigerator; Kei's jewelry business, suggesting I come home for Christmas; forever asking me to write or call my mother. These, I remember them clearly. The waver that took over Arnie's hand, making his script seem weak and uncertain. The Christmas and birthday cards, with the checks I was willing to cash so they would know I was still here—I *am* still here—but even these were written out by Arnie.

There was no day that would have been too late for a letter from my mother.

"We're both getting old. Your mother is still a beauty, compared to my old bones. We'd love to see you."

I can recite them all. Each word, run over and over in my head from the day I got it, even when I tried to shut down my mind.

"Happy to buy your ticket home whenever you want to come. They changed my blood pressure medication, but there's not much to be done about it—it runs in the family."

"I hope you are getting some spring flowers there for your birthday. You know what we have here. Same old thing every day. I do most of the weeding now since your mother can't get out into the garden anymore."

"A little remodeling to report this fall. We moved the bed into the living room. That way, your mother can still see her favorite flowers. Nifty solution, don't you think? She's a fighter."

"Neither one of us is well, Hana. It can't be said any other way. If you can't come home, then please at least call and surprise your mother. She'll be so happy to hear from you."

And then, finally: *"The important thing is, no regrets. Right? Your mother is happy. That's all you need to know. When you get old like us, you want to look back on your life and know that you wouldn't change anything. If you did, you wouldn't be where you are."*

That was the last one. Why hadn't I called her?

Maybe it was the fact that he never wrote the word *cancer*. There was nothing in the cards that said Mama was riddled with it, that she had brain cancer, breast cancer, cancer in her liver and bones, more cancer than any one person could possibly survive. The doctors had never seen anything like it, not in someone so young. There was no point in treatment, which was what I learned only from the neighbors at the funeral; the options were a slow, painful, and expensive death or a suicide, a lovers' pact in the snow. Snow. *Fragile as thread, balanced as a ripple, brief as a blink*, as Arnie once described it. They say death from hypothermia is like drifting off from an overdose of sleeping pills. You slowly lose consciousness. You don't feel it, and you don't know where you are.

What does one do in the end? What do *I* do? What do I do with the truth that I am the one who left my mother to die alone, without me, and with all these empty years? How foolish was I that I thought I could change things, even after Mama and Arnie died; that I could relent a little and answer a letter, that there could still be a day when I could pick up the phone and hear my mother? How I long to hear it: her lilting voice, rising, checking to make sure everything is okay. Even now, with the truth spread out before me, I can imagine it: that next time it rings, I will hear her on the telephone.

I waited too long. It was my fault; I can admit that now. And I am waiting again, and I'm tired. Tired of not sleeping, tired of living a life that has been turned upside down and shaken. What is Kei *doing* in there? I can't help it: I imagine her as willful, in hiding, maybe even watching me, while Bree monitors her vitals and looks more doubtful every day. I have been convinced that our childhood can save Kei, but now I am beginning to appreciate Dr. Shawe's total lack of concern for the blanks in my past. Who would want to relive so many betrayals? Who would choose the endless loop over questions about who did what?

But if the past cannot save either of us, it has given me a gift: a reminder, not of who I am or what happened, but of what I can do. If I can't save my sister, cannot wake her just by willing it, the fact is that there *is* a way for me to find the person who hurt her and bring him to justice.

Justice, like I never had. I know what I have to do.

Shadow Child

KEI

Missy is your new sister. She is the popular one, the beautiful one. She has an air about her...of air. Of drifting off. You see that about her from the very beginning. Would she disappear if you tried to call her back? In that moment of being startled, would her spirit get lost? If that's what you imagined you were—a lost spirit—it is Lillie who Missy reminds you of. Lillie, the girl who appeared out of nowhere, stayed for the stories, and then disappeared.

You have become a talk-story hero: the Red Cross Angel, the girl who stumbled into the intermediate school with the child you snatched from certain death in the Big Wave. You handed out coffee and Band-Aids. You helped make beds for the refugees sent by the fire department. There was even a story in the *Herald* about you. This is who Kei is now. What the town has decided you should be. But you are also the runaway, the girl who got away with sneaking out, who got picked up by Missy's brother. Would Eddie have kept that a secret from his sister? Who knows what *his* stories are about that night?

Arnie brings you together. In those first days of the tidal wave cleanup, he volunteers you for everything a girl can do. People almost pet you when they see you—*Good girl*—and you are getting practice at not shying away. You make people smile, not because your actions that night were so unusual, but because you are so young they can believe that anyone can be a hero. That's how you end up at the river, helping to wash out the fabric from the dry goods stores for the tidal wave sales.

It is a day just for women: mothers and daughters, sisters and aunties. The men drive their flatbeds down into the little valley north of town where the river meets the sea. There, they dump the crusted bolts of fabric amid the keikis who come to greet them. "Pee-u! Pee-u!" The stink of the wave is met with laughter. The children scatter. Then the men themselves are shooed away.

Mama is still in the hospital. The day she will return home, with crutches and medication, a new diet, and a bandage that needs to be changed, is still weeks away. Hana acts as if Mama is dying and won't leave her side. So you are the one Arnie sends to the river with Miss Shima. Your job is simple: to catch the bolts of fabric as they unfurl down the river, spread them out in the shallows, and wash them as best you can. Women are scrubbing, sometimes in pairs or threes. When you are done rinsing, you wring the fabric hard and give it to the children, who grab the ends and run around. Theirs is the fun part. The bolts of flowers lift into parachutes, then fall, bouncing on the little ones standing beneath them. Then the mothers swoop over and help them lay the next ribbon of color on the grass to dry.

When the flocks of kids part, Missy is there. She is crouched alone in the shallows of the stream, trailing a piece of purple plumeria fabric like a long, flowered eel. She is close to the ocean. You are closer. Both of you near the high bridge that takes the road from the top of one side of the valley to the other. She is intent on something far away.

She doesn't notice you, but then the cloth pulls out of Missy's hands and gets taken by the river. You grab it as it slithers toward you. It ripples back on itself, tugging at your arms so you have to step deeper into the water.

Any normal girl would splash over quickly to retrieve her fabric. But Missy just gives you a long, sad look you can't shake. Her onyx eyes seize you, and you wonder if she's remembering the conversation you overheard about Charlene's grandmother tumbling to death in what has now become the "first" wave. And if not, then at least she feels—she *is* feeling—all those lost souls that are the talk of the town.

What *you* can feel is the stillness of Missy's body. And the time it takes her to respond, as if the little ripples of this world are slow to reach her. You can see beyond her popularity. See *her*: profoundly alone. There is a tenderness in that recognition. There is mystery, possibility, and loss. And she can see inside you, like no one ever has except Hana. When she finally moves toward you, she's entranced by her feet scything through the water. That is the beauty of this girl: her otherworldly mystery. In her first, startling question, she confirms everything you feel, and your own aching loneliness:

"When you die, do you think, will you be all alone?"

There are flowers in the river. Flowers in the air and on the grass. After high school, when you start making your jewelry, you will think back to that floating fabric for possible combinations for your charms. But Mama is insistent: You will create only the simplest blossoms, all in a gold-edged white. She wants plumeria, Hana's favorite flower; and pikake, her favorite perfume. She is the one who chooses, and she is the one who gives your store its name. Flower Child. Mama doesn't know the peace-and-love hippies have already claimed the term for your generation, but it wouldn't matter. The name is simple, happy. It lights Mama's drawn face with a secret sparkle.

Your friendship with Missy ignites in that moment. Hangouts, like Kress, are mostly destroyed, so you meet at her house, the house she lives in with her aunt and uncle and, at least in the beginning, with Eddie.

At first, you don't want to see her brother, but you don't want to admit that. She might think you have a crush on him, but what you're really afraid of is that he'll put you down and make you look like a too-little kid. Somehow, you manage to avoid him until the town no longer smells— or perhaps you've all grown used to it. Until the empty spaces along the waterfront are no longer shocking when you walk by. Then one Saturday, he's there in the carport of his uncle's house playing pool with his friends when you come to see Missy.

You pad along the edge of grass that ruts the driveway, approaching sideways. When you get close enough, you can hear him bragging about how he was called on to patrol the waterfront that night.

"First, you know, da police wen deputize me to get everyone evacuated. Den, da fire department wen arrive and I was in charge of going into da buildings to get out da people who was trapped. Oh, an' I was helping da volcano guys get all de'ah gear out, too. When da wave wen come, we went running up da hill so fas'..."

His pidgin is much thicker than you remember. He is hamming it up for his friends. Eddie shoots while he talks, dominating the cue. You have forgotten the lengths you have gone to, to be unnoticed. He is lying. Grandly and cheerfully. Now, you want him to see you there, listening to his lies.

But of course, he has already seen you. And, far from being embarrassed, he has slipped you into his story.

"De'ah was a bunch of us deputized, not jus' me. It was some night. You might'a heard'a one little girl, well, not *so* little, but..." That's when he glances over at you. "We was out da bridge together, and when da scientists wen say da wave was coming, we wen start yelling out de alarm and pounding on da buildings. Get up! Get up! Li'dat."

Two of the boys around the table were in the truck that night, but neither one contradicts him. Missy is rapt, too. You realize she's heard these stories before. You have no idea if she believes them, or if their truth matters to her at all.

Missy is different in the presence of her brother: breakable, and full of longing. You feel that way also. So aware of your skin and edges and flushed blood when he is there. Why don't you see this, about her, about you? Why don't you understand what this means? She is smiling. You are smiling, too. You have been joined with her brother in the biggest thing that's happened in your lives, and what occurs to you is...it would be rude to correct him. Or maybe the truer thing is this: He is a junior in high school. He's on the basketball team that the whole school parades down to the Armory to watch. He's got soft hairs over his lips in his still-baby face, and he's looking at you. Including you.

If you could see into the future, would you save yourself? Would you turn around and walk away? But you have already lingered too long and the chance to step out of the world of Eddie's stories is gone.

At first, Eddie is mostly away, hanging with the latest of his high school girlfriends, all of whom treat you and Missy like little girls even though you're only three years younger. When they're in the house, Missy can't stay away. She is drawn into any room Eddie is in like a magnet. The girlfriends tell her to get lost and Missy tells *them* to suck eggs. Then whichever girl is today's favorite raises a knowing eyebrow at Eddie and he swats at Missy from his still-reclined position—*You like lickins, eh, sistah?* In many ways, it's a relief when Eddie gets into a fight with his uncle and moves out. It is peaceful at Missy's house for the next several years.

In the beginning, you and Missy lie around on her bed together and make up stories about her missing mother. You pretend her mother was sent away to a sanitarium, then you kill off her father with a broken heart. Missy is a magical storyteller, and she tells you all about Eddie, too. How kind he was when they were younger. How every night before bed, he'd bring her a treat and sit with her while she ate it. The treat was usually a candy from his pocket that never got paid for, but the point was, he took care of her. That is the Eddie of her dreams—the Eddie of your dreams, too, since you can almost feel him bending toward her, smoothing her hair as he whispers good night. You never tell her any stories about you and Hana, though, about your years as *two girls* with Mama. Even in those first few months, Missy bristles at the thought of your "other" sister if you even mention Hana. Besides, that world seems so long lost now.

You will teach Missy to cook. In return, she will try to teach you to dance the hula. First, you will watch her. Here she is, bending her knees so deeply her bottom sticks out and sways with a grace that steals your breath. You are hopeless. Missy tries. She arranges your body like a doll's: pushing your shoulders down, floating your fingers, and finally even standing in front of you with her hands on your hips shoving them from side to side. You are growing, already too slippery and tall, your shoulders too broad from swimming. She will have more success teaching you how to smoke. Those days will feel so dangerous: your throats seizing on the years-old tobacco she steals from Eddie; you holding Missy's hair back as she vomits into the toilet bowl. You are finding your edges. Testing your effect on the world. Testing your image inside that world also, since now you are like Arnie: Everyone in town accepts you.

You are two. Instantly. Although you often hang around with Charlene, you and Missy complete each other. You have found the new family you were looking for when you decided to throw yourself into the wave.

The year you and Missy and Hana are seniors yourselves, Eddie comes back into your life.

You have been doing cannonballs with the kids off the rope swing at the Ice Pond, where the freshwater comes in and you can shock yourself in the summer when it gets really hot. You don't remember where Missy was that day. Hula maybe, or just smoking with Charlene at the beach. After three years of being everything to each other, you and Missy have hit a bump. You are the captain of the varsity swim team and Missy is jealous. She didn't mind last year, when you were the star and kept winning everything. But being captain takes too much time, calls for too much responsibility and perfection. *Just like Hana*, she says when she really wants to insult you. As if swimming in a pool and being the valedictorian were in any way the same.

You are on your own, then, and you haven't seen Eddie for so long it takes you a minute to recognize him in his sunglasses, with the thin goatee on his chin. Once you do, you add a little somersault to your cannonball.

He claps.

You pretend to notice him for the first time. "You try."

"Nah."

"Scared?"

You are taunting him from the water, shielding your eyes from the sun. He's staring at you like you're someone new. That's the only way you can explain it—suddenly, you *feel* new. It's the same feeling you had when you first met him, first met Missy: that they could see inside you, and were delighted with whatever it was they saw. But in Eddie's eyes, you can sense the outline of your bra under your T-shirt, the lace on the swell of your breasts under the clinging cotton. You can feel your heart beating against the fabric, blood flooding to the surface of your skin to meet his gaze as you search for words to deflect him. "Missy said you're a jumper."

Eddie raises an eyebrow at the challenge. He unwinds himself and stands up, taking off his hat and sunglasses. That movement dances all the way to his smile. He walks over to the rope and begins his swing. At the top of the arc, his body throws itself forward but too casually to get the height he needs, or too lazy to tuck: He lands flat on his belly in the water. As you laugh, he shoots up sputtering, slinging the water off his hair like a dog, and in two splashing lopes, he grabs you by both shoulders.

"Too low," he gasps, laughing himself.

He isn't embarrassed that you bested him. His hands hold you firm, the heat of his body melting over the ice of your skin. What does he see in you that is so amusing, as if he has just opened a birthday present? And why does it make your face burn to match his heat?

All the Eddies you thought you knew get mixed up in that burning. All the futures you might have had disappear.

"You like jumping, Gutsy Little Keiko? Come with me."

HANA

The next morning, I am sitting at home inside an angle of early sun through my front windows, an unused sketchbook in my lap. Arnie sent a set of five with me when I left for college, and I kept them in the back of my closet behind my winter coat. The sketchbook is oversized, overly optimistic. I have my colored pencils, pastels and crayons and charcoals, too.

Images have power. A power, I am realizing too late, that I have denied myself. Once I stopped drawing my mother's ghosts and started trying to fulfill my school assignments, I lost my creative spark. As a child, I knew the thrill and terror of seeing my emotions spilling onto the page, but in primary school, my teachers were much more concerned about realism and perspective. Technique was the focus of intermediate school art classes, but the assignments kept changing, each one just a hint of where we could take our ideas, delivered so quickly that there was no chance to perfect anything we began. By the time I got to high school, I understood that absent a personal urgency, there was no way for my art to match my own expectations, let alone whatever unfathomable rubric my teachers brought to their grades. I was only adequate. And I was not interested in being adequate, so I stopped.

But to catch the *perpetrator*, I need to find that spark again. I am no Nancy Drew: I don't have the courage to sneak through back alleys searching for bad guys, nor the strength to fight them off. But if stories of our childhood are not enticing to Kei, surely safety must be? If I can tell her that we caught the guy...I can feel the pit in my own belly aching to deliver that news.

Justice and safety. Maybe it's me who needs it. I am afflicted by voices, tormented by a lack of sleep. Will Kei's attacker come back for me, and can I find him before he does? There is something in that bellyache that reminds me: I am the only one who can see his face.

I can draw him myself. I never needed a sketch artist to create a wanted poster; I guess I've known that all along. I am the only witness, and I am an artist: that much my memories assure me of. But my art is risky and unreliable. If I do this, I have to be accurate so the wrong man is not arrested. And accuracy is the obstacle that has always shut me down.

I begin with a pencil. First, I try to capture the shape of his face. Then his nose. I can feel my throat seize every time my pencil falters. I experiment, skipping around and taking shortcuts, imagining what I want to see instead of reproducing what's no longer there. It's more of an exercise for the lead and my eraser, both of which seem to be working equally. The eraser is a nice touch; it blurs the lines, opens new possibilities. But still, he's slipping away. With every mistake, he moves further out of my control. Eight days feels like so long ago, I might never reach him.

No, Hana. You can do this. In high school, I found a way to reach much further back than eight days for the painting I did for the senior art show. Not just to images that I barely remembered, but also to faces I had never seen.

It was shortly after our Home Ec teacher had gotten bored with meat loaf recipes; she had given us some watercolors and declared that the best pictures would go in the year-end show the art department was organizing. Usually that was a showcase for the Honors Art class, but this year, they opened it as a competition, with a first, second, and third prize for seniors. The winners would be exhibited in the public library next door.

I wasn't interested, but I did the assignment. I roughed out a quick impression of the town. Over a black silhouette of buildings along the waterfront, I introduced a heavy yellow fog shadowing the bay. It was a fluid, impromptu image, and it was fun to hang a specter of loneliness over a home where I had never fit in. But it wasn't a great painting. Certainly nothing that would have moved the art teacher, Mr. Kealoha, to grab me one day and ask that I come to the studio to talk to him. And I was right. When he sat me down to suggest that I enter something into the show, the picture he had in front of him was not the watercolor. It was a page out of one of my old monster diaries.

Kei had submitted it, and not as her own work but as mine. I was shocked first, then confused. What was she thinking? Mr. Kealoha said that the energy and naïveté were excellent, but that they would need something bigger, something not rendered in crayon. Oil, he suggested. Or encaustic. How familiar was I with the different media? If I didn't have my own materials, I was welcome to work in the studio with the school's supplies. And, if he could make a suggestion, perhaps an image with more of a narrative would be more compelling. A connection between the figures. A story.

Naïve? At first, I was angry, then embarrassed. I hadn't thought about the diaries in years. Of course, it was naïve; I had drawn it when I was five, six, no more than eight years old. Had Kei been trying to humiliate me? How could she think it was okay to rip a page out of my old sketchbook and flash it all around the school? Or was she trying to help me? What help she'd thought I needed, though, I couldn't conceive of.

Those days, it seemed that I barely knew my sister. It was as if the tidal wave had picked up my family, swung us around, and left us marooned on different shores. We still resembled a family, but Mama was better after her stay in the hospital. Healthier, more vibrant. I stuck around her, still the "good, smart girl," but she didn't need me. Instead, she leaned on Arnie; they entered into some strange, unspoken devotion, and I was cut loose.

As for Kei, she had been reborn in the tidal wave. At first, she was famous, but after that, she had friends. She had a community. She was accepted. Even by Missy, the stuck-up queen of our class. Kei was free, no longer the daughter of crazy Miya Swanson. She still didn't finish half of what she started, and she was just as happy to be known for what she did wrong as what she did right. Her talent for getting boys to like her *for* her mediocre grades helped me understand that the ones who didn't like smart girls were no loss. But for all of her continuing embrace of her identity as the shadow child, it was me who was living in the shadow of my sister. I longed to be seen, to make something of myself. I had a plan to go to college, to get as far away from a town that looked right through me, and the people who seemed to no longer care that I was there.

But suddenly, whatever her reasons, Kei had singled me out.

I had to admit that she hadn't chosen badly. The picture that she had ripped out was, ironically, of three figures: two smaller on each side flanking one in the center almost double the size. They were standing, each in the same posture: legs apart slightly as if taking a step but with no feet; backs hunched identically; both arms slightly raised in front of them and held out, feeling their way without sight. Each figure's head was also bent forward, all at the same angle: their round heads sitting on their necks like marbles and just a topknot of hair falling forward directly off their scalps. They should have been looking ahead, zombie-like, but instead, their faces were swiveled, confronting the viewer directly out of the plane of the paper, their simple features twisted into black-eyed screams. I had drawn the figures in red and yellow crayon, along with some lines of black ink pen, slashing in a suggestion of blood, skin, and shredded clothing.

It wasn't the fact of the trio that caught my eye, because these were Mama's monsters, not us. It was how I had rendered a clear image without an outline of a body to follow. I remembered what Mama used to say about this particular kind of skin-walker when she was hallucinating: that their skin hung in rags off their arms. From the crayon slashes, I couldn't tell if I'd drawn them naked; if the red was raw meat and muscle everywhere, or just blood running from a discrete set of wounds. Though they were almost replicas of each other in posture and color, the figures were not a family. I could see, even now, the complete isolation of each one.

I heard my *yes* before I understood that I would do it. The page had squeezed my heart, and even the ease of the watercolor of the waterfront urged me to find my creative voice again. I was thinking as an artist, not a daughter, when I accepted Mr. Kealoha's offer to do it in the department's studio. But I didn't want anyone to know I was painting, in case I changed my mind or failed. Thankfully, I already had class scheduled during Honors Art, so he agreed to let me come by after school, when no one else wanted to be there. As for Kei, I didn't know what to say to her, so I settled on saying nothing at all.

I set up a canvas and an easel, but I didn't know where to start. What did he mean, a narrative? Despite the echoes between the three figures from my diary, Mama's ghosts never inhabited a scene. I tried sketching lightly in pencil to locate different elements and decide how they would interact with each other, but I ran into the same problem of control that I'd been having since middle school. I decided to work small at first, to try out some ideas in a sketchbook before I committed to the paint, but I spent most of my time tearing up the paper I had barely started on. I spent more than a week with nothing to show for my efforts except some pointed questions from Arnie about where I was spending my afternoons. I didn't think of what I was doing as dangerous then. Time was surging by me, running out, and I was struggling to find my voice. I had no choice but to return to the source: If I was going to draw anything halfway important, I needed to pull one of the monster diaries out from the carton under my bed and study it. A narrative. How had I ever put Mama's monsters together on a page?

I could see Mama again, in her night garden. She was lying in the dirt, as if dead, beneath drowsy but plentiful stars. How old was I? Maybe three or four. I could hear myself yelling, my screams billowing into the night air. Within moments, Kei was in sight, dodging green onions, tomatoes, and nasturtiums, jumping off the terrace walls toward Mama, who had scrambled to her feet in surprise and then was strangely frozen at the sight of her desperate daughter.

When I reached them, Kei was sobbing, still caught in the thrall of an unknown fear. Mama's face held no questions as she looked toward the house for whichever of her monsters might emerge. Maybe it was the violence of her dreams in those days, or the fear in her eyes when a car pulled up to the house, but I understood that my mother was a fugitive. From what, we never knew.

That was all I needed. Fear. With our childish terror racing through my veins, I picked up the largest brush I could find and loaded it with black. I started with a single stroke, then added the next one without thinking. I built it one stroke at a time, surprising myself, changing direction. The black paint slashed across the canvas in some places, but in others, I began to recognize what was emerging. Bodies, naked. I grayed them out with my elbows, smudging the paint so they looked like they'd been rolled in ashes. One figure was standing—a woman, a mother?—but most of the rest were lying in a jumble. Dead. After a while, there were a pile of bodies, then a river. My initial slashes became a bridge. I grabbed another canvas, put it next to the first, and continued. Then I added a third. Now there were people beneath the bridge and on top of it, reaching out for help, reaching out for water. They were thirsty. Crawling, falling into the river of the dead.

It was horrifying, even just with the thrown-back heads I had roughed out and the impossibly twisted limbs. But still, it wasn't enough. I took a much smaller brush, the equivalent of a writing pen, and began to fill in. The faces in the river were contorted, nightmarish, like the diary drawing of the skin-walkers, but I wanted them to have features, too. That was the terrible beauty of the skin-walkers: their faces. I needed to make these people real.

When I was finished, the three panels created a bleak garden of bodies: some blossoming, some trailing, some withered. The juxtaposition of the thick brush and fine lines was arresting: Your eye didn't know whether to be affronted or drawn in. But still there was something missing in the monotone. I looked at the panels for two more days until I knew what to do. Finally, on the afternoon before it was due, I squeezed tubes of red and yellow paint into the bottom of a shallow tray and used my fingers to swirl it loosely together. With every possible combination of the two colors on my fingertips, I picked up my hand and added fire. I raked the pads of my fingers and the scrape of my nails around and sometimes over the ghosts in my river until the entire canvas ran in blood and flame. When it was done, I stood back and started to cry.

People said it was an antiwar protest. Others thought it was supposed to be the Big Wave. I called it *Ghost River*, and it won first prize. The art teacher declared I should give up the idea of college and enroll in a school for fine art. Everyone was talking about it. Everyone but my mother.

I had wanted to surprise her. On the evening the show opened in the library, she still didn't know that I had entered it, let alone that I had won. I took her arm and escorted her over to my painting, approaching it from the side so she could get the full effect at once. Now, I don't know what I was thinking. Mama hadn't fainted in so long. I had been carrying my mother's demons around inside me forever, and they were so familiar that I didn't think they would upset her. The more important thing was to let them out, let them be seen so they could be conquered. After all, that was what the monster diaries had always been for, how Kei and I had exorcised Mama's ghosts together. It wasn't the monsters, but me I wanted her to see: how carefully I had listened to her, how deeply I felt. My heart fluttered as I pointed to the little plaque with a description and my name as the artist. Then, as I looked at her expression, the flutter became bubbles, and the bubbles swallowed each other until there was a pressure in my chest that I could barely breathe around.

Why are you haunting me? It was something she used to say to her ghosts when we were little, and at that moment I heard it clearly in my head. The clouds spread over her eyes and she stuttered—her body stuttered—swaying toward the painting and also away. She looked shocked. She looked at me but also through me, as if there was someone else she expected to see. Was *I* haunting her? What did she see in me?

Neither one of us could get a breath. In her face, I could feel the gut punch of every gruesome detail I had rendered, but wasn't that my point? I had felt all the things that she had, but I had also painted through them. Seeing gave me a control that Mama's invisible ghosts couldn't. It was a way to come out the other side. I never considered that the opposite would be true for her. I could feel the room around me begin to slide as I waited for the splash of pinpricks across her face. I waited to catch her as she started to fall. But instead of fainting, the haze over her expression cleared, and I watched her emotions move through disbelief to dread. My mother of old; there she was, and

I was shredded with remorse. Then, I saw a new specter rise from my mother's eyes, something I had never seen before.

Revulsion.

She spun away from me then, wrapped her arms around herself and turned, looking for the exit. I was trying to jump-start my heart when Arnie reacted, reaching her quickly with his long steps, gathering her into his arms. I watched him whisper into her hair. She clung to him like a buoy, but she didn't faint. How long was it before she could turn to see me and my painting from where she stood? It might have been seconds, but it felt like my entire lifetime.

She didn't move, but that meant she didn't leave, either. She stayed in Arnie's shelter in the middle of the room, her face twisted, rubbing at her arms like there was something on them that she had to shed. Other guests moved between us, but Arnie didn't let her go. She kept looking back and forth from me to the painting, as if I was someone, or something, she hoped never to see again.

I got swept up by Mr. Kealoha then, and the ceremony started. When he announced my first prize, I didn't look out into the audience to see if Mama was still there; I couldn't bear to find her face, nor could I bear to find her gone. He talked for a long time, and I didn't hear any of it, though once I got home, Arnie was full of compliments, mostly about the nice things the art teacher said about my style and my finger painting technique when they gave the award to me. Mama never said a word, and it was just as well.

The painting was effective: That was what I had to hang on to. Art moved people; it disgusted people; it made them do terrible things and fall in love. Mr. Kealoha had said this, and it was true. *Ghost River* had nauseated my mother; her body wanted to expel everything inside her, and she had to keep her jaw locked so her bowels would not end up on the floor. In that horrible moment, I became a true artist. I had proof that I could render something from nothing, something from history and memory, that I could make it so real that someone seeing it might want to throw up.

So real that I vowed never to draw or paint again.

But now, with my sister in a coma, I have no choice. I put my pencil down and pick up a crayon. If no one in their right mind would create a wanted poster in finger paint, I still have my favorite tool. With single, sure strokes, one at a time, I begin to build a face. When I make a mistake, I rip out the page and start over. But with every almost success, I can feel a sense of self that I barely recognize flooding back—my surety and my creative energy.

Kei's attacker begins to take shape.

1945

The train thumped slowly through the patchwork landscape. Hiroshima had been untouched for so long—and then completely obliterated—but the rest of Japan had been burning in random smatterings of bombs for years. Lillie had heard about the fire bombings when she was working as a monitor. By virtue of her job she was better informed than most, but the news, delivered as it was by a staticky short-wave radio in the shrouded communications room, had lacked a visual component. She didn't expect to see acres and acres of black on the way to Tokyo.

She hadn't planned to go to Tokyo, either. But August 6 had changed everything.

Hanako was dead. She had watched them place her best friend's body in the fire. They were trying to burn as many as they could, but still, only those who were lucky were cremated, and even luckier if the fires didn't go out before they were completely burned. The smell of it—she couldn't bear it—that was why she couldn't go out to claim any of Hanako's ashes. But it wasn't better inside.

Inside, people were rotting. Without their skin, there was only pus and maggots. With nowhere else to go, Lillie stayed at the hospital for those first days, in shock: dabbing dying bodies with iodine until there wasn't any left, then just water and some salt.

She was so tired, and then she was ill, too. Throwing up; her bowels were gelatin. There wasn't much food, so there wasn't much to come out, and once she was empty, she couldn't keep conscious. Lillie lay on the floor, unresponsive. On the outside she was burning, the same way all the victims had burned, but even as her fever broke through her skin in a rash that resembled a scouring of pinpricks, on the inside she felt cold to the bone. There was blood in her stool, and then her menses came, after a year of being so skinny she didn't bleed at all, and there was so much blood, weeks of it, clotted and dark, that the nurses thought she might not survive.

To have their mysterious sickness without being there when the bomb dropped: *that* was punishment. She was not the only one. No one knew what the bomb contained. At first, they thought it was a new kind of poison. Then a contagion: a mysterious plague that was felling not only those who had been in the city at the moment of the pikadon, but also, days and weeks later, those who came in after to help. Boatloads of people began escaping out to the islands of the Inland Sea in hopes that the freshest air might save them. But for most, it was already too late.

They didn't deserve this, Lillie knew, but she did. She knew every choice she had made to get here, and still, she thought: *I want to go home.* Lillie didn't have a home. She hadn't spoken with her mother in years, had been unable to find her own child. But there was no reasoning with despair. She wanted to be lifted out, to be somewhere safe, and maybe that was punishment, too, to want what she couldn't have. To want to hold a little boy who was dead or may as well be. She was never going to find Toshi. To admit it felt like it might stop her heart from beating, but she had seen enough of this ruined world to know it was true.

Lillie wavered in and out, of sickness and also time. She knew the days were passing only because there were fewer bodies on the floor. She was in the hospital, in the river, with Hanako; she was with Toshi again. When her fever broke and she could lift her throbbing head to see through the ruptured walls of the hospital, she understood that it was not just the rooms around her that were emptying. The city had cleared out as well. Once it had been looted of what the survivors most cherished— the dead, the dying, the possibility that someone they loved was still out there waiting to be found—it was left for what it was: a burial ground.

Hibakusha who had anywhere to go, any family who wouldn't turn them out, went.

She had been too sick to hear the news of the second bomb, of the Emperor's surrender on the radio. Later, she heard people's unease: how tinny his voice had been. How small, and how human. Japan's returning soldiers drifted back to the city, carrying their humiliation with them and perhaps also their relief. They must have expected that those feelings would be the worst and best parts of their reunions with their families. But by the time Lillie emerged from her illness, people were counting themselves lucky if half their family members were still alive, and the soldiers who came back to nothing had devolved into marauders, peddling stolen goods and dog meat in the black markets that sprung up around the train stations.

She could have stayed in the city, at the hospital, helping the injured, but she didn't. These people wanted to die; Lillie wanted them to die. What was the point of hanging on? She was living in a world where children kicked bones and even skulls out of their way as they crossed the sudden fields that stretched between the few, staggering buildings. Where the starving children who had been sent out of the city were the more fortunate of the orphans simply because their clothes were not yet in tatters. She felt as dead inside as the two bodies she passed on her way to Hiroshima Station, still seated at their breakfast table, charred hard and black in their ruined house in exactly the poses they must have been sitting in when the bomb fell. She envied them. It was harder to be a survivor than to be dead.

She had nowhere to go, nowhere to be, and nothing to eat. She only went to Hiroshima Station because it was one of the few places people gathered, and it wasn't until she was there that she found out the trains were running again. There were rumors of jobs in Tokyo for people who could speak English; the Occupation Forces had arrived. She didn't know if they would take her, but when she turned to leave, falling back into old patterns—as if she would go home, maybe gather her things, check the train schedule and pick the best time for her departure—she remembered that she had no home. She had no "things" besides her small handcase. She was wearing everything she owned.

The world was just too big and too broken. Even if Toshi and Donald had survived, she would never be able to find them now. Nor would they come looking for her; not her husband, who had twice abandoned his father to save his own skin. That was what she had to do, too. Not to haunt the pile of sticks and rubble that used to be their apartment. She had to continue, to move forward somehow.

She didn't know how she forced herself onto the train, but she remembered the twenty hours that followed, standing in a compartment that was so crowded she could fall asleep and not fall down. When the train stopped in Osaka, she pushed her way out between cars for a breath of air and ended up trapped there, her fingers hooked onto the window ledge; her entire body, even her face, covered with soot. She was stranded for what seemed like hours until another woman pushed her way out between the cars. Then, Lillie tried to get back in, but even a small adjustment in each person's posture had filled all the space that both women had taken up and no one seemed inclined to make room for her. She didn't get back inside until the other woman shoved Lillie like a cork in a bottle so that she could close the door.

Once they arrived in Tokyo, Lillie found that Shinjuku Station, too, was filled with beggars and the homeless, but the center of the city rose around her, tall and square, with working streetcars and arcades. The Allies had taken over, bustling in and out of the huge department stores like there was something to buy. Later, she would learn where the PX was, and which buildings had been commandeered for housing. She would know the map of the new city and which places were reserved for Americans, and which for Japanese. But that day, the atmosphere was like a carnival.

Jeeps were swarmed by children chanting for chocolate. The soldiers cheerfully threw handfuls of it into the streets, calling out "Ohio!" as if it was a greeting, not even waiting to see if it was retrieved from the ground. There were lines everywhere, wrapping the sidewalks: lines for jobs, for papers, for rations. Anyone who could speak English, or who could cling to someone else who could, was chasing after one GI or another. Lillie was cautious. After years of being spit on in the streets because she was American, of having to excise every borrowed word, every mention of America—even pastimes, like baseball, that the Japanese used to love—this fawning was shocking.

The Americans looked so big, so fat and shiny.

It was clear, from the reports of the people standing in lines, that she wasn't going to get very far with a job. To claim she was actually an American, she needed papers, and even so her skills were limited to changing bedpans and bandages. One of the GIs directed her south, to the Army hospital in Tsukiji, watching her curiously as she fumbled to orient herself in the unfamiliar city, trying to create a map of it in her mind.

—Where are you from?

Even then, before anyone had heard the phrase *radiation poisoning*, Lillie knew that "Hiroshima" was not a good answer. She couldn't think of a better one, so she pointed vaguely in the opposite direction.

—Oak-key, he drawled. Then he repeated his directions, using broad arm gestures and the loud, slow speech one reserved for the stupid. "Away from the palace, toward the water. You can't miss it."

She was halfway there, moving out of the nest of skyscrapers toward a section of town that was more wooden and worn. The pace here was slower. There were fewer cars, fewer people in Western dress. But it was still a place for the living.

In front of her, an old man in a rough, patched kimono, barely more than a robe, was shuffling his way across the street. She had almost overtaken him when a weapons carrier full of careless GIs came careening too fast around the corner. The truck fish-tailed in the intersection, the brakes screeching. On instinct, she leaped forward and shoved the old man out of the way, her own handcase skidding across the pavement and out of reach as they both went down. The truck stopped so close she could feel the heat of the engine waft over her, and more than a couple of uniformed men spilled out over each other like puppies.

—Are you okay?

Lillie nodded and tried to help the old man to his feet. But it was immediately clear that the old man was not okay. He was in a panic. Scramble as he tried, he was unable to put even the lightest weight on his leg—when she looked down, the bones jutted out. It was broken. The soldiers stood back as she tried to settle him down on the ground and keep him from moving, but he was wailing and clutching at his leg, casting around for help from anyone other than the girl who'd pushed him. A small crowd of pedestrians had gathered behind the soldiers, watching.

Lillie felt a panic of her own coming on. The old man wouldn't accept her help, and her handcase was beyond her reach, having skidded to a stop beside the curb. "That's mine," she warned sharply in Japanese as she pointed, hoping to preempt the street urchins and perhaps inspire someone to bring it to her. Her own leg hurt—she'd fallen awkwardly and pain was shooting up her side. She felt a rush of fury at the soldiers.

—Why don't you slow down? Why don't you watch where you're going?

—Hey! one of them said, unfazed by her anger. "Where'd you learn that American?"

The old man flinched when he heard them speaking, then—as Lillie looked up at the soldier, considering what to say—he began pouring out a story of two sons dead and a wife waiting with no food...He insisted that Lillie translate, to help him get payment for his leg. She owed him. But she knew that if she started to barter for him, the soldiers would suspect a scam. And if they left, she would never have the strength to take the man to the hospital alone.

One of the GIs had retrieved her case and was watching her mutter at the injured man. The soldier's hair was a spiky blond crown, and he wore a splash of pink sunburn on his nose and the tip of his prominent chin. She would come to find out later that the little leaf on his jacket meant sergeant. He wasn't young or old, nor did he seem particularly kind or evil, but she was too distracted to notice more. Her attention was split between the frantic pleas of the old man and the fate of her entire worldly possessions, which were dangling from the soldier's barely curving fingers. Then he crouched down to her level and looked at her.

—Miya? he asked, holding the case out to her.

—What?

—Miya, right? I met you last night. Miya, Miya, Miya. I never forget a face.

It was such a bizarre little song that she almost corrected him, but the old man could tell from the sergeant's voice that he thought he knew her and that set him off again; he had decided she was one of those bar girls in the shadows, just as the sergeant must have. Lillie felt oddly liberated, suddenly, by their judgment. She owed them nothing, especially not some soldier who clearly thought all Japanese women looked the same. She rubbed the corner of her case, trying to smooth a new abrasion away with her thumb, imagining the shock on their faces if she walked away and left them there with their shouted words and their hand gestures. Then it occurred to her: In this devastated country, she could say she was anyone—American, Japanese—and no one could prove any different. She could define herself.

—This man needs to get to the hospital, she said.

—Sure. Sure. You're good with him, you know? Talking like you do, so calm. You're American, right? That's what you told me. It's like I said the other night—we could sure use someone like you.

Anyone watching might have thought she answered instantly. But a million thoughts exploded in her head. The long lines in the street full of women who had surely touched a typewriter before. The fact that she hadn't eaten in two days. She would have nowhere to sleep tonight unless she retreated to the train station or went into the subways with the rest of the homeless.

And then there was the question of Miya: the possibilities and pitfalls of this new, American woman. Who was Miya? Would Lillie get caught?

—I don't have any papers.

—Such a worrier, Miya. Never fear, there are a lot of filing clerks here. Hey! It's a rhyme.

It was the delight on his face that got her. How simple he seemed then, and soft. Or maybe it was the possibility of file clerks.

—Why are you crying? No, no, don't do that! Don't worry, little Miya. I'll help you. Once we get this mess set to rights, we'll all be going home.

KEI

Y ou get into a rhythm. Kicking, breathing, pulling until your arms are coming out of their sockets. During the off-season, Arnie works with you on breathing, deep into your belly, but in a race it's no calm meditation. It's sucking air in as deep and hard as you can. Everything synchronized, yes, but not relaxed. Arms cycling, legs. Just like now. Can you feel it? Faster and faster until you're swimming for your life.

Arnie comes to every meet, even the exhibitions. He's one of those parents who arrives too early for pickup, who coaches from the edge of the pool. But it's good to have his company, now that you understand his purpose in your lives. He came to be Mama's savior. And also Mama's voice.

When you first tried out for the team as a freshman, you didn't realize who you'd be swimming against. Girls who could tuck and turn in their sleep before you learned that a race could be longer than a single length. You had never lost before that moment, so you stopped once you fell behind so no one could beat your best attempt. But Arnie was there, and patient, and he helped you break it down. "What's the one thing you would have done differently, Kei-girl?" he asked, as if winning was only one choice away.

"Do what you love and forget the rest," Arnie always says. "There's nothing you can't do. Nothing you can't try."

He was right about 1960. It *was* a turning point.

* * *

When you scan the crowds, sometimes you still see Missy. She comes to cheer when you're competing against one of your hot rival schools and everyone knows you are going to win. Even though she's annoyed that you are the team captain, still your success reflects well on her, since you two are best friends. But sometimes, she'll also come to reward you, when she's managed to coerce you into giving her something, or doing something you didn't want to do.

Lately, being good means being with Eddie. Your connection to her brother has rekindled your own friendship. For three years, you two have been skirting the edge of trouble, being sisters. You saw yourselves in each other, and it wasn't until this year, now that you are a senior, that you began to realize how constricting that was. Just when you began to feel you had to break out of the box Missy had put you in, Eddie came between you, and he's the one who did the breaking. Now, you are more than the half that completes her, but also less: You are a third of a new triangle that you created. But you are also the one who brought Missy's beloved brother back to her.

Mama comes to your meets more frequently than Missy does. She is out of the house often these days. After the tidal wave, whatever had afflicted her was driven under, and she left the hospital restored. The intensity of your childhood is gone, but in its place, Mama's own youth is rising. She looks more beautiful than you have ever noticed her to be. At the state meet, she wears a green-and-white shift, with a belted waist and round neck that sits at her collarbone, dabbed with her favorite pikake perfume. Her hair rests on the tips of her shoulders. It is this, her most vibrant moment, that you will hold on to later.

This, and the growing inkling that she might be proud of you.

Mama's face is in the water. That's how you see her. Isn't that odd? Her hair floats above us, long and drifting. Are we hiding beneath her at the bottom of the pool?

Or... are you rising? The surface around her is bright silver now with darker spirits inside it. The voices around her are muffled. Can you hear them? You don't know who is speaking. Hana, maybe. You should listen better. It sounded like her before.

Hana is the only one who's never seen a single swim meet. Not that you need more of a cheering section—you haven't lost the 200 freestyle since you were a sophomore swimming against seniors—but you miss your sister. She's so bent on leaving the island for college, she won't take her nose out of her books, even though her applications were already submitted. She thinks she is better than everyone else, and the truth is, she probably is. You don't beg her to come. You let her spend her time as she likes, studying the Greek roots of a word like *sophomore*.

Hana is leaving. Even though the acceptance letters haven't come yet, still you know. She'll get in everywhere, invited to cities you can't even visualize, and she'll go. She's been talking about it for months, looking at brochures and maps in the library, exchanging letters with alumni. But it's only now that you have begun to feel the ache beneath your breastbone that the thought of Hana living off the island brings.

You don't want to stay behind and teach kindergarten or get married. You don't want to spend your life working in a store. That's what piques your sudden desire to show up all the teachers who decided you weren't intelligent. How many months, even years, has it been since you first started making pretty patterns on multiple-choice tests, seeing how much effort it might take to score a perfect C minus every time? Flip-flopping your smart, succinct essays so the right answers were in the wrong places?

In the evenings, you find yourself gorging on dead philosophers and old battles you should have learned about years earlier. It's too late for you to apply to college, but still, can't you borrow a space? Hana can only go to one school. How would the others know the difference? You know it's delusional, but still, you want to be ready. With this new clarity you realize it would be a simple thing, really, to be Hana.

Maybe you are walking in Hana's footsteps on the day you see the poster for the art show. You've never paid attention to it in past years— why would you?—but there is a senior prize. It would be perfect for

Hana. The ghosts and monsters she used to draw when you were still Koko gave you chicken skin. You know Hana would never enter it, but what if you did it for her? She's got several notebooks of old drawings under her bed.

Are you hoping you will derail Hana's college plans, even inspire her to stay at home? Or do you just want people to see her the way you do? You don't know, will not even think about it, because it feels right, doesn't it?

It feels like something good.

After Mama died, you used to dream of the last story about Lillie. The one when she had to leave. By the time she told it, you had already begun to notice the way Mama's stories kept shifting. At the time, you wondered whether you just understood more. Over time, she changed the world.

By the time you were in high school, there was a war on in Lillie's life. Maybe Mama sensed the war brewing between you and Hana, or maybe you were all just talking about Vietnam. Arnie was against the idea that the country might send troops there, and he used to expound upon that over dinner. Mama never shared her own feelings about the war.

The last time you remember that she told it, Lillie's leaving felt so real, with so many details and dialogue you'd never heard before. Mama was recounting the moment Lillie said good-bye to her parents. She was traveling light, with only what she could carry in a carpetbag and a hard-sided case that banged into her shins when she walked. Usually, at that point in the story, Mama stopped to warn you that the world was big, and good-bye was forever, but this time, you asked her a question about the young man who came to save her.

"Did she love him because he was Japanese?"

Mama's response that afternoon was that Lillie thought the young man recognized her. Not that he knew who her parents were and had come out of the blank spaces in the story to reunite the orphan with her real life, but that he could tell her who she was. You tried to absorb this, to make the distinction Mama made: not just that he knew her, but that he could *tell* her who she was—that he could gift her with her own description. It was a thrilling idea. After a pause, Mama offered: "There's danger in that."

That was all she said. You didn't hear her. As much as you loved your Lillie stories, you didn't realize how profoundly you didn't understand. That day, you thought she was talking about passion. But very soon you would be learning what Mama was trying to say.

You are at Eddie and Missy's house during the last school period. Eddie insisted you sneak away before swim practice because he needed you. After only a few months together, his idea of need already consists of having you wash a couple of the dishes in the sink so he'll have something to eat off the next morning, or to get his jacket for him from across the room, but you came anyway. Missy is there, too. Once, you and Missy had a special connection, then it was you and Eddie. But now, she is always beside you, between you, and around you and Eddie. She is sprawled on the couch asking for advice about which boys she should lead on.

Missy doesn't believe in love. There aren't a lot of Prince Charmings in her family tree, nor in the town for that matter. Men provide for the family. They don't ride up on white horses with spangled bridles unless they're roping cows and drinking beer afterward. It seems ironic that you and Eddie are the one exception Missy has made for great romance until you remember that it is her romance, too.

Right now, Eddie is rummaging through your gym bag for cigarettes because he is out of his own again. Of all days, this is the one when the art teacher finally returned Hana's sketchbook, which you had loaned him when he asked to see more of the monster pictures, and you just stuck it on the top of your clothes. Eddie thinks he has the right to pull it out, that he has the right to everything about you.

"What's this?" Without waiting, he flips it open to a drawing of one of Mama's faceless ghosts.

"Give it back!" Too late, you realize you should have pretended not to care about the sketchbook. Now he is really not going to let go.

"What crap is this? These are like, kid's drawings! Have you been failed back into preschool?"

You look over at Missy. She's the one you are worried about. Last week, you let it slip that Hana was invited to submit to the art show even though she hadn't taken a single class in high school, and of course Missy was instantly jealous. You knew better than to mention that you and the diary started it all.

"What are these?" Missy asks. She starts flipping through them. "Creepy." She seems thoughtful at first.

"They're, umm..." How to describe them? You can't say they're your mother's ghosts. They are the monsters that united the three of you before Arnie. Your mother, the hero who stood between you and the creatures who would come. And if they were invisible, even figments of her imagination, still, Mama's ghosts were proof that she would protect you from the devil himself. She would not let you disappear. "They're Hana's."

Missy's expression doesn't harden until you explain what happened. Then she slams the notebook shut and tosses it on the table. "Wow, maybe she really is a baby if she can't even enter a contest herself."

"A retard baby," Eddie offers.

"For God's sake, Eddie! Could you be a bigger baby yourself?"

As annoying as Eddie is becoming, he seems to know where your mind goes even when you haven't spoken. "Your mom was always loco, yeah? Maybe your twin sister wen catch 'um. Crazy cooties. How 'bout you?"

"Shut up!"

There is an edge in your boyfriend's voice, the one you have been hearing too often since he got fired from the gas station for pocketing cash. Eddie says it was bull, made up by the old man since Eddie was better with a timing belt. But since that day, Eddie has been pushing at something. Cheating his friends at pool in the carport. Sending you to the kitchen to get him another beer while he jokes that you're too young to drink.

"Ooh, you're so cute when you're angry!" Eddie grabs Hana's sketchbook and starts paging through it himself. "These are some freaky ghosts."

The sketchbooks were ghost catchers. That's what you remember. You did them together. Hana drew, but you told her the stories, recalled the details, put the figures in their places. Then, when they were captured, rendered harmless on the page, you could be the ones who protected Mama, not the other way around. Is that why you keep defending Hana? "It was just stuff she said," you say, caught between the two of them and not thinking clearly. "Stories. Your mother never told you stories?"

Missy has been waiting for you to disown Hana and Mama. No, she assumes that you will and is puzzled that you haven't. But now, she flinches and you remember: Missy's mother wasn't there to tell her anything. Maybe that's what puts the heat in her voice. "You can't think these stick drawings are sane? They aren't even any good! They're like kindergarten."

They *were* kindergarten, but you don't say that. "They got her in, didn't they? Mr. Kealoha asked her to submit. They must have some value you don't see."

"Oh, but you do?" Eddie asked, looking toward Missy for approval. There's something dark in his eyes now. Something that demands soothing. "Mental art if you ask me. By a mental kid of a mental mother..."

"Shut up, Eddie." You know you should back off but you can't help yourself. "Let's not start comparing mental mothers. People who live in glass houses..." It was a story from the Bible that Mama used to tell them. She never had to say more than the first half of the proverb, but Eddie wouldn't know the rest. You know he'll hit back at you somehow for making him feel stupid, but you are too furious to care.

But instead, Eddie seems pleased that he has you off balance. He holds Hana's sketchbook high in the air, trying to make you jump to get it. He's so tall you both know there's no way for you to grab it without knocking him over or trying to climb up his body, which is what he wants you to do. When your body collides with his, he grabs you with his other hand and pulls you to him, then tosses the notebook back to Missy so he can circle you with his other arm. "No, I'm wrong. You're kind of sexy when you're angry. What do you think of our gutsy little tiger, Miss-Miss?" he asks his sister.

You try to twist out of Eddie's embrace, but he pulls you tighter and brings his lips down to your ear. "Stop it. Eddie. Please."

Eddie's smile crawls across his face like a spider. He likes it when he can cut you deep. "You don't beg nearly often enough," he growls, delighted, and begins to nibble at your earlobe.

"I said stop!" You push him away, hard. You must have caught him by surprise, because he moves easily as your hands shove his ribs. "Leave me alone."

"You, alone?" The space between you vibrates. His face is twisted. This is not how he expected it to go. "You, who's always over here like a little puppy dog? And now you say you want to be *alone*?"

He's making you choose between him and Mama. Missy and Hana. He thought he knew which choice you'd make, and he's pissed at the dawning understanding that he is wrong.

"Take it, Miss," he says to his sister without looking in her direction. There is something flat and final in his words. For a moment, you think he might move toward you, then he decides he's had enough for the day. Missy looks crushed, both of you drained and shaking, waiting to see what he'll do. But he only grabs his baseball cap and heads for the door.

Over his shoulder, he gives his sister her final orders. "Don't give it back until we decide what we should make our little tiger do."

He leaves the two of you together in appearance only. Missy gives you a drowning glance, then tightens the sketchbook against her chest. You can't fault her. Blood is thicker than water, as the saying goes.

Except that in your family, blood is thin and treacherous, and that's what gives you hope.

HANA

I draw all day: a kind of therapy. One stroke. One stroke. One stroke. I could fill a whole book with the face of Kei's attacker, except that I rip the pages out freely, crumpling some of them and spreading the ones with at least something of him around me on the floor. He is there, in pieces—the profile of a nose, the hollow of a cheek—in the same dismembered way that he litters my thoughts.

But I am getting somewhere. I recognize an expression in his eyes especially, and that spurs me on. I run my black crayons down to small nubs, then change to charcoal. By then, I am no longer controlling anything, and I can shade him freely. His hairline. Did I see his ears? It is that double take, that expression, that I finally capture.

He is here. Finally, on the page. Not 100 percent, but enough that I can feel the malice pouring off him, and I know that he recognizes me as clearly as I recognize him. The pressure builds behind my eyes as I look at his image. I don't know whether to expect jubilation or vertigo, but after all that, I am empty. I have recovered my voice, and I have survived it. I want to share it with Kei; she's the one who has always understood me. Will she recognize the picture?

But of course, Kei cannot see.

What more can I do? What have I overlooked? I am coursing with energy, finally taking action. My nerves are jangling, but I want more. There has to be something else that can bring my sister back to me.

I have searched through my mother's case. I've been through Kei's things, too. She came with clothing. With gum. She wore that chunk of jade, a tapering, deep olive obelisk, thumb-sized, on a knotted cord. My sister didn't even have socks with her—that's how unprepared she was. How light she was traveling.

But there are, still, the contents of the case. Nothing I haven't tried to understand already. Some of these have given up their stories. Others will forever remain a mystery. Maybe because of the night I just spent puzzling the pieces of Kei's attacker together, I go into my bedroom and take every item out of it, then spread them around me on my bed. It's a circle of life, Mama's life. My attention catches on the two photos labeled "Hiroshima." The first one, of an empty concrete bridge, is particularly strange as there are no people in it. No bomb debris, no scenery. In the second one, a gray water tower is etched with the dark shadow of a ladder.

What could Mama have seen in a picture of a water tower? In the shadow of a ladder, broken as it is on the third rung? It must have been made from bamboo, handmade, lashed together in the smudged bulges at the joints. On the top, I can see where the lashing itself seems to be unraveling, its frayed edge etched into the bleached metal.

Except, there is no ladder there. I have to do a double take to realize what I am looking at. Few things on earth could imprint the shadow of something as flimsy as a frayed piece of cord into steel. I am looking at the blinding flash of the atomic bomb. At its aftermath. How did I not notice it before?

Shadow child.

I was young when I learned what Kei's name meant. It was offered to me with a certain ghoulish interest, but that's no excuse now. The point is, I used to tease her, and she pretended it was the ideal name for her, which spoiled my fun. It was Mama who put an end to it. One day she heard me calling Kei a shadow and she became very still. "Oh, Hanako," she said, and for a minute, I thought she might not speak again. And then she said, "The shadow is the proof of the soul."

She didn't tell me not to tease my sister. I didn't even know what she meant. *The shadow is the proof of the soul.* Was she saying Kei had a soul, and I didn't? She looked so grave that I knew it was important, and more than that, the way she used my full name, which almost never passed her lips, disturbed me.

"Flower child," I said, showing her I understood where my name came from also. "Flower child. Flower." She looked at me thoughtfully for a moment, as if trying to catch up with what I was saying, and then the sun broke over her face and she smiled. That smile was enough to prove that I had not lost my mother completely, that mine was the simple, straightforward name. I never mentioned the shadow again.

It wasn't until I was in college that another possibility was offered. In my junior year, I met a girl named Keiko, so I told her, without thinking, my full name. She translated it for me, "flower child," as expected. Then she pointed to herself and said, "God child." Then she thought about it further and clarified. "Blessed child."

Had I given Kei the wrong name? The girl explained that the meaning of *Keiko* depended on the kanji. *Shadow*...she considered what I told her. It was not the most common usage, but she admitted slowly that it could work. By then, it didn't seem to matter; I was sure I would never see Kei again to tell her. But in Mama's pictures, I found a deeper understanding of Kei's name. There were shadows on the bridge in the second photo, too: shadows of the railing imprinted in concrete. And what's more, the spots that had first seemed like the dappling of an old photograph were actually very specifically shaped shadows that had been left wandering all over the foot bridge. *Shadows are proof of the soul*, my mother had said. A reminder that our lives were dappled with clues we might never notice, with hints we must decipher for ourselves. These shadows in Mama's pictures were imprints where, in the instant before the blast of radiation incinerated them, people were standing.

Human footsteps. Feet.

Once upon a time, there was a little girl named Lillie—Mama told me this story one afternoon, when I was a teenager. I'd come upon her in the garden, in front of a small fire. I thought she was burning trash, but she was throwing paper across the top of the fire, page after single page. Mama's face was bright and her eyes sticky as she read each word off each sheet of paper to herself silently before feeding it into the flames. She waited for each page to ignite and then to sail, lit, on the draught of the rising heat like a fiery little fairy. She kept reading, and burning, even when I sat down with her.

They were wishes, Mama told me. When Lillie was just about my age, her mother taught her that she could send all her wishes and prayers to Heaven in the smoke. There, God would hear them, and all the spirits and the angels, too. You could even send messages to your past or future self, or to someone else who was still living.

"It's a big, big world," she said. "And sometimes you lose people. But just because they are lost to you doesn't mean that they are gone."

It was a clumsy explanation, and I knew it. Christian preachers prayed in church, or kneeling by the side of the bed, not in a garden by a fire. I knew of girls in my school who went with their families to the temple to burn gifts for the dead and prayers written on wooden planks every new year, but that was a Japanese church. But I kept quiet.

Mama's wishes were densely written on each page. Some looked like they were addressed as letters. I tried to read them, but from the distance, I couldn't make out any words.

"What did you wish for, Mama?"

She didn't answer at first. And then she said, "Sometimes I wish I could talk to my mother."

I watched the letter spark and dance and carry, mostly turning into ash. There were little singes in the grass, too. Lillie left her parents and never went back, I remembered, and the coincidence unnerved me as much as the thought of a mother separated from her child. Maybe it was the sadness in my mother's eyes, so close to spilling over, but I didn't say anything. We sat together, watching the smoke sway, dissolving into spirit. We watched her letters becoming a part of everything in the big, big world, until all the pages were gone.

I know all that I ever will about my mother now. Her mysteries will remain mysteries, and it will have to be enough. If I lie on the floor, like

Mama used to, I can feel what she must have been feeling. The way the floor holds you up. The fact that you have already hit bottom and can fall no further. This is the true inheritance my mother tried to give me: the truth of losing everything and the courage to be reborn. I never understood, and now, it's just me. No trio. I don't have anyone to bring me water or to hold my hand. That was so long ago I'm not even sure it really happened.

But here's what I do know: I should not have left. It's that simple. At least not without seeing my mother again. Arnie used to say we could change the future with just one choice, but if I could do it over, I would never scream at Arnie in the hospital. I wouldn't blame Kei or Mama; I wouldn't have to be sedated. I would come home, instead, to find out why they never visited me. There must have been a good reason. And I would have chosen a different college, closer to home, just like I'd promised Russell. Despite the way our relationship ended, he was right: So far away, I'd miss my family. I'd miss my Mama, and walking barefoot, and the salty trade winds off the sea. Hawaii was my home. If I left it, he'd warned me, I'd be just the shadow of who I could be.

It was early spring, in our senior year, when I noticed Russell watching me.

After the award ceremony in the library, the paintings had been moved to the school hall. *Ghost River* had the most prominent spot. Sure, I was getting some cockeyed looks, some comments about how dark I was inside. Like, *You seem like such a nice person—where did that come from?* And others along those lines. I knew where the darkness came from, and I'd seen it clearly in my mother's face. I'd wanted to shake the viewer, just like we had all been shaken, and every comment I heard only proved I had succeeded.

Which is why I wasn't entirely shocked that Russell approached me. I must have known some basic facts about him—our town was small and we'd both grown up in it; he wasn't one of the haoles with names like Smith and Phillips who were moving here with more regularity now that Hawaii was a state. Still, I'd found myself observing him whenever he appeared in the halls or with his buddies, which seemed to happen between almost every class. He was a regular guy: medium brown hair, medium build, medium intelligence. He wasn't rich or poor, though his style leaned toward surfer in the wide-striped shirts he often wore, and his hair was *'ehu*: highlights reddened by the sun. He didn't hang out near the auditorium with the troublemakers, nor was he the captain of any team as far as I could tell. His grades were above average; he played a little basketball; he was an only child. He was bland, normal, a regular guy like Arnie. He seemed kind. If he hadn't, I never would have let him come close enough to ask if I would go with him to the dance.

I remember: After the bell rang at the end of the day, the students used to pour out of the buildings, down the wide steps and onto the grass where they slowed down and puddled. I had never noticed them, not until I put myself out there with the painting and realized that, to balance out being so vulnerable, I had to see them, too. There were the surfers, and the "Wreckers," and the kids from the different plantain camps; they gathered according to where they lived, the sports they practiced, what they liked to do. The buildings all had walkways along the outside, facing the square courtyard and open to the weather. I was leaning into one of the big arched openings to feel the breeze when Russell came up behind me and leaned, too, both of us side by side, looking off into a shared distance.

"So," he said, still facing forward, "you going to the dance?"

It was not an invitation, exactly, but I had been waiting for this very question, rehearsing it at night before I went to sleep. Now that it was happening, I couldn't make myself speak. I kept my eyes on my classmates: the snakes of kids who slipped obediently along the walkways; the odd ones who struck out on their own. I was a path taker, and it seemed like most of the other kids were, too, even though the ones who set off across the grass got where they were going faster.

What to say?

I'd pulled away from him in case anyone was looking. He'd been coming over to talk to me for several weeks, but what if it was all just a practical joke?

"You know who I am, right?" I kept it light, jokey. I was ready with a follow-up, something like, *I'm the one who can't dance.* But I had to know that he wasn't there just because of some ghoulish interest in *Ghost River*, and, more important, that it wasn't Kei Russell thought he was talking to.

Russell must have felt the space grow between us. He pushed off the ledge and straightened, looking around. He seemed hurt. I'd ruined everything; he was leaving.

"I could," I almost gasp.

"What?"

"I could go. I mean, if you are."

He relaxed back toward me. "Cool," he said. "That would be cool."

He looked like he would say something more, and for a minute we stared at each other. His thick hair, glinting with the color of an old penny, fell over his hairline in a soft, cowlick curl that drew attention to his flecked-with-gold eyes. But it was his neck I was looking at, or rather the hollow between his collarbones. He opened his mouth, but I was nodding again, my eyes darting away, so his did, too.

"I *would* like to know you, Hana," he said. "Better."

As I watched him walk away, my fingers dipped into the indent at the base of my own neck to see if I could feel my beating heart. My fingers were amazed by the softness of my skin.

He liked me, and who knew where that could lead? We could become one of those couples who danced so close that the teachers had to measure the space between us with a chopstick. The thought of it made me blush. It put an unfamiliar weight into my limbs.

Now, when I look back, I realize that I still don't know what he was doing. Wouldn't it have been wonderful if he had been just interested in me? What would it be like to turn back time, make space for the possibility of a little bit of happiness for that girl, who was stronger and more trusting than I am now? The artist. The former Koko. The girl who once believed she could be loved?

Suddenly, more than anything, I want to know.

KEI

Missy has a secret smile now, the one with sharp edges, getting sharper. The one you have to try to smooth down if you are ever going to get your sister's sketchbook back. Hana hasn't said a word about her missing monster diary. She never said *thank you*, either, or acknowledged that she knew your role in her first-prize win. You don't kid yourself: She knows exactly which book the drawing you submitted came from, and probably which page. Still, her silence gives you space, and time. Which means you spend your Saturday mornings sitting under the trees at the beach watching Eddie and his friends surf.

While you wait for the surfers to get tired, Missy mentions Russell. "Hana's in love."

"No way." You shake your head, squinting at black dots bobbing on the white break lines so far away. You can't even tell which one of them is Eddie. "Hana? She'll never let anyone close to her."

"Wrong again!"

Maybe it's that your best friend is all knives now. Or maybe you are finally paying attention. On Monday, when the bell rings, you know Hana will lag behind the rest of her classmates as always, choosing to jot down every last note and detail over taking a few extra moments of fresh air. You know her patterns cold. But when Hana is actually one of the first people out of the building, you recognize this, too. It's the new norm since they announced the exhibition selections, and, in fact, you have seen it. You have also seen her talking with the boy who comes out beside her, rolling his eyes about something someone must have said in class, some new and safe stupidity to share.

Russell Robello. Missy was right. He is standing a respectable distance from Hana, but you can see how easily they slide into talking, even if she hugs her books to her chest.

You notice Missy's smile. Her favorite pastime is disrupting other people's crushes. Her record is thirty seconds. She's by far the most beautiful girl in school. It's going to be ugly to see how fast Russell crumbles, but there is nothing you can do. Eddie's pride is wounded, but Missy is still fixated on Hana.

So Hana's heart will break, you think. There's nothing you can do about it. At least she can take solace in the fact that she's leaving soon.

But Hana looks so happy, and whatever Missy is planning for her, you can't deny it's because of you. You brought her to Mr. Kealoha's attention. You lied to Missy, your best friend. How can you stand there between them and watch Hana shatter when you can buy her some time? You know what Missy wants: to be the one you chose. You turn to her. "All right! Enough! How can I make it up to you?"

When you jump, there is air, first, before the water. A sleeve of wind to slip into. The higher you are on the cliff, the longer the sleeve. To feel it tingle all the way from your toes to your ears, you have to jump from the top rocks, where it's tricky because they're set back from the water's edge. You have to leap out, launching yourself like a track star, but with no running start. Cycling your legs to get beyond the shallow spots, and always feetfirst.

Thirty feet is only one second of falling.

On the old train bridge, though, you can dive. Hands- and headfirst into the wavering dark patches of safety beneath the surface. And *that* is beauty.

River water is cold. Much like Ice Pond. And it's a different kind of chill when it begins headfirst, in your ears and throat. When it travels down the whole long length of you, gets caught in the hollow of your belly, then releases, to your inner thighs and down. The shock of the water will fade. The body moves to equilibrium. But what if it doesn't?

What if it stays, ice against your skin until it burns hotter than any summer sand on your instep, hotter than prickly lava? This is what you don't know. What Mama, who chose to lie down in the snow to die, could tell you. *How do you sleep your way to death?*

When you die, will you be all alone? That was Missy's first question to you all those years ago. Being alone was her greatest fear, which she reminded you of at Mama and Arnie's funeral. You hadn't seen her more than a couple of times since Hana's "accident" in the cave, when you and Arnie went to confront your friends together, and Missy cried and denied it all. What she offered you at Mama and Arnie's funeral was the greatest comfort she could muster: *At least they weren't alone.*

Those words bothered you then, and they kept bothering you.

Mama was in Arnie's arms, that's how they found her. That was what the coroner said; maybe what he says to all the sobbing children. He told you she probably went first, frail as she was, so Arnie might still have been whispering in her ear when she passed. You like to imagine Arnie conscious, but then he could have gotten up, too. He could have stayed with you awhile longer. He could even have been the one to travel to New York to bring your sister home. But that's not why you keep dreaming of Mama and Arnie, lying together in the snow. Mama always warned you that people would disappear but, in Arnie, she had finally found someone who wouldn't. She found a man who would keep the promise that Lillie's stranger made to her mother:

He said he'd take care of her forever, Mama used to tell you.

Only then did Lillie's mother finally let her go.

Gutsy Little Keiko, that's always been Eddie's name for you. And it's true, you're not afraid to jump.

They pick you up after school: no warning. The gang of four, as the boys like to call themselves, has found a new spot. This time, it's a pond on a river just out of town, past the main swimming hole where the little kids hang out. Missy comes with you today, which, since she doesn't dive and has never been interested in watching, is your first tip-off. She hops the guardrail with the rest of you and climbs down to a waterfall. It plunges straight down, higher than anything you've ever tried, into a dark green, oddly round pond. There's one small platform notched into the top of the cliff about four feet down, but that barely shortens the distance.

Other people have jumped this one, or so they told you in the car.

You will, as always, do this right. Start with a jump, feet first, screaming, arms flailing, loose cannonballs of delight. From the top, the pond is a shifting blue-green; the sound of the falls rises up from the plunge and wraps you. You are a goddess on top of the world: the clouds, the sky, even the weather at your command.

You jump.

You can feel the sleeve of air. You have just enough time to point your feet straight down like an arrow and then ball up at the last minute into the safest, cannonball position. Style counts, and you have it. The boys are just goofy blobs of energy.

Clyde goes after you, then Billy, then Eddie and Damon.

For the boys, it's about twitching and flexing before the jump, and then whooping and hand slapping afterward. You've caught your breath by the time they're all in, so you lead the scramble back up to where Missy is still watching. Most of the way, the guys crow over how brave they are. When you get to the top, Eddie turns to Clyde, who is one of the school's top divers, and challenges him to dive.

"Nah."

"You can do it."

"You think I'm stupid?"

"No. Just chicken."

"Kei would do it."

The guys are just pushing each other like guys do. It's Eddie who throws your name in. You have the record: all the highest jumps, the best ones with the spins and somersaults. You are fearless, just like Arnie said once. It fascinates Eddie.

But this is a big drop. Maybe two seconds, maybe fifty feet.

He's not looking at you when he says again, "You guys are more chicken than a little girl." If he had given you that sunny smile that once won you over, that said your success is his own and would save him, maybe you wouldn't have hesitated. But he's not the same guy you started going steady with months ago. Once, Eddie and Missy both looked into you like you were exciting, but now, Eddie seems more excited about what he can do to you.

"Nah," Billy says. "Clyde should do it. He's the *star*."

Clyde looks at you. He isn't happy with the challenge, either.

Then Eddie says, "Kei goes. Right, Missy? Kei goes first."

And that's it. That's the deal for Hana's sketchbook. She looks at you, hopeful, uncertain, and a chill rushes through you.

Eddie's looking between you and Missy as if he can't decide whether you will dive or chicken out. He can't decide which one he'd rather. That's his expression. Like he's the puppeteer.

You want to take that power back.

The pool is blue-green. Fringed with rocks, and overhung with trees. It's like looking into an eye. You are standing on the edge, knees bending, wondering whether to push off, run, and then try to dive, or to trust your legs to take you all the way out and into the center where it's deepest. You are always the first, because you are the lightest and bravest.

You are Kei.

You launch yourself, flat out to get as far from the cliff as you can, and dive.

Thirty feet is one second of falling. Thoughts are even faster. As your toes leave the ground and your body is light, midair, only then do you remember Damon, the biggest and heaviest of the guys, whooping out of the pond, almost shooting out of it, screaming, "I touched!" as he high-fives all around.

The pond is too shallow. And you are in the air.

1 9 4 6

The heir hostess slid the screen open, her face appearing first, bent and bowing, her eyes flickering over them even as her gaze swept quickly down to the floor. Behind the woman, Miya could see the small, spare tatami waiting room, and the tall green vase placed on a pedestal that resembled a cloth-covered book in the corner. Proud, but empty of flowers.

—Ohio! the sergeant greeted the hostess cheerfully as he kicked his shoes off and onto the stone floor of the genkan, then stood there in his socks.

He was delighted that he knew this place; that it belonged to him by the virtue of his knowing. He took Miya's arm as she navigated out of her shoes, trying to step up so her feet landed, not on the ground in the stone entrance as his did, but on the worn but glowing wood floor. She could see the displeasure in their hostess's face and knew it was not his shoes, which were still hanging from his fingers, or even his dirty feet that made her frown; it was that Miya herself was not the person the hostess expected to see. Or perhaps it was the Western blouse and skirt she'd bought at the PX, which would not have seemed so indecent if she were Caucasian. She *was* indecent. She was desperate; that was why she was here.

Their hostess's kimono was not as muted or as worn as she might have expected. It was a deep indigo blue with a thin tracing of red cranes near the hem, and an immaculate white silk undercollar. She wondered if the colors were intentional, and if they were the only guests. The woman was alone, and old enough to be her mother. Her face was carefully prepared: powder filling in the lines she had earned; charcoal drawing the ones she wanted.

—*Irrashaimase*, Tai-la-sama, the woman said as she fussed over the sergeant.

Miya had always known there were places like this: establishments that catered to GIs who wanted more than sukiyaki parties and bingo nights; they wanted a taste of real Japan. That he frequented this one, knew it well enough to arrange this dinner on no notice, meant there was some truth in the jokes and comments about the certain bar girl he was often seen with, in a disreputable section of town. The girls at the clinic in Tsukiji where Miya worked, and her dorm mates who stumbled in from their own adventures long after she had gone to bed, all teased her for losing her chance with "her sergeant" because she didn't understand the currency.

—Don't you know what those Jap girls will do for silk stockings and cigarettes? they asked. "You can't afford to be such a prude."

He used to stop by the radiologists' clinic to bring her *Reader's Digest*s and *Ellery Queen's Mystery Magazine*s. She wouldn't go out with him, not even when he begged—on mock bended knee with his eyes twinkling— for an "innocent lunch." It was only once she had read every English language magazine and article he'd ever given her through twice that she realized her dorm mates were right. Miya couldn't remember the last time he'd stopped by.

She thought she didn't care, at first. She had lived through much more than any of the silly Red Cross girls who'd come here to play the victors. Girls not much younger than she was in years, but so far behind in suffering. Miya was weary, and ruined in a way that she tried to keep secret, a way she knew none of them could ever understand.

But now, the city was emptying out. August 15 was V-J Day, when the Allied victory would be celebrated. The sixth was nothing. A lonely day in Tokyo. If there were survivors of the pikadon here, they were in hiding. Even those who had an interest in Hiroshima had moved on. At the one-year mark, the Occupation was scaling back and spreading across the country, and there was a new commission established in the two bombed cities to study the damage. She knew of several girls from the clinic who'd gone there to help collect the data on radiation poisoning in the victims of the bomb.

Less than half the girls in her dorm were still in Tokyo. The rest were traveling, doing a little sightseeing before they went home.

Miya had never imagined she could end up here, living in Japan. Each time she applied for repatriation to America, they told her there was no way, not ever, not with her records or the lack of them. She might as well give up trying to get home.

Home. Where was that anyway? America didn't want her. Where did she belong? One country was no better than the other, but she didn't relish the options in this one: waiting to find a new set of in-laws who would consider her lucky to have caught even the disdain of their son. Working in a bar.

Her future had not changed; it had just caught up with her. And with the truth of it right in front of her, she made it a point to discover where her sergeant could be found. She was relieved that he still recognized her, that he seemed happy to see her when she "just happened" to run into him on the street not too far from a strip they called Hooker's Alley. She was just glad she had found him alone. That day, her biggest criticism—that he was so simple in such a complex world—seemed like an asset. She remembered what she had liked about him. That he had never killed anyone.

She was used to forcing a smile, but once they were settled at the table in their private room and the food began to come, happiness was easier. Their hostess shuttled it in in courses, small to be sure, but the flavors were delicate and the service so prompt the woman might have been hovering outside the sliding door. The main course was a small gray fish, and whole—the meat was wet and sweet; she could see that before she tasted it—and their hostess seemed touched by Miya's barely stifled squeak of pleasure. Miya felt the earth slide under her as the heady smell of sake and shoyu reached her; she should be ashamed of being so easy on their first date, she thought, but she didn't care. She had been so many things for so many people that she no longer knew how to recognize herself. Not a mother any longer. Not a wife, not even a daughter. What did it matter, really, that the man she was sitting with had been in Japan almost a year and still used the bastardized, GI form of "good morning" every time he tried to say hello? She could endure much more than that if he could get her home.

She hated the GIs for how privileged they all were. They had their pick of everything, even the teenaged girls. If you were white, and American, the grand PX had anything you could wish for, while entire Japanese families stood in line for beans because the rice rations had run out and there was nothing else to eat. She hated the Japanese soldiers, too, hated everything she'd heard about the human shields and the young boy pilots committing suicide by smashing their little planes into aircraft carriers. But she also hated to see the veterans shining shoes, or selling old metal in the black markets, or begging in the streets with their missing limbs wrapped in old cloth because the people they were once ready to die for now actively shunned them.

These were the thoughts she walked with, slept with; they held her together. But tonight, on the anniversary of the bombing of Hiroshima, with a real meal in front of her, she was tired of being so angry.

—*It's not our place to hate*, her father used to tell her. *It's not our place to judge, or to forgive. God is the only one who can stand in judgment.*

Back then, she hadn't yet seen enough of the world to understand him. Now, though she could no longer believe in her father's God, letting go of judgment was a huge relief.

Her sergeant was going home soon. He didn't have his orders yet, but they both knew it was a matter of time. She thought of his happy future: his return to South Dakota and the welcoming arms of some blond fiancée whom he insisted did not exist. But what if he was lying? She wouldn't be the first girl in her dorm to be seduced by a soldier who had no intention of keeping his promises. If she gave in to him and he left her? It was more than she could bear.

She let him sing his little song of the name he gave her, "Miya, Miya, Miya." She let him tease her when she couldn't finish her food. He bumped her toes with his own under the table, where any touch could be an accident, and she did not pull away. His hand would be next, grazing her thigh. She was not a stupid girl.

It was then that she brought up the subject of Hiroshima. And though he knew almost nothing about it, still he was well versed in how excellent it was that a single bomb could stop a war cold and save all the lives that would have been lost had America had to invade by land. Miya could say nothing to this. It was not just that she'd never told him she had been there, nor that it was beyond her to stand up for either side. On that night, on that anniversary, Hanako was all she could think of: her charred face; the raw, red, puffy swathes on her body where there had once been skin.

She had mentioned the bomb to him so that she could force a real connection, but suddenly, she was exhausted. The pikadon was still exploding in her mind, and in her body, too. She could feel it deep in her bowels, a heat that still broke into a cold sweat when she least expected it. Whatever poison the bomb had left inside her, it had not gone away. It burrowed deep; she imagined it like a snake, curled around her spine. Sinking its fangs into her, a hot, icy poison, whenever she thought she might at last be healed. She could feel her belly clenching, and imagined, almost idly, that her insides might come pouring out, draining her in front of him, leaving her a shell. She was already empty. Already erased. What bothered Miya the most, though, even as she struggled to stay attentive, was that she could no longer hear the sound of Hanako's voice in those moments when she tossed and turned and lost consciousness. That Hawaiian lilt that she had come to rely on had been overwhelmed by all the accents of the Occupation.

She missed her voice so fiercely. Missed her companionship. Missed Hanako almost as much as she missed Toshi, who she could still feel with her every day.

Her sergeant was still talking, though he had moved on to the war in Europe and what they had found in those German camps. A buddy of his from high school had been there and they had been exchanging photographs. Now that the fighting was over, the censors had gotten lax, or they were too busy checking the outgoing mail to search the lining of a care package. Her sergeant had sent him copies of some pictures from Hiroshima that he'd gotten. Some artsy ones of shadows from the blast. But his buddy's pictures, well, the people they liberated in those camps were so skinny, he told her, it seemed impossible that they were still living. He tried to describe the dents in their bodies where the skin wrapped around knobs of bone.

He wasn't saying it right, but did she understand what he was getting at? Even though they were technically still living, with everything that happened to them, how could they really be *alive*?

Was it possible to survive the death of the spirit? she wondered. Was it possible that a man she'd thought too simple-minded and innocent could think about such things? She found herself wondering what he would look like when his hair grew out, in civilian clothes. It was time to tell him the truth if she wanted more than one night with him, but where should she begin?

—I had a...she began, then she started to cry. There were too many possible endings to hang on such a simple beginning. *Son. Friend, family, life...Son.* Those words, even if he could hear them, could never carry everything she had lost.

—Oh, Miya, Miya. And then his body was against hers, his arms around her, and she realized she couldn't remember the last time someone had touched her. The name he had given her rocked her gently. Truth could come later. So could food. First she would shut out the world for one night, she thought. One night was all she needed to find out if the dead could be revived.

KEI

By the time you get home that night after cliff jumping, Mama's hand is on the doorknob. You are cold and wind whipped, and Mama is on you immediately, your crazy mother of old. *What happened? Oh my God...* She is fingering you, pulling at your hair, your clothes, turning you around to see the worst, to see the damage.

How is it possible you are standing here alive? How is it possible you're unhurt? In her tears, in her pacing—she can't stop that flight from the window to you and back again, as if she's still waiting for a different you to fly in between the louvered glass. Or perhaps she's pacing because Arnie has gone out to look for you, is still out there, searching in circles. How to find him? How to call him back?

You can't tell her about the dive, how you changed your mind in midair and hit the water full force, still trying to flip your body 180 degrees from head down to feetfirst. You made it only partway, knocking your head back and the air out of you when you hit the water. You blacked out, but it couldn't have been more than a few seconds. You were close to the surface, but you couldn't get your bearings. Which way was up?

Your body lifted you. Your body brought you to the light. The gang was yelling from the cliff, but they couldn't jump without jumping on you, and you were still in the middle of the pool. You were floating in the icy water, your face barely above the surface. The rest of you was submerged, hanging like moss, and the cold helped. It kept you awake.

It kept you from feeling your neck ache, and your skin, and how your stomach had exploded. You heard a splash, and it was then you started puking. Puking in the water, choking, almost drowning.

Clyde had jumped down to save you, pulling you to the edge like a lifeguard, swimming through your vomit. At the top, Eddie: "Ew. Gross."

You don't know how to tell Mama all of this. You want to tell her you're alive, that you're lucky to be alive, but you can't think.

Your head is pounding. You are lucky to keep your head on.

Mama continues to flutter around you. *Thank the Lord. Where have you been? You missed the relay tryouts and Arnie was so worried. I was so worried. Thank the Lord...*

You didn't expect this. This suffering. You didn't think it through. You've always glided by, with bad grades, with ducking your chores; even your tidal wave escapades were never punished. Mama hasn't fainted once since the tidal wave. Had you forgotten? You didn't think—

That's your problem, Kei. You don't think.

That's what Arnie would say if he were here now, and it robs you of words.

You can see Arnie, driving the roads. Going slower than the usual island crawl, stopping any kids who look to be your age. Though maybe not. It's getting dark. It was a while before you were able to sit up, let alone hike back to the car. When the sun set, though, they half-carried you.

When no one's on the street anymore, Arnie stops by the police station. Then he goes to his friends' houses. Together, they get into their trucks and drive through town or search along the riverbanks while their wives poke their heads into the darkened bedrooms of your classmates to see if anyone knows where you are. Is it that late? Reports trickle in, kids extrapolating from other nights when you weren't where you were supposed to be—at the movies, in a car with Eddie and his gang heading toward beach run—reports that make it clear to all his friends that Arnie doesn't know what his daughter is doing. And yet he keeps searching, so they search, too.

* * *

You are dizzy the next morning and your head is pounding. Even when the pain has gone, it's hard to get out of bed. You find yourself weepy for no reason. Mama sighs a lot. She must think you're trying to play hooky, and, yes, you are the rebel, but surely she can tell when you are truly ill? This is your mother, who used to monitor your health for any flush or sniffle. Your mama, who was afraid of strangers and the bloody, walking dead. *People will disappear*, she used to say, which could have meant anything from contracting a sudden illness to exploding into flame. But she is only normally worried when the doctor tells her you have whiplash and you'll have to rest in the dark to keep your brain from swelling. When you won't tell Arnie how it happened, he promptly grounds you.

The first weekend after you've been released from your bedrest, you find Arnie under the house, running new pipe to replace the sink drain. You watch him without speaking and he doesn't acknowledge you. He's said maybe ten words to you since you got home that night, so his silence isn't a surprise. You're here to say you're sorry for missing the relay tryouts, and you know it's your turn to speak and you should just say it. But the back of his head is making you nervous. You're having a hard time finding the words.

You watch him wrap the thin, clinging tape around the threaded end of the pipe, bandaging it as if with a skin to fill the gaps. "Remember when I used to help you?"

He looks at you now, as if you've suddenly gone insane.

"I did. We...remember?" You are trying to think of the last time you helped Arnie with one of his projects. "We put the porch light in together?" When you see yourself stripping the ends of the wire for him, though, you look much younger than you are now.

"What do you want, Kei?"

"I thought, maybe we could go to the pool on Saturday. I could float and maybe just do some kicking. You could help me..."

"What do you *want*?"

Arnie has finished tightening the pipe and he's sitting now, slouched a little on a large rock, his legs spread and his elbows on his knees leaning forward. He's looking at you as if this question is terribly important, but you have no idea what he's asking, except that it makes you want to cry.

"I don't know—"

"What *do* you know, Kei? Do you know why you treat yourself like crap? Christ, how much damage can a person do to herself? If it was someone else treating you this way I swear I would knock his head off. But it's you."

You don't know why he's attacking you, or what he's saying, exactly. You were supposed to be at tryouts and you went cliff jumping instead. Is it just that you missed swimming, or does he know how you almost killed yourself? Maybe he's heard something. Surely Hana knows. The story of Clyde swimming through your vomit must be very popular in the school halls.

Arnie might understand, if you could find a way to tell him. But you can't, and anyway, this isn't what he's talking about.

Why do you treat yourself like crap?

Even then, you feel like you've been caught red-handed, but not in the way you could have expected: the way you could deny, explain, blame on someone else. And not for anything you even knew you were doing. Your mind is spinning and Eddie's voice comes back to you: "Ew. Gross." Eddie, who calls you a little girl and never asks what you want.

What you *want*. This is what Arnie is asking.

"I forgot."

"You forgot three times in a row. Three Saturdays. You don't even know that, do you?"

Three times. How long have you been lost? Why didn't anyone tell you?

The look on Arnie's face tells you he's through. He's disgusted, and for the first time, you feel disgusting.

"You aren't stupid, Kei. I don't know why you try to blow every chance you have. Forget the swimming. I know what kind of mind you have. Always pulling things apart to see how they work. How can you hang out with those friends of yours? You must be so bored."

It's like he's speaking a language you don't understand, except you hear his words clearly. It's your response you can't manage. You came here to apologize. And you expected that he would try to make you feel better. But this is something else. A truth he's offering. You have to stand in it and let it wash over you as he says, "When are you going to love yourself as much as your mother and I do? Christ, Kei, I give up."

You can't breathe. And right then, you are suddenly so tired. How can he know you better than you know yourself? How can he say he loves you, that Mama does, and then withdraw that love before you can take it? You start to say it again, *I don't know . . .* , this thing you keep saying, which is the only thing that comes to you, but it is also a deflection.

A plea for him to stop saying what he's saying. To give you something easy to hold on to, or at least a chance to breathe and understand.

Though it has been a long time since you were home alone with Mama, your body remembers those steamy afternoons when you and Koko took care of your mother. What you *want* is to be grounded, you realize, following Mama from room to room. *Let me carry that*, you say when she's on her way outside to do the laundry. And, *Don't bother with the stool. I'm taller than you are. I can reach.* You smile at her. You have things to make up for. How would she have endured it, if you had dived headfirst and died? But mostly you do it because it feels right, because when you are with her, really with her, you feel layers peel off you. Masks and skins you never knew you wore. You are moving backward in time, and you can feel the contours of the real you, where they have waited. You are remembering who you really are.

What you don't notice is that Hana should be here, too. You should be tripping over each other in the afternoons to get to the ironing, but instead, you have slipped neatly into your sister's chores and she slipped out at the same time. The truth is, it's been a long time since you paid enough attention to Hana. You didn't notice her leave, since you never had the experience of being two high school girls in the house together. But that means it's simple enough to slip Hana's sketchbook back under her bed when you find it shoved into the side of your gym bag. And it's telling when, just as she never mentioned its disappearance, Hana never acknowledges the sketchbook's return.

You remember how worried Missy was when you could barely stay conscious on the bank of the pond. She gave you back Hana's diary in the car that night, didn't she? You can't picture it; you were too out of it in the dark, but it must be true. But Eddie is another story. You have no interest in being his "gutsy little Keiko" anymore. Your eighteenth birthday is coming up, and you won't be grounded forever. Eddie has been waiting for that birthday. *Wen you one adult, girl*, he often says, *they no can tell you what to do.*

You want what you want. To learn how to love yourself. You break up with him in a letter, letting your imagination go a little wild.

We can never see each other again, you write, heart-dotting your *i*'s. You tell him that Arnie knows about your diving accident and wants to knock Eddie's head off for pushing you. After all, he's an adult and you're still a minor, if barely. You nearly died, and Arnie says Eddie better stay very far away from you and Hana, or Arnie will have him arrested for endangering a child.

Never mind that there are cops in Eddie's extended family. Never mind that almost no one in town ever got arrested. If there could be any world, any slip in time, that would let you write that letter over, you would get on your knees in gratitude. But instead, you were still congratulating yourself on including Hana under Arnie's protection when you gave Missy the sealed envelope to deliver on your first day back at school.

When you dream, your voice is different. Not the pidgin lilt, the words in Japanese, Hawaiian, the slang you learned to pepper in and always sounds right to your friends. But this dream you're having now—it's a different kind of dreaming. It's you, your own voice in your head, slipping into here and out of now to remind you of why you came. You have been gathering, gaining strength, but are you ready yet to wake up and face your sister? To tell her what you know, and apologize for what you did?

* * *

Do you remember the quilt Mama made for Hana?

At first, she worked on it in her own room when Hana was out. You came in one afternoon, poking your head in the doorway, and there she was. You thought maybe it was a birthday present, so you started to leave, but she called you back.

It was Hana's going-away quilt. Mama put her favorite flowers on it. Plumeria. Pikake. Hana always picked the fragile ones. Hana was going farther than any of us had ever been, and the quilt was to help her remember, and to find her way home. You didn't understand it then, though surely you would have noticed how strange that sounded? You were looking at the blossoms, cut out and stacked in order. Mama had just begun, and she thought she had the summer to finish. She couldn't know what was about to happen. Neither could you.

For a long time after Hana left, Mama didn't have the strength to sit up, let alone do quilting. You were surprised when she picked it up again. She spent years going over and over the stitches, trying to root her perfect daughter in hardier plants. During your college years, Mama's spiritual invocation of invisible stitching seemed to work: Arnie got regular reports from Hana's psychiatrist that suggested she was healing. That she had even started to paint again.

Much later, after Arnie received a letter from Hana's college about her missing final credits, Mama put the quilt away. She was dying by then. She never said so, but you could tell.

Toward the end, Hana was beginning to flower, at least according to Arnie. She had a painting in a group art show. Then her own exhibition in her new gallery, which was why she could never come home. You wanted to go get her, drag her back to say her final good-byes to your mother, but Mama wouldn't let you. Children are supposed to leave, she told you. Hana's choices had to be her own.

There was one quilt. For the valedictorian—the one who could make her parents proud. Not for the twin left on a dead-end island, still looking for a way to love herself, relying on her parents to help her find a way to live. You would never leave. You would never even get on an airplane until Mrs. Harada died and left her pendant to Hana in her will.

After Mama and Arnie had committed suicide, the Haradas were all the family you had left, though you'd never thought of them that way. You sat together in the wake of Hana's breakdown, trying to forget how she had walked into the funeral already broken, then proceeded to explode. To distract you, Mrs. Harada told you what she could remember of your mother's stories. You recognized Lillie slowly: her voice in the children's choir; her iconic quilt. But then Mrs. Harada told you about the internment, and Lillie's trip to Hiroshima, and you realized that the old woman was not mixing fairy tales with reality. That was when you finally understood.

All your lives, Mama had been a mystery. First you thought she was sick, those fevers that would come over her. Later you began to understand that her heart and mind were damaged, that something beyond horrifying had happened to her. But no matter what terrible truths Mrs. Harada had to tell you, she was also Lillie. She changed her name, but she never changed who she was.

Mama is Lillie. The little girl who lived on a farm, scattered flowers with her mother, and sang the songs that brought the congregation. Lillie was Mama's gift to you: the good-luck charm who was loved and who loved her parents. You inherited your gift for storytelling from your mother. And also, her stories of her own childhood. This is why you came to New York. One of the reasons. Hana needs these stories. There is so much she doesn't know.

Once you are back at school, Missy sweeps you back into her circle like the dive never happened. And you go along because, what else are you going to do? You eat with the same girls, complain about the boiled vegetables, and covet each other's musubi. But Missy also keeps passing you notes, insisting that Eddie still loves you. You shake your head and shove the notes in the garbage, as if even reading them might severely compromise you. You can't tell her that her brother is a loser and you are happier without him. All your conversations—what Eddie is doing, who's holding him back, what you're all going to do together that weekend—have disappeared overnight, and there's nothing to replace them. Missy's dreams are still about getting a house together where you can string up side-by-side hammocks, with Eddie. About driving to the other side of the island to the blowhole where there is a secret underwater cave that has air in it to breathe. Yours involve going much further, and you keep them secret. You snap at each other, even as you try to hold on.

You never see Eddie himself, not even from a distance, which surprises you even with Arnie escorting you back and forth to school each day. The truth is, both of you are done with each other. When Missy can't make you jealous about Lorna, Eddie's new girlfriend who is as old as he is, she changes her story to warn you that Lorna's trying to get pregnant with Eddie, like that's something that should matter to you. Now you understand all the drama was coming from Missy. She is the one, of the three of you, who would not let go.

You've been back at school only a couple of days, when Missy goes up to Russell in the school yard. You see it happen but are slow to recognize the problem, so it takes you a few minutes to go running over to join them.

"Sooo...Russell," Missy is saying, pulling out the two words so they last as long as it takes her to push her hair over her shoulder, twist the length of it in her hand, and let it slide back again around her face. "We're going to Four Mile on Saturday. Why don't you invite her?"

Russell looks as surprised as you are. "Who?"

"You know. Hana. I've seen you two together."

Missy hates Hana, now more than ever. Why would she want her anywhere near them?

Russell flushes at the thought that the most beautiful girl in school has noticed anything about him, but he's pleased to be included. "Sure. We can...I can..." He stops and looks at you in panic in case you know something he doesn't, then takes a chance. "For sure."

What is Missy hatching? You know it can't be good.

You look around then, and you see Hana watching. Maybe she was heading over to meet Russell, but she stopped when she saw you. You have to squelch this idea before your sister hears about it, so you thread your hand in Russell's, and steer him away from her.

"Nah," you say, as if you are tossing the idea around, as if it's still in play and you're being consulted. "Hana's...you know. She can't even swim."

Missy snorts and smiles at you from Russell's other side. She waves away your objections like the breeze. "Who swims?"

"Well, you know." You hear yourself pushing. Russell is beginning to look confused. He can't figure out why you've come over to debate this—why bring him in before it's planned? "We don't want to be dragged down."

"Hana? A drag?" Missy asks, and all the mocking Russell doesn't notice is clear in her voice. She pats his arm. "We'll make her feel right at home. Won't we, Russell? And Eddie will come. He can teach her to swim. It'll be a great day."

When she says *Eddie*, you finally understand. You can see that poor girl, Emily, again. They invited *her* to the beach, too, then pantsed her in the water and left her stranded in her underwear. That was Eddie's idea. You saw him take her out there. You saw him getting closer, smiling and slipping his arms around her waist. But you didn't know what had happened until you saw her head drop beneath the surface as her feet were swept out from under her and Eddie came leaping out of the water swinging her shorts around his head. You had wanted nothing to do with their pranks, or with this girl who'd thought she could steal your boyfriend in front of you, but you had stayed to make sure they returned her clothing. When one of his friends finally flung the shorts back into the whitewash, you caught a flash of her underwear when she crawled in to snatch them. Then you could go.

But the art show is old news by now. So why is Missy still after Hana?

Then it hits you. You are the one who keeps pointing her in your sister's direction. Missy must think Hana told Arnie about the cliff-diving accident. Why else include her in the note? Though it is also possible that Missy is so angry about the breakup that she has to punish someone, and she's decided to use Hana to strike back at you.

You got away from Eddie. But in return, you gave them your sister. You can't leave Hana alone with them, even if it means you have to see him again. It doesn't matter anymore whether he likes you, or whether Missy does. Of all the things you need to tell yourself, this is the most important one. You put Hana in danger then, and she is still in danger now.

Only you can help her. That's what Harada-san told you at the airport when you were leaving for New York, and you know what he meant. You saw her at Mama's funeral. Some part of her is still lost in that cave. You came here to tell her the truth, but instead you have been hiding. But you are long past the safety of childhood, and far beyond the luxury of blame. Stop talking to yourself, Kei. You remember everything you need to know now. The time for guilt and punishment is over; you have Hana's inheritance to give her.

Wake up and talk to your sister instead.

HANA

The sky is like shave ice—crisp and sweet and tingling on the tongue—
it's a candy blue not found in nature, except there it is above me. Not a
cloud in sight. I am laughing. Am I laughing? I feel it in my face, still lifting the corners of my eyes.

I am walking with Russell along the side of the road.

His arms bump mine from time to time. Our shoulders too broad, fan-
ning out from our necks: They need space. Our forearms, the backs of
our hands, held out even wider than our shoulders. His skin is warmer
than mine, and smells like soap.

It's Saturday morning and the air is just losing the last of its cool edges.
It swirls around my ankles and the hem of my skirt. Small puffs of dirt
pillow my feet as we walk. Russell is saying something about some prank
after basketball, but I would rather watch how the tip of his nose bobs
just slightly when he talks. Some days we're just silly, like today. Some
days we talk about the draft for Vietnam and whether they'll call the boys
from our island. This is how I imagine it: that it starts in the East, in the
big cities like New York and Boston, and then spreads slowly westward.
I think of the draft as a storm, a patch of rain and lightning moving slowly
across the continent, hovering over one place and not leaving it until only
the women and children are left. The world will be depleted of young
men before it gets to us. It seems impossible it will come so far.

There is nothing for me in the world these days but these Saturday
mornings, when I just happen to run into Russell outside Kress, when

we both *just happen* to have nothing else to do, so we walk along Front Street, along a waterfront that still feels new. Spending time together even as we pretend not to notice it's become a habit. Sometimes we go all the way to Coconut Island to watch the kids jumping in the water. Sometimes we follow the sounds of balls and bats. It's part of what we count on— that each of us will be there, with a little time and nothing else to do and we will do that nothing together. Nothing but walk, sometimes so close I can feel the hair on his arm rise up to touch me. Bumping each other:

Oops, sorry.

Oops, no, I'm sorry.

No, me.

Then we laugh, exaggerate our stumbles so that when we right ourselves the momentum will take us into each other again. Arm against arm. Hip against hip. Arm against hip.

"Hey, Russell!"

Russell has just grabbed my hand to keep me from falling when we hear his name. A sampan has pulled over across the street and some of his friends are calling.

"Hey, Russell! Kei! Hurry up!"

Kei, they called me. I don't know if Russell heard. I start to pull away but he squeezes my hand and twines his fingers in mine. In public.

"Hold up, hold up!" one of the boys is yelling as the sampan driver starts to move. "They're coming. C'mon. Hurry up!"

Russell looks at me, like *Shall we?* and seeing no real resistance, starts to move.

I am running across the road with Russell, with Russell's hand beating against my palm.

"Hey, howzit!"

"Howzit."

"So—"

"Hey, we waited for you..."

We climb past the driver and into the back. The horseshoe of benches are full of Kei's friends. There is Missy; there's Charlene. Everyone squishes together to make room, but Russell and I get stuck on opposite sides. Russell is shrugging, like, *Things happen*, but I can't tell if it's aimed at me and he's reacting to how we got separated, or if it is in response to the cryptic comment about waiting. The sampan is heading out of town toward beach run. That's where we're going. They had been expecting Russell to meet them, I realize. He must have stood them up for me.

I am sandwiched between Charlene and a big girl with dark, glowing skin who I don't really know. Of course she's the one who turns to me.

"So, what 'choo bin up to? I nevah wen see you round no moa'."

Kei, they called to me from the inside of the sampan. I'm wearing a flowered blouse my sister and I sometimes swap and a cotton skirt, but these are Kei's friends; they would certainly know the difference. Did they not know Kei has been grounded for weeks? And why would they expect to see my sister and Russell holding hands on the street?

"Oh my God, did you see Miss R at the basketball game?" Charlene asks, and my fumbling silence goes unnoticed.

"Some fancy, yeah, da dress?"

They don't require me anymore. I can smile and nod and be quiet, even when the conversation turns to Russell and the layup he made to end the first quarter at the last game. The girl I don't know asks if I saw it.

I am thinking of the way he snuck into the key, how his arm hooked the ball into the basket in a singular swoop. "Some fancy," I say. It just comes out that way, in the lightest pidgin, exactly mirroring the big girl's speech.

Russell does a quick double take when he hears me, but he's smiling. No one takes it as an insult that I'm mimicking her; no one seems to notice at all. Maybe no one here has ever heard me speak, outside of class where we're all expected to speak standard English anyway. Or maybe they actually do think I'm Kei—but how could they?

What I know, though, inside, is that it's Kei's voice I am using. I'm dipping my toe in, seeing what it's like to live inside Kei's life. The only thing more absurd than trying to pretend you're someone else in the midst of that person's inner circle is to try to balance being two people at the same time. To answer to two names and hope no one notices. But still I wonder: Can it hurt to let this play out?

It's a small tremor, a shifting ground, as I decide it can't hurt. Even as I wish Russell would say my name and rescue me from this limbo, I am also basking in the possibility of being new.

When we get to the beach, some of the guys call for a stop. Most have towels under their legs, but neither Russell nor I had dressed to go swimming. We are quickly left on our own as the others take off, pushing through the bushes, looking for a good spot. We walk more slowly, Russell holding some of the branches so I can pass.

Most of the places around the tide pools have families around them, so the group has gone over to a point, where the open ocean is broken up by rocky croppings, and a little island with a clump of ironwoods and a couple of palm trees sits just off the shore. The winter swells are over and the ocean is getting calmer, but there's still some surge around the rocks and along the outside of the island on the ocean side, and the bottom is rocky and not easy on the feet.

I'm still admiring the gorgeous day: Every color is saturated, and glazed by the sun: the black of the lava, the spectrum of blues in the sea and sky. The guys are in the water already. The first ones in stop and turn around to send big rooster tails of water into the faces of the others when they come up for air.

Russell and I are sitting and talking, waving off Missy, who keeps coming over like a stray dog. Although she's Kei's best friend, she's never said much to me, but today she's all about throwing her arm around my neck as she tries to coax us into the water. I wish she would say my name so I could be sure all this attention is really for me. She wants to pull us over to say hi to Eddie, her older brother and Kei's boyfriend, who was set up like a little king under one of the ironwood trees when we arrived. Eddie's a bit of a playboy, and he clearly hasn't wasted any time while Kei's been unavailable. The girl from the sampan is under his arm, leaning into him. Russell is not inclined to move.

"C'mon in. It's hot. Russell, Sammy has some swimming trunks for you."

It *is* getting hot, as Missy points out, and, besides Eddie and the girl, we're the only ones who have not been in the water. If I noticed a hint of whitecaps when we got here, there is now a small break developing on the other side of the island. The stretch between me and it seems an easy swim away, if I could swim.

"You love to swim!" Missy is looking at me.

"Yeah...I do." I can feel the lie twist. But Missy looks so delighted.

"You want to?" Russell asks.

Can I? I wonder. I would almost like to. Kids are in the water, though they're over where the stairs are. Even kids can do it.

I gesture to my clothes. "I can't."

He nods. Then: "Boy, it's hot, though."

He could take the offer of the trunks or we could join Eddie in the shade, but neither one of us makes a move. Missy flits down to the surf, then back, then down again, ankle deep in the water, calling us to join her. Much as I'd thought I would love a group of friends, I would much rather be left alone with Russell, just us two, to feel that personal gravitational force we both must lean away from lest we fall into each other. But my sister's friends are watching, as if we are the stars of a play staged in the round. I can't figure out why, unless they really do think I am Kei, and maybe they're wondering when I became so close with my sister's boyfriend. None of it makes sense, but for whatever reason, I can feel their active interest, even though each time I look up, they look away.

"I can teach you to swim," he says. "Or...we don't have to go out far. We can just get our feet wet."

"I meant..." How does he know I can't swim? I don't want him to think that, even if it's true. I've never lied to him, and I overdo it. "Of course I can swim. Who do you think I am? It's just...my clothes."

"Oh, that. They'll dry."

"I'll race you!" Missy is back, dripping wet. She challenges Russell.

"Nah."

"Oh, Russell, you're so boring. Both of you, all snuggled together. So boring." Her charm is powerful; I've never wanted to be in her orbit before, but suddenly I understand the force of her personality, why Kei has been drawn to her.

Missy pushes Russell away, playfully, and plops herself down behind me, curving her legs around me on either side. Before I can react, she starts combing her fingers through my hair. I can feel the difference in our body temperatures, and how the water from her suit pools in the tiny pukas in the lava we are sitting on and cools the rock down. I don't quite know what to do. She's so close, surrounding me, her breath on my shoulders. She's already separating out hefts of hair and braiding it into a crown. It's been so long since my mother sat me in front of a mirror, combing my hair from the tips to the roots and then roping it into pigtails to keep it from becoming a hopeless knot when Kei and I played outside. I forgot how good it felt.

"There," Missy says. "Now it'll stay out of the water and your mother will never know."

It is, at best, a curious statement. Is this what Kei does? How she gets away with things? Does she even worry about what Mama thinks anymore? I feel exposed, vulnerable. I can't shake the feeling that this sudden intimacy is all for Kei. I am cheating, letting it happen, pretending to be my sister. But in that masquerade, the vertigo of saying and not saying, I feel alive. I feel seen and loved for the first time in years.

"C'mon. I dare you. Let's go."

I'm surprised at how much her friendliness means, how I fall into it and accept that it belongs to me, when I suddenly see Kei. I freeze. She's there on the beach, walking up to Eddie in shorts and a red blouse, looking just like me. Two months ago, Kei would have been here and I would have been in the house with Mama, but now, isn't Kei supposed to be grounded? It's been a month, and I can't remember the last time I ran into her outside of school. It seems impossible that on the one day in my life I find myself at the beach with her friends, she is here. But here we are: two girls, both girls, at the same time.

I confess that I wish her gone in that moment. Whatever it would take to make her disappear, just for one more day. I want to stay with the warmth of the sun on my shoulders, Missy's fingers in my hair and

Russell smiling at me. Kei is walking toward Eddie and the girl from the sampan whose name, I have learned, is Lorna. It is a matter of seconds until everybody sees her.

This is not my place. It's time to leave. I try to rise, but Missy's hands are on my shoulders, pushing me back down, then snaking around so her upper arms are resting on my collarbones. At the same time, she glances over in the direction of her brother and Kei. Missy doesn't seem to react, doesn't pause or do a double take. Instead, she looks at me and smiles.

"Kei!" she calls. "Over here, Kei!"

Had she known all along, then? Had all this intimacy really been aimed at me? My sister turns toward her name, and doesn't look happy to see her best friend embracing me. I am caught—in Kei's narrowed eyes and pointed glower, and Missy's tightening hold on me. Will Kei run me off? Will she humiliate me for pretending I belong here? But then she turns back to Eddie, ignoring me.

Missy stands up and takes both my hands, then pulls me to her. "Race you," she says, as if I have already agreed to go into the water. I don't know what to do.

Russell gets up with us. "Are you really going in?" He's seen Kei, too, but of course he's always known who I am. None of the others have reacted with any surprise, either. I had given myself over to a silly fantasy, but with my sister standing there, I realize I am the only one who's confused and Kei is the only one who is angry.

Seeing me hesitate, Missy takes off, splashing into the water and then doing a smooth flat dive.

I take a step toward Kei, then stop. Something new has occurred to me. What if I don't give all this back to her, this gift of her friends' friendship? What if I stay?

Everything I am in this moment. Everything I am feeling. This can be me.

I smile at Russell and gesture down at my clothes. "Well, to the ankles at least. Or maybe to the knees."

He takes my hand—it's becoming a habit—and we walk into the surf together. The water's always colder than it looks, and it tingles against my calves. Missy is about five lengths away, bouncing and hollering and drawing attention to us. Russell and I are in almost to our knees, and I am holding my skirt with both hands. I'm in deeper than I should be— I can't raise my skirt much more without being indecent. We must look ridiculous, I think. Shipwrecked.

I wonder if Kei thinks so. The hems of Russell's madras shorts are swimming in the water, banding him in a wet ring up to his mid thighs, but he's teasing me for acting like a movie star who sees a cockroach. He isn't thinking about Kei, or the two of us here together. I am the only person he sees.

Back on the shore, I can see that Kei is still not happy. She's asking Eddie something and he's ignoring her. I assume it has to do with Lorna, but the girl seems bored by the exchange, not threatened. It isn't until Eddie turns away and Kei grabs his bicep that he gets into her face with his own and she drops her hand.

"C'mon, Kei! Eddie! Come join us!"

It's Missy again, her voice sounding like she can't see that things are tense on shore. But when I turn back to her she is treading water, waving to Kei. Eddie turns and walks away. Kei shrugs but doesn't acknowledge Missy's offer, signaling clearly that she wants nothing to do with me.

She looks so much like me then, so much like I must have the many times I was pretending nothing was wrong, I was fine, just lost in thought and weighing my options. Like it was my choice to eat alone, to study alone, to be the only one in class without a science partner. Kei is the one on the outside now. For just a little longer, I want her to stay there. Is that so terrible? I want, just for a minute, to savor being the one who is "in."

I feel a rush of adrenaline. "Last one in is a rotten egg," I call to Russell. I have been dared enough. I dive into the water, headfirst, fully clothed, before he realizes I'm serious. *Hold your breath. It is only one breath*, I think, calling back the few words of advice I allowed Mr. Torres to give me. *Don't suck in with your nose until you are all the way up*. My feet cycle for the sand almost as soon as I raise them, and then I'm up in a panic, gasping for air in waist-high water.

"You!" he says. Russell has followed me in and now he is laughing and swinging the water from his hair off to one side as boys do. I realize that I pulled the back of my head out of the water first like a drowning cat—it would be a mess except for Missy's braid. The bottom goes up and down but where I am it's shallow, and he creeps closer, keeping the lower edge of his face submerged with his body, as if he's a sea monster or a shark. When he bursts out of the water next to me, he is so close I can feel it pouring off him.

"You are really something, Hana."

In fact, I am. I am the only one in the water in a skirt. I am the only girl who has dared to walk into the ocean in street clothes. That Russell has done it with me, that it will be simple to dry and we will be respectful, if slightly salty, in an hour, is not the point. I am the one who did it.

Missy gives me a thumbs-up. Russell is circling around me, splashing me gently to get me to sink down to my neck, or maybe that's just his way to bump against me with the water. I settle in, as the water warms around me, matching my skin so exactly I can barely feel where I end and it begins. When I lift my feet, even in my tucked position, I can float a little.

My sister is sitting on the beach, legs splayed out in front of her. She's watching me intently, raking her fingers in the sand. I know the conversation with Eddie didn't go well, but there are more important things than boys, I want to tell her.

I don't know yet what Kei is doing here, but I want to put my smile on my sister's face. I want to tell her that there is room for both of us. There has to be. I want to slip inside her, just as our mother used to slip in and out of the spirit veil, so she can see herself through my eyes: beautiful. I want to show her that it's a perfect day, a day of utter belonging, when all futures are still possible and there's no separation between you and the world. Even though I know now what they are planning—even though this day is the end, the last day I remember before the cave—still it is the best, most beautiful day, and I refuse to believe it has to end here. I am me, and I am *really something*. Can't there be a world in which that is allowed?

We were Koko once. Before there was a Kei or a Hana, we were two girls, never apart. In all the lives I never lived, here is the one I long for the most: I am the girl who waves to my sister from the water; who saves her from Eddie; who is unafraid to be seen. I am the one who calls out, with the lightest lilt of pidgin entering my voice, my new voice, that is my own.

"Come on in, Kei!" I am calling to my sister. "Come in with us. The water is fine."

HANA

I pass through the vestibule of the police station without a tremor, this time with my sketch in my purse. It's a bright afternoon, but still, my lack of fear is a good sign. Maybe the high school Hana is resurfacing, after all. Her flash of confidence is more than welcome now.

The officer at the desk, Sergeant Cole, is a younger, pleasant-looking man with round glasses. "I'd like to speak with Detective Lynch, please? Or Detective Tapper?" I tell him. "It's about the Keiko Swanson... Hanako Swanson... case? On Claremont Avenue? A week ago?"

He picks up a phone, not quibbling about the double name, and listens to it ring. Then he asks me to wait for a minute while he locates the detectives. I sit in one of two wooden chairs along the wall. It's quite a bit more than a minute, enough that I wonder if I should have made an appointment. When he returns, he says Detective Lynch will be back in twenty minutes but that in the meantime, she asked him to show me a lineup.

I imagine myself standing behind one of those special viewing windows I've only seen in the movies, picking out the man in the lobby and then pulling my sketch out to show Sergeant Cole precisely how well I have captured his essence. But that vision is short-lived. He takes me back to a desk and hands me six plain file folders, each containing the photograph of a different man.

"I thought you said this was a lineup?"

"This is how we do it." His voice matches his mild face as he explains that I should look at them one at a time, and let him know if I recognize anyone.

There I am again, with mug shots, only these are bigger. And again, none of the men are white. Why do the police keep ignoring my description?

"No." I flip through them too quickly. "This can't be right."

Sergeant Cole has stepped away, out of my sight line. He tries to look encouraging. "I know it's hard. But if you put him back into the room where it happened, you might recognize him."

I have never seen any of these men before. Even allowing for the most liberal use of the word *swarthy*, each also has some defining feature: a strange, twisted nose, a scar, a stoop, a potbelly. My sketch loosened something inside me, and I thought it was almost over. But now, I could not feel more suffocated than if I was swimming in a pool of tar.

Do the police know something I don't? Could it be that the man I saw in the lobby was a random stranger, maybe readying himself, as I searched for my keys, to ask if I needed help?

Showing them my sketch now would just make me seem even more crazy. And what do I know? Maybe Kei's attacker really did go in and out the window. After all the effort I went through to draw him, maybe there was no double take at all?

I feel the possibility as if it's creeping up behind me. Why does it feel so dangerous?

I look back at the mug shots. If the cops are right, if Kei's attacker is there, would I feel him? At least Sergeant Cole is beside me to keep me safe. "It's okay," he says, after I ask twice for more time. He takes pity on me then and says something he probably shouldn't. "We have him."

At first, I assume he means that the man is in custody, and therefore can no longer hurt me. Then I realize he means evidence.

"Was any of it from my apartment?"

"There you are!" Detective Lynch interrupts us. She is weaving through desks on her way toward us, traveling in a waft of stale frying oil and Chinese food. When she reaches us, she spins a chair from a nearby desk around and pulls it over. "I didn't know that we'd finally gotten ahold of you. By the way, I heard you were having a hard time last time you left here. Broken shoes or something?"

Is she being snippy, or is she testing me? "I'm fine. Thanks. I heard you caught the guy?"

Detective Lynch gives Sergeant Cole a flat look. "We've made an arrest in another case. That might be what you heard. We have eyewitnesses from some of the other buildings."

"*Some* of the buildings?"

"Another girl saw him when he attacked her," Detective Lynch continues, appraising me. "He's a thief, making that little enclave around your sister's place his own. The attacks were accidents—he picked an apartment that wasn't empty and got surprised." She shrugs. "Shit happens. It's just bad luck."

Shit happens. How to wrap my mind around this? Shit happened to the poor burglar who picked the wrong apartment? Or to my sister?

"And this other woman?"

"He knocked her over, but she faked blacking out and called 911 before he was even down the stairs."

If only Kei had been smart enough to fake it. This thought replaces *If only she had screamed for help*, which goes along with *If only she had thought to lock the door.* These are all that stand between me and the accusation: *If only I had gone out to the airport to meet her, or had been home to greet her when she arrived.*

But now, there's another possibility. Shit happens. It is Kei's worldview, and my worst nightmare. How could we live in a world where people get hurt, killed, even, for no reason? How can a person protect herself if she can simply be in the wrong place at the wrong time?

And yet...if he was there to steal, why leave behind a hefty chunk of jade? Why not at least open Mama's leather case? "He didn't strangle this other woman?"

"Each break-in is not identical, Miss Swanson. It only happens that way in the movies."

I can't mention the necklace or the case, since I left them out of my original statement. But why would a thief leave them?

This magical thinking has to stop, I tell myself. They have him. Whoever he is. I have to stop believing that my intuition has anything to offer Kei and let it go. We are safe now, Kei and I. That's something to celebrate. I can stand in my living room and look out at the night without the fear that I, as a witness, have to be silenced. There was no half-glimpsed truth in my hallucinations; no perfectly intuited double take. No role for me.

Shit happened, and now it is over.

I have almost convinced myself of that when she continues. "We did find your sister's driver's license in the alley under the fire escape window. You should fill out a claims form to get it back."

"Really? No one told me."

"You haven't been answering your telephone."

Now I am sure I don't like her expression. "You found her wallet in the alley? So your suspect didn't have it on him?"

"No wallet. Just the license. Sometimes they dump them."

It's all coming at me so jumbled. The fact that I can have her ID back, that the window *was* the key. Detective Lynch doesn't trust me, and why should she? I told her I worked late at the restaurant, and then told her I didn't work. But she checked my alibi, and I can still help.

"I drew this. It's what I remember." It's my last chance to right any wrongs I made in cleaning up the apartment in my shock. I pull out the picture and hand it to her.

She looks at me with a mixture of exasperation and annoyance, but also something more. In her expression, I can see a flash of Arnie: the way his brow furrowed when the faucet was still leaking after he had replaced the washers and the tape and tightened all the joints, after he had searched his toolbox for inspiration and even switched out parts that were perfectly good. It was the expression that said he had arrived at that point when he was torn between continuing to fiddle until the fix was found and smashing the pipes with a hammer. But still, she looks at the sketch.

I look at it, too. Only this time I can see it upside down, and I recognize him.

I have drawn Eddie.

With that, the vertigo slides in. I am fragile, exhausted. The police flooded my brain with predators, and I was so determined to prove them wrong. But the monster I drew this time was my own.

I was only trying to help. I was trying to be a good witness, a good sister. Being good, I thought, would protect me. *They* would like me, whoever they were. They wouldn't hurt me.

Being good would keep me safe.

But the joke—on me—is that I have lived my whole life that way and it never worked. I am still afraid. I'm afraid of men, afraid of being robbed, afraid of being strangled and left to die in my own bathtub. I'm afraid of being misunderstood, and of being the victim. I am afraid of losing my sister, and losing my mother. I am afraid of drowning, and so very afraid of the dark. My fear hasn't protected me. It has eaten me alive, literally poisoning me, and the question is: How long did I refuse to notice?

Time flows in all directions. Our past has almost filled itself in. And the truth I must face is this: I am *not* good.

We are not your friends, Eddie said to me. And he was right. *Not your friends, not your friends.* The words play in my mind—I can't stop them—in the singsong voice that has been with me ever since I came out of the cave.

That's when the final blow hits me. I realize what I am listening to. Kei's voice.

The voice in my head is Kei's. The singsong I thought I created to help keep me sane is now an endless, taunting loop winding tight inside my brain. How is it possible that I never understood that before now? I thought all along that I was healing, when in truth, I was invaded. By a voice I thought was my own.

Suddenly, I am running. Out of the police station, four blocks to home, with no concern for what strangers might think of the only white girl on the street racing like the devil himself is behind her. I run through my lobby and up three flights of stairs, unable to wait for the elevator. But my apartment isn't the sanctuary I am looking for. I can hear Kei's voice in my head, whispering to me. *Jus' one joke. Jus' one joke. Jus' one joke.*

How could it have been her all along? The singsong proves that I *am* crazy, that Kei has driven me crazy by luring me into a cave the same way she tried to lead me into the ocean on the day of the tidal wave. For the last six years, she's been hounding me, haunting me, directing me like a paper doll.

She made me. And now, I have something for her to see.

I walk into the bathroom where I found my sister and strip off my clothes, baring myself in a blast of cold daylight. I yank the duct tape off my mirror, strip by strip. Through the ghosting of old adhesive, I can see myself, fully naked for the first time since I left home. There they are: my scars, each one just as I mapped it. The long pink keloids that hug my calves. The buckling, misshapen little brains that used to be my knees. Even the crosshatched skin on my upper back, like a rusty plaid blanket, which I can't see.

Or, rather, where my scars are supposed to be.

The bathroom mirror gives me my body in pieces. There's a bump on my shoulder, but more of a slight asymmetry, unnoticeable unless you look. On my triceps, where the angry red snakes of scar tissue should be, raised lines of pearly white trail like icing, thick enough that I can't feel my fingers running lightly over my skin. It isn't the old tape residue on the mirror, or the distance. My forearms and hands look more textured than angry. My knees are knobby, blunted, but not so noticeably. And on my legs, patches of skin are slick and off color, but the effect is delicately marbled and not entirely unpleasant. Nothing that a pair of sheer hose won't conceal.

I look nothing like myself. The drawn, suffering version of my mother that I imagined doesn't look back at me in the mirror, nor does the soft, startled seventeen-year-old version that I last saw. My face is flushed, and sloppy from crying, but that isn't what's so shocking.

Where is the person I knew myself to be?

I grab my purse and pull Kei's pumice stone out of it. I have to see myself. I have to *be* myself. I am crying, stuttering sobs, but I won't let time and healing take away who I am. I grasp the stone in my hand and scrape the scar on my left tricep. The thickened skin pushes back against the pumice, so I dig in harder. I am digging for the pain. Looking for myself, and also looking to escape myself. It doesn't work; the stone's too round and smooth. I palm it in my hand and smash it on the corner of the sink, shattering it. I know the monster I became, and I need to recognize her. I pick up a jagged shard and place it against my forearm. And push.

Red dots spring up as my skin bursts. Blood. I can see it in the mirror. Suddenly I can feel, in a rush of heat, how the lava kissed that same line once, how the glassy, spun shards of rock shredded my innocent skin. I close my eyes and rake the rock from the inside of my elbow to my wrist.

A hot shot of life lights the inside of my arm.

See me, Kei.

I am here, at last, in the place where you abandoned me.

Time slips, and I slip with it. The shower recedes behind me and the endless darkness of the cave moves in. It's on the edges of my sight, suffocating: the memory I've been avoiding. This is it: the moment Dr. Shawe always warned me about. I expected to be a mess—straitjacketed, hallucinating—but my mind has never felt more clear.

I am back in the cave.

1 9 4 7

That many days into the Pacific, the stars were as bright and close as tiny searchlights in a blackout. The constellations looked different here. Every night, unless the wind was slapping spray from the black sea onto the pitching deck, Miya slipped past the riggings and cranes and turrets toward the stern of the transport ship. There, in the shelter she'd found between the bench where the life jackets were kept and the stacks of cargo lashed down with oilskin, she looked up and tried to recall the stars. She could always find the warrior, Orion; the two Dippers; and Pleiades; but the names of the others escaped her. Was it her memory that was unfamiliar and shifting, or this sky itself, as she sailed into a new world?

She liked the night, with its varying shades of disappearing. And the lights off the ship that dappled the ocean with silver, tipping the little waves in long lines before fading back to black. And the wake, too, the water instantly cleft by the prow of the boat, each half carried helplessly apart from the other—good-bye, good-bye—before being consumed by the enormity of the sea. Above her, the Milky Way was a band of bright clouds that seemed to catch the full moon, though of course it was too far for that. Too deeply past. That was what she liked the most about the stars: that when you saw their light you were looking back, past the beginning, to where time began.

Time before she was the mother of a beautiful boy she would never see again, except in a photograph. Before she was remarried and pregnant for the second time.

During the day, Miya stayed in her quarters, with its soft scent of old vomit. She shared a compartment with five strangers. There were three bunks on each wall with a passage between them that was barely wide enough to stand in, and one small porthole that didn't open. From here, through the hazy crust of salt on the glass, she could watch the ocean in the sunlight, almost as black as it looked under the moon. On the decks, the day was harsh and loud. The heat magnified the smell of the fuel, and the close press of the baking sun made her more nauseated than usual.

She took most of her food in her bunk.

The transport ship was a large village, or a small city. The troops, coming home. Of the thousands on board, only a handful were Japanese American, and not too many more than that were women. The women banded around her whenever she appeared. Calling her dear, clucking at her. Poor thing, barely more than a girl. What were the generals thinking, sending her home without her husband in her state? They counseled her about what to eat, and what not to eat; they debated whether she should worry about the deep circles beneath her eyes and her sallow skin, or the fact that she was always sleeping. They didn't know what the doctor had warned her in private: that her body was weak and there might be complications, even hemorrhaging, due to—he put it delicately—her time in Hiroshima, which meant the poison from the bomb. When they thought she couldn't hear, the women murmured about how she was all wrists and collarbones, like one of those skeletons. Except for her pregnant belly, which rose like a hot air balloon pushing even her small breasts up toward her chin.

Four hands, four eyes. Two hearts. She had never told her sergeant the doctor said there were *two* babies. Funny how she still thought of her new husband that way.

She fingered the pendant in her pocket. The long, green thumb of jade, her passport "home," to Hawaii, a place she'd never seen. There were palm trees and sand, Hanako had said, and little rivers running to the sea. When her best friend had talked about her home, there was no one listening who couldn't taste the ripe, scented mangos dripping through their fingers or feel the daily rain that left the grass sparkling and the trees and flowers heavy. It was safe, a place where everyone was welcome. And when the war was over, Hanako had always promised, they would go there together with Toshi.

Now Hanako was gone, and so was Toshi. Lillie, too, was a figment of the past. Miya was going to Hawaii alone. But she told herself that that was what Hanako would have wanted: the return of the pendant to her Aunt Suzy, and the welcome that would surely follow. It was what Miya herself would have wanted for her best friend if their positions were switched and she had a home to give. Since Miya left her parents' farm, the war had tossed her from place to place. Hawaii was *her* choice; a place of safety where she could finally stay.

A home, she thought, with her hand on her belly. A true home, for a family that no man and no country could ever take away from her again.

Tomorrow, they would dock in Honolulu to load more fuel and supplies before the last, long leg to San Francisco. Miya had looked for land all day through the cloudy glass of the porthole but didn't see it. She liked the idea of that: islands so small, you'd have to stumble on them. Hawaii was not a place where her sergeant would think to search for her. Her plan would hold. It had to. Even if passengers weren't supposed to go to shore, she had an excuse—milk, and fresh fruit; she needed perishable food. She was skin and bones, after all. Even if they spotted her, they would have to let her pass.

She was a free woman, and now a citizen once more. She had to remember that.

The babies kicked her. They were always kicking now. She was exhausted, and her blood felt as thin and weak as water. Miya knew, once they landed, that she wouldn't have much time to find passage to the island Uncle Joe and Aunt Suzy lived on. Once, she'd planned to send them a telegram, but now she knew she couldn't wait for an answer. The babies were coming early, she could feel it, and Miya couldn't take the chance of being so sick that she would get stranded for months in

Honolulu with infants in a hospital where her husband might eventually be able to track her down.

In her mind: the first sight of Aunt Suzy's face. Suzy Harada. She would look so familiar: the sharp lines across the bridge of her nose, the pincushion frown on the tip of her chin. The soft pouches under her eyes would be new, but otherwise Hanako's aunt would look just like she had in Hanako's picture. Hanako's pendant would be her message, too hard to voice, that Miya was the only one coming. She couldn't bear to see the hope drain from Aunt Suzy's face when she realized Hanako wasn't with her, but at least Miya could give them some answers to what happened so they weren't left to guess. She could tell them how much Hanako loved them, how her beautiful stories about them and their island were a lifeline during the war that kept her friends alive.

In her mind, she practiced walking off the gangplank with only her small handcase and her enormous belly, trying not to stumble this time when both feet reached solid land. Her freckled bunkmate, whom she'd paid with a golden silk fan and bewitched with stories of her terrible mother-in-law who would beat her when she arrived in San Francisco, could be counted on to vouch that she had returned to the ship. By the time anyone else found out Miya was missing, they'd be deep into the ocean crossing. They'd assume she had become despondent and thrown herself into the sea.

No sane person would run away, abandoning the four trunks full of silk kimonos, family scrolls, lace, and lacquer bowls. Her sergeant was giddy with all he'd collected, a bounty—a dowry, he called it—that would ensure her smooth acceptance into his family in South Dakota. He'd wanted to show her each item, but when he got to the long, bound tails of glossy hair that his mother could sew into exotic wigs, she couldn't take it any longer. She'd passed through plenty of black markets both in Hiroshima and Tokyo, where scavenged bits of what would be garbage anywhere else were proudly displayed on pieces of tin and cloth, and the more valuable family heirlooms were only a private conversation and a secret meeting place farther away. Didn't the Americans care about the lives they had taken? Miya wondered. Her sergeant was better than most. So why couldn't he, why couldn't any of them, see what they were doing, picking away every bit of value that was left in the remnants of those conquered lives?

But she had already married him. And behind the facade of romance and in the quiet acknowledgment that the troops were being recalled back to the States in waves now and quickly, what had once seemed impossible became easy enough: She had papers to go home. The Occupation suddenly had all the deliberation of a fire sale—everything must go, all bets off, everybody grabbing whatever they could carry and moving out—and all Miya had to do was to tell her sergeant that she was afraid. She was afraid of going into labor on the voyage. She was afraid of being left behind to give birth without him if he was ordered to leave when she was too pregnant to travel. It was a simple thing now for him to take care of her. Ships were sailing. He arranged for her to get on one. She could stay with friends—*his* friends, his buddy who was already home in San Francisco and who had plenty of room—and he would follow as soon as he could. They would travel across the country to South Dakota together when the baby was old enough. They would see the world by train. He would show her an America she'd never even dreamed of, with its sweeping prairies and huge mountains. They could stop to see the Grand Canyon.

These were his dreams. In the short time they were together, he, at least, had kept his promises. She worried for him a little: What would he do when she went missing? Would he suspect a grisly cover-up of a birth gone wrong? She imagined him pounding on all the compartment doors and forcing open the holds to look for her, but of course he wouldn't be there when the ship docked. He was still in Japan. It would be days before he got the news; it would be weeks, maybe even months, before he could follow her, and by then she would be long gone. Safe and hidden on a different island, sheltered with her babies, and the trail would be cold. The boarding cards would show that his wife had boarded in Yokohama and only hearsay and scattered memories might say what happened next. All her belongings would be accounted for.

Leaving, she thought. It's not so bad when you have somewhere to go.

The last two nights, the sky had been overcast with only a few points of light peeking through the blanket of clouds, but on her last night before her disappearance, the wind picked up and the stars were clear once again.

And in that moment, with so many stars winking and most of them close enough to touch, Miya remembered how she used to lean against her father to keep warm as they took turns making up names for the stars. That was how Pleiades, the Seven Sisters, became a cloud, became the Golden Egg, became the Baby Jesus. Just like a baby swaddled and left on a doorstep, her father had said. They had gazed up together at the constellation, tracing the outlines of the little bundle of joy. Though she had been a young girl then, she would not forget the night that they'd changed the name of the Pleiades constellation to the Blessed Child. It was her father's idea, in honor of the swaddled orphan.

He had raised her to be strong enough to be okay without him. She had to believe that, too, when she gave up her son. Love was not connected to a presence. She could love despite loss, beyond death. Miya knew she had done her best for Toshi. He was alive because of it, living in a country that was beginning to heal, where everyone would look like him. She was alive because of him, too. If she hadn't left to search for him, she would have been killed by the bomb. They had survived, and though in separate worlds, happiness was still possible. Toshi's unborn siblings were proof of that—she knew she would always see him inside them—and it was up to her to make a good life for them, too. Still, she felt her tears come as she looked up at Pleiades, smudging her vision so at first it seemed like there were two constellations, touching each other, before they resolved into one. Two babies. She had been looking for their names, and it gave her an idea.

When the sun rose in a few short hours, Miya would see the volcanic peaks of Paradise rising out of the ocean in the distance. The ship would stop for supplies, and she would totter her way down the gangplank to shore, barely memorable amid all the other passengers getting off to stretch their legs. There, she would find a large, browned man with a big laugh who said he could get her on a boat. The dull ache in her lower belly, a tight band around her hips, would confirm that there was, once again, no time to send a telegram to Uncle Joe and Aunt Suzy before she boarded the empty cattle transport, its engines already running and about to cast off the dock. On it, she would set course for the new life Hanako had offered her.

This time, she would make sure that no one would stop her from taking her children and going home.

HANA

I wake like the dead: heavy legs and arms, groggy. The first thing I notice, as I try to get my bearings, is that my head is empty of dreams. I am lying on my floor, naked, wrapped in a sheet dried brown and stiff with bloodstains. When I move, hard disks of blood crackle and peel themselves off my skin.

The cave rushes back, then wraps around me. I remember. And that memory turns my stomach over, turns me inside out. Of all the possibilities that the blank in my mind could have been hiding, the truth is something I would never have suspected. It's inconceivable.

Yet, I know.

I have to tell Kei. I have to see her. This is a story she will surely wake for, if I can just bring myself to form the words. I imagine myself sitting beside her on the edge of her bed, holding her hand, just as I've been doing for so many days, but with a difference. The girl I was before was numb, stunned. Uncomprehending. There's no way she could have reached her sister in such a weakened state.

I sit up, dump the sheet in the kitchen sink before taking stock of my wounds. The new ones are just an echo of what they were after the cave. The first cut, under my left arm, ends in a ragged pucker that might need a stitch or two, but the rest are just a little oozy in the cracks of the scabs when I move. I find some old gauze, left over from the days when an extra layer felt good between my skin and my clothing, but I have to tape it on with Scotch tape, which makes for a stiff-legged walk and some telltale crinkling. I know Eckert has hospital tape and anything else I need, and that there will be time enough for dealing with this once I get there. With six years between us, my recovered memories can't wait another hour.

I keep to myself when I get to Kei's floor. The last thing I need is Bree's usual perky morning greeting. *Hey there, Coco Chanel,* I can almost hear her saying. *You look like death warmed over. I didn't think we were going to see you today.* There will be no more need for more stimulation therapy, not once I tell Kei what really happened. She can hear—isn't that what Bree said? What I remember will free us both.

"Kei?"

The halls are quiet, and she seems peaceful, alone in her room. I half expect that she's gone through some kind of similar revelation in the night, that she woke up already knowing what I can't quite figure out how to tell her, but that is wishful thinking, too. As usual, she doesn't answer. My left arm aches, so I roll up my sleeve and am applying a thin layer of ointment on the cut on the underside of my forearm when Bree appears in the doorway. She glances at my arm and hesitates, as if some other duty calls, and I flash on the first time I ever saw her at Eckert, how she was on her way elsewhere that day, too. But she lets herself be drawn over to Kei's bed.

"Bike accident," I offer, rolling my sleeve back down as quickly as I can. The fabric sticks to the ointment. My excuse is believable. In the light of day, my arm looks like I suffered no more than a shallow scrape I could easily have gotten from sliding along the pavement.

Bree seems tired. I've been through hell, and I know I look it, but she doesn't ask how I am.

Instead, she stands beside Kei. "Why do you call her 'K'?"

"Oh." Was she lurking in the hall when I came in? I drop down onto the corner of Kei's bed, too exhausted to come up with a good answer. "It's just a nickname. From childhood."

"What does it mean?"

"Well," I begin, "we both have a *K* in our names..." Almost anything else would sound more plausible. There is a momentary silence.

"How could you think you would get away with it?"

We both keep our eyes on my sister's body while I try to sift through all the things I'd hoped to get away with. Or at least all the things I have been trying not to face. I still have not answered when she relents. "It might have helped if we had at least been calling her the same name."

Bree sighs and seems to want to sit. Instead, she straightens, professional and clearly wanting to get what she has to say next over with. "Her insurance denied payment. It seems there's some discrepancy with the police report."

I would have panicked once, but I'm so weary that it's almost a blessing to be caught. "Really?" It doesn't sound like a question.

"She's being transferred off the ward tomorrow."

"But..." Kei doesn't look any different. "To where? I don't understand."

"She's not responding to our treatment. There's some concern about her fever and a possible infection. If she's unresponsive when they test her, as long as she's not septic, she'll be transferred to a long-term care facility. An evaluation team has my notes."

"You're giving up on her?" How long has Bree been calling Kei's condition unusual? How many times has she said there's no significant damage, no medical reason why Kei shouldn't wake up? "I thought we had another day? Another week if I was here to help you? I thought you said she wasn't really in a coma? How can you make a decision like that?"

"I'm sorry." Bree picks her words carefully. "These things are hard to predict. And look into her insurance, Koko—I mean, if that's what your name is. Without it, she'll end up at City, and that's not where you want her to go."

Bree is angry with me for lying about Kei's name, but what's a stupid name, anyway? Does it really matter what we're called? Kei would answer to either name, just as we did when we were still Koko, before our names finally stuck. Or perhaps she's mad because I didn't come in yesterday? Is that why this is happening? "You said she wasn't in a coma."

Bree doesn't point out that I'm repeating myself. "I did. But apparently your 'K' disagrees."

"But..." How could this happen just as I got Kei's driver's license back? Of course, I ran out of the police station without it, but the point is, I can sort out the documents now. I just need a little time. Time is the one thing Bree keeps insisting we can't afford to waste. How can she abandon us? "There have to be some other tests. I'll pay for them."

Despite all Bree's talk about the mystery of Kei's condition, I realize that she also holds the opposite view: that Kei was attacked and the answer lies there, not in some past family drama. What if she's right? What if there is no wishing away whatever's happening in Kei's body, just like there's no wishing away cancer? Insurance, mug shots, what if none of it was ever important?

What if it's out of my hands?

But Kei is a fighter. She could never be hurt. She's the lucky one, the one who gets away with everything, and I need her to fight now, just as she did after the Big Wave, and at every swim meet, and in the school yards. I need her to fight, not just for herself, but for me. Now more than ever, knowing what I know now, I cannot bear to be alone.

Before I can say more, I hear the tone in Bree's voice, clubbing my words back to earth. "Go home, Koko, or wherever you have been the last two days. There's nothing more you can do here. Find someplace for your 'K' to go."

This can't be the end of hope. There are things I need to say. Truths that have to be sorted through and amends to make. I am suddenly hollowed by the thought that during this whole week sitting beside Kei, I haven't even heard her speak, and now I might never hear her.

"They'll be by to start her testing in the next half hour. If I were you, I'd make sure I wasn't around for that until I get my answers straight, because they'll have questions."

Is Bree kicking me out? How is that possible? "Please. I need some time with her." Bree starts to shake her head, but I talk over her. "Give me a few minutes with my sister? Please. You asked me to tell her stories and I have one I know she'll want to hear."

On Kei's left wrist, my name. But in her right palm, the proof that it is her. On the edge of Kei's bed, I pick up her hand, tracing and retracing the wiggles and turns of the scar in her palm. It's a symbol of her resilience. A reminder that Kei is like a phoenix, who can burn everything around her and rise from the ashes.

But I have no such regeneration skills, for me or for her. I am finally at rock bottom: a place beyond blood, or exile. It's a place of nothingness. Nowhere. And despite what I just promised Bree, it's a place without stories. For stories have always been a lifeline; a way to get out. And in this story, there is no escape.

Bree lingers at the door as I swing my legs around to lie down on Kei's bed, curling beside her. I nestle her head against my shoulder so her cheek lays on my collarbone. She is warm against me, but there's no response. I rake my fingers over her scalp and sink them into her long hair. Then I simply hold her. This is my fault, and now, without my sister, I am no one.

What to say? Where to start? Bree lingers to hear my next words, the most important words I'll ever utter. There's no time left and no excuses.

"It's all my fault, Kei," I whisper to the top of her bent head just like Mama used to do when we were Koko. "I'm so sorry. It was me."

Rising

K E I

There is light on the other side, now. I see it.

There is moonlight. A half circle. Everything black and white along the winding road. I can see the gnarled ohia trees, the ones that are pocked and gray even in the daytime. Petrified trees, against a petrified landscape. Their red pincushion flowers disappearing against the tufts of rock.

On this road, the weather changes, bend after bend. The rain drifts. The mist moves in from between the trees like an eerie forward army. It flits from one side of the road to another, hovering just above the pavement without leaving a darker footprint. The stars above are bright.

I can see all of this, and more, under the moon.

You and I are in the back of the pickup truck, Hana. All of us pressed against the cab to stay out of the wind. I don't know the name of the driver, though I'm sure I recognize him. He's one of the guys who got suspended in high school for breaking a door. He's a big guy, with a struggling goatee and a flattop buzz cut, and Missy tosses her hair more when he's around. Missy and Lorna are in Eddie's car. Charlene is here with us, and Russell. Until tonight, I never noticed how soft he looks, with his curling hair and thin arms.

You and I left the house together, but you shrug off my warnings. Since I came to the beach to save you, you haven't once allowed yourself to be alone with me. I know there's a plan, though Missy scoffs at my suspicions. I know that smile, which she can't keep off her face. It's not much proof. It's not something anyone else would notice. That's why I don't say more, not that you will let me. All I can say to you is: These aren't your friends.

I have followed you to the beach. I have watched you in the water. I made sure I planted myself on the shore right in front of you where I could grab anyone racing back onto the beach with your skirt. I didn't know which of them might do it: Missy or Russell. They were both flittering around you, but I knew I could outrun either one. I could tell that you didn't know what to do with all Missy's attention, but with Russell, you suspected nothing. I saw you flush as he got close. I could feel it. I watched how you kept your bodies under the surface of the water so no one could see you touch.

That was then, and nothing happened. I had guessed wrong. But tonight is the dance.

Mama got into the truck with Arnie to drop us off at the theater. It was the last senior dance, and the first one we had ever been to together, and she said she wanted to see us off. Arnie teased her, told her not to worry. "She's with Hana. Hana won't let anything happen." Mama smiled and patted your hand as we got out. "Good girl," she said. And then, "Have fun."

Even then you ran to Russell and wouldn't let me speak to you. Once everyone gathered, we headed out of town. Back up the hill, past our house, where we all lay down in the back of the flatbed. That road runs for hours through the saddle of two volcanoes, all the way to the other side of the island. And in between there is rain forest, lava fields, a military camp, and, sometimes in the middle of the winter, a glimpse of snow on the peaks.

But we are not passing over the saddle. Eddie's car pulls over barely a mile past our house, and then we, too, are bumping along gravel and grass. Across the road from where we park is the cave.

The cave was an underground lava tube until the roof fell in. Now it's two caves accessed at the bottom of a pit, some thirty feet or so below the surface of the earth. On one side, it opens like a huge mouth: Fangs of ferns and long, hanging roots drip softly onto the moss-covered rocks. The opposite entrance is small, more secret. I have been here before with Arnie. We stopped on a whim that day, and walked in only until we couldn't tell if the chills we felt were the result of the cold or the ghosts. As we sat and looked out at the glowing portal to the green world outside, he told me the cave snakes along for miles. It dips and drops and squeezes through holes, but it keeps going.

When Arnie and I came here, we weren't prepared. Even so, he could reach under the seat to grab the flashlight he kept there, the one that banged back and forth in the well of the floor and was almost never used. It cast a brown-tinged light, ringed by the concentric circles of low batteries.

It is one of Arnie's mantras: Never go anywhere without a flashlight in your car. Never get into a car without flares, and a jack, and a lug wrench. The truck he dropped us off in was equipped like that.

Where is Arnie when you need him?

I know you hate caves. You've always hated close spaces, and more than that, you hate the dark. When we were two girls growing up, you couldn't sleep with the curtains closed. You needed the light in the eaves outside so there was no mistaking a dress for an old straggly-haired *obake* appearing at the foot of your bed. I would like to take comfort in the fact that this cave is one of the two places I can be sure you will never enter.

Except that the other was the ocean.

Don't cross the road, Hana. We could stay right here. We could walk home together, you and I. It's not so far. If they won't take us to the dance, we'll make our own fun, together.

But you are too happy that Missy and the others have included you.

You are wearing a yellow spring dress you made yourself. A tiny, hand-sewn line of white lace edging the round, open collar. That's my sister—so much more beautiful than the flower Russell has pinned on your chest. Your arms are bare beneath your cap sleeves. I try to give you my sweater, since my sleeves are longer, but I think you'd rather have a reason to shiver under Russell's arm.

I took *him* aside at school before the beach trip. He seemed oblivious, but you never knew. I told him, "You better watch out for Hana. If anything happens to her, I will make you pay."

Now, as we walk down the steep steps into the pit, Missy's chattering about how this is "our hideout." I don't even know who "our" is. She has never mentioned the cave to me before. Who do I know here? Charlene, Missy, Eddie—who do I really know? There's no one I can trust, nothing I can say that might be safe, but I still venture a single word. "'Our'?"

"It's no fun being left out, is it?" Missy asks me.

You almost nod, as if Missy's truth is undeniable, but then you just pull Russell tighter. You don't know Missy and I are having a different conversation, beneath the one everyone else can hear.

"Let's go this way," I suggest, pointing to the smaller entrance once we reach the bottom. This side is just tall enough to walk into without crouching but it leads down. I am counting on the fact that you will refuse to sit on the wet rock to slide inside. "Scared?"

"Nah," Eddie says, *tsk*ing like I'm the one who's trying to pull something. He takes the group into the root-hung, cathedral-sized chamber Arnie and I sat in, hugging our knees and looking out.

It's cooler down here in the bottom of the pit. The air is clingy. There's no ducking in this end of the cave, not for a while, not past many lengths of the light of the two flashlights. Eddie and his friend are the only ones who brought lights—the rest of us are dressed for the dance, not prepared for a cave hike. We are at their mercy, down here in these unhinged jaws.

At first, the lights are strong enough, slicing into the darkness at random. They catch flashes of walls and a ceiling—black, white, and broken—and a floor that shivers with brick-red ridges. On one side, the cave is a pile of loose rocks, but there's a natural path along the right wall: It's like a mouth with the tongue pressed down, and the sides curl over to form a ledge that will catch our calves if we aren't careful. The cave sucks up all the chatter we came in with. I can hear breathing, an occasional comment, but our voices shrink instinctively to whispers. As we move in deeper, there are smooth reddish bands on certain ledges, into which names have been carved. The rock is rough, pocked by air holes and bristling with buds and filaments of black glass.

The flashlights stay ahead of me, forcing me to keep up. I nudge my feet forward, trying to slide the soles of my flimsy sandals along the ground, knocking my toes on rocks and sudden steps. It's getting more rocky and harder to maneuver. We are going around a bend.

As quickly as that, I lose track of you.

"Can we have a flashlight back here, please?" I don't like how high my voice sounds, how strained in the thickness of the dark.

"Watch your head!"

The ceiling is still high where I am. He must be warning of more ledges ahead. But it's Eddie's voice, and when I hear it, I know which light is his. It's hard to judge distance with the lights always moving, but he's closer than I thought. I keep my eyes trained on his light, moving as quickly as I can manage with my hands straight out in front of me. I've made up some of the gap between us when his light blinks off. The flash of it, there and then gone, imprints itself green on my retina. Then I see him. He's holding the light beneath his chin. Laughing. Pleased with himself.

The light goes out again. With all the switching on and off, my vision, or lack of it, is a patchwork of yellow-edged shadows. "Hey, quit it!" I try to keep my voice light, joking. I can hear the others laughing, too—no one seems concerned. I have to feel my way forward with my hands out in front of me, but Eddie's still enjoying his joke and is not moving away.

"Give me the flashlight!"

"Get your own!" He was not expecting me to grab him, but he's still much stronger, and my fingers slip away before I can get a firm hold.

"We need one in the back." I have lost his arm and the dark rushes in between us.

"Turn them both off," Eddie orders. His voice comes from off to my left when I was sure he was on the right of me. Sound and light pinballing in a space I can't make sense of, except that every time I think I have my bearings, I get turned around.

We are still walking. The two lights go on and off at whim, lighting the way only for those near them.

"Careful!" Hana, hear me. "Hold your hands out in front of your head."

I feel like a fool. It'll only egg them on if they think I'm frightened. But I know you must be terrified, and I need to know where you are. "Everybody look for the lichen. It glows in the dark."

"Ooh...lichen!" Eddie mocks. "Don't get eaten by the lichen!" He sounds much farther away.

I try again, sounding as casual as I can. "Everyone all right?" I am willing you to reply, but Eddie's cackle explodes against the cave walls, drowning out any other sound. Is it my imagination, or is he zigging and zagging to throw us off? In the dark, it would take more skill than I would have credited him with, but he's proving impossible to follow. He is climbing, or is he holding his occasional flashlight above his head? "Last one to the clubhouse is a rotten egg."

There is no clubhouse, Hana. No one hangs out here. Surely you have figured that out by now.

I make one last attempt to close the distance between me and Eddie, but manage only to smash my toe. I can feel the end of it slice open and begin to burn. Eddie wasn't faking. I have hit a steep pile of rocks. I know the cave continues, because the lights keep blinking on and off ahead of me, and also above me, so there must not be a way around. I keep going: climbing over the pile on all fours, testing each rock. It's so slow; I don't know how I'm going to reach them. It's ridiculous that I'm still trying to go deeper but I am. It's better than being in the dark alone.

That's when my hand grabs an ankle. I pull on it before I realize what it is, and pull her body down into me.

Hers is a soft body, balled up in front of me. My fingers slide through her hair. My other hand, as I reach out to keep myself from pitching forward, lands on her back.

"Hana?"

"Kei? Oh, Kei. Thank God!"

The voice is trembling, both of us whispering. It takes me a minute to place it.

"Charlene? Are you okay?"

"No. I mean...no." Charlene's voice is low, yet I've never heard her so close to wailing. "What the heck are we doing here?"

"You don't know?"

"No. It sure wasn't my idea. I hit my knee so hard!"

"You don't have a flashlight?" I don't know why I asked. "C'mon. We have to keep up, then. We can't lose the lights."

My sister is in the cave, Charlene. That's what I don't say. *She's not safe with them.* "They're leaving us."

"I can't. I'm so...I'm scared, Kei. I feel like I'm burning up. Feel my head."

I put my hand out and fumble for her forehead. She *is* hot, and sweating.

"I have to get out of here. Please."

We're both whispering. I have lost my bearings. I can hear the clatter of rocks ricocheting as the rest of the group continues somewhere ahead, but much farther now, and I'm having a hard time identifying the true direction of the sound.

"They have to come back this way," I say at last. "Let's just wait. We'll hear them coming. They'll stumble right over us."

"Please, Kei. Get me out of here." Charlene is crying now in earnest, though she is still trying to choke back her tears so no one hears. There is no response from our so-called friends, if they can even hear her. "I can't bear it. I have to get out."

"Okay, then."

There is nothing else to do. The lights have disappeared altogether, but I know from the slide of the rocks which way is out. We sit, facing the direction we think we need to go in, and crawl like crabs. Feet first, then butt, then hands. The rocks tip and roll under us, smashing my fingers. Every step seems so tiny compared to the distance we have to travel. Charlene is still whimpering and I have to stop occasionally to hold her hand so she knows I haven't left her. We are so close we can hear each other breathing, and yet it is still so easy to panic. Even her tight squeeze on my throbbing fingers feels much better than being alone.

At last I feel the ledge, and the path that leads out to the entrance. Here, we can get to our feet, and we can almost see. Even though the night is dark, it's a different kind of darkness.

"There it is!"

The moon is higher in the sky. When we step out into the open, Charlene throws her arms around me and squeezes her full body against mine. She is so short, her cheek rests on my clavicle. I hold her for longer than I've ever hugged another person, feeling the adrenaline pass through both of us, leaving us shaking and drained.

At last, we break apart and Charlene sinks down on a boulder. Her right knee is mottled black and red with blood, the edges what Arnie would call "quite a strawberry" puffy. Even though we're both banged up, this is the worst of our wounds. Still, she circles it with her thumbs and index fingers, pressing into her knee as if to corral the pain.

"Thank you, Kei. I was so hot, I couldn't even think."

Her body is cooler. Clammy, but no longer fevered. "I don't know what happened. Suddenly, I was so dizzy and I just couldn't move."

"You're safe now," I assure her. "You're okay."

But I am not, though I can't say that out loud. Hana is still in the cave. I came here to save my sister, and I saved someone else instead.

Call her. Bring her back.

That's what Mama said. But Hana never listens.

Call Koko. Keep calling her until she answers. Look up her address, then. Get her back here.

A long time later, five of them emerge. Eddie's bodyguard friend, whose name I refuse to remember, comes out first, then Lorna and Eddie himself. They are laughing and shoving each other and swinging their dark flashlights. Next come Missy and Russell.

Russell seems confused by the fact that it's Missy who's hanging on to his hand. He stops and tugs away, looking around her and then right at her, as if she might turn into you. Missy is making *Ooh, you're so brave* cooings to distract him, but no one else seems to notice that there is no sign of my sister.

"Where is Hana?" I ask Eddie first, since I'm sure that whatever he did, it was his plan. He swings his head around with extra extravagance, then shrugs.

"Where. Is. Hana?" Three words. Unmistakable. I give up on Eddie and deliver them directly to my best friend, the girl I have given everything to for the last four years of my life. Standing in plain sight, without Russell's hand to protect her, she's having a hard time finding something safe to look at. "Missy?"

She doesn't answer.

"What is she, your babysitter?" Eddie steps into the fragile space between me and his sister. "Who's the baby now?"

"I thought..." Russell is looking around, still trying to put together what he's seeing. "When we did that switching thing in the circle..." It's clear what he thought. How stupid he is, how easily duped.

"What thing? What did you switch? What did you do to her?" Now I'm just broadcasting, hoping someone might be shamed into an answer. "Where is my sister?"

Missy has spotted Charlene and rushes over, as if a scraped knee is the worst thing in the world. "We should probably get her to a doctor," she says, keeping her eyes on a tight line from the knee to Eddie.

Look at me, Missy, I think. Tell me what you did. I remember the first time I saw Missy's onyx eyes staring right at me. I remember thinking how otherworldly she was then, possessing secrets no one else was special enough to know.

But now, Missy sets her gaze beyond me. Her face is as blank as a doll's.

"Where is Hana?" I keep saying it. If I say it over and over, someone will have to respond.

"How should we know?" In all the time I spent with Eddie, I've never seen him come to his sister's defense quite so strongly. "It was dark in there. She'll be out soon."

"Give me the flashlight."

"No way. Get off me. Don't be a baby. She's probably right there inside, listening to everything we say."

My former boyfriend is smirking at me and suddenly I can't take it anymore. "What a jerk you are, Eddie. If you were so pissed I dumped you, why didn't you take it out on me? Huh? Why turn on some poor girl who can't defend herself? Didn't have the guts to face me, did you? You've never had the guts."

He's in my face again. He grabs my hair and yanks my head back. I'm sure he's about to hit me. I want him to try it. If he has hurt my sister, I will kill him myself.

Russell steps in. "The flashlights don't work, Kei."

My head immobile under Eddie's fist, I shift my eyes to Russell in disbelief.

"The flashlights...I mean, that's what you said, right?" Russell is looking from person to person, at the flashlights in their hands, the truth slowly coming to him. "Eddie's died and then there was only the one that we had to shake in order to get a connection. That's what you said, right? That's why we had to come out in the dark?" He's so pathetic. All of them.

Eddie has released my hair. "Let's go," he says. "We can't wait around all night."

"What do you mean, let's go? I can't just leave my sister."

"Your choice. Cars are leaving. Ray, you give Charlene a piggyback to the car."

"For Christ's sake, Eddie. At least leave me a flashlight!"

"They don't work, Keiko." He says it with a laugh as Charlene climbs onto the back of her latest savior.

Russell stands beside me, watching them go. "She should be out soon. Don't you think? We could just wait for her here. She should be okay. I mean—"

"You're the one who *switched* her. You tell me."

"She'll come out. In a minute. Don't you think? I mean, we were all together, weren't we? We must have been."

I can't believe I'm stuck here with this loser. I can't believe I relied on him to protect you. I shouldn't have relied on anyone but myself.

"Hana!" I start yelling into the cave. "Hana! Where you stay?"

Water dripping. My own voice sinking into the rock, but no answer.

"You're going to get in trouble," Russell says, worried. "It's late. You should go with them. I can—"

"What are you, nuts? No one knows she's even missing but us, and all we know is she's somewhere in there!"

The rest of the group has reached the top. "Cars are leaving!" Eddie calls again.

Russell takes a step in their direction. "Maybe..."

"What *is* your problem? You're going to run away, too?"

He's protesting, but I'm not listening. Charlene is calling, trying to keep Eddie's friend from carrying her away. "Kei, please. Come with us. We'll get help. You don't want to be left here."

Yes, I do. I'm tired of them. They can all leave.

"Hana! Godfunnit!"

Answer me. Please answer. I am coming to save you.

I am yelling your name in the entrance to the cave over and over. Telling you I am here. Hoping you are right there, that any minute you'll step out of the shadows. Maybe all of this is a joke on me. Maybe this is *your* joke, wouldn't that be a turnaround? I would laugh along at my own expense, I would laugh with you, anything, as long as it meant you were okay.

Scare me, Hana. Make me pay. Just come out.

Above us, I can hear one of the cars start up. Russell hears it, too.

"Wait for me!" He makes up his mind and takes off, running. "Wait for me!"

I am in the cave, searching for my sister. I can't see anything. You can't be too far.

"Hana! Please! I'm here! Where are you?"

No answer.

"Call back, eh, Hana? I know you can hear. I'm sorry, Hana!"

I am counting my steps. I have counted to fifty. It's so dark. Did the clouds pass over the moon? I know how to walk now—one hand against the wall, one out in front, feet shuffling forward slowly, right foot first to protect my left toe. I can get down the tongue like this, and around the first corner, to where the rock pile begins.

It takes a while, but I have made my way back to where I was when I found Charlene. I can't go any farther. I have no way of knowing what's ahead, no way of getting out if I get lost. The cave could fork. I could fall through a hole in the ground, and then there'd be no one to save Hana, no one who would know either of us was still in here. It's so dark, so stubbornly, utterly dark that I can barely breathe.

"Hana!" Why won't you answer? How far away can you be? "Oh God, please. Just please be okay."

Mama said, *Call her. Bring her out.* Was it Mama who said it? But how can I save my sister if I don't know where I am?

Arnie will come. Even if it takes all night. Even if it's tomorrow before anyone tells him where we are. He will have lights and blankets. He will have a first aid kit. Maybe he'll have food this time, especially if he doesn't leave until daylight. People have survived on deserted islands for weeks, Arnie told me. We can survive here until the morning.

How long before he comes?

This is a joke. Sometimes I think so. Someone's going to turn on the light switch and I'm going to see that I could throw a stone and reach the opening of the cave. If I could throw a sidearm slider, maybe. If I could skip it along the wall. This is your joke, isn't it, Hana? What else could it be? How does one lose one's boyfriend? How does one just sit silently and not follow when everyone walks away? If there's one thing I can count on you for, it's not to trust anyone. If they told you to do something stupid, you wouldn't have listened.

But what if you are still walking, deeper into the cave? I smashed my fingers and my toes. You could have done the same. You could be injured, unable to move. What if you hit your head and knocked yourself out? Or, my God, what if they did something worse to you? What was Eddie—or Ray, his hulking friend—capable of? Or what if it *is* a joke and you are hiding near the front and let me pass you? I could be the only one in the cave. No, you wouldn't do that to me. Would you?

"Can you hear me, Hana? Jus' one joke?"

I am coming for you.

HANA

It's dark in here. Where is Russell? He promised not to let go of my hand. But his hand is gone, and in his place Kei's boyfriend, Eddie, has moved in like a magic trick. He's behind me, his head slinking forward before his body. Then, when his face is inches from my own, he flips his flashlight on high and yells, "Boo!"

Eddie's face flashes green—his skull explodes on my retina. I am blinded in his laughter when his arm wraps around my neck. His lips brush my ear. Will he bite me, or kiss me? But he only whispers: "You thought you'd get away with it, didn't you? Kei was right. We're not your friends. Unless you want to join your freaky ghosts in the river, you better do what I tell you. When everything goes quiet, don't move."

I do what he says—I don't move—and now, the gang is gone. Is it a joke? What does Eddie think I tried to get away with? I am alone, underground, breathing air so old no one has ever breathed it before. I trusted my sister. I trusted Russell. But they left me. How did this happen? I am alone in the cave.

Kei? Can she hear my thoughts? *Where are you, Kei?*

Where am *I?*

I am, I must be, very deep inside this cave. The darkness is so complete that there are no shadows, no gradations; it doesn't lift or part or thin. It is *so* dark, in fact, that I have lost track of my actual body. I can't see my hand; I can't feel it. When I bring it toward my face, I don't know where it is until it hits my nose. If I walk my fingers down my legs to my toes, I can feel that, but just for an instant. Then the sensation fades and my legs disappear.

How can it fade so fast? How can *I* fade?

There is nothing I can use to get my bearings—to say, *This is where I am*, or even, *This is who I am*. I have become my own shadow, and in the darkness—how could this be possible?—I have lost my body.

I have disappeared.

It's time to join your freaky ghosts.

Don't scream. Don't cry. He said not to move. They must be hiding around a corner. Surely? Ready to laugh at me if I scream. They will return.

Kei will return.

Count to one hundred, I tell myself, but I can't. My breath catches. The darkness bulges in my throat. There's no telling how much time has passed. I know it isn't hours, or days, but it might as well be. I am disintegrating. I am alone, buried alive, disappearing into the dark.

And then it comes to me that no one is coming back. I should have seen the signs. I watched Kei strolling with Russell, her arm in his and Missy with them after school when they thought I couldn't see them. I should have known at the beach, when Kei sat down in the sand, glaring at me. With the sudden clarity of a punch line, I understand exactly how each one of these events, even in this past week, have led us to this moment.

I stick my arms out in the dark and feel nothing. Where is the wall of the cave? I extend my hands, first with caution, but I cannot find anything to ground me or help me get my bearings. Soon, caution is gone and I am stabbing my arms into the darkness, but there is still nothing there. I slide one foot forward, waving my hands now, but there is no wall, no direction, no exit. Only the blackest of blackness.

Only nothingness—everywhere. And I am nothing, too.

My chest is crushed, pulling, but I can't get air. I throw myself forward, but I've lost any sense of balance. My body is disconnected, and my feet roll in loose rock. They shoot out from under me and the cave comes up so fast. My head snaps back and I can hear the thud before I feel it when my skulls hits the ground.

And then, the pain. Sharp first where the lava smashed it, then getting duller, stronger, thumping in my ears with every heartbeat as it curls around to my forehead. I know I'm bleeding, though I can barely feel the sticky warmth on my hands. I dig my fingers into my scalp, imagining I could split my skin open if I pulled on my hair. I can feel my head—all of it—beating with every heartbeat. The throbbing pain is a sound, is a feeling: *I am here, I am here, I am here.*

The gash behind my ear beats in my pressing palm; yes, it hurts, but I can *feel* it. I can feel myself, and the pain is not going away. I can feel the backs of my calves, too, which must have scraped along the cave floor when I fell. I push them harder into the rock, scrubbing them, forcing hot, tiny shards of lava into them. My skin responds. I am no longer missing. It screams at me: *I am here.*

I crawled on my knees, pulling my shins and the tops of my feet across the ground so they, too, would be lit up by the lava. I remember it now. I dropped forward, flat on my forearms and, one by one, I welcomed them, too, banging one elbow into a rock and wallowing in the hot shot of life through my arm. The tops of my feet lit up, stinging; my toes danced around them. I lay down on my back and swept my arms and legs wide, making broad, luxurious strokes, swimming to reach every inch of my skin. I gave in to the urge to move—not to escape, but to retrieve myself, through the pain, with each motion. Was I trying to get out? At that point, did I even think it was possible? Or was I just trying to find a way to feel the limits and movements of my body in that terrible dark?

Finally, after I'd awakened every part of me, I hit the wall, and even though I was no longer looking for it, I pressed the length of my back against the side of the cave, content to feel the barbed lava caress me as the front of my body glowed. After a while, there was a glow in the cave, too, in the distance, a congratulatory glimmer in the tunnel of my mind.

I could hear my breath for the first time since Kei left me. I had saved myself, and in that blessed moment of discovering that I was alive, I could hear the lava, too. Reverberating at first, and then, very faintly, speaking.

Where you stay, where you stay, where you stay, Godfunnit, Hana?

Whispering my name.

KEI

K ei-girl! Hana!"

Were my eyes closed, or were they open? How long have I been here in the cave? Have I been asleep? I feel like I am floating, shapeless, adrift in the dark.

There is a voice, and an edge in front of me, glowing. The beginnings of the wall. This is more than the dark shimmer of the night at the end of the tunnel.

"Kei! Hana! Girls, are you there?"

Girls. The cave knows us. It is speaking in Arnie's voice. *Arnie?*

What's wrong with my brain that I can't think? Maybe that's why you never answered, Hana. In all this darkness, you fell asleep. Arnie is here. How much time has passed?

"Arnie! Dad! Here I am, over here!"

I stand up, sliding and tripping down the rocks I managed to climb, then fall into Arnie's arms. He's hugging me and I'm trying to tell him that I searched this far at least. I covered this ground. I am sobbing and I can barely see the others with him. I can barely hear Russell telling me something about jumping out at the stoplight, how I warned him to protect Hana and he was only leaving to get help. But his voice is unimportant next to Arnie's arms around me.

He is here.

Your mother and I love you. That's what he told me once.

"Are you okay, Kei?"

I am nodding. So many voices mumbling now, I can't always hear. Arnie puts his hand on my shoulder, as if he's guiding me through a crowded room. But we're walking in the wrong direction, turning toward the entrance. There are several men with him and at least three spotlights. "Chuck, can you take her out of here?"

"No! We can't leave! Hana's lost in here."

"You're bleeding, sweetheart. We need to get you out."

"It's only my toe. It's only—" I can see blood on my hands and I drop them quickly. "It's just a scratch. Please."

I want to find you. I can't have saved so many other people—the little girl in the wave, Charlene—and not save you. Arnie doesn't press. Maybe he understands. He takes my bicep and hooks it firmly into his. "Can you walk?"

Charlene's father, Chuck, is leading the way with one of the searchlights, and we are in the middle, fully lit. The light is so bright. I can see the scrabble of rocks I was trying to climb. It seems so much smaller in the light, so much easier to manage. Beyond it, a ways in the distance, I can see a small opening, where another chamber of the cave begins.

To get through it, we have to duck, making ourselves as small as possible. A couple of the bigger men can't fold themselves so small and need to lie flat and pull themselves through, over the jagged rocks. On the other side, the cave opens up into a long tunnel, the walls almost pinkish and rounded. It looks like we're in the belly of a dragon. The cave is narrow compared to the first chamber and bends around a corner, but the ceiling is high and the center of the path surprisingly smooth.

We can move so fast when we can see where we're going. Arnie's almost lifting me off the ground to keep me up.

Call your Keiko. She's in there. She's fighting to get out.

"Oh my God, is that blood?"

You have gone deeper in than anyone expected, Hana. You are leaning against the wall of the cave. You look like a doll someone left propped on a pillow, like someone painted you in red mud. Petals from your corsage are scattered around you. Your face is the only part of you that's clean. Your eyes are open, but blank; you are facing toward us, but you don't respond to the lights or to your name pulled, ragged, from deep inside my belly. Arnie lets go of me, and we are all converging, trying to get to you first.

My god, Hana—Koko—what have they done to you? You look like Eddie bounced you off the walls. Tossed in a washing machine: that's the image that comes to me. Your new dress is hiked up, or ripped off, and you are bleeding everywhere except your face. How could they do this and come out without more than a scratch or two on them? You must have fought. You must have begged for Russell's help. How is any of this possible? How could he look me in the eye and pretend he didn't know? And how could I, your twin, have been so near and yet not have heard you screaming?

I am the first one to try to touch you. My hands slip in your blood and you scream. It's like you are waking from a nightmare—you stiffen at my touch, arching yourself and thrashing away from me. Your screams are surging through the cave, echoing. They're wheeling like a trapped bird, beating itself against the window glass. The cave is full of you. My breath is full of you. I have your blood all over my hands.

"Don't let her move."

"Here, take my sweater. Wrap her up. Careful!"

The lights have been set down as we hover around you, trying to figure out what to do. They cast prolonged shadows off our bodies. Our spirits, black spirits, recoiling and trying to leave.

"Don't just stand there. Lift her head. I've got her. Someone help her hold her head."

It still feels so wrong. The lights bouncing off the walls, off the blood on the ground, off your body. Your screams, and even when you pause in your screaming, your moaning and writhing in Arnie's arms. The lights waver toward you every time you make a sound; they dip with your every movement. At first, we try not to jostle you, we try only to touch the parts that aren't raw—the backs of your knees, your neck, the small of your back—but every step jars. At last, Arnie gives up, lengthening his stride to get you out as quickly as he can without the bounce of an actual run. We have to pass you through the narrow opening, but I am small enough that I climb in along with you and try to hold you off the rock. I can't tell what's worse for you, our hands or the ground. You are screaming, you keep screaming, and then suddenly we have you through. Arnie lays you on top of his own body as he slides himself down the rock pile. One of the lights has jumped ahead of us, and one is trained on your body. The lights are rolling, jumbling everything, making it impossible to imagine how something like this could have happened.

Kei, it's okay. I'm here. It's Hana.

Stop mumbling. Everyone is talking at the same time. How can I understand anything you say?

She's moving. Look! She's moving.

Are you moving? There's so much light in my eyes. Move the light.

The moonlight is so bright when we get to the entrance. No, it's not the moon. It's the third searchlight, Charlene's father, who has come out ahead of us to warn Mama that her daughter has been found.

Mama doesn't move as we approach her. She waits for us to emerge fully from the dark. Her face is grave; it holds no questions. It's as if she knows the worst has happened and there's nothing to be done but to deliver the news.

The tight knot we wove around you has loosened in the final chamber of the cave, and the tension goes out of your body. Your head falls backward, and Arnie's afraid to shift his arms.

"Hold her head," he says to no one in particular.

I am holding you, Hana. But now our mother is here.

Russell has been waiting to be useful. He cups your head as I break around him and run.

I fling my arms around Mama, sobbing. She feels so small in them—smaller even than Charlene and so light. How can her shoulders tuck into my armpits? Where is the safety her body once offered?

Mama's body yields when mine hits, absorbing the shock of my weight. Her arms come up reflexively to keep her from falling backward, but I count it as an embrace. I want her to cry with me. I want her to move, to scream, to try to make things better. Anything but to accept the limp form of my sister coming toward her as something that cannot be changed.

Mama, are you here, too? Go to her. Call her. Hanako.

Kei!

Your rescuers are approaching, fanned out and silent. At last Mama leans against me, but still she doesn't move. You could be an armful of red laundry in Arnie's arms, except for Russell bobbing sideways beside you still trying to cradle your head. *Go away*, I will him, this boy who has ruined everything. *Go away.* How can Arnie turn and head up to the road without saying a word? How can Mama fall in, trotting behind you as if to pick up any scattered pieces, without trying to touch you?

When Arnie gets to the top of the pit, you suddenly see the moon. You begin screaming again, a much thinner sound amid the dripping, bending trees, and here, the scene changes: jangled and pitching as we run, yell; we reach the cars; we try to plan. Arnie says, "Get the door open, Miya, get into the cab. I'm going to put her over you so you can hold her.

"Hana, don't move. If you can. We are trying as best as we can not to touch you. Stop. Please."

Mama gets into the truck and Arnie tries to drape you over her. Each time you move, each time your wounds scrape something new, you scream. Mama's arms hold you tight. Her arms are sliding in blood but she won't let go. You settle into her embrace. Maybe you are numb now, but you have stopped trying to fight it.

I can see Mama holding your head, pressing her face to yours, forehead to forehead. She is trying to pull you into stillness. Your blood is on her face. She is kissing your forehead, saying your full name over and over again, and I'm right there beside you standing in the open door.

"I'm so sorry I left you," I hear Mama say to you. "Rest in peace, Hanako. Rest in peace."

Arnie meets my eyes, helpless. Both he and I are covered in your blood. There is no room for me in the truck. When I close the door gently, Mama is still pressed to your forehead, whispering, fretting— *Peace. Rest in peace*—as Arnie inches the truck away from me. Then all of you are gone.

Russell is standing beside me. His lips are moving. He needs to say something, but I will not hear him. He sits down and holds his head between his hands, and I wonder what it's like to hold his own head, to feel his own fingers, after holding Hana's.

You warned me to protect her, he'd said when he returned with Arnie. And he was right. I knew something was going to happen. This is all my fault.

There's nothing to do now but go home, me and my few scrapes and bruises. There are still two cars here, and Charlene's father putting away the searchlights. I wonder where Charlene is, and what her father has been told. Is he here in penance or in solidarity with Arnie? Will he go to the police station next and have Eddie and the others arrested for what they have done? Penance and punishment: They are both pounding in my brain. Mr. Chow will deliver me safely to the Haradas' house, but he can't look at me.

At the hospital, after they've stabilized you and given you so much morphine you are quiet at last, Mama will climb onto your bed and try to keep her balance on the edge of it. There's not much room, but her body is tiny, and she can almost fit beside you without touching any of the bandaged parts. She can nestle her face near your neck, even if you won't respond, and whisper to you. She can tell you secrets. She can be there even if they say you are unconscious. She knows you're still there. She has seen this before—minds and bodies separated, one freed from the other—and she has to believe her daughter will experience this moment, even if you don't remember.

I don't know how I know this. Perhaps Mrs. Harada told me later. But this is what it feels like now to me.

They might have let Mama stay if she'd gotten up when they asked her to. Or if she'd allowed herself to be changed into clean clothes. She refused to acknowledge the nurses when they told her she couldn't be on the bed. Every second she could still touch you would be imprinted on you, Hana. She was there. You would know.

They probably whispered about her. Wasn't she the one people used to say was crazy? The Cowgirl? The Calrose Rice Queen?

Arnie let Mama do what she wanted, held the nurses at bay, until the doctors all came into the room at the same time, saying she would have to go. Mama would be better off at home—it was a stressful time, but more so for you, Hana, and it would only hurt you to have her there, acting so deranged. They let her stay for a full day, but she kept crawling back into the bed, incoherent, stroking your hair. They couldn't know that you were the only thing keeping Mama from fainting, that once she got home she would sink into her own bed and not get out. By the time Arnie gave in and brought Mama home, I had more than a day of being left behind with the Haradas, desperate about where everyone was and what was happening. It was fitting that I was the one waiting. The one pressed against the window yearning for someone to approach; listening for the footsteps on the porch to tell me that, at last, there was someone on the other side of the door.

I want my sister, but no one can see you. Arnie tells me this, his eyes averted. Not me, not Mama, who doesn't get out of bed until after my graduation, weeks away still. Not even Russell, who has been coming to the hospital every day. *Not even,* Arnie says. Of all the words out of his mouth, this priority for a boy over me is the strangest. I'm your sister, your other half. I can reach those wounds in your mind that Arnie says are too deep—we can't risk making them worse. I can heal you, tell your story, Koko. That's what I do.

I can explain.

Except, I couldn't then. No one could. Arnie started by trying to get everyone arrested, but the police only held Eddie and Ray, and then only for one night. There was no proof, and barely any blood on either one of them. All of us had banged up something that night, however accidentally. Eddie denied hurting you, and their stories were consistent, though as Arnie pointed out, he and Ray had had all night together in a cell to rehearse them. You could have just gotten lost or wandered off. That's what the police said. You could have fallen. They hadn't seen you when we found you in the cave, so they couldn't know. If you had just told the police what happened they could have helped us... But you didn't.

No one had the guts to tell me the day you left.

Arnie never stopped trying to bring those two boys to justice. Even when some of his friends grew cooler to him, tired of picking sides. As for me, I crossed the street rather than talk to any of my former friends, even Charlene. But I couldn't forgive myself, even if Mama did. I told her how I had put you in the center of the gang's attention, but she just waved my words away. I couldn't have known, she told me. I couldn't freeze time and judge it from the worst moment. You never knew what terrible things would bring something good in the future.

People make their own choices: That was always Mama's mantra. And Hana... Mama paused then, as if she knew something, but whatever it was, she didn't say. Her final words on the subject were the ones she often said to us: Each one of us has to make our own way in a big, big world.

Kei?

I remember lights. New York City, flashing through the windows of my cab on the way from the airport. It wasn't until I walked into your apartment that I realized Arnie had lied. All his talk about your friends at the galleries had been made up to protect Mama, just as he used to pick me up when I was in middle school so Mama wouldn't know about the fights. There was no sign of the "big city success." No sign of any painting at all. You had one plate, one cup, one set of utensils. You had three library books, but no books on a shelf, no possessions. No wonder you hadn't wanted me to come.

The walls were bare. That's when I knew my trip was for nothing. All those lost years, and it was my fault. You were hiding; you had stopped living after the cave incident, and no necklace, not even Mama's history, would make you better. I could still hear you screaming at Mama's funeral, the same scream you had been screaming since I left you. I couldn't save you. You would never come home.

I needed a cigarette.

I carried my bag into your bedroom and turned on the radio. Then I rummaged in my duffel for the small folding case where I kept my emergency Kools. You have always abhorred the smell of cigarette smoke, so I tugged the window open and unlatched the safety gate so I could stick my head all the way out into the fresh air before I lit up.

I was leaning on the windowsill, trying to blow the smoke downwind. I was trying to figure out what to do. I had been counting on your success, on your curiosity about Mama's secrets. On a promise that we could start over, and the assumption that you felt as I did: that you missed me every single day. I had come to give you your inheritance.

Your name.

Hanako sent your mama to Hawaii, Mrs. Harada told me, in one of the very last stories she told. She was dying—her voice was full of pauses, barely more than a whisper. Her shaking, fragile fingers tucked the pendant into my palm, and she held it there with what little strength she had left as she told me about her niece. Maybe I had heard her talk about Hanako when we were little, but I never understood. But after a lifetime of assuming that it was *my* name that held the secrets, I realized that the world was not so big that I couldn't fly to New York for my sister. You couldn't make your own choices without knowing what I knew. Once upon a time, you gave me my own name, and it was time to return the favor.

You were never a Flower Child. You were named for the best friend who saved our mother's life. But now that I was here in New York, with the truth of what your own life had become, I was no longer sure whether that name would be enough to save you, too.

The night air was cool. When I was finished with my cigarette, I grabbed Mama's quilt off your bed and was pulling it around my shoulders when I heard a door slam across the hall. It wasn't you, but as I whirled around, the stiff edge of the quilt swept my cigarette case off the sill and down into the narrow alley between the buildings, four stories below. I could feel it falling. I never thought about my cash and my driver's license tucked in with my cigarettes, perhaps because I was falling, too. My ankle gave out beneath me as I turned, off balance after a long plane ride, a head rush from the tobacco, and no food. I slammed my ribs hard on your bed frame and lay there, groaning.

What did I do then? I hobbled into the main room and drank some juice to get the sugar back into my system, had a few bites of your leftovers. I was exhausted, and still waiting, so I decided to take a shower to clear my head. I hadn't brought a robe, and couldn't find one in your bedroom, so I wrapped the quilt around myself after I undressed, then left it on the lid of the toilet when I got into the tub.

When I turned off the shower and went to dry myself, there was no towel. You clearly had no interest in making yourself comfortable or at home. Still dripping in the tub, I glanced at the mirror above the sink as I squeezed my hair out, and it was only then that my brain finally registered the tape.

When you die, will you be all alone? That was Missy's first question to me, all those years ago. Being alone was Missy's greatest fear. She had reminded me of it at Mama and Arnie's funeral, when her first words, her only words to me since the cave incident, were the greatest comfort she could muster: *At least they weren't alone.* It had bothered me then, but it wasn't until I got here and saw how lonely your New York life was that I understood why.

I could see you again, sitting by yourself in the back of the chapel at the funeral in your fancy New York suit. You had reappeared just as suddenly as you'd disappeared, and no one in town knew how you wanted us to approach you. There was a buffer of breathless space around you; even those of us who would never stop reliving that night weren't sure what to do. Your story had become gossip, then rumor, and then forgotten. And then, there you were, resurrected in the form of a black-clothed specter perched on a wooden pew: so forlorn, in the flesh. Silent. So...alone.

Growing up, as we did, as Koko, I knew the one thing that neither one of us could ever bear was the feeling of being just one girl. That was what the tape on the mirror told me: the piece of the puzzle I had been missing all along. There was one thing even more terrible than being attacked by one of my former friends in the cave that night.

And that was being left in the dark all alone.

In that blacked-out mirror, I understood you were still there, Hana. That you were still haunted by monsters you could not face. I could see them: your loneliness as the perfect daughter, and your terror in the dark. But I could also see something else: you on the beach with Missy having your hair braided. You were shining, in love with your life and your possibilities. I wanted you to remember yourself that way.

I stepped out of the tub and wrapped the quilt around my shoulders, the rest of me still naked and wet, putting myself directly in front of the mirror. I didn't touch the careful strips of tape covering it; instead, I chose what I would see. I was crying as I parted my own sopping hair with my fingers and began to twist sections of it into a French braid. This was your beauty, Hana. Your reckless joy at conquering your fears. I was lost in that day—the candy-colored sky, the laughter of the children in the tide pools, and you standing in the water, the ocean streaming from your dress—when the door to the bathroom opened. The sound of the radio came rushing in. I spun around. There you were, my actual sister, standing there.

You looked worn. Defeated. Still white and drawn, as I had seen you at the funeral, and still dressed in black. You must have heard the water, heard me turn the shower off, and yet you looked at me, surprised. As if you had both expected and not expected to see me.

You had taken a step into your tiny bathroom with the swing of the door. You were only an arm's length away. I could feel the connection between us, all our history sizzling back into being as our postures adjusted to mirror each other without any thought. Your eyes were so close, looking directly into mine, but also far away. My own must have been equally startled, and surely puffy, running with my tears. I was caught in time, wet and hopeful, hair half braided, in the escaping steam of the shower. I was waiting to hear you speak, to see if, despite everything, you would welcome me.

It happened so fast. You reached toward me, and I was so happy to be with you, to be so close to you, at last. It wasn't until I felt my throat closing that I recognized the clouds that had come over your expression. Mama's world used to slip the same way. Mama lived with us, but also in the world of Lillie. And also in a world of ghosts she never wanted us to see. And there were times when she couldn't tell the difference. Just like, at that moment, you couldn't.

Your fingers dug into my neck. And then I heard a whimper. *Don't.*

That raw. That aching. You were pleading. Were you pleading?

With all our history between us, known and unknown, there is one thing I know to be true. My sister would never hurt me.

But before I could say your name, the force of your lunge carried us both over. I hit my head on the corner of the shower enclosure as we went down. I didn't fight, because I knew it wasn't me you were seeing.

The twin you were trying to punish was yourself.

What was the bedtime song Mama always sang to us? I keep hearing it in my head. Two girls. Lillie's light is on the other side with the girls.

But now I'm here, in your cave, Hana. I'm the one trapped without you. But I am also the one who became the storyteller, and now it's my turn. I can change the story if I want to: It's me and you, here together in the cave. You've been waiting for me. My sister.

The story begins here: in the dark.

Arnie, give me your flashlight.

It's a dim beam in the darkness. Not really even a beam. It's a yellowish splotch, brown around the edges, that lights the bits of dust in the air and the bugs when you point it too far forward. "Good enough for government work," Arnie says. He likes to say the same thing over and over. Good enough to see your feet if you point it down.

"Point it down, Kei," he says. "You won't trip. You won't cut your toes. Flash it up and it will catch the levels marked on the walls. The lava stream must have dropped to there, see? And the center of the smaller flow still ran hot while the ledges cooled."

See how beautiful it is?

Take your time, Arnie told me. *Admire your surroundings. It's a natural wonder. Good that we can experience the world this way. Look for the crickets—did you know there's a rare cricket that lives here? Watch out for the lavacicles, the big ones look like shark's teeth. No, they didn't chisel those rocks. They break that way naturally, on straight lines, like bricks. That white stuff on the walls? It smells metallic. Use all your senses, girl.*

That's the thing about life, Hana. That's what Arnie tried to show me in the cave. There's so much we are given that we can't appreciate. But only because we don't know where to look.

You are here, Hana.

I can feel you.

I can hear you laughing that day on the beach with Russell. Your hair braided like a crown. Stray tendrils around your face. A water nymph, my sister who doesn't like the ocean, transforming in front of me. You are fearless, facing the world down, looking it in the eye and then embracing it. Your clothes are soaked, and you have no idea how beautiful you are.

This is the life our mother gave us. The paradise of the two girls.

Laugh for me when I find you in the cave. Arnie's flashlight is brown, it's almost out, but you are here. Wave to me. Your dress is pale yellow, a little smudged but no blood, no screaming. You are here, so happy to see me, then the battery finally gives up and the light goes out.

Dark in here, so dark we cannot see our hands before they touch our faces, but we have found each other. We can whisper—entwine our fingers together to keep ourselves safe in the dark. Let's sit down. Careful— the ground is rough here. Feel for a smoother patch. Let's sit down.

Remember how Mama used to dress us? White cotton momohiki and tabis on four feet? She would give us gloves, too, if we didn't keep flinging them off and losing them in the flower beds. We were always losing things when we were little, weren't we? Who cared, when we had trees to climb and streams to cool off in? Those were such innocent days, and we had each other.

Like now. We can wait together. It won't be long. Remember how we used to run down the hill, crawling on our knees beneath the umbrella of heart-shaped leaves and sweet, crushed flowers under Mama's huge hau tree? That was our favorite place to be.

It's cool here. The sweat on my neck and face itches. Hold my hand. They will find us, see? Can't you hear them already? Over there, where the dark is ebbing. It's getting brighter. Listen to the people. You can almost make out what they're saying.

There she is. Look, she's coming to!

Oh God, Keiko, can you hear me? It's Hana. I'm here with you. Open your eyes.

Am I coming, too? Are we both finally together?

I can see the lights now. Let's go toward them. Whatever you do, don't let go of my hand. We can open our eyes now, Hana.

Two girls, together. The light is here now, with the girls, and it's been dark for too long.

Acknowledgments

This book was born of a rape. Although I was very much on the periphery, that terrible night has haunted me, and it is that haunting that helped this story stick for nearly two decades. *Shadow Child* has taken many different forms over that time: It was two books, then one; a historical novel, a quiet family drama, a failed thriller. I have changed the setting, immediately altered the attack itself, killed off characters, and then revived them. I wrote the first hundred pages in the year 2000, then I went to Japan to research the character of Lillie, which led me to write a memoir instead. So much time later means I have a lifetime of people to thank, including those who've helped me with false starts, dead ends, and abandoned narratives, and those who just smiled and stuck with me.

My first thanks go to the people I interviewed in Hawaii, including Dr. Billy Bergin, Patricia Bergin, Anderson Black, Ralph Black, Fumi Bonk, Robert "Steamy" Chow, Tim DeSilva, Walter Dudley, Leningrad Elarionoff, Doug Espejo, Esther Fujioka, Dr. Samuel Gingrich, Claudette Hagar, Izumi Hirano, Miyoko Kamikawa, Chizuko Kawamoto, Claudia Kobayashi, Arte McCullough, Fumiye Miho, Susumu Sugihara, Jean Yamanaka, Karen Yamasato, and others. Thanks to Hanae Tokita and Michael Nakade for early guidance in the Japanese language and customs. In California I am grateful to Dorothy Stroup and Kanji Kuramoto, and Friends of Hibakusha, an organization that compiled numerous oral histories with Hiroshima and Nagasaki survivors, including the indispensable testimonies of Judy Aya (Misono) Enseki, Kay Yoshioka, and Chieko Fravel. Also instrumental was the time I was able to spend with

Violet Kazue de Cristoforo. And, of course, my great aunt who started it all, Mary Hamaji.

I have enormous gratitude to the U.S.-Japan Commission, the National Endowment for the Arts, and the Japanese Agency for Cultural Affairs for the life-changing gift of time in Hiroshima that I received through the U.S.-Japan Creative Artist Fellowship. Although I had thanked them in the acknowledgments of my memoir, I could not have written this book without the support, time, and generosity of many people and organizations in Japan. These include the tireless Keiko Ogura, my mentor and inspiration; and Megumi Shimo, who still reads my work and fixes my Japanese after all these years; as well as Isao Aratani, Christopher Blasdel, Dr. Kohei Daikoku, Kazuko Enami, Shoichi Fuji, Pierce Fukuhara, Dr. Hiroe Hamano, Mamoru Hamasaki, Nobue Hashimoto, Shizuo Inoue, Katsuko Kaimatchi, Mr. Kanaoka, Professor Kan Katayanagi, Yachiyo Kato, Dr. Fumiko Kaya, Chioko Kono, Tadashi and Sumako Matsuyanagi, Kenji Mito, Keiko Miyamoto, Hiromu Morishita, Keiko Murakami, Akira Nakano, Dr. and Mrs. Takeko Nakayama, Dixie Setoyama, Kosuke Shishido, Professor Rinjiro Sodei, Suzie Sunamoto, Rev. Ryoga Suwa, Chieko Tabata, Masumi Takabayashi, Yasuhiko Taketa, Pe Hak Te, Hiko and Nancy Tokita, Hajime Tsukamoto, Marie Tsuruda, Yasuko Uemoto, Nobuko Ueno, Mitsuko Yamamoto, Michiko Yamane, Tokio Yamane, Michiko Yamaoka, Tatsuko Yasui, Mika Yoshida, and others who chose to remain anonymous. I was given great support by the Hiroshima Interpreters for Peace, the Hiroshima YMCA, the Hiroshima Peace Memorial Museum, the *Chugoku Shimbun*, the International House of Japan, the U.S. Embassy & Consulates in Japan, the World Friendship Center, and the Radiation Effects Research Foundation. It is deeply appreciated.

I will forever be grateful to Hedgebrook for giving me a place to gather the pieces of this story into my arms. Truly, you have become my writing home. To Amy Wheeler and Vito Zingarelli for making sure I remained part of the family. To Evie Wilson-Lingbloom, who found me documents I didn't know existed, and Sherri L. Smith, who became my Friend of the Book during my first residency. Hedgebrook also gave me my incredible

Borg and Erratics, whose support and friendship have been everything, as well as my PowderKeg writing group, who graciously read a much earlier version of this book. The Asian American Writers' Workshop continues to be a part of me. I am grateful to everyone in the Goddard MFA Creative Writing program who has heard me read from this book over the past fifteen years and encouraged me not to cut the scenes I was threatening to cut. Special Goddard thanks to Kathryn Cullen-DuPont, John McManus, Victoria Nelson, Rachel Pollack and her Shining Tribe, and to Jane Wohl.

My publishing family began with Susan Bergholz, a dear friend and still a great supporter of this novel. Thank you also to Ellen Levine. I am beyond thrilled to be in the hands of Samantha Shea, who fell in love with this book on Christmas Eve, and the extraordinary Millicent Bennett, who leaves no word untouched and no wild and wonderful idea unexplored. The team at Grand Central Publishing has been a dream, and I am deeply grateful for their instant belief in this novel, and for their passion, vision, and expertise: Ben Sevier, Karen Kostolnyik, Brian McLendon, Andy Dodds, Andrew Duncan, Karen Torres, Ali Cutrone, Siri Silleck, Anne Twomey, Meriam Metoui, Erica Scavelli, and everyone whose brilliance and dedication has brought a better book into the world.

Abiding, heart-stopping gratitude to Ruth Ozeki, Victoria Redel, Dani Shapiro, and Hannah Tinti for your support and generosity, and for your kind words.

Then there are the people who have read countless drafts, brainstormed, taught me things I would never use about painting, who listened patiently or simply loved me through it all. They are my cherished family: Kathryn Bischak, Kathleen Boeger, Carole DeSanti, Linda Duggins, Eloise Flood, Kenny Fries, Jannifer Jones, Elena Georgiou, K. J. Grow, Beth Kephart, Kate Moses, Tina Nguyen, Bino Realuyo, Kai Rizzuto, Amy Scholder, Alix Kates Shulman, Majo Tinoco, Kalei Tooman, Elizabeth Woodhouse, and Ming Yuen-Schat. I am so grateful for each one of you.

This book is dedicated to my parents. My first teachers, unfailing supporters; my guiding lights.

A NOTE ON PLACE AND HISTORY

Though the characters and incidents in this novel are entirely a product of my imagination, it is set against the background of very specific historical events, and I have done extensive research to ensure that these are as accurate as possible. History is integral to Lillie's story in particular. Actual events have made her who she is, just as they have forever changed the lives of real people, and it is my hope that this novel can help to show how consequential they were, and still are, today.

The same is not true of the story of Hawaii. There is a town that inspired the one I created here, where I did extensive interviews and research to catch the nuances of a certain life and time. Unlike Lillie's story, however, the story of the twins is in no way representative of that particular town or of its people. Hawaii is a rich and diverse place, and it requires many voices to bring it to life. Much like the conflicting accounts of the tsunami I heard during my interviews, the beauty of Hawaii is that no two stories will be the same. I encourage you to explore the many local authors who are writing from their indigenous, multicultural, and diverse experiences. And if you are curious about what really happened during the tsunamis that have affected Hawaii over the years, I recommend *Tsunami!* by Walter C. Dudley and Min Lee (University of Hawaii Press, 1998) and a trip to the Pacific Tsunami Museum in Hilo, which offers extensive oral histories, archives, scholarship, and science.

After two decades of writing and rewriting, I have undoubtedly made mistakes and forgotten details. For the facts, I want to acknowledge some of the sources I leaned on most heavily: *And Justice for All: An Oral History of the Japanese American Detention Camps*, John Tateishi (Random House, 1984); *Dear Miye: Letters Home from Japan, 1939–1946*, Mary Tomita (Stanford University Press, 1995); *Hibakusha: Survivors of Hiroshima and Nagasaki*, ed. Gaynor Sekimori (Kosei Publishing, 1986); *Hiroshima Diary: The Journal of a Japanese Physician, August 6–September 30, 1945*, Michihiko Hachiya (University of North Carolina Press, 1995); *Our House Divided: Seven Japanese American Families in World War II*, Tomi Kaizawa Knaefler (University of Hawaii Press,

1991); *Personal Justice Denied: Report of the Commission on Wartime Relocation and Internment of Civilians* (University of Washington Press, 1997); *Prisoners Without Trial: Japanese Americans in World War II*, Roger Daniels (Hill & Wang, 1993); *Unforgettable Fire: Pictures Drawn by Atomic Bomb Survivors*, ed. Japan Broadcasting Corp (NHK) (Pantheon, 1977); *Were We the Enemy?: American Survivors of Hiroshima*, Rinjiro Sodei (Westview Press, 1998); *Years of Infamy: The Untold Story of America's Concentration Camps*, Michi Nishiyura Weglyn (Morrow, 1976). For their collections and archives, I am also grateful to the Japanese American National Museum; the UCLA Asian American Studies Center and their publication the *Amerasia Journal*; and the Bancroft Library at the University of California, Berkeley.

About the Author

Rahna Reiko Rizzuto is the author of the memoir *Hiroshima in the Morning*, which was a finalist for the National Book Critics Circle Award, among other honors. Her debut novel, *Why She Left Us*, won an American Book Award. She is also a recipient of the U.S.-Japan Creative Artist Fellowship. Reiko was the first woman to graduate from Columbia College with a bachelor's degree in Astrophysics. She was raised in Hawaii and lives in Brooklyn.